ALFRED HITCHCOCK'S CRIMEWATCH

ALFRED
HITCHCOCK's
CRIME-
WATCH

Edited by Cathleen Jordan

The Dial Press
Davis Publications, Inc.
380 Lexington Avenue, New York, N.Y. 10017

All of the stories in this book were first published in *Alfred Hitchcock's Mystery Magazine*. Grateful acknowledgment is hereby made for permission to reprint the following:

You Can Get Away with Murder by Charles Boeckman; copyright © H.S.D. Publications, Inc., 1974; reprinted by permission of the author. *Sam's Conscience* by Douglas Farr; copyright © 1958 by H.S.D. Publications, Inc.; reprinted by permission of Scott Meredith Literary Agency, Inc. *A Husband Is Missing* by Fletcher Flora; copyright © 1957 by H.S.D. Publications, Inc.; reprinted by permission of Scott Meredith Literary Agency, Inc. *A Good Kid* by James Holding; copyright © 1971 by H.S.D. Publications, Inc.; reprinted by permission of Scott Meredith Literary Agency, Inc. *My Escaped Convict* by Donald Honig; copyright © 1959 by H.S.D. Publications, Inc.; reprinted by permission of Raines & Raines. *Farewell Gesture* by George Grover Kipp; copyright © 1971 by H.S.D. Publications, Inc.; reprinted by permission of the author. *You Can't Win 'Em (at) All* by Ed Lacy; copyright © 1967 by H.S.D. Publications, Inc.; reprinted by permission of the Estate of Ed Lacy. *Sweet Smell of Murder* by Allen Lang; copyright © 1957 by H.S.D. Publications, Inc.; reprinted by permission of the author. *No Small Problem* by John Lutz; copyright © 1968 by H.S.D. Publications, Inc.; reprinted by permission of the author. *The Donor* by Dan J. Marlowe; copyright © H.S.D. Publications, Inc., 1970; reprinted by permission of the author. *Footprints in a Ghost Town* by Donald Martin; copyright © 1959 by H.S.D. Publications, Inc.; reprinted by permission of Raines & Raines. *A Woman Is Missing* by Helen Nielsen; copyright © 1960 by Helen Nielsen; reprinted by permission of Scott Meredith Literary Agency, Inc. *Enter the Stranger* by Donald Olson; copyright © H.S.D. Publications, Inc., 1974; reprinted by permission of Blanche C. Gregory, Inc. *The Plum Point Ladies* by Henry T. Parry; copyright © 1976 by Davis Publications, Inc.; reprinted by permission of the author. *I Had a Hunch, and . . .* by Talmage Powell; copyright © 1959 by H.S.D. Publications, Inc.; reprinted by permission of the author. *The Greatest Cook in Christendom* by S.S. Rafferty; copyright © H.S.D. Publications, Inc., 1975; reprinted by permission of the author. *A Debt to Doc* by Carl Henry Rathjen; copyright © 1964 by H.S.D. Publications, Inc.; reprinted by permission of Larry Sternig Literary Agency. *The Crime Machine* by Jack Ritchie; copyright © 1960 by H.S.D. Publications, Inc.; reprinted by permission of Larry Sternig Literary Agency. *The Fly Swatter* by Frank Sisk; copyright © H.S.D. Publications, Inc., 1975; reprinted by permission of Scott Meredith Literary Agency, Inc. *Item* by Henry Slesar; copyright © 1962 by H.S.D. Publications, Inc.; reprinted by permission of the author. *The Patchwork Quilt* by Pauline C. Smith; copyright © H.S.D. Publications, Inc., 1973; reprinted by permission of the author. *Water Witch* by William M. Stephens; copyright © 1960 by H.S.D. Publications, Inc.; reprinted by permission of Larry Sternig Literary Agency. *Who's Innocent?* by Lawrence Treat; copyright © 1959 by H.S.D. Publications, Inc.; reprinted by permission of the author. *The Wells Plan* by Thomasina Weber; copyright © H.S.D. Publications, Inc.; 1970; reprinted by permission of the author. *The Invisible Cat* by Betty Ren Wright; copyright © 1958 by H.S.D. Publications, Inc.; reprinted by permission of Larry Sternig Literary Agency.

INTRODUCTION

If one undertakes to look out for crime, one must keep a sharp eye out for hot tempers and dark alleys, for lost love and sudden wealth (tiresome spouses are particularly vulnerable, and anyone at all who has put his name to a Last Will and Testament). One should keep firmly in mind that things are rarely what they seem to be, but nevertheless, one should *always* adopt a guarded stance around guns, knives, bottles of poison and bottles of sleeping pills (and therefore around cups of hot chocolate and bottles of wine, especially sealed ones). One should look out for jewelry cases, revelatory diaries, unlocked french doors, packets of white powder, and rare stamps. One must, however, be careful Not To Know Too Much if one does not wish to cease to know a thing. Which can make crimewatching tricky.

It gets even trickier—but nine times out of ten even more interesting—when the crimewatching involves the printed page, and when the imagination of crime-story writers goes to work. On those occasions, a tale of crime can include

the smell of wintergreen
a stack of old hymnals
a deep sea diver's flashlight
an unmarked grave
a determined ghost
the murderer's crabby mother
a series of young people's adventure stories and a heroine
    named Penelope
a pigpen
a paper wrapper for diamonds
a handbag at a thrift shop
a gardener in traction
a mysterious "V"
the morning paper
and a pair of dancing slippers,

all of which have roles to play in the twenty-five stories collected in this volume.

In its nearly three decades of publishing new mystery stories, *Alfred Hitchcock's Mystery Magazine* has come upon thousands of such important details. The stories that follow are all taken from its archives, and they suggest, at least, the range of clues and confoundments that crimewatchers can get mixed up with.

And be entertained by.

Cathleen Jordan

CONTENTS

ALFRED HITCHCOCK'S
CRIMEWATCH

Who's Innocent?

by Lawrence Treat

To begin with, two things should be clearly stated, for they were important in what happened. That Doc Selby had the gun, and that Carlie usually got what she wanted—and preferably by means that were devious.

She was fair to behold. She spoke softly, liked to flout convention, and wound her hair in a circlet of tight, pearly braids. She had other assets, too, notably a sixteen-year-old daughter, a suitor, and an absentee husband, whom she refused to divorce for fear of inflicting a hurt.

"Poor Jeff," she used to say, gently. "He has no one except me." Which was not strictly true, but since the statement was accompanied by the soft dazzle of a smile, it was not questioned.

Doc Selby was the suitor and he lived next door to Carlie, about a mile out of town, in a big, rambling house as befitted a country doctor. He was a widower in his forties, with children who were not around at the time of the murder. But Carlie's daughter was.

Doc Selby had heard a good deal about Carlie, even before she arrived. He knew that her husband was Jeff Bedrick, a TV actor, that she was moving to the country for reasons of economy, and that her daughter Myra would be a senior in high school. But Doc did not know what Carlie looked like. It so happened, however, that he took a moment off from a proctoscopic examination of old Mrs. Dunning and glanced through the window just as Carlie and Myra were driving up to their new home. To say the least, the momentary break was decidedly pleasing.

In the evening, Doc went to pay his respects. He was not a polished man, but he was well-constructed—both inwardly and outwardly—and he was much occupied with kindness. He took the shortcut through the patch of woods that separated the two houses, and he came around the corner of the porch and stepped wide to avoid the broken drain pipe. Then he saw her, framed in the antique tracery betweeen the porch columns. Her hair was prematurely gray, but she looked ridiculously young to be the mother of a teenager.

11

"I'm your neighbor, Dr. Arthur Selby," he said. "I was wondering whether there was anything I could do."

She smiled softly, thereby creating a complication. For Carlie drew love the way an astringent draws pain. "Thank you," she said, in her quiet drawl that always had a suggestion of teasing. "You could do a lot. You could find me a gardener. Someone a little old and feeble, I think, to go with the house."

The doctor laughed. "Old Neeko isn't feeble, but he does go with the house, and he loves flowers. He's Hungarian, and I'd better warn you—he has a violent prejudice against actors. In fact, with Neeko's temperament, there could be serious trouble."

Carlie frowned without even wrinkling the perfection of her clear, ivory skin. "My husband won't be with me," she said.

But he was. In the months that followed, during the long, slow, hot summer days, Jeff Bedrick was like a thunderhead on the horizon.

Doc Selby, being a man who knew his mind, closed his office two afternoons a week and dedicated them to the pursuit of Carlie. They used to go on picnics. Myra and old Neeko would lead the way. Myra skipped and Neeko plodded, but they shared a delight in nature and in finding new ferns and berries, which Neeko always discovered with a grunt and Myra with a shriek of excitement.

Doc carried the heavy picnic basket that Carlie loaded with delicacies, and they followed slowly, up the long hill that rose from the pond and flattened out on wooded uplands. There, Doc would set the basket down under the shade of the apple tree, and Carlie would unpack while Doc rested from the climb. Then Myra would dash off in search of wildflowers.

That was before she met Bob Roberts. Afterwards, she would sit quietly and gaze into space, while Neeko squatted next to her in silent communion.

Bob Roberts was a clean-cut, honest boy who came from a good family and worked hard. At twenty-one, he had his sights set on a small store, and expected to have his own TV repair shop in the fall.

"I hate him," Carlie said vehemently.

Doc studied her face, as he often did, and found nothing but pleasure in the occupation. "Why?" he asked. "What have you got against him?"

"Everything."

Doc sought to interpret the remark. "You mean you don't like Myra falling for him?"

"She's too young. Arthur, I married Jeff when I was seventeen, and I won't let Myra make the same mistake. I won't." She spoke so firmly and looked so innocent that Doc refrained from further probing.

"Well," he said mildly. "I'm sure Myra will be sensible."

He was wrong, for no sensible girl would have gone out with Buddy Aston. Buddy was blond and careless and spoilt. He had the twisted brain of a psychopath, but he came along in a red sports car, which made snatching up Myra a lot easier. Moreover, since his father owned the bank and the local paper and most of the real estate in town, including the store that Bob Roberts had his eye on, Buddy was in a position to exert considerable leverage.

Meantime, Jeff Bedrick returned from the west coast, where he'd failed to get the TV work he'd counted on. He settled in New York and Myra visited him every two weeks, and on at least one occasion Buddy went with her.

Carlie took the news hard. "I wonder how much he asked Buddy to lend him," she said. "Or whether he merely gave Buddy a bad check."

"Forget about Jeff," Doc said harshly. "He's not your responsibility. Divorce him, Carlie, so that we can get married. You're wasting your life over him."

She gazed up, and her eyebrows arched ever so slightly, giving her an added whimsical allure.

"I'm sorry," Doc said. "I shouldn't have said that."

Carlie's smile was tender. "But you're perfectly right. It is unfair of me, but I can't help it. There are things way, way back and deep, deep down, and I just can't give Jeff up."

"You don't have him at all. He's gone. He's out of your life."

"But I'm not out of his. Arthur, I can't throw him over, he has to do it to me."

"He never will."

Carlie leaned back and half-closed her eyes. "He will, someday. When he has a great triumph and feels important. when he gets a movie contract or a glamorous part on Broadway. But now he needs the thought of a wife who is waiting for him, ever faithful. Do you see?"

"That," said the doctor, "is a sweet thought and would make a nice Victorian story, and often has. But how about us?"

"Arthur, be patient with me. Something will happen."

Doc Selby clamped his lips tight and went home.

Around two in the morning, he heard voices raised in anger, and he saw the lights go on in Carlie's house. Then Buddy's red sports car raced out of the driveway and turned into the highway with a roar. Doc got dressed and rushed over.

Carlie was doing her best to quiet Myra down, but Myra was in a state bordering on shock. She had a bruise on her face, and she kept moaning that all she'd done was to ask Buddy to let Bob Roberts have the Oak Street store; it was a perfect location and exactly what Bob needed. And now Bob wouldn't get the lease. She'd promised to help him and she'd tried and she'd failed—just everything had gone wrong.

Doc questioned her and obtained a disjointed account of what had happened. Myra had asked Buddy to help Bob Roberts, and Buddy had reacted by calling Bob a low-down bum who'd never amount to anything, which last item he would see to, personally. In the course of the quarrel that followed, Buddy had gotten violent and hit her. Then, in a rage, he'd driven Myra home and dumped her out of the car. He'd almost run her over in the process of racing off.

Doc examined Myra. After he'd given her a sedative and put her to bed, he returned to the living room. Neeko was standing there and cursing in Hungarian, and occasionally turning to Carlie and shouting in a fierce voice, "I keel him, I keel him!" Carlie was trying to talk him out of it, but Neeko wasn't even listening.

Doc grabbed him roughly and shook him. "None of that," he snapped. "Stop that kind of talk."

Neeko answered laconically. "I fix my gun now, I keel him tomorrow." And he swung around and left the room.

Carlie said helplessly, "Arthur, he really means it."

Doc put his arm around her. "Just leave it to me," he said. "I'll handle him."

She gave Doc a look of worship, and he would have braved a goon squad, let alone an elderly Hungarian with a gun which might or might not be loaded. Thus, feeling like a hero, Doc strode outside and marched upon the cabin at the rear of the house where Neeko lived in bachelorhood. When Doc burst in, he found Neeko oiling the gun.

"Give me that," Doc said immediately, forcefully.

Neeko grunted, and Doc grabbed at the gun. Neeko hung onto it with a sullen stubbornness, and although Doc, who was stronger and younger and heavier, tore and yanked, Neeko remained permanently attached to the trigger guard. In desperation, Doc gave a sudden, jiu-jitsu twist, while his foot hooked Neeko's and spilled him neatly. Neeko slipped and went crashing to the floor. And broke his leg.

It was a nasty break, and Doc took him to the hospital that same night. Thus Neeko, with his leg in a cast and suspended from a traction frame, which was in a room with two other patients and supervised by a floor nurse, had an adequate alibi and can be counted out of the story. His gun, however, remained behind and entered into the events that were yet to come.

The following day was cloudy, and the barometer went down to twenty-nine point ninety, and was falling. Myra's spirits were even lower, although she ate three scrambled eggs for breakfast and phoned Bob Roberts. She told him she wasn't going to the party at Cora's that evening because everything had turned out worse than anybody could imagine. Under Bob's prodding, she consented to see him in the afternoon, but only for five minutes and he had to behave himself.

Carlie, who overheard part of the conversation, told Myra she had to go to the party.

"But I can't," Myra wailed. "I'm too ashamed."

"Nobody has the faintest idea of what happened," Carlie said firmly. "And if you don't go, they may very well wonder why."

"Buddy will be there and I can't face him. I'd rather die!"

"He will not be there," Carlie said. "I promise it."

As fate would have it, she met Buddy on the street that afternoon and slapped his face and said how dared he, and told him he ought to be put in jail. Buddy laughed and called her Mother Dear, and Carlie remembered what she'd promised Myra, so she turned sweet and made a date with him.

That, then, was the situation. It was as transparent as Scotch tape, and far stickier.

In the afternoon, Doc Selby had an emergency call that took him up to the hills. It was late when he returned, and he was dead tired. From work, from the sultry heat, from worry. He made himself an eggnog, tumbled into bed, and fell almost at once into a heavy, dreamless sleep.

The thunder woke him. There was a resounding burst that nearly split his eardrums, and he opened his eyes to see a sheet of blue light sweep out of the floorboards and crackle at the chandelier. He smelt the sharp odor of burnt oxygen, and for a moment he was afraid he'd been struck. He was surprised to find that he could still move. He got out of bed and pulled on a pair of trousers and a shirt.

The thunder smashed again, a great, rumbling peal that rocked the house. In the next sheet of lightning, Doc saw the white shingles and the dark green roof of Carlie's house.

There was no sleeping after that. Doc was excited, and some atavistic instinct was roused in him and he stayed there at the window, fascinated by the celestial fury.

He could see a light burning in Carlie's living room, and he supposed she was scared and had gotten up. He felt an overpowering loneliness, and a bitterness so intense that he had to clamp his jaws tight. For minutes afterwards, they ached from the pressure.

He belonged over there, with Carlie, and in his mind's eye he saw her clearly, tall and long-limbed and moving with charm and with grace. Then a stab of lightning split the darkness, and he noticed the sports car blocking Carlie's driveway. Not far from it, a long convertible was creeping slowly out to the road. Doc wondered who was in that car and why it was leaving now, when in ten or fifteen minutes the storm would probably let up.

Puzzled by the presence of the two cars, but not liking the idea of spying on Carlie's house, Doc turned away, crossed the room, lit a cigarette, sat down. But after about a minute, his curiosity was too much for him, and he returned to the window and waited for the next flash of lightning. What he saw made him wish he had stayed right in the chair.

Buddy Aston was leaving Carlie's house and he was angry. His head was turned, and he was shouting at Carlie as he stamped across the porch. And Carlie stood in the doorway, grasping the jamb with one hand, while her other arm was concealed and yet in the middle of a threatening motion. Then darkness obliterated the scene.

Doc swung around. He thought of phoning Carlie, but he had no right to interfere. He supposed she'd demanded that Buddy apologize and promise not to see Myra again. Buddy must have defied Carlie, and probably insulted her, besides.

But at least, Doc told himself, they'd parted. He returned to the window again, telling himself he wanted to see if Carlie's light was still on.

It was. And Buddy's car, dark and motionless, was still blocking the driveway. The next flash of lightning showed Doc why Buddy hadn't gone, and perhaps never would.

Slowly, Doc put on a slicker and an old hat. Slowly, hoping his eyes had deceived him, that Buddy had merely slipped in the mud, sprained his ankle, stunned himself for a moment or two, and would get up, climb into his car, leave. Slowly, with a dull foreboding and the sense of imminent catastrophe, Doc trudged out.

It was still raining, and thunder rumbled in the distance. Doc noted that the ditch was cascading with water, which had swept down Carlie's driveway and washed out whatever marks there might have been. He approached the car and bent down.

Buddy Aston was dead, and a gun lay a few feet away from him. Doc picked it up, and in a brief flare of lightning he thought he recognized Neeko's gun.

Doc groaned, glanced at Carlie's house. Then he put the gun in his pocket and went home. He wiped the mud from his rubbers, hung up his slicker where it would dry by morning, and broke open the revolver. It was definitely Neeko's, and one bullet was missing. Doc placed the gun in the bottom drawer of his desk, next to his spare stethoscope, and went to bed. He did not sleep.

Early next morning Mert Tagle, the town cop, knocked on Doc Selby's door. The doctor, in pajamas and bathrobe, came downstairs.

"Morning, Doc," Mert said. "Turned out pretty nice, after all that rain. Lightning struck the Dexter barn and split that apple tree up the hill. The storm wake you?"

"Sure it woke me."

"What did you do, Doc?"

"What in blazes could I do? I couldn't stop the blasted storm, so I rode it out under my pillow. What's the trouble, Mert?"

"Buddy Aston got shot."

Doc showed surprise, but not sadness. "Shot?" he said.

"Murdered," Tagle said somberly.

Doc said, "Where did it happen?"

And Mert said, "In the Bedrick driveway. And an interesting thing, Myra stayed in the village last night. On account of the storm."

"Come in and have a cup of coffee," Doc said. "Nobody's going to cry over Buddy except his old man. But he's certainly going to want action."

Mert nodded. "I called in the state cops because this is too much for me. But privately, I'm wondering why Mrs. Bedrick slapped Buddy's face good and hard yesterday afternoon."

"I hadn't heard about that," said Doc. "Why not ask her?"

Mert asked, as did many others, and Carlie's explanation was that a few nights ago Buddy had had a date with Myra and kept her out late, despite a specific promise to the contrary.

Under heavy pressure, Carlie insisted that she had no gun, and no way in the world of getting one, and that she didn't kill teenagers for keeping her daughter out after midnight. She said that, although she'd lost her temper and slapped Buddy on the street, she'd been thoroughly ashamed of herself and had asked Buddy to come see her, under a flag of truce, and that he'd done so. She said that their talk had been friendly, they'd sat in the living room munching potato chips and sipping a very weak vodka drink, because she wouldn't waste good liquor on him. She said Buddy had left before the worst of the downpour. The autopsy bore out the weak drink and potato chips version, and she stuck to it doggedly.

Local opinion was divided. Half the town thought Carlie was concealing something and should have been arrested, and the other half thought that her motive for doing away with Buddy was mighty slim and that the police should look elsewhere.

But the police were stymied. The storm had washed away all tire marks and other clues, and they were at a complete loss as to what weapon had been used and what had become of it. Naturally, nobody thought of looking in Doc's desk drawer.

Doc saw Carlie as little as possible, for fear of blurting out what he'd seen. But he kept thinking of her and yearning for her, until one afternoon the need to see her rose up like a lump in his throat. He closed his office and told his nurse that he couldn't be reached. He went next door.

Myra let him in and announced that her mother had a new hat, and Carlie floated in and exhibited it.

"Do you like it?" she asked. "It cost me a fortune, but it gives me poise and confidence, so why not?"

"Carlie," Doc exclaimed, "you've got to divorce Jeff and announce our engagement."

"Why?" said Carlie.

Myra giggled and sat down to study her elders.

Doc looked embarrassed. "It would stop some of the gossip," he said. He laughed, a forced little laugh. "It would give them a chance to say, 'At their age—just imagine!' "

Myra admired the way her mother moved towards Doc and placed both hands on his shoulders. It gave her dignity, she thought, and yet made her available for the first pass.

"Arthur," Carlie said, "what is your real reason?"

Myra felt quite certain that, under similar circumstances, Bob Roberts would have kissed her passionately. But Doc made a speech.

"I belong with you," he said with a tortured emphasis. "I want to be on your side, helping out in every way and by every means I can find. It burns me up to live next door and be just a good neighbor. I've been trying to stay away from you, but it won't work. Carlie, I'm going half crazy."

Carlie touched Doc's cheek lightly, in a tender, familiar gesture that Myra noted carefully. Then Carlie backed away. "Why, Arthur," she said in a low, teasing voice. "You'd think I was really involved in the murder."

It was the wrong thing to say, for Doc seemed shocked and repelled by her words, and he turned and walked over to the window. Myra expected her mother to follow, but instead, Carlie spoke. And in a hard, crisp voice.

"I have an appointment with the district attorney this afternoon," she said. "He's no fool, and he knows perfectly well that I'm hiding things. But he doesn't know what, and he can't *make* me talk, can he?"

"I hope not," Doc said earnestly.

"Well, he hasn't managed, yet, but I'll admit I'm a little nervous. Arthur, will you drive me there?"

"Why, of course," Doc said.

Myra's eyes widened. All that, and her mother settled for a chauffeur.

Myra always regretted not being a witness to the drive. She would, however, have been disappointed, for Carlie sat in the corner of the car's front seat and never so much as touched Doc's sleeve.

"Arthur," she said, "they've found out all the facts they can, and this afternoon they have to charge me or else clear me." She leaned back, and she glowed softly. "If I'm arrested, I want you to go away on a long vacation. Will you promise to?"

Doc supposed she was being practical, because his testimony would of course clinch the case against her. But didn't she realize that he'd perjure himself before he'd do that?

He answered obliquely. "Carlie, I'm not the kind that runs away."

"Neither am I," she said. "And I have no reason to be afraid. They know nothing about the gun, and juries don't convict attractive mothers who act in defense of their daughters. I've no worries, Arthur. I *know* I'm safe."

She was in the D.A.'s office for two full hours. Doc waited outside and thought of how he used to laugh at expectant fathers pacing the floor, and how wrong he'd been.

At the end of two hours Carlie emerged, tired but gay and jaunty in her new hat. She was free.

On the way back they spoke of small, inconsequential things and laughed without reason. When they reached her house, she said, "Arthur, come in and have a drink. I'd like to celebrate."

"Celebrate what?" he asked dourly.

"My luck. It's surprising, isn't it? A person like me, alone and inexperienced, not too good a liar, pitted against the police and the district attorney and all their resources. And I won. I got away with it, and I'm happy."

For a moment, Doc didn't answer. This was more than a confession, it was an admission of callous disregard for the sanctity of human life. He could have understood a Carlie who had acted on emotion, with no thought but of her daughter, and whose penance had been the deep sufferings of conscience. But a Carlie who bragged about committing murder—he neither understood her, nor cared to.

He cleared his throat, and he spoke stiffly. "I'm not exactly in the mood to celebrate. My heart wouldn't be in it."

"Oh," she said. "I hadn't thought about how you'd feel."

"Well, think about it now."

"I prefer not to," she said, and got out of the car.

As a result of the quarrel, Doc went through a bad time, but when she called him a couple of days later and he caught the worry in her voice, he went to her house immediately.

The convertible in the driveway warned him that someone else was there, but Doc was not prepared for Jefferson Bedrick.

Doc recognized him from a photograph Carlie had once shown him. Jeff's face was gaunt. He was older and thinner, but his smile was confident and he had the strong, dominant personality of an experienced actor.

"Doc," he said in his deep, rich voice that was replete with the tones of a full orchestra, "Carlie has told me about you, and I wanted to meet you and give you my blessings before I leave."

Doc frowned, and Carlie said. "Jeff is divorcing me. He—I—" She appeared to choke up, and her eyes lifted in pleading.

Jeff rescued her with a gesture of magnanimity. "Carlie's trying to say that I can tell you the truth because you're in this up to your neck. And besides—" Jeff paused in order to build up his effect. "And besides, I'm sure Carlie would tell you anyhow."

"What are you driving at?" Doc asked.

Jeff glanced at Carlie to make sure that he had her undivided attention. Then mindful of his audience, his lips curled in the wry, repressed smile of an actor deliberately underplaying his role. "Doc," he said, "I haven't been an ideal husband, but when Carlie needed me, I came through. I took care of things, in my own way."

"What do you mean by that?" Doc asked.

"Exactly what I said. *I took care of things.*"

For a moment, Doc was stunned. Then, with the realization that this meant Carlie was innocent, he exclaimed, "You—you killed him! That second car was yours!"

Jeff inflated his chest, and his voice vibrated with a low, confidential quality. "I had a strange feeling that night. I still can't explain it. But I kept thinking of Myra; she seemed to be calling me. Storm—distance—money—they meant nothing to me. I hired a car and drove out here, as fast as I could. I found Carlie weeping, and she told me what had happened. She said Buddy Aston was due in a little while, and she asked me what to do.

" 'Do?' I said. 'Give him a drink and some potato chips, and look lovely. I'll handle him.' And I left."

Doc sat down glumly. So Carlie had protected Jeff from the police because she still loved him. Even a divorce wouldn't change the way she felt about him.

"You waited for Buddy?" Doc asked.

"That's right." Jeff said. "I stayed out of sight, but I saw him come and I saw him go, and when he stepped from this house, I was there. I called him a rat, and I shot him. Just like that." And Jeff snapped his fingers.

"And the gun?" Doc asked, in a flat voice. "How—"

"Perhaps, in my way, I loved my family too much," Jeff said, interrupting, "but I cannot ask Carlie to be tied to me any longer. Doc, I'm setting her free. Look after her well; I cannot." And, biting his lips, holding back the deep flow of his emotion, Jeff turned and stalked out.

Doc stood there, tired, dull, beaten. He was not even aware that Carlie had approached him until she touched his arm and spoke. "Arthur, didn't he do wonderfully?"

Doc spun around. "What are you talking about?"

"It was his finest role; he actually convinced himself. He forgot that Myra had phoned him. He even forgot what he said to me when

he got here. He'll be so proud, Arthur. For the rest of his life, he'll
believe he committed murder to save the honor of his daughter."

"Didn't he?"

"Of course not. You surely know he didn't."

"I guess I do," Doc said. He had to clear his throat before he spoke
further. "Carlie, isn't it about time for us to be honest with each
other? Because I know you killed Buddy. I saw you."

"Saw me?" she said, in a shocked voice. "Arthur, *I saw you.* In
that flash of lightning. You were standing there with the gun."

"Sure. I took it because it was Neeko's and would be traced to you.
I still have it. Oh, Carlie—you mean you went through these last
two weeks thinking you were protecting me?"

"Of course I did. Why else would—"

Doc laughed in relief. "Then Jeff did kill him. You said once that
you'd be free of him when he had some great triumph, some glamorous part to play. He did this crazy thing and thinks he's a hero,
but it turns out that he wasn't playing a role at all."

"But how could he have gotten the gun? It was in the cabin, wasn't
it? He didn't even know there was a cabin, and nobody went near
it except Myra when—" Carlie stopped short. She shook her head.
And then she started to cry.

Doc put his arm around her. "Carlie, don't think that. Listen, we'll
go there; we'll turn the place upside down. Maybe we can find some
evidence."

"After two weeks?" she said shakily. But she went nevertheless.

As they approached the shack they heard sounds from inside it,
and they walked apprehensively, afraid of what they'd find. When
they were a few feet away, the door shot open and Myra, in Levis
and an old shirt, stepped out.

"Myra!" Carlie exclaimed. "What are you doing?"

Myra sneezed and wiped at a smudge on her cheek. "Cleaning up
for Neeko's return, and I never saw such filth. Mouse droppings,
cobwebs, old beer bottles." She started to giggle, and broke off.
"Why're you both looking at me that way?"

"Nothing," Doc said. "Nothing." He elbowed past her and entered
the tiny room. He kept thinking of a teenage party with everybody
coming and going, stepping outside for a drink or else to neck in a
parked car. How easy to sneak away for a half hour, and no one the
wiser . . .

"The gun was here," he said, dropping his hand wearily on the
table.

Myra looked perplexed.

Doc didn't dare look at her. "It was my fault," he snapped. "I started it, hitting an old man. What came over me?"

"Nobody's blaming you," Carlie said.

Doc moved restlessly, with no fixed purpose. He thumbed a magazine, tapped at the table, flipped on the radio. There was a humming sound and the smell of something burning. Doc spun around.

"That's funny," Myra said. "I thought Bob fixed it. He promised he would."

"When?" Doc asked.

"The afternoon Buddy was killed. I told Bob about it. I'm sure he came here. And he's so good at fixing radios."

Doc took a deep breath and exchanged a look with Carlie. Then, half-closing his eyes, he switched off the radio.

"Myra," he said slowly. "Did Bob Roberts stay at that party all evening? You must have been with him. Did he stay there all the time, or did he go out somewhere, for a little while?"

"Why—" Myra thought about it for a moment. "Now that you mention it, he *did* slip out for—Oh!" Her eyes widened and she flung herself into her mother's arms. "Oh, *no!*"

Carlie's troubled look over Myra's head as she comforted her daughter asked Doc what he was going to do about it.

Doc sighed. He wasn't sure what he was going to do about it, but a thought was beginning to shape itself in his mind: *I've already meddled too much in matters that don't rightfully concern me, and after all, I'm not God, am I?*

Item

by Henry Slesar

"It was the craziest thing," the woman on the stretcher said. "Me and my husband Milton were having breakfast this morning, around ten o'clock because Milton likes to sleep late on a Saturday. And as usual, he was half man and half newspaper; I didn't see his ugly face for the whole meal. Then all of a sudden, he acts like a bomb went off. He jumps up, tears an item out of the paper, and shoves it into his pocket. Then he runs to the hall closet, gets his hat and coat, and busts out of the house like a rocket. Not a word, you understand, not a single word about where or what. The next thing I know it's eleven thirty, and I hear the front door opening. 'Milton?' I says, going out to the hallway. Sure enough, it's Milton, and what do you suppose he's doing? He's pointing a gun at me? I thought he was kidding, and was I surprised when he pulled that trigger and *bam*. My gosh, a bullet feels just like a hard slap, did you know that? I don't suppose I'll ever wear this dress again, will I?"

"Take it easy," the police interne said, slitting the cloth shields from the rayon sleeves. "You've lost some blood, but the bullet only struck the fleshy part of the arm. You're a lucky woman, Mrs. Hanley."

"Lucky?" she snorted. "With a husband like mine?" She turned her dull gray eyes toward the lieutenant. He was on the phone, talking quietly. When he hung up and came towards her, he looked like a diagnostician with bad news.

"Sorry to tell you this," he said, "but a prowl car spotted your husband on Grand Street and ordered him to halt. He didn't listen, unfortunately. I'm afraid he's dead."

Mrs. Hanley's face did a muscle dance. Then it relaxed, with a sigh of either relief or acceptance. "Poor Milton," she said. "I suppose you want to know about him?"

"Yes," the lieutenant said.

"Well, Milton was a pretty ordinary guy in most ways, but I never saw such a man for squeezing a nickel. I guess that was the real

24

cause of all the trouble between us. I mean, Milton was so tight that he hadn't bought a new pair of shoes in six years, and the suit I'll bury him in is at least nine years old. Listen, you want to see something kooky? Take a look in the basement. Milton's got the biggest ball of tinfoil you ever saw in your life. He's got boxes full of string and a crate full of soda bottle caps. Don't ask me what for, maybe he was going to retile the roof with 'em. I never saw a man so cheap.

"Anyway, we've been having fights about money for years. I tried to stretch his miserable salary as best as I could; me, I'm the national bake-off champion when it comes to leftovers. But every once in a while, I *had* to spend some money on myself. I mean, a woman needs a new hat or dress now and then or she goes to pieces.

"Well, things got pretty bad in the last few months. We were having some real fights about money, Milton and me, and he was getting tighter by the day. Once, after a hot argument, I walked out and came back with half a dozen bundles from a woman's shop. I must have spent fifty dollars, just to spite him, and he got so worked up he was frothing at the mouth. He would have thrown things at me, but he was too cheap to break anything.

"I guess the fight we had yesterday was the last straw. I never had much sales resistance, and a vacuum cleaner salesman came to the door with a real smooth talk. Before I knew what I was doing, I signed an agreement for their fanciest cleaner with all the trimmings. The bill was around a hundred and sixty dollars, and when I told Milton about it, he looked at me sort of peculiar and didn't say a word. Not a word. I should have realized that was the kookiest thing he could have done, and started to worry. Instead, I didn't give it another thought. And look what happens."

"I see," the lieutenant said. "But what I want to know is, what was the newspaper item your husband clipped? The one that got him so excited?"

"I don't know," Mrs. Hanley said. "I never got a look at it. It must have been really something."

"Is that paper still in the house?"

"Yes, but it's all torn up."

"Harry," the lieutenant said, turning to a patrolman, "search the apartment for that newspaper, and get me another edition of the same issue. Find out what item Hanley removed."

"Yes, sir," the patrolman said.

They had it in their hands an hour later.

"What is it?" Mrs. Hanley said eagerly.

"It's an ad," the lieutenant said. "An advertisement for a sporting goods shop."

It read:

"GUN SALE. Were $18.95, now $11.95."

I Had a Hunch, and . . .

by Talmage Powell

After a strangely timeless interval, Janet realized she was dead.

She experienced only a little shock, and no fear. Perhaps this was because of the carefree way she had conducted her past life.

She had never felt so free. A thought wave her propulsion, she zipped about the great house, then outside, toward the great, clean open sky. Above, the stars were ever so bright and beautiful. Below, the lights of the suburban estate where she had been born and reared shone as if to answer the stars.

Janet was delighted with the whole experience. It confirmed some of the beliefs she had held, and it is always nice for one to have one's beliefs confirmed. It also excited the vivacious curiosity which had always been one of her major traits. And now there were ever so many more things about which to be curious.

She returned to the foyer of the house and looked at her lifeless physical self lying at the base of the wide, sweeping stairway.

Whillikers, I was a very good looking hunk of female, she decided. *Really I was.*

The body at the foot of the stairway was slender, clad in a simple black dinner dress. The wavy mass of black hair had spilled to rest fanwise on the carpet. The soft, lovely face was calm—as in innocent, dreamless sleep.

Only the awkward twist and weird angle of the slim neck revealed the true nature of the sleep.

A quick ache smote Janet. *I must accept things. This—this is really so wonderful, but I do wish I—she—could have had just a little more time . . .*

The great house was silent. Lights blazing on death, on stillness.

Janet remembered. She had returned unexpectedly to change shoes. Getting out of the car at the country club, she had snagged the heel of her left shoe and loosened it.

"I'll only be a little while," she had promised Cricket and Tom and Blake.

"We'll wait dinner," Blake had said, after she'd waved aside his insistence that he drive her home.

At home again, she had reached the head of the stairs when she heard someone in her bedroom.

She'd always possessed a cool nerve. She'd eased down the hallway. He'd been in there. Murgy. Dear old Murgy. Life hadn't begun without the memory of Murgy. He was ageless. He had worked for the family forever. Murgatroyd had been as much a part of Janet's life as the house, the giant oaks on the lawn, the car in the garage, over which Murgy lived in his little apartment.

She simply hadn't understood at first. Crouched in the hallway and peering through the crack of the partially opened door, she had seen a brand new Murgy. This one had a chill face, but eyes that burned with determination. This one moved with much more deftness and decisiveness than the Murgy she'd always known.

He was stealing her jewelry. He was taking it from the small wall safe and replacing paste replicas. They were excellent replicas. They must have cost Murgy a great deal of money. But whatever the cost, it was pennies compared to the fortune he was slipping under his jacket.

She saw him compare a fake diamond bracelet with the real thing. The fakes were so good, she might have gone for years without knowing a large portion of her inheritance had been replaced by them.

As she saw the genuine diamond bracelet disappear into his pocket, she had gasped his name.

He had responded like a man jerking from a jolt of electricity. Frightened, she had turned, run. He had caught her at the head of the stairs.

She had tried to tell him how much his years of service meant, that she would have given him a chance to explain, a chance to straighten the thing out.

But he had given *her* no chance. He had pushed savagely at her with both arms. She had fallen, crying out, trying to grab something to break the fall.

She had struck hard. There had been one blinding flash, mingled with pain.

Murgy had followed her down. He had stood looking at her, wiping his hands on a handkerchief. He had listened, and heard no sound. She had come alone. Everything was all right. Even the heel on her left shoe had come off during her fall.

Murgy's decision was plain in his face. He would go to his quarters. Let her be discovered. Let her death be considered an accident.

Janet broke away from the study of what had once been her body.

Murgy, you really shouldn't have done it. There is a balance in the order of things and you have upset it. There is only one way you can restore the balance, Murgy. You must pay for what you have done. Besides, my freedom won't be complete until you do.

Janet was aware of a presence in the foyer.

Cricket had entered. Cricket and Tom and Blake, wondering why she hadn't returned, beginning to worry, deciding to see what was keeping her.

A willowy blonde girl, not too intelligent, but kind and eager to please, Cricket saw the body at the base of the stairway. She put her fists to her temples and opened her mouth wide.

Janet rushed to her side. In her world of silence, she couldn't hear Cricket screaming, but she knew that was what she was doing. Cricket's merry blue eyes were not merry now. They strained against their sockets with a terrible intensity.

Poor Cricket. I'm not in pain, Cricket.

She tried to touch Cricket with the touch of compassion.

Cricket wasn't aware of this effort, Janet knew instantly. She wasn't here, as far as Cricket was concerned. She would never again be here for Cricket, or for any of the others.

Blake and Tom were beside Cricket now. Tom was helping her to a deep couch. Blake was taking slow, halting steps toward the body at the foot of the stairs.

Blake kneeled beside the young, dead body. He reached as if he would touch it. Then his hands fell to his sides. He rose, his dark, handsome face pained.

He turned, stumbled to Tom and Cricket. Cricket had subsided into broken sobs. Tom sat with his arms about her shoulders. Shock and fright made the freckles on Tom's lean, pale face stand out sharply.

They were discussing the discovery. Janet could feel their horror, their sorrow. She could sense it, almost touch it. It was as if she could almost reach the edges of their essence, of their being, with her own essence and being.

Blake was picking up the telephone now. This would be for the doctor.

Before the doctor arrived, Murgy came in. Janet strained toward him. Then she recoiled, as from a thing dark and slimy.

He was speaking. *Saying he had heard a scream, no doubt.*

Then Blake stepped from in front of Murgy. And Murgy looked toward the stairs.

Cosmic pulsations passed through Janet as she slipped along with Murgy to the body at the stairway.

She could feel the fine control deep within him, the crouching of the dark, slimy thing as, in its wanton determination to survive, it braced the flesh and ordered the brain and arranged the emotions.

The emotions were in such a storm that Janet drew back.

Murgy went to his knees beside the body and wept openly. *There was Blake now, helping Murgy to a chair. Everything was so dreadfully out of balance.*

She tried to get through to Blake. She strained with the effort. She succeeded only in causing Blake to look at Murgy a little strangely, as if something in Murgy's grief struck a small discord in Blake.

Blake went to fetch Murgy a glass of water. Janet turned her attention to Cricket and Tom. Tom's mind was resilient and strong. She battered at the edges of it, but it was too full of other things. Memories. Janet could vaguely sense them. Memories that somehow concerned her and the good times their young crowd had had.

Cricket was simply blank. Shocked beyond thinking.

Janet perched over the front doorway and beheld the scene in its entirety.

Look, people. He did it. Murgy's a murderer. He mustn't be allowed to get away with it.

Dr. Roberts came into the house. He spoke briefly with the living and turned toward the dead. He stood motionless for a moment. His grief spread like a black aura all about him. It spread until it had covered the whole room. He had delivered Janet, prescribed for her sniffles, set the arm she'd broken trying to jump a skittish horse during a summer vacation from college. He had sat by her all night the night he'd broken the news to her that her parents had been killed in a plane crash, that now she would have to live in the great house with Murgy and a housekeeper to look after her wants.

She flew to Dr. Roberts, remembering the way the big, square face and white goatee had always symbolized strength and intelligence to her.

You must understand, doctor. It was Murgy. He was ever so lucky; everything worked devilishly for him, my arrival alone, the broken shoe heel.

Then she fell back, appalled. It was as if she had bruisingly struck a solid black wall, the walls of a crypt where Dr. Roberts had shut away a part of himself. *She would never reach him, because he didn't believe. When a man died, he died as a dog or a monkey died. That's what Dr. Roberts maintained.*

Janet moved to a table holding an assortment of potted plants. She studied the activities before her.

She saw Dr. Roberts complete his examination. He talked with Blake. He looked at the broken shoe heel and nodded.

He put a professional eye on Cricket. He reopened his bag, took out a needle, and gave her a shot. Then he spoke with Tom, and Tom took Cricket out.

The doctor was explaining something to Blake. At last, Blake nodded his consent.

Janet felt herself perk up.

Of course, they'll phone the police. It's a routine, have-to measure when something like this happens.

She felt the dark, slimy thing in Murgy gather and strengthen itself, felt its evil smugness and confidence.

This was her last chance, Janet knew. The balance simply had to be restored. Otherwise, she was liable to be earthbound until Murgy, finally, died and a higher justice thus restored the cosmic balance.

But what if they send someone like Dr. Roberts?

The policeman came at last.

He was a big man, had sandy hair and gray eyes and a jaw that looked as if it had been hacked from seasoned oak. His nose had been broken sometime in the past and reposed flagrantly misshapen on his face.

Janet hovered over him.

Look at Murgy!

For Pete's sake, one second there, when you walked in, it was naked in Murgy's eyes!

Intent on his job, the policeman walked to the stilled form at the foot of the stairway. He looked at the left shoe, then up the stairs.

After a moment, he walked up the stairs, examined the carpet, the railing. He measured the length of the stairs with his eyes.

Then he came slowly down the stairs.

He paused and looked at the beautiful girlish body.

His compassion came flooding out into the room. Janet felt as if she could ride the edges of it like a buoy.

It was a quiet, unguarded moment for him. Janet threw her will into the effort.

It was Murgy. Look at Murgy, the murderer!

He glanced at Murgy. But then, he glanced at the others, too.

He began talking with Dr. Roberts.

Janet stayed close to the policeman.

If she could have met him in life, she knew they would have enjoyed a silent understanding.

I met a lot of people like that. Everybody meets people whom they like or distrust just by a meeting of the eyes.

You're feeling them out, forming opinions right now, by looking into their eyes, talking with them, letting the edges of your senses reach out and explore the edges of theirs.

I feel your respect for the doctor.

I feel you recoil now as you talk with Murgy. The dark, slimy thing is deep down, well hidden, but somehow you sense it.

But for Pete's sake, feeling it isn't enough. You must pass beyond feeling to realization.

Murgy killed me.

The balance simply has to be restored.

The policeman broke off his talk with Murgy. More official people had arrived. They took photographs. Two of them in white finally carried the body away on a stretcher.

Except for the policeman, the official people went away.

Blake went out. The doctor departed. Murgy was standing with tears in his eyes. The policeman touched Murgy's shoulder, spoke.

Janet was in the doorway, barring it. But Murgy didn't know she was there. He went across the lawn, to his apartment over the garage.

Only the policeman was left. He stood with his hat in his hands, looking at a spot at the base of the stairs with eyes heavy with sadness.

He was really younger than the rough face and broken nose made him appear.

Young and sad because he had seen beauty dead. Young and sad, and sensitive.

Janet pressed close to him. *It's all right, for me. You understand? There's no pain. It's beautiful here—except for the imbalance of Murgy's act.*

It wasn't an accident. You mustn't believe that. Murgy did it. You didn't like him. You sensed something about him.

Think of him! Think only of Murgy!

Don't leave yet. Ask yourself, are you giving up too easily. Shouldn't you look further?

He passed his hand through his hair. He seemed to be asking himself a question. He measured the stairway with his eyes.

She could sense the quiet, firm discipline that was in him, the result of training, of years of experience. The result of never ceasing to question, never stopping the mental probe for the unlikely, the one detail out of place.

Yes, yes! You feel something isn't quite right.

The shoe—if a girl came home to change it, would she go all the way upstairs and then start down again without changing it?

Oh, the question is clear and nettlesome in your mind.

It's a fine question.

Don't let it go. Follow it. Think about it.

He stood scratching his jaw. He walked all the way upstairs. Down the hallway. He looked in a couple of rooms, found hers.

In her room, he opened the closet. He looked at the shoes.

He stood troubled. Then he went back to the head of the stairs. Again he measured them with his eyes.

But finally, he shook his head and walked out of the house.

Come back! You must come back!

She couldn't reach him. She knew he wasn't coming back. So she perched on the roof of his speeding car as it turned a corner a block away.

He went downtown. He stopped the car in the parking lot at head-quarters. He went into the building and entered his office.

Another man was there, an older man. The two talked together for a moment. The older man went out.

The policeman sat down at his desk. He picked up a pen and drew a printed form toward him.

Janet hovered over the desk.

You mustn't make out the form. You must not write it off as an accident.

Murgy did it.

He started writing.

It was murder.

He wrote a few lines and stopped.

Go get Murgy. He was the only one on the estate when it happened. Can't you see it had to be Murgy?

He nibbled at the end of the pen.

Think of the shoe. I went up, but I didn't change shoes.

He ran his finger down his crooked nose. He started writing again.

Okay, bub, if that's the way you want it, go ahead and finish the report. Call it an accident. But I'm not giving up. I'm sticking with you. I'll throw Murgy's name at you so many times you'll think you're suffering combat fatigue from being a cop too long.

Ready? Here we go, endlessly, my friend, endlessly. Murgy, Murgy, Murgy Murgymurgymurgy . . .

He drove home. He showered. He got in bed. He turned the light off.

After a time, he rolled over and punched the pillow. After another interval, he threw back the covers with an angry gesture, turned on the light, sat on the edge of the bed, and smoked a cigarette.

There was a telephone beside the bed and on the phone stand a pad of paper.

While he smoked, he doodled. He drew a spiked heel. He drew the outlines of a house. He wasn't a very good artist. He looked at the drawing of the house and under it he wrote: "No sign of forced entry. Only that servant around . . . "

He drew a pair of owlish eyes, and ringed them in black. He added some sharp lines for a face.

Then he ripped off the sheet of paper, wadded it, and threw it toward the wastebasket. He snubbed out his cigarette, turned off the light for a second time, punched his pillow with a gesture betokening finality, and threw his head against it.

He reached the curtain of sleep. He started through it. Cells relaxing, the barriers began to waver, weaken.

She pressed in close.

MurgymurgymurgyMURGY!

He tossed and pulled the covers snug about his shoulders. Then he threw them off, got out of bed, and snapped on the light.

He was still agitated as he dressed and went out.

He sat in the dark car for many long minutes, before starting it. He drove aimlessly for a couple of blocks, his mind a pair of millstones grating against themselves. He stopped before a bar and went in.

He sat down at the end of the bar, alone. He had one, two, three drinks. His face was still troubled by nagging questions.

Two more drinks. They didn't help. The creases deepened in his cheeks.

Janet balanced atop a cognac bottle. *Better give Murgy a little more thought. Why not follow him, shadow him? He isn't resting easy. He'll want to get rid of those jewels in a shady deal now and be ready to run if the fakes are spotted.*

The policeman raised his gaze and looked at the television set over the bar. He stopped thinking about the long stairway, the broken heel, Murgy, and various possibilities. His mind snapped to what he was seeing on the TV set.

A local newscaster with doleful face was talking about her, her death. He was only a two dimensional image and she could sense nothing about him from this point. He was taking considerable time, and she could only guess that he was talking about her background, her family. There were some old newspaper pictures, one taken when she'd been helping raise money for the crippled children's hospital. She hadn't wanted any publicity for that, and she wished the newscast were less thorough.

There was a sudden disturbance down the bar. A fat man with a bald head and drink-flushed face was giving the TV set the Bronx cheer.

Janet felt quick displeasure. *Really, I was never the rich, degenerated hussy you're making me out, mister.*

The force of the mental explosion back down the bar caused Janet to rise to the ceiling. She saw that the fat man's exhibition had also disturbed her young policeman. He slammed out of the bar. And he was so mad he started across the street without looking.

Janet became a silent scream.

He looked up just in time to see the taxi hurtle around the corner. He tried to get out of the way. He'd had a drink too many.

Instantaneously, he became an empty shell of flesh and blood, shortly destined to become dust, lying broken in the middle of the street. A terrified but innocent cabbie was emerging from his taxi, and a small crowd was pouring out of the bar to join him.

This was defeat, Janet knew. Never had a defeat of the flesh been so agonizing. The stars could have been hers. Now the stars would have to wait, for a long, long time. For as long as Murgy lived. It wasn't the waiting that would be so hard. It was this entrapment in incompleteness, this torture, this unspeakable pain of being inescapably enmeshed in cosmic injustice.

She took her misery to the darkest shadow she could find and lurked there a while, until the scene in the street had run its course, from arrival to departure of the police.

A bitter thought wave her propulsion, she returned to the estate. She filtered through the roof and hovered in the foyer.

While there had been hope, the foyer's full capacity for torture had not reached her. Now she felt it.

"Hello, Beautiful."

Where had the thought come from? She swirled like a miniature nebula.

"Take it easy, I'm right here."

He swirled beside her. *Her policeman.*

"You!"

"Sure. I was so amazed at where I found myself I didn't get to you while you were hiding near the accident. You know, you *feel* even more beautiful than you looked."

"Why, thanks for the compliment. And your own homeliness, fellow, was all of the flesh. But don't you concern yourself with me."

"Why not?"

"I'm stuck here. You didn't catch Murgy."

"I had a hunch about that guy . . . "

"Hunch? Hah! It was me trying to get the guilt of the old boy across to you."

"Really? Well, I was going to keep an eye on him."

"I was after you to do that, too. See, I caught him stealing my jewels."

"I had to go and ruin everything!"

"But you didn't mean to barge in front of that cab."

"Just the same, I'll spend eternity being sorry. Sure you can't come with me?"

"Nope. Just go quickly."

He was gone. She felt his unwilling departure. It was the final straw of torture.

"Look, honey, my name's Joe."

He was back.

"I got this idea. It's worth a try at least."

It was so good having him back.

"My superior officer, Lieutenant Hal Dineen. He's the sharpest, most tenacious cop ever to carry a badge. That report of mine, to start with, is going to raise a question in his mind. The same facts you were trying to get over to me are there for him to find. I just bounced over to headquarters and back. Just a look told me my fray with that taxi has knocked his mental guards to smithereens. He was at his desk, reading that last report of mine. If you alone could do what you did, consider what the two of us trying real hard can do if we hit Dineen, in his present state, with full thought force."

Janet bounced to the rooftop. Joe was beside her.

"Janet, Dineen is razor sharp at playing hunches. He believes in them. All set to hit him with the grandfather of all hunches, the results of which he'll talk about for a lifetime?"

"Let's." *Let's, darling.*

Lieutenant Hal Dineen was talking to a fellow officer, "I dunno. Just one of those things. Comes from being a cop, I guess, from having the old subconscious recognize and classify information the eyes, ears, and hands miss. Just a hunch I had about this old family retainer. We all get 'em—these hunches. Me, especially, I'm a great one for 'em. And this one I couldn't shake and so I figured . . . "

The Fly Swatter

by Frank Sisk

Twice a day every day Sr. Giampietro Saccovino, l'americano ricco as the Portofinese referred to him, descended from his villa in the pine-shrouded foothills above the Via Roma and refreshed himself for a while at a table on the piazza outside the Trattoria Navicello.

He came first in the morning not long after the carabiniere had unpadlocked the heavy chain that stretched across the narrow road at the town's entrance from one stone post to another—about seven thirty. He came again late in the afternoon, a few hours before sunset. Generally he was alone, although there were those rare occasions when he might be accompanied by a woman—one of a number who visited the villa with some degree of regularity; women who, in the eyes of the parochial natives, looked suspiciously like high-priced sgualdrine down from Genova. The Signore nevertheless was adjuged il gentiluomo, for man is not born to be a saint.

Besides, Sr. Saccovino tipped most handsomely all who served him.

Also, he wore shimmering silk suits of a conservative cut. The third finger of his left hand shone with a stone worth perhaps two million lire or more. Another fortune was represented by the ruby-studded clasp formed like a scimitar that adorned a succession of hand-painted cravatte. Then there was the thin gold watch, not much larger than a Communion wafer, which told not only the hour down to the split of a second but the day of the week as well. Not to be overlooked either was the slender pen of (some said) platinum that the Signore employed with a smile and a flourish to sign the presented chits, never failing to write down that generous gratuity. Then—the pearl-handled fly swatter.

This fly swatter was final proof, if ever such proof were needed, that Sr. Saccovino was not only a rich American gentleman but eccentrico in the bargain, and this could be the very best kind to have around.

He entered Portofino toward the middle of March on board the yacht *Santa Costanza*. The marinai who operate the taxi craft in the harbor quickly learned that he had chartered the yacht at Bastia in Corse and had sailed here by way of Livorno and La Spezia.

Five boat-taxi and three mule-cart trips were required to transport the Signore's luggage from the yacht, which soon thereafter raised anchor, to the villa that had been unoccupied since the previous spring when the owner, a crusty old port-drinking inglés, had succumbed to il colpo apopletico while watching, as was his diurnal wont, the evening sun sink like a big orange into the Ligurian Sea.

Sr. Saccovino made his first exploratory visits to the quayside a few days after settling in. Flies being scarce at this time of the year, he came armed only with his warm engaging smile and his soft but authoritative voice. His "buon giorno," his "buona sera," his "venga qua, per piacere," his "mille grazie," were all uttered without the trace of a foreign accent. When he ordered lasagna al pesto (a regional manifestation of squared pasta covered with a green sauce in which basil is prominent, and sprinkled with grated goat cheese and crushed pine nuts), he obviously knew exactly what to expect.

These pleasant aspects of the man, combined with the dignified swaths of gray in his sleek black hair and the corded wrinkles in his mastiff-like face, earned him immediately a certain homage from the townspeople.

The pearl-handled fly swatter didn't appear until the last days of May. By then the mosce were growing bold and bothersome. While strolling from shop to stall and along the quays, the Signore carried the fly swatter as inconspicuously as possible. Often as not he concealed the greater part of the beautiful handle up the sleeve of his jacket in the fashion of a professional knife thrower, but whenever he sat at a table he always laid it out in plain view on the cloth to the right of the place setting, ready for instant use, and he could use it with remarkable accuracy.

Each morning the Signore broke his fast with the same nourishment—caffe ristretto, warm rolls with sweet butter and tart marmalade, a bottle of mineral water, more caffe ristretto. Mercia was usually the cameriera at his table and she batted her brown eyes outlandishly as she served him. She was a plump young widow with two small children.

In the evening, when he consumed a bottle of white wine with perhaps pasta con frutti di mare, he was most respectfully attended by a gaunt middle-aged bachelor named Silvestro, whose voice and mien were as funereal as an undertaker's at the obsequies.

During the noontime repast in the trattoria's aromatic kitchen

these two—Mercia and Silvestro—were forever dissecting and ana-
lyzing every nuance of Sr. Saccovino's utterances and behavior. The
following colloquy, typical in mood, occurred one day in July:

"This morning the Signore praised the cool breeze coming in from
the harbor."

"Last evening he spoke well of it, too."

"Did he dine alone?"

"As if you didn't already know, Mercia."

"What did she look like?"

"Her hair was as black as a raven's wing . . ."

"You have a poet's tongue, Silvestro."

". . . Her eyelids were tinted green. A tiny black star occupied her
left cheekbone. Her skin was the color of fresh cream. She possessed
a pair of mammelle the like of which you see on—"

"Ah, one of that type again."

"What else?"

"What else indeed. He is a man with blood in his veins. His nature
is affectionate."

"Last evening he ordered two bottles of Cinque Terre and permitted the lady to drink a bottle and a half."

"He is an abstemious man. His name is a gross misnomer. What
did he eat?"

"Fish soup with an extra pinch of basil. Squid simmered in oil and
garlic. Anchovies and capers in lemon juice. Bearded mussels in
mustard. Pasta with clam sauce. Wild strawberries in brandy."

"The food of love."

"I must say he appeared to be wonderfully prepared for the lady
by the time she had finished the last of the wine."

"I can well believe it. Did he kill many flies?"

"Only three in my presence. The lady was a powerful distraction."

"And the gratuity, it was generous?"

"More than generous. Eight thousand lire."

"So it goes. This morning he presented the carabiniere with two
long cigars and bought a dozen lace handkerchiefs from old Camilla."

"The dark hours of night rewarded him."

"Over coffee he inquired after my bambini by name."

"He is a most courteous gentleman."

"He asked why I do not marry again."

"How do you reply to such a question?"

"To the Signore I said that a good man is not to be found in the
market as readily as a good fish."

"Alas, that is the truth."

"And he answered— Do you wish to hear what the Signore said to that, Silvestro?"

"I think so."

"He said that many a sweet-fleshed fish is overlooked because it is thought to be not fat enough or young enough."

"That also is true."

"Such a fine fish is Silvestro, he said."

"He actually said that, Mercia?"

"I swear on the cross."

"Ah."

"He spoke in jest, of course."

"Of course."

"Then with his platinum pen he wrote out a gratuity of thirty-five hundred lire on a chit of half that sum. A night of love is a wonderful experience, Silvestro."

Toward the latter part of September—sabato, settembre ventisimo primo, as it would be remembered locally—the Hairy Tourist arrived in a rented Fiat just as the carabiniere was making fast the chain across the Via Roma. The time was ten-oh-four A.M.

"What's the big idea?" the Hairy Tourist asked as the carabiniere snapped shut the padlock. "I want to drive this heap into town." He spoke abominable Italian with an atrocious foreign accent.

"No motor vehicle is allowed in the town, signor," said the carabiniere, whose name was Umberto. "Except between the hours of seven and ten o'clock in the morning. And then we allow only those vehicles authorized to make deliveries of essential commodities."

"What the hell kind of a town is this anyway?"

"An old town, signor. A peaceful town. A town as yet unblessed by the fumes of benzina."

"Okay, admiral. Where do I park the heap?"—using the word mucchio.

"You may park the mucchio where the mucca grazes," Umberto said, pleased at the way he had worked a cow into the conversation.

It was Sr. Daddario, manager of the Hotel Nazionale, who dubbed this man the Hairy Tourist. The proffered passport identified him as Henry A. Scotti of St. Louis, Missouri, U.S.A., but Sr. Daddario was more impressed by the bushy black eyebrows, the sweeping black mustachios, the dense black beard, and the flowing black hair that fell nearly to his shoulders.

"You are fortunate, signor," Daddario said. "Because of a late cancellation we have a single room available."

"I'll take it," the Hairy Tourist said, setting his luggage, an airlines flight bag, on the counter as he signed in.

"On the other hand, you are not so fortunate. This room is available for three days only."

"That's all right with me, captain. I'll be checking out early tomorrow morning."

"In that case, signor, you must pay in advance."

The room, a small one as are all the rooms in the Hotel Nazionale, was situated on the second floor and overlooked the town square. The Hairy Tourist remained in it just long enough to drop the flight bag on the bed and then he was outside wandering around the town and asking questions of everyone about everything.

Where is the Church of San Martino? Who lives in the Castello Brown? Are there dolphins in these waters? Where is the Church of St. George? Is the fishing good outside the harbor? How cold does it get here in the winter? How old are some of these old arches? Do many tourists come here? Where do most of the tourists come from? Are there any Americans in town now? Has Sr. Giampietro Saccovino been living here long? Where does he live? When he dines here in town does he dine alone? How many miles is it to Rome? How much is a kilometer?

Sr. Saccovino strolled down from his villa an hour before sunset, graciously greeting all whom he met on the way, and finally settled down at a table outside the Trattoria Navicello. The chair he sat in, his favorite, afforded him a view of the harbor, with its flotilla of pleasure craft, impeded only by an occasional passerby. He enjoyed the warm glittering look of the water at this time of day.

Silvestro materialized at his side with a mournful "Buona sera" and "Desidera, signor?"

The Signore ordered a bottle of Cinque Terre and the antipasto and placed the pearl-handled fly swatter on the table. The flies of September are obnoxious and hardy. In a moment one of the creatures buzzed past his ear and settled on the corner of a folded napkin. The Signore's veined right hand moved stealthily toward the pearl handle, grasped it firmly, lifted it slightly, slapped it down unerringly.

The crumpled fly left a spot of black blood on the white napkin. Using the rubber palm of the swatter, the Signore meticulously shoved the small corpse off the table onto the cobbles.

"This I had to see with my own two eyes," twanged an American voice close by. "Old J. P. Sacco killin' flies for his kicks."

The Signore raised his eyes from the spot of blood and saw the Hairy Tourist standing where Silvestro normally stood, with what appeared to be an exultant grin breaking its way through the hirsuteness. The Signore's eyes grew suddenly slitted but his voice, when he spoke, was toned to its usual softness. "Buona sera, signor. A que ora c'è l'omicidio?"

"Let's talk United States," the Hairy Tourist said.

"As you wish," said the Signore. "Since you probably plan to stay a while, take a seat."

The Hairy Tourist, sitting in a chair that placed his back to the harbor, said, "You got a very quaint scene here, J. P."

"It's restful."

"I guess. A man could rest in peace here. Forever."

"There are worse things. What is your name?"

"What's the diff? We ain't gonna know each other long enough to get acquainted."

"We're already acquainted," the Signore said, lifting the swatter and striking down a fly in mid-air. "You're acquainted with me by sight and reputation. I'm acquainted with you because I've known a dozen of your kind."

"It takes one to know one," the Hairy Tourist said.

"Don't equate me with yourself, young man. I never did a thing in my life for just money alone."

"Oh yeah."

Silvestro arrived with the wine and cast a look of sad inquiry at the newcomer.

"Bene, grazie, Silvestro," the Signore said. "Un altro bicchiere, per favore." To the Hairy Tourist: "What will you drink?"

"What's good enough for you is good enough for me."

"Would you care for an antipasto?"

"Why not?"

The Signore gave instructions to Silvestro, who left for a moment and returned with another glass. He poured a dram for the Signore's taste of approval and then filled the Hairy Tourist's glass to the brim.

"Can this ginzo understand English?" the Hairy Tourist asked after Silvestro's departure.

"No more than ten or twelve simple words," the Signore replied, his attention on a fly that had landed a few inches from the tip of his fork.

Taking a swallow of wine, the Hairy Tourist watched the Signore slap the insect fatally and flick it from the table. "What's all this business with the fancy fly swatter?" he asked.

"Swatting flies is second nature to me," the Signore said. "The first money I ever made was paid to me for swatting flies."

"You're tryin' to put me on, J. P."

"Not at all."

"This is Cutter Moran you're talkin' to."

The Signore took a thoughtful sip of the wine. "I knew a Cutie Moran back in the old days."

"None other than my old man."

"You don't say. Like father like son. As I remember, Cutie got too cute for his own good. And suddenly he wasn't around any more."

"Just like you, J. P. Suddenly you weren't around no more and one hell of a lot of bread went with you."

"I took my retirement fund, Cutter. That's all."

"I ain't interested in the details, man. All I'm gettin' paid for is findin' you and finishin' you."

"How did you find me, by the way?"

"It wasn't easy."

Silvestro served the antipasto and asked whether there would be anything else. The Signore thanked Silvestro and promised to signal when further service was required. Silvestro bowed somberly and left.

The Hairy Tourist fingered a slice of red peperoncino from the dish in front of him and popped it into the whiskery opening in his face. "One thing's for sure, J. P.," he said, chewing, "you got off the beaten track when you picked this burg. They don't even let cars inside. Wow, these peppers are hot!" He downed a big draft of wine. "Now, if you'd gone to Rome or Naples, we got connections there and could've dug you out in a couple of weeks. In fact, that's where I was goin' first, to Rome, but then I decided I better see an uncle a mine in Corsica I hadn't seen in four, five years, a nice old guy retired like you but clean, and that's where the old coincidence come in. I'm in a waterfront joint outside Bastia a couple nights ago and I get talkin' baseball with this cat speaks United States pretty good and it turns out he goes to sea whenever a job turns up, except he ain't been to sea since way last spring when he gets a berth on a yacht chartered by a rich American named Saccovino, this cat says—Jampeetro Saccovino—and I think to myself, I wonder. Plain dumb luck, but here I am, two days later drinkin' wine with old J. P. Sacco himself."

"Do your employers in St. Louis know about this dumb luck?" the Signore asked, laying another fly low.

"Not yet. Until I seen you in person I wasn't a hundred percent sure you'd be the same cat who chartered that yacht. Besides, I hate to use the phones in this damn country. I don't trust the damn phones, you know what I mean."

"And quite right too, Cutter."

Beads of perspiration began to form on the bare area of the Hairy Tourist's face, that space between the bushy eyebrows and the low bangs. "That pepper was *hot*." From the lapel pocket of his jacket he flicked a handkerchief embroidered with a blue *M* and patted his brow. "Do you eat these damn peppers as a regular thing?"

"Yes," the Signore said. "I find they sharpen my wits."

"Like swalleyin' a lighted match."

"Well, you've got to be properly dressed to eat these peppers."

"Oh, sure you do."

"That turtleneck sweater you're wearing, for instance, and the tweed jacket. Absolutely no good for **any**one who plans to eat a few red peppers."

"Yeah, you gotta be naked to eat them."

The Signore chuckled. "It might help at that, yes it might. But I can promise you one thing, Cutter, you'll definitely be more comfortable without that heavy wig and those phony whiskers."

The Hairy Tourist registered confoundment, at least to the degree that it was able to seep through the camouflage, and then tried to cover it up by pouring more wine into his own glass. Finally he said, "A real sharpie, ain't you? They told me that about you—a real sharp cookie. Don't ever rate him low, they said. He's got a sharp eye for a lot a little things nobody else notices. That's why he live so long. He keeps an eye open for the—"

The Signore's swatter took toll of another fly.

"Flies they failed to mention. Little things like flies. What's this fix you got on flies, man? You act like a cat with a bad habit."

"It's an old habit anyway," the Signore said. "I've already told you that."

"Yeah, you made money at it. Tell me more."

"Are you really interested, Cutter?"

"Until the sun goes down, J.P., you're my main interest in life."

"That's very flattering, Cutter. *Silvestro!*"

"Keep it cool, man."

"That's why I'm ordering more wine."

"Whatever you do, you talk United States."

"That wouldn't be cool at all, Cutter. I always converse with Silvestro in Italian."

"Then keep it short. My old lady was Italiano and I capeesh and don't you forget it."

Silvestro materialized and leaned deferentially toward Sr. Saccovino, who ordered another bottle of wine and two plates of lasagna al pesto. The Hairy Tourist followed every word with the big-eyed concentration of a bloodhound.

"My first flies," the Signore said as Silvestro withdrew. "I was eight or nine at the time, a small boy, small for my age, my father already dead, my dear mother forced to work long hours in sweatshops . . . Are you sure you want to hear this, Cutter?"

"With violins it would be better, but keep talkin'."

"My mother had a younger brother Isacco—Ike to all who knew him—and somehow he got enough money together to rent a small shop in our neighborhood. Much later I was able to guess where the money came from. Anyway, for sale in Ike's shop were olive oil, cheeses, prosciutto, sardines, salami, tomato paste, figs, mushrooms, peppers hotter than even these in this antipasto, braciole—"

"Skip the Little Italy part, man, and get to the flies. That's the part I'm interested in. How you started out makin' money by killin' flies."

"Of course. Well, my uncle's inventory attracted flies in the warm weather. And although this inventory was merely a front for his real stock-in-trade, he had a fussy prejudice against—"

"You mean he was like hustlin' somethin' else out of the back room there, I guess. Right, man?"

"That's right, Cutter. This was during the time of the Eighteenth Amendment. Ever hear of it?"

"Sure, the no-booze bust."

"Right again. Uncle Ike didn't sell enough Italian food to pay the rent. He moved what was known in those days as hooch. Still, he had a certain number of food customers, old-country people, who came in for a pound of provolone or something like that, and he honored them by keeping the front of the store neat and clean. No flies allowed. He let me hang out there after school and on Saturdays for the express purpose of keeping the place free of flies. I used a rolled-up newspaper to kill them and earned a penny a corpse. At the end of a good day I often collected as much as . . ."

While the Signore was talking Silvestro served the lasagna and more wine and the sun slipped into the shimmering sea and violet shadows crept rapidly over the pines on the uplands behind the town. Soon the darkness lay everywhere outside the meager light from the old fashioned street lamps and the boats moored in the harbor.

The Hairy Tourist washed down the last morsel with the last of the wine. "I feel so good right now," he said, "that I almost might grab the check off the waiter."

"Don't strain yourself," the Signore said. "I have a weekly account here."

"This could be the week it don't get paid." The Hairy Tourist chortled mirthlessly in his beard.

"That depends on how well you do your job."

"I ain't flubbed a job yet, J.P."

"*Silvestro.*"

The Hairy Tourist, sobering, leaned across the table. "Watch yourself with the waiter, man. One word outta line and I'll put a shiv in your gut so fast you won't have time to say scusa."

"Don't worry, Cutter. I have due respect for any man with a name like yours." The Signore took the proffered tray from Silvestro and signed the chit with his renowned pen, adding a fat gratuity.

"Mille grazie, signor," Silvestro said.

"Prego, Silvestro," the Signore said benignly.

"Buona notte, signor."

"Arrivederci, Silvestro."

A few minutes later the Signore and the Hairy Tourist passed from the town square side by side. The Signore was carrying the fly swatter, pearl handle up, under his right arm, much in the manner of an NCO with a baton on parade. The Hairy Tourist was smoking a cigarette silently, all talked out.

As they proceeded around one of the stone posts that held the chain across the Via Roma, the Signore said conversationally, "Did you come by car?"

"Yeah, that's right."

"Where did you park it?"

"You'll see soon enough."

"You plan to give me a ride?"

"Just a short one."

Out in the darkness, away from the lights of the town, a thousand stars became visible around a nearly full moon. In a moment the Signore's searching eyes caught a metallic glint ahead on the side of the road—a steel wheel disc.

"Do you have another cigarette?" he asked.

"Sure do," the Hairy Tourist said.

"I could use one."

"Okay, but no tricks." The Hairy Tourist took a pack of cigarettes from one pocket of his tweed jacket and a switchblade knife from the other. "Just in case," he said, snapping out the business end of the knife.

With his left hand the Signore pulled a cigarette from the pack. "Do you have a match?"

"You want me to spit for you, too?" Returning the cigarette pack to his pocket, the Hairy Tourist came up with a butane lighter. "Here you are, man," he said, clicking a blue flame into life. "Enjoy it. You got time for maybe five good drags."

The Signore was standing ramrod straight, a few inches shorter than his companion. He still held the fly swatter tucked under his arm like a baton. As the Hairy Tourist leaned forward to touch the cigarette in the Signore's mouth with the shimmying flame, the Signore's left hand went swiftly to the pearl handle and gave it a double twist. There was a vibrating sound—*piing-giing-giing*—and the lighter shook convulsively.

"Aaah gug ach," the Hairy Tourist said, dropping the switchblade and reaching for his throat. In a few seconds he got down on his knees and in another few seconds he prostrated himself at the Signore's feet.

After rolling the body over on its back, the Signore squatted beside it and began to remove the wig, the eyebrows, the beard, the mustache. The face thus revealed struck a chord of memory. Cutie Moran all over again, twenty years later, with a few minor variations. Still stupid, still inept. Like father, like son.

He raked the nearby ground with his fingers until he located the butane lighter. Then with the lighter's help he explored the throatal region until he found what he was looking for—the tip of a narrow stainless-steel shaft protruding a tiny fraction of an inch from the folds of the turtleneck sweater. With a pair of jeweler's pliers taken from the pocket of his silk coat he grasped the tip of the shaft and gently pulled, presently extracting a needle six inches long. He wrapped it carefully in the monogrammed handkerchief which he took from the breast pocket of the dead man's jacket and set it on the ground next to the fly swatter for reloading at a later time. He stripped off the jacket and went through the pockets. Wallet, money, traveler's checks, *two* passports.

The first passport, containing a photograph of the Hairy Tourist, identified him as Henry A. Scotti of St. Louis, Missouri; the second, depicting a living likeness of the hairless corpse, was issued to Charles Moran, also of St. Louis.

"Addio, Enrico," the Signore muttered. "Addio, Carlo."

He spread the tweed jacket on the ground. Onto its lining he dropped the passports and the switchblade. The turtleneck sweater followed. Next went the slacks, in the hip pocket of which he found the car keys. When the corpse was stark naked he dragged it several yards off the road and propped it in a sitting position with its back against a boulder.

He made a bundle of the tweed jacket by tying its arms together. He carried the bundle to the car—a rented Fiat, he noticed—and locked it in the trunk. He climbed into the driver's seat and drove the car in the direction of Paraggi until he reached a place where the road hung recklessly over the Golfo Marconi. He got out of the car, its motor idling, and walked it with some effort to the brink of doom. As it began its irreversible tilt he lit the butane lighter and tossed it into the front seat. Then he began the longish walk—three kilometers, at least—back to the villa, reloading the pearl-handled fly swatter en route.

The next day was domenica, God's day, but the Portofinese weren't talking about God. The main subject of conversation was the discovery of the nude body of an unidentified man on the Via Roma outside the town. The man was generally assumed to have been a Mafioso because of the tattoo on the left forearm—a serpent (evil) climbing a cross (good). Though not yet officially determined, the cause of death was attributed by Umberto the carabiniere, who had seen such things, to a fishbone's lodgment sidewise in the man's gullet. Nobody seemed to wonder why a naked stranger would be eating bony fish out there at night.

A minor topic of conversation that same morning concerned the fact that Henry A. Scotti had departed unseen from the Hotel Nazionale without taking along his airlines flight bag which contained, according to the manager, Sr. Daddario, a safety razor, a package of razor blades, an aerosol can of shaving cream, and a bottle of lime-scented lotion.

"Why should such a hairy devil carry around articles like these?" Sr. Daddario was fond of asking whenever the subject arose, which was not often.

On this same day Sr. Saccovino killed twenty-seven flies.

The Patchwork Quilt
by Pauline C. Smith

I didn't think Tommy should go up on the mountain that morning, but it was the day for Miss Mattie Jackson's quilt, and since Tommy's got a calendar in his head instead of brains, he was, of course, determined. I argued thieves and killers until I was out of breath, with Tommy's only rebuttal a firm and stolid reiteration that Miss Mattie Jackson would be finished with her quilt and expecting him.

Tommy takes his responsibilities very seriously, probably because it's the first time in his eighteen years he has had any. He does all my running around for me, and believe me, that's some running around. I own and operate the Jane Flagg Old Time Store in Mountain Hollow, specializing in stitchery done in the old-time manner—cross-stitch mottoes, appliqued coverlets and patchwork quilts, crewel and other embroidery, needlepoint, wax-work, feather-work, quill-work, all lovely, and offering these hill women a pride of achievement and a bit of independence they have never known.

My best worker, Miss Mattie Jackson, lives alone, high up in a narrow gulch of the mountain. She was old when I was growing up in these parts, so she must be ancient now. Nobody ever sees her; nobody except Tommy, who drives the jeep up those treacherous roads on the first day of each month, carrying supplies and materials, and returning with her newest quilt.

Her patchwork quilts were wonderful, the stitches fine and true—with, each month, an old and different historical pattern, such as "Tippecanoe and Tyler Too," reminiscent of the William Henry Harrison campaign, and "Clay's Choice," a memory of the bitter Calhoun and Clay days. She does the old and favorite patterns and those that are old and rare.

My mother was a quilter, as were her mother and grandmother before her. They all lived in this house and left here records of the quilts of their times. I can identify most of Miss Mattie Jackson's patterns by searching through the detailed and titled sketches carefully recorded by these women of my family and stored in a suit box. Sometime I plan to copy them on graph paper for publication, except

51

that nobody quilts any more, nobody but the hill folk who quilt for
the few traveling customers willing to leave the fast traffic of the
superhighway and slow down for the old Mountain Hollow road.

I don't know exactly when I decided to come back to Mountain
Hollow to stay, but it was long after I finished college, married, and
had Tommy. Probably Tommy and his father Brian finally decided
me—poor Tommy, whose body grew but whose brain did not, and
arrogant Brian who accused my hillbilly blood of causing the re-
tardation.

I didn't argue the matter. Who could argue with an uptight businessman who thought of a wife as decorative background to his
ambition, and a slow-witted boy as something to hide? I just went
on getting my hair done each week, being nice to the right people,
and trying to find someone who could spark the few brains Tommy
was born with to make of him a reasonably functioning facsimile
son of a rising executive.

Well, after a series of pathologists, psychologists, and special
schools, at last I did what was best for him—for me, too—and came
home to Mountain Hollow where the people wouldn't know the difference between a rising executive and a falling star, and where
Tommy was accepted with love and admiration both for the calendar
in his head and his way with a jeep.

"Tommy sure can drive that jeep," Mountain Hollow folk exclaim
in wonder; and he can. He also understands what is under the hood
and keeps it in perfect running condition. Tommy has realized his
potential and now I don't have to get my hair done each week, which
is a big relief.

I like breathing the clean air and living the slow life of Mountain
Hollow. I like the unsophisticated goodness of the people. Nothing
touches us here; nothing until those hoodlum killers got close—or
were they close? Nobody really knew. Actually, nobody knew who
they were, how many there were or what they drove. Nobody knew
anything about them except that where they had been, they'd left
death.

The radio newscasts dropped separate announcements: liquor
store robbed, all witnesses killed; drugstore looted, proprietor
slashed to death— until the separate announcements made a chain
of identical iniquity along the superhighway, still far away, but
heading toward the turnoff that entered Mountain Hollow. Then,
after seven murders, the newscasts reported nothing new. It was as
if these phantom killers had vanished, evaporated somewhere be-

fore, beyond, or between the roadblocks set up along the highway—they and their phantom vehicle.

The hillbillies of Mountain Hollow, not having any great imagination, breathed a sigh of relief and I began to worry. If the killers weren't killing, where were they now? I worried more actively on the morning Tommy insisted on driving up to Miss Mattie Jackson's cabin in the gulch because he had this calendar in his head instead of brains, and the page had flipped to the day Miss Mattie's quilt would be finished.

"All right, all right," I finally cried, "go on," and he loaded the jeep with supplies, as happy as a dumb lark, doing his thing on the day he was supposed to do it.

I had a radio going in the shop, which used to be the parlor of the house when my folks and my folks' folks and their folks lived here. Tommy and I live in the rest of the house. I didn't give much ear to the country music, which is about all we have on the local radio station, but I did listen to the news spots that offered such shameful items as Big Jed Bartlett's drunken tangle with the law at the local tavern and juicy little bits about Mary Louise Plunkett's latest hair-pulling melee; but nothing new about the killers who were "at large," the newscaster vaguely announced.

It took Tommy an hour to make the trip up to the gulch . . . what was it they used to call that place . . . ? Well, I can't remember now. Anyway, it was about an hour's trip up there, then fifteen minutes to unload the supplies and load on the new quilt, so all in all, I figured Tommy should be back in two hours and fifteen minutes, if everything went all right. . . .

We've got a sheriff; well, actually, we don't have him, the county has him, and it's a pretty big county. After Tommy had been gone a little over an hour, I phoned the sheriff and got him, too. He wasn't out chasing killers or standing beside roadblocks, he was right there at the sheriff's station, answering the phone!

"What makes you think, Mrs. Flagg, that they're around Mountain Hollow?" he asked with slight surprise.

"I didn't *say* I thought they were *here*," I shouted quickly and vehemently. "What I *said* was I thought they *might* be here, holed up somewhere."

"Well, I suppose they might be at that, Mrs. Flagg," he said with the drawl all mountain people have, probably because they live so slowly their thoughts slow down and their tongues, too, to match. "And if they come out, Mrs. Flagg, we'll try to catch them."

I sat there at the phone, shaking with inward rage. I could see the sheriff in my mind's eye, lolling back in that old swivel chair of his. How could he catch anything, lolling in a swivel chair—even flies?

"If they're holed up somewhere, Mrs. Flagg," he said, "they're probably holed up maybe fifty miles from here because that's where the hoodlums were last heard from . . ."

I banged down the receiver in despair, thinking: *These people! There's not an ounce of imagination in all their pea-brains rolled together.* I set about to rearrange the entire shop, hoping to keep my mind off what *my* imagination was conjuring up while I waited for Tommy—who drove up to the shop, exactly on time, two hours and fifteen minutes from the time he had left it! Thank heaven!

I hugged him between the quilt he carried in his arms, and plied him with questions: Had he seen anyone on the way? Had he heard anything—like shots? Were there any dead bodies around? Was Miss Mattie Jackson all right? To which he answered, *Heck-no-Mom*, and *Sure-by-golly-Mom*, and went outside to shine up the engine of the jeep.

I stood there in a grateful daze, holding the quilt, and looking through the big window I'd had put in the front of the shop, at Tommy leaning lovingly inside the open hood of the jeep. I stood there quite a while with a heart full of thanksgiving and a bit of regret for banging down the receiver on the sheriff, who had probably been right in his assumption that the killers were holed up fifty miles away.

Then I spread the quilt out on a table. It was a bright and cheerful pattern, done in different shades of orange and yellow, the sunshine colors, and I ran for the suit box to find out whether it was the "Sunbeam" or "Rising Sun" pattern. I couldn't be sure, as they are very similar; the one a circle with curved triangular patches forming a larger circle, around which are stitched smaller sunray triangles on a block; the other, a square with alternating shaded triangles. I studied the sketches.

It turned out to be the "Sunbeam," simpler of the two blocks, and very lovely. I admired it for a few minutes, reached down for the part of the quilt that draped over the table and extended almost to the floor, then bent frozen, with my hand outstretched in rigid shock as I saw the bottom blocks of the quilt, which had none of the "Sunbeam" pattern, but were all in somber color, each different from the other!

I cried, "Oh, no!" and moved at last, yanking the bottom of the quilt to a heap on the table. "Oh, no!," thinking for sure that Miss Mattie Jackson had flipped her lid.

I had here a quilt, five twelve-inch blocks wide by six twelve-inch blocks long, regulation size, regulation "Sunbeam" pattern in variegated shades of orange and yellow, a beautiful and classic quilt *until* that very bottom row with its dark colors and strangely blocked patchwork. I leaned over the quilt in a kind of limp supplication—poor Miss Mattie, she must have popped her cork.

I brooded for a while, then I went to the front door of the shop, opened it, and called out to Tommy. "Tommy, did Miss Mattie Jackson say anything strange when you were up to her cabin today?" I had to call Tommy's name four times before he pulled his head out of the jeep engine long enough to stare at me blankly. Then he said, "Heck no, Mom," and stuck his head back under the hood.

He wouldn't know.

I closed the door and went back into the shop. Well, if Miss Mattie Jackson had become psychotically senile after a lifetime of living alone up there in that mountainous gulch, she had the right, I guess, and the years.

I picked up the phone and called Mrs. Frankie Mae Pangborn, who said she'd be right over even though she was cluttered with trouble and busy as a bumblebee in a bucket of tar, which was probably true, what with a bunch of grandchildren and great-grandchildren always underfoot. Mrs. Frankie Mae Pangborn was as ancient as Miss Mattie Jackson and had just as much right to go crazy with senility, but probably wouldn't since she lived in the valley with all her posterity to keep her mentally alert.

I showed her the quilt, with the last row tucked under, as soon as she arrived all out of breath. "Look," I said. "Look at that!"

"As pretty a 'Sunbeam' pattern as ever I did see," she admired.

Then I whipped the last row of blocks free on the table and watched her expression, which didn't change one iota.

"Well . . ." I said at last.

"Looks like Miss Mattie Jackson changed her mind a bit before she finished this here quilt," she offered.

"It looks like maybe she *lost* her mind," I said dryly, and Mrs. Frankie Mae Pangborn studied me with the remote gaze of the hill folk for outlanders.

"I mean," I said desperately, "it looks as if maybe something is very wrong; a quilter like Miss Mattie Jackson, an expert, an artist, suddenly going off the beam like this, throwing in just any old block pattern . . ."

"Maybe it ain't just any old block pattern."

"She might be sick. She is, after all, very old. And living alone the way she does . . . Well," and I spread my hands helplessly in an attempt to explain senility to one who was ready for senility, "she might not have really known what she was doing. What do you think?"

"I ain't had time yet to think," Mrs. Frankie Mae Pangborn chastised me. "I am still at the ponderin' stage."

So there she stood—pondering—without intellect, without imagination, while her friend, a poor little lady alone on the mountain, went crazy with old age. "What I mean," I said, "I think she needs help and somebody ought to go up there and bring her down where she can be taken care of."

Mrs. Frankie Mae Pangborn nodded, but instead of racing out of the shop to round up some able-bodied nonworking men to go up the mountain and bring down that poor crazed woman, she leaned over the quilt and drawled thoughtfully. "I reckon Miss Mattie Jackson is offerin' up a message and it's up to us to unscramble it. Now this, what would you say this block meant?" as she pointed at the first block in the last row of five, a seemingly helter-skelter design of different colored patches forming a staggered diagonal pattern.

"It's a crazy-quilt block," I said impatiently, and Mrs. Frankie Mae Pangborn tolerantly answered that no, it certainly was not, it was an "Old Maid's Puzzle" block, probably put there purposely to make me read the rest of them, or for *someone* to read, she added with the barest hint of scorn that made me suddenly feel like a dullwitted clod before such bright perception.

"Miss Mattie Jackson is sharp as a pin. Always has been, always will be. These blocks ain't just staggerin' off course. They're tryin' to tell us somethin' here."

Looking down at them, I regained my equanimity. Those blocks weren't trying to tell us anything, not unless they were trying to tell us that poor Miss Mattie Jackson had finally come unstrung after all the years alone up there on the mountain and, each time she made one of those blocks for that last row, thought she was starting a whole new quilt . . . "For instance, that block," I said, pointing at the second one, right after "Old Maid's Puzzle," "that's a 'Bat in Flight' and, really now, what meaning could it have?"

Mrs. Frankie Mae Pangborn cocked her head and studied the block. "It does look like a 'Bat in Flight' and that's for sure," she said with wonder.

I began to riffle through the open suit box for a sketch of the block in question, when she stopped me dead. "But 'Bat in Flight,' as I remember, flies outward toward the corner of the block, and this one sure is flying inward and looks a heap more like a 'Bear's Paw' to me."

She was right!

It was a tricky little pattern, the block sectioned off in five squares across and five down, the center being dark, its corner squares dark, with those adjacent to each corner square, triangled dark fabric patches, forming the wings and tail of a bat, four bats to a block; but, in this case, the pad and toes of a bear's paw, four paw prints to the block.

I looked at Mrs. Frankie Mae Pangborn with dawning respect, and then I said, "But 'Bear's Paw' doesn't mean any more than 'Bat in Flight.' "

"Not," she said, "unless you remember that 'Bear's Paw' is the name of the gulch where Miss Mattie Jackson lives."

I remembered at last. They used to say, when I was a girl in Mountain Hollow, "Miss Mattie Jackson, up at Bear's Paw." Now I was sure that Miss Mattie Jackson, of Bear's Paw, was sending a message through the "Sunbeam" quilt—an "Old Maid's Puzzle" to be worked out, block by block.

The next was obvious: a patchwork house set in a ground of flowered material. I called out the name of the pattern almost as quickly as did Mrs. Frankie Mae Pangborn: "House on the Hill." The cut patches were not as true, nor the stitches as tiny—Miss Mattie Jackson had become nervous or hurried, or *frightened?*

The fourth block was a teaser. Mrs. Frankie Mae Pangborn frowned over it and I riffled through the patterns, whispering names: "Drunkard's Path," a block of four squares; "Wild Goose Chase," no, that was sectioned off into diamonds . . . " 'Jack in the Box'!" I cried. My voice rose and Mrs. Frankie Mae Pangborn nodded.

I ran for the phone and called the sheriff.

Thank God he was still sitting on his swivel chair at the sheriff's station. I yelled into the phone that Miss Mattie Jackson was being held prisoner up at Bear's Paw in her House on the Hill, and just as I banged down the receiver, Mrs. Frankie Mae Pangborn added that she was being held by five people, or had been held for five days, or something five anyway, because the last block was a "V Block," and what else could it mean but five?

I raced back to look down at the "V Block," formed of narrow V's, four of them, so placed on the block that their points came together in the center; the final stitches, not Miss Mattie Jackson's fine overcast, nor her hurriedly wavered stitch on the "Jack in the Box," but an uneven basting that made me fear for her life.

"Well, jump down my throat and gallop my insides out, if Miss Mattie Jackson ain't in a heap of trouble now," breathed Mrs. Frankie Mae Pangborn, and reached out blindly for a place to sit down. I led her to a chair and she dropped, sitting stiffly with her hands folded on her lap.

I finally got Tommy's head out from under the hood of the jeep and into the shop, and questioned him while we waited for the sheriff to arrive. "Now, Tommy, this is important," I said seriously. "What did you see when you were up at Miss Mattie Jackson's this morning?, " remembering suddenly that it was no longer morning, but afternoon, and Miss Mattie was still being held by five people, or had been held for five days or—my goodness—would be held for five more hours before they killed her and took off!

"Tommy, think!" I cried. "What did you see at Miss Mattie Jackson's?"

He furrowed his brow, then he smiled. "Why, Mom, I saw the trees and the chickens like always."

"No, Tommy," I cried, grabbing his shoulders and shaking him in desperation. "Did you see anything *different*? Were there any *people* around?"

He shook his head, attempting to break away and head out for the jeep that was the love of his life.

"You see, Tommy," I said, my voice shaking, "we think those killers are in Miss Mattie Jackson's house. Did you go *in* the house?"

He shook his head vigorously, and I knew that he never did. He took the monthly supplies up to her door and she handed the quilt out to him. Tommy was not gregarious nor was Miss Mattie sociable. They had that together, the rapport of two loners. "Did you *hear* anything?"

"Heck no, Mom," he said, smiling. "Not even the chickens. She told me where to drive so the chickens wouldn't squawk and stop laying eggs. She said, 'You drive clear off the road down below and through the trees and up to—' "

"All right, Tommy," I interrupted him. "All right, you can go on out now and shine up the engine of the jeep again," and I gave him a little shove.

From the minute the sheriff drove up in a jeep, Tommy stuck to him like a burr, probably feeling close kinship with another jeep driver, and stood right behind him while the sheriff and his two deputies leaned over the quilt and Mrs. Frankie Mae Pangborn explained the message.

"This here," she said, pointing to the first block of the last row, "is the 'Old Maid's Puzzle,' that's how I knew Miss Mattie Jackson wasn't just throwing on any old piece of patchwork because her brains was dusty, but that she was giving us a message, starting right out with, 'This here is Miss Mattie Jackson talkin'.'

"Then the next one, 'Bear's Paw' being where she lives, and adding the 'House on the Hill' to it, I knew she was tellin' us that something was going on there. 'Jack in the Box' was real inspirational—I don't know of anything else she could have used to let us know she was bein' held prisoner. This last one, though, has kinda got me," admitted Mrs. Frankie Mae Pangborn. "Maybe it means there are five of them cowardly dogs there in her cabin. Maybe it means they been there five days. Whatever, she's sure trying to convey a message in that there 'V Block' . . ."

"That's the V," said Tommy pointing over the sheriff's shoulder. "That's the V of trees where Miss Mattie Jackson tells me to drive the jeep so the chickens won't set up a ruckus and stop laying eggs. That's the V right there. Miss Mattie Jackson says, 'You drive clear off the road down below and go on up to that stand of trees . . .' The V, she calls it. 'It looks like a V,' she says, 'and that V of trees cuts off the sound so the chickens won't be bothered.' "

"And so, whoever's in there with Miss Mattie Jackson won't hear us until we get right up on them." The sheriff thrust out a hand. "Son," he said, "you've got a brain and a half on you," and I wanted to cry with pride. It was the first time anybody had ever told Tommy he had any kind of brain.

"You put that boy's brain in a jaybird's head and he'd fly straight and true," announced Mrs. Frankie Mae Pangborn. "Why don't you deputize him, sheriff, and let him drive you up to the V? He knows right how to get there, and he's the best jeep driver around."

Before I could protest, Tommy had become a smiling-faced deputy and was on his way up the mountain, carrying three officers of the law loaded down with guns!

Mrs. Frankie Mae Pangborn sat with me through part of that long afternoon. The spot newscasts on the radio continued to offer no news as to the killers. However, Mrs. Rachel Peabody, at the south end of the county, swore she saw what looked to be a very suspicious character fishing on the river bottom, and Mrs. Frankie Mae Pangborn snorted out her opinion that Mrs. Rachel Peabody's mouth was so wide that if it weren't for her ears, the top of her head would be an island. I walked the floor, looked at the clock every ten minutes and, in between the country music, listened to the weather reports, crop and hog prices, and the local news items—until Tommy arrived home at near-dark and told me all about it. He told it as only a boy with the sophisticated, arrogant, ambitious part of his brain left out, and the homespun, down-to-earth, ready-to-help part left in. He told it chronologically, with few words and little emotion.

"I took them up there to the V place, and told them how to get to the house. Then I watched. They made me the lookout, Mom," he said proudly, and I patted his shoulder and swallowed.

He told how there were three against three, the sheriff and two deputies against the girl and two boy killers, and some shots fired, ". . . but they didn't do any hurt except to get the chickens to squawking so they probably won't lay any eggs for a while."

"Well," I said, "I guess Miss Mattie Jackson won't never mind about that," dropping into the vernacular of the hill people—my people and Tommy's—these wonderful people with great imagination and the talent to send a message on a quilt and have it read correctly. The country radio music stopped abruptly to allow the latest news report to come through, all about the apprehension of the three young killers, found in their mountain hideaway. They didn't know the half of it!

"Miss Mattie Jackson is all right?" I asked Tommy.

"Sure, by golly, Mom," he said. "She told me she was going to make a special quilt for me. She said it would be like a letter. How can she make a quilt like a letter, Mom?"

"Well, she can," I said. "Miss Mattie Jackson can send a beautiful letter on a quilt. Now, would you like to shine the engine of the jeep before supper?"

Tommy didn't get a chance before darkness fell, for the sheriff came to pick up the county jeep and told the story again, more graphically and more in detail, but not nearly as well as Tommy, who knew what the "V Block" really meant, and because he knew, Miss Mattie Jackson can make patchwork quilts until she dies a natural death.

Farewell Gesture

by George Grover Kipp

Detective Doug Temple got his first inkling of the case as he passed the open squad room door on his way out of the station house. What piqued his curiosity primarily was the number of men assembled in the squad room. Actually, Doug shouldn't even have been in the building, but the records clerk had loused up some of the papers pertinent to Doug's retirement, and he'd had to come in and sign a new set. On a sudden hunch, Doug took a seat just inside the door, his back to the wall. At the far end of the room the commissioner, Chief Muldoon, and Hal Tobin, from the FBI, sat behind an elevated table. The final report had been given and the chief rose and faced the gathering.

"Well, that wraps it up, men. The five kilos of heroin did *not* come in on the *Singapore Mail*. So the problem now belongs to either San Francisco or Seattle. Let's get back to work."

Doug leaned back in his chair, eyes closed, and ran the bit of information through his mind.

"What's the matter, Doug, do we bore you?" a voice gibed gently.

Doug opened his eyes slowly, a faint grin playing around his mouth. "Not really, Henderson. It's just that the thought of hanging up my gun and badge and turning the city over to you scares me. I shut out the sight every chance I get."

Henderson was one of the new breed of lawmen. Somewhere in his late twenties, he was blond, crewcut, and college educated. He grinned at Doug and passed through the door with the others.

When Chief Muldoon remained alone at the far end of the room, Doug brought his lanky frame erect and moved to the table. He scanned the reports lying there, then scratched his chin thoughtfully. "You were expecting a shipment of heroin on the *Singapore Mail*. How come I never heard about it?"

Muldoon shuffled the papers into a pile. "It was strictly a short-notice deal. We just got word ourselves as the ship docked. You were too far out in the boondocks looking for a getaway car to get here in time. Henderson hit Terminal One with two squads of men and gave the ship a real going-over, but she was clean. One truck had been loaded, but they overtook it at the corner of Holcomb and Second and escorted it back to the terminal. Like the ship, it was clean." The chief leaned back in his chair and shook his head hopelessly at Doug. "Why don't you ease off a bit? According to my figures you've got something like seventy-two hours left out of thirty-three years. Day after tomorrow you're sixty-five. You get the pension, the rocking chair, the whole bit. Then you'll *have* to turn Chinatown, the warehouse district, and the waterfront over to somebody else."

Doug nodded soberly, his pale blue eyes intent. The very thought of retiring left a cold knot in his stomach. "But not today. And since I'm a cop for seventy-two more hours, give me a rundown on this heroin thing."

"It's fairly simple," the chief said indifferently. "An Interpol agent followed the shipment from the border of Nepal and India to the south of France, where he was almost wiped out in an automobile accident. He was in a coma, in critical condition, for several weeks. When he regained consciousness he got a list of the ships that were in the port of Marseilles that day, ships that were headed this way. There were four of them and the *Singapore Mail* was the first of the four to arrive. The other three are slated to arrive during the next three days. Two of them go to Frisco, the other to Seattle. According to the Interpol agent, the shipment consists of five kilos."

Doug's brows rose perceptibly. "Five kilos means real big operators are pulling the strings on the operation. Why don't I ease off a bit like you suggested and snoop around on this thing?"

The chief shook his head despairingly. "What is there about that part of town that gets to you, Doug?"

The detective thumbed his hat back and grinned. "Sentiment, I guess. My first job with the force was to help break a narco ring down there. That was in 1937, the biggest case in the city's history. We scooped up two kilos and seven hoods on that one. Uh, what was on the truck the boys stopped at Holcomb and Second?" he asked offhandedly.

Muldoon shuffled through the papers. "Wire. Reels of steel wire from Kobe, Japan. Weston Aluminum uses it in the cores of their electric cables. And before you point out that the truck was off course, Henderson already did that. The driver said he was on his way to get a cup of coffee. When his rig checked out clean, there was no reason to doubt his word."

"There's just one small flaw in the picture," Doug said slowly, "and it's right there in Hencerson's report—the part where the truck turned right onto Lander and then left onto Second Street. As near as I can figure it, the truck was completely out of sight for something like thirty seconds."

The chief's jaw sagged. "Aw, come on, now Doug. I've known you a lot of years and I've never known you to split hairs before. Thirty *seconds?* You *must* be kidding."

Doug stared out the window to where storm clouds were falling into formation for their march on the city. "The highway runs straight from the docks, and anybody in that truck could have seen the police cars coming up behind them. There would have been enough traffic at that hour to slow our boys up for a good thirty seconds after the truck turned onto Lander. Just for the hell of it, let's assume the dope *was* on that truck. A hood running scared with five kilos of horse under his arm could cover a helluva stretch of real estate in thirty seconds."

Muldoon threw up his hands in surrender. "So you've spent a lifetime prowling Chinatown and the warehouse district, and you're going to use this deal as an excuse to go back one last time. All right, go. Giving you a free rein for the last three days sure won't break the city, and you've earned that much. Go on. Get out of here."

Doug touched a finger to the brim of his hat and moved toward the door, his mind probing the various aspects of the case. An Interpol agent involved in a near-fatal accident while pursuing five kilos of pure heroin? It was possible, of course, but the odds were against the accident's really being an accident.

"Don't prowl down too many dark alleys," Muldoon called as Doug reached the door. "I'd hate to have to tell your beautiful granddaughter that after thirty-three years on the winning team you went out and bought yourself a slab in the morgue."

Mention of Jenny brought a warm smile to Doug's lean features. When Doug's son and daughter-in-law died in the plane crash, Jenny had been a knobby-kneed eleven-year-old. She'd been with Doug and Emma five years when cancer took Emma away. Now there were just the two of them.

"Don't worry about Jenny," Doug called to Muldoon. "She's a junior in college now and going with a fourth-year law student. She's a real levelheaded kid."

Doug drove the route the truck had taken from the *Singapore Mail,* then circled back to Terminal One and drove it a second time. After completing a third such trip, he parked his car at Holcomb and Second, where the truck had been stopped, and began walking.

The wind had come up, giving fair warning of the storm that was moving in. Eddies of dust whipped around his legs and pirouetted crazily across the street as he paused at the corner of Lander and Second and studied the towering rows of warehouses that lined the streets.

He backtracked slowly toward the car, his eyes noting every detail. Midway along the block he passed an opening, barely eighteen inches wide, between two of the buildings. Then he moved back and stared into the opening, his eyes squinted in deep thought. He went to his car and got a flashlight.

Moving sideways into the opening, his chest to one building, his back to the other, he inched his way along. He halted twice to gather a minute smattering of fibers clinging to the craggy tongues of dried mortar protruding from between the bricks, and once to pick up a piece of tarred roofing paper. When he could find nothing else that interested him, he drove back to the station and turned the fibers in to the lab for an analysis.

When he returned from having a fast cup of coffee in the squad room, the technician had the report waiting for him. "Alpaca fibers, Doug. Dusty yellow in color, sort of a dried mustard shade, and expensive. Offhand, I'd say they came from a sweater in the fifty-dollar class."

Doug nodded a silent thanks and returned thoughtfully to his car. With the piece of roofing paper in his hand he began a tour of the better shoe shops. At his sixth stop the clerk studied the distinctive sole print on the veneer of tar coating the paper, then disappeared into the back room. He returned with a pair of heavy brogues in his hand. "This is the shoe that made the print. One of our better items. Size seven."

Doug studied the points of similarity between the sole and the print on the tar paper. "How much do they sell for?"

"Eighty-five dollars a copy," the clerk said indifferently.

Doug thanked the man and moved out the door. The furrows in his brow deepened as he walked back to his car. Fifty-dollar sweaters and eighty-five-dollar shoes . . . They didn't go with the scroungy hole between the two warehouses at all. Back at the station Doug leaned back in his chair, eyes closed in deep thought.

"I don't know why you'd want to retire and leave such a soft touch," the chief's voice broke into his reverie. "You never had it so good."

Doug opened his eyes and came slowly erect. "Did Henderson run a check on the guy driving the truck this morning?"

Muldoon shook his head. "There wasn't any sense in it after the truck turned out to be clean." He grinned. "Why don't you give it up?"

Doug rose and stretched. "I suppose I would if I was half smart, but the possibilities inherent in those thirty seconds still intrigue me. Besides, I've helped keep this town clean for too many years to turn my back now. There's probably nothing in it, but I'll push it a little farther before I sign off. What was the truck driver's name?"

"Orchard," Muldoon said. "Harry Orchard."

Doug caught up with Harry Orchard at a pre-stress firm on the edge of town. The trucker was waiting for a crane to load his truck with concrete blocks. At Doug's question he shook his crewcut blond head wearily. "Now it's a passenger? Well, I didn't have a passenger this morning, just like I didn't have any contraband. I'm beginning to wonder about you guys. I've got a beautiful wife, two beautiful daughters, and a nice home. I have to keep scratching to make the payments, but I do make them, and with legitimately earned dough."

Doug had checked Harry Orchard thoroughly and then driven past the Orchard home before setting out in search of the man. There'd been nothing anywhere to suggest the trucker was dishonest. "It's like this," Doug said slowly. "I'm running a double check on the matter, sort of playing a real long shot. I'm looking for a guy about five six or seven, as near as I can figure his size. He probably weighs a hundred and fifty pounds, and goes in for expensive shoes and alpaca sweaters."

Orchard shook his head. "He can have the alpaca sweaters. My wife's brother has five of them—his status symbols, no less. He's tried to get me into the used car business with him so I could wear them, too, but who needs them? I was thinking of him this morning on the pier when the photographer came by. He was wearing an alpaca sweater."

"Photographer?" Doug prodded softly.

Orchard looked toward the crane but it was still loading the truck ahead of him. "He came along the pier this morning when my truck was being loaded. He had a camera around his neck and the leather carrying case slung over his shoulder. About all I really noticed, though, was the alpaca sweater. It reminded me of the brother-in-law."

"Build me a picture of the photographer," Doug invited, his voice still soft.

Orchard squinted in concentration, then his eyes widened comically. "He was just about the size guy you said you were looking for—about five foot six, a hundred and fifty pounds. He was somewhere between thirty and thirty-five and real swarthy."

"His sweater?" Doug probed.

"Kind of an off-color yellow. Say a dull, brownish yellow."

"Would you know him if you saw him again?" Doug asked.

"You'd better believe it," Orchard said emphatically. "He was a real sourpuss. He was at the corner of the warehouse watching two cops in the parking lot when I said, 'Don't give your right name,' but he didn't appreciate it at all. I worked with an old ex-con once and that's what he'd say every time he saw a police car or heard a siren. I just said it out of habit."

"There were two police officers in the Terminal One parking lot *before* you drove away?" Doug asked warily.

Orchard turned to check the lane again. "Yup. Two of them. They were parked beside a dark green Pontiac. The way they were leaning against their patrol car, I got the impression they were waiting for somebody to show."

"You didn't happen to notice the license number of the sedan?" Doug persisted.

The trucker waited until a loaded truck groaned past. "Nope. But the letters in front of the number were MEE, and there was one of those big stuffed snakes lying in the back window. I wouldn't have remembered the letters, but some of them stick in your mind—MEE . . . JUG . . . PIP . . . PAP." Orchard crawled into his truck and moved toward the crane.

Back at the station, Doug called both daily newspapers and also six weeklies in the outlying districts, but none of them had sent a photographer to meet the *Singapore Mail*. "Probably a free-lancer," one of the editors suggested.

Moving down the hall, Doug halted at the dispatcher's desk. "One of our cars was parked in the Terminal One parking lot this morning *before* the raid on the *Singapore Mail*. Find out who was riding it and get them in here."

From the dispatcher's desk Doug proceeded to the record room and began thumbing through the files. He was still looking for a hood with a love of fine clothing when two officers entered the room. One was fiftyish and stocky, the other slim and just out of the rookie class. "You send for us, Doug?" the older man asked.

Doug shoved the file drawer shut. "Yeah, I sent for you. You guys were parked in the Terminal One parking lot this morning, Larsen. Sometime before the raid on the *Singapore Mail*. Why?"

Larsen hooked a thumb at his companion. "Because Jonesy here has a big thing going with the sexy blonde who drives the canteen truck. It comes time for a coffee break, we always manage to find the little white wagon. Sometimes we even manage to find it at lunch time." Larsen's eyes slitted. "Somebody put in a complaint or something?"

Doug emitted a soft chuckle. "No complaints, Larsen. But I should have suspected a dame figured in the picture. I *must* be getting old. What I wanted to see you about was the car you were parked next to, the dark green job. What can you tell me about it?"

Larsen scratched his head thoughtfully. "Not much, I'm afraid. It had one of those big stuffed snakes in the back window, and the back seat was loaded with camera accessories and boxes of film. There must have been two, three hundred dollars' worth of stuff. When I saw all that stuff I checked the car to see if it was locked. It was. About then the call came in on the radio to hit Terminal One, so we just stayed where we were and waited for the other cars to show up."

"You didn't happen to notice a small, dark guy in a yellowish sweater, with a camera hanging around his neck?"

When both men shook their heads, Doug wasn't the least bit disappointed. As closely as he'd been able to figure it, the man with the camera had scrambled onto the back of Harry Orchard's truck as it pulled away from the pier. Hidden behind the reels of wire, it would have been simple for the man to spot the police cars coming up behind the truck. In his mind's eye Doug could see the hood, eyes wide with fear as the police car edged closer. The man had been doomed, unable to get off the speeding truck in the freeway traffic; then had come the real fluke—Harry Orchard had turned off the freeway to get a cup of coffee. It couldn't have been timed better for the character on the back of the truck. He'd bailed off and cut out bare seconds ahead of the police.

Larsen studied Doug for a minute. "You got something going, Doug? Something to do with the raid of the *Singapore Mail?*"

"I could have," Doug said slowly. "But right at the minute all I've got to go on is intuition." He described the man who had been on the pier that morning. "He goes in for eighty-five-dollar shoes and fifty-dollar sweaters—and maybe million-dollar packages of heroin."

Doug checked his watch. "Time to call it a day. Maybe I can find him in the files tomorrow."

Doug was watching the evening news and Jenny was at the kitchen table, bent over her homework, when the telephone rang. It was Larsen. "Doug? After I got home I got to thinking about a slob who might fill the bill for you. I couldn't figure why you hadn't mentioned him, and then it came to me that you didn't know him. He heisted a loan office five years ago the first of last May. Harcourt and I busted him before he got three blocks. If that was him on the pier this morning, I can understand why he was making himself inconspicuous. I'm the last guy on earth he'd want to see."

Five years ago the first of May . . . Doug had been off for two weeks then. There was the funeral and all that goes with it, and then the search for a suitable lady to stay with Jenny for a while. "Thanks, Larsen. What was the guy's name?"

"Rinaldi," Larsen said. "Joey Rinaldi."

Rain driven by a north wind was hitting the window in great splashy drops the next day as Doug leaned back in his chair and studied the file on Joseph Albert Rinaldi. Rinaldi had been busted four times in his life, three times upstate and once locally. According to the file, his last parole had expired six months earlier. Doug put five other photographs in with Rinaldi's and set out to find Harry Orchard.

The trucker was back at the pre-stress plant waiting for another load of concrete blocks. He went through the pictures like he was dealing cards and stuck his finger right between Joey Rinaldi's eyes. "That's him. Old sourpuss himself."

Doug's next stop was at the office of Harrison White. He found him in a closet puttering with an electric percolator. The two men had had a speaking acquaintance for years. Doug handed White the picture of Joey. "You were his parole officer, Harrison. What can you tell me about him?"

White fumbled around on a shelf for a pair of cups. "I had a feeling about Joey. I didn't think he'd make it."

Doug reached for a chair. "I didn't say he'd done anything wrong, Harrison."

White arched a critical brow. "Of course not. You're looking for him to award him a merit badge." He poured two coffees and handed one to Doug. "He had a good job hopping bells at the Savoy-West. The pay wasn't much, but the tips were terrific. He was going with a damn fine girl, had a wardrobe you wouldn't believe, and was driving a brand-new car. The day his parole ended he quit the job and moved out of his pad. There hasn't been any sign of him since. It figured that somebody would be along looking for him."

Doug spooned his coffee silently. "What kind of car?"

"Olds," White said. "Pale blue. It was a real beauty. A lot better than what I'm driving."

"And the girl?" Doug said gently.

"Margaret Eleanor Ellis, a leggy blonde. She's a secretary-photographer for Foss Real Estate in the Hawthorne Building. You've seen their ads in the Sunday supplement."

Doug nodded understandingly. A girl with the initials MEE, who was going with Joey Rinaldi, was also a photographer. Doug thanked the parole officer and made his way back to his car. The rain was half-frozen slush now, and coming in more on the horizontal than the vertical. Doug reached the Bureau of Motor Vehicles just before noon and checked the files. Margaret Eleanor Ellis owned a dark green '69 Pontiac, license number MEE-2114. The number on Joey Rinaldi's new Olds was JAR-7262.

"And why," Doug mused aloud, "would a guy with a new car go out and borrow a car?" He moved on to the dispatcher's desk and left a description of both cars. "But don't have either car picked up," he said pointedly. "Just give me a buzz when they're spotted. The green car should be in a parking lot by the Hawthorne Building. Have somebody check at the lot."

When no report had come in on either car by a quarter to five, Doug shrugged into his raincoat and reached for his hat. He passed the squad room and continued on down the hall. He found Muldoon behind his desk, glowering at a prodigious pile of paper work. "Any word on the three ships yet?"

The chief chomped disgustedly on his cigar. "The two slated for Frisco have both arrived, and they were clean. That passes the ball to the boys in Seattle. You satisfy your curiosity on this thing yet?"

Doug shook his head. "Not really. I've got a collection of unconnected pieces. Not enough to make a case, but enough to keep working on."

Muldoon took the cigar out of his mouth. "Jenny called a while ago and said to tell you to be sure and wear your rubbers, and that the pork chops would be ready at five thirty."

Doug grinned. "That girl is having one helluva time raising me."

His first stop the following morning was the dispatcher's desk. The girl's sedan had been parked at the Hawthorne Building at eight thirty that morning. There was still no sign of Rinaldi's Olds. Doug went to his desk, but at ten o'clock he grabbed his hat and coat and headed for his car. For a while he simply drove as the traffic dictated on the ice-slickened streets. Then he found himself on the fringes of Chinatown. On a sudden impulse he parked the car before a towering office building and took the elevator to the top. From the roof he stared out over the panorama spread out in the wind and cold. He'd come to love the warehouse district, the ships and piers, and the hidden crannies of Chinatown that could have been lifted right out of old Hong Kong. Finally, he turned away.

The call was coming over the radio as he opened his car door; the Olds was moving north on Third with an unmarked car a half block to its rear. Doug grabbed the speaker and gave his call number. "Temple here. I'm at the corner of Third and Dixon. I'll pick up the tail as they go by." Three minutes later he slipped into the flow of traffic two cars back from the Olds, but he'd managed to get a good look as the car went past him. Joey Rinaldi was behind the wheel. The other guy was a stranger to Doug.

Doug kept a discreet distance to the rear. At the parking lot of a posh hotel, Rinaldi turned in and let his passenger out. Almost leaping from his own car, Doug made it to the lobby in time to see the man collect a key at the front desk. When he disappeared into an elevator, Doug flashed his badge at the desk clerk. "The big guy in the sloppy gray suit who just got a key, who is he and what's his room number?"

"Room 918," the clerk said. He turned to the files. "He's listed as Samuel Greene, Chicago."

Warning the clerk to maintain a discreet silence, Doug headed for the manager's office. The official listened attentively, then nodded agreeably. When Samuel Greene left his room an hour later and entered the coffee shop in the lobby, the manager let Doug into Room 918 and witnessed his acquisition of a water glass from the bathroom. Then he dutifully replaced it with another. Doug made a swift examination of the room, but it was clean.

Twenty minutes later he handed the water glass, carefully wrapped, to the sergeant in the fingerprint bureau. "Get a make on these as fast as you can."

He checked his watch. Twelve o'clock . . . five hours left in a lifetime behind a badge.

He had *almost* all the pieces to the puzzle but *almost* didn't get it. The big piece, the location of the heroin, was still missing, and without it the rest of the puzzle was a bust.

He returned slowly to his car, running the matter through his mind as the cold wind swirled around him. Then, on a sudden hunch, he returned to the hotel. The manager was on his way to lunch, but he returned to his office and listened to Doug's request. Then he punched a button on the intercom and told some unseen person what he wanted. A few minutes later a leggy, black-haired secretary placed a folder on his desk.

The manager thumbed through it rapidly. "Mr. Greene wired for reservations from Chicago at six o'clock yesterday afternoon. His time of arrival was to be at six o'clock this morning."

Doug nodded slowly. "Which means he came in on a plane that landed here about five thirty this morning . . . " He left the office and found a pay phone in the lobby.

Three different female voices guided him through the strange world of the airport before he found his man, Wesley Farmer, manager. "Wes? Doug Temple here. Could you check out the planes that landed about five thirty this morning and see which one a Samuel Greene was on? It should be a flight from Chicago. And find out what, if any, arrangements he's made for his return trip." He gave Farmer the pay phone number. "Call me back here as soon as you find out. It's quite important."

Twenty minutes later the phone rang. "Doug? Your man Greene came in on Flight 606, which landed at five twenty-two this morning, and he's got a reservation for a return flight at four thirty this afternoon on Flight 620, Northwest Orient."

"Thanks," Doug said, and after Farmer hung up he dialed the number of the police detail stationed at the airport. After explaining what he wanted to the officer in charge, Doug returned to the lobby. With a newspaper in his hands he kept watch on the man called Samuel Greene, still feeding his face in the coffee shop. Shortly, Greene crossed the lobby and entered an elevator. Doug checked his watch and settled back to wait. At a little after three Greene emerged from the elevator, suitcase in hand. When he moved through the big front doors and onto the street, Doug sauntered along behind him. At the corner Joey Rinaldi was waiting in his car.

Doug hurried to the parking lot, executed a swift turn with his own car, and fell in behind Rinaldi's. One thing was bugging him: was Greene in on the five-kilo caper, or was he somebody else altogether? It was a possibility that had given him some bad moments.

He was pondering the distasteful thought for the tenth time, when Rinaldi swung west, directly away from the street leading to the airport. Keeping well back of the car, Doug followed it to a large apartment house in the west hills. Both men got out and entered the building, Greene carrying his suitcase. They reappeared minutes later, got into the car, and began moving back across town.

"So far, so good," Doug breathed relievedly to himself. He pulled the speaker from its bracket and gave a description of the Olds to the airport detail, adding that he would be right behind the suspects and not to move in on them until he gave the signal.

When Joey eased his car into a parking slot on the south side of the hangar, Doug stabbed the brakes, jerked the emergency, and hit the ground at a run. He could see four men from the airport detachment converging on the Olds.

Doug reached the car first. He jerked the door open with his left hand, his gun in his right. "You're under arrest," he told a white-faced Joey Rinaldi calmly.

The man called Samuel Greene eased his right hand inside his coat, but the door on his side opened and a police revolver nudged him meaningfully below the right ear. He slumped resignedly in the seat, then cut loose a torrent of invective that scorched the ears.

Both men were relieved of their guns and handcuffed together in the back of Doug's car while he examined the contents of the suitcase. Then, with one of the airport guards in the back seat with Rinaldi and Greene, he tossed the suitcase into the front seat and headed the car uptown.

Most of the men from both day shift and swing shift were in the squad room when Doug came through the door. Silence fell swiftly over the room. Muldoon was at the head table with the commissioner and FBI agent Tobin. Finally Muldoon growled loudly, "Where in hell have you been?"

"Why? Is something up?" Doug asked slowly.

Muldoon waved a sheet of paper at him, "This is what's up—the report on the fingerprints that were on the water glass. They belong to one of the biggest Mafioso dope merchants in the business. The bureau's been after him for years. We were afraid you'd gone after him alone."

Tobin cut in pointedly, "The guy has a reputation for being real mean in a pinch."

Doug accepted a cup of steaming coffee from someone. "I'm growing old, chief, not stupid. I assume the sudden appearance of this top narco dealer jibes with what *wasn't* found on the ship that just docked in Seattle."

The bleak look in Muldoon's eyes was answer enough. "She was clean. But you've got your teeth into something juicy, or did you win that set of fingerprints in a church raffle?"

Doug started at the beginning and filled them in on his activities of the last three days. They hung on his words as if mesmerized.

When he was through talking, Henderson scratched his head in wonderment. "And the thirty seconds the truck was out of our sight was *all* you had to go on in the beginning?"

Doug sipped his coffee. "That's the size of it. I really wasn't sure anything had happened, but I knew that it *could* have. I just kept checking on the possibilities."

"But you were shooting in the dark all the way," Henderson said slowly.

"I wasn't in the dark very long," Doug said, "not after Harry Orchard identified Joey Rinaldi as the man on the pier. If he'd been a legitimate photographer he'd have walked right up to Larsen and his partner instead of lurking around the corner and spying on them. Ex-cons who have really gone straight get a boot out of rubbing shoulders with cops. They can't be touched, and they like the feeling."

Muldoon's Irish features broadened into an admiring smile. "You've wrapped it up beautifully, Doug. Two men and five kilos." He turned to address the others. "You can get to work now, or go on home. We're through here."

Doug stood up and quietly handed his gun and badge to Muldoon. He felt naked as he walked toward the door. Then the men behind him began moving, some home to their families, the others out into the concrete jungles for their tour of duty. A faint smile uptilted the corners of Doug's mouth, and he kept walking, not looking back. Outside on the steps he paused. The wind had died down and the melodious chime in the courthouse tower across the street resounded five times.

Beyond the tower the dirty gray clouds were giving way to a patch of blue.

The Plum Point Ladies

by Henry T. Parry

The hand protruded from the water, the wrist caught in the yellow nylon line that slanted from the buoy to a vanishing point in the black sea. Eddie Morse saw it when he reached with the gaff to snag the line and leaned over the side for a closer examination. Deciding that its present mooring was sufficiently secure until he could return with help, he pushed the throttle forward and headed back through the harbor mouth toward the town dock, leaving the hand to ride gently in the swell among the buoys over the lobster ledges.

He found Pursell Small in the one-room police station, the telephone hunched between shoulder and ear, listening with raised-eyebrow patience to a complaint about outboard motor noise near a private dock.

"I found her, Purs."

"Who?"

"You got any other prominent member of the summer colony who's been missing two weeks except Mrs. Turner?"

"Where?"

"Off Plum Point. There's a body snarled up in the line of one of my lobster traps. I didn't look close enough to identify her for sure. I figured you'd be the one to pull her out of the water."

"I bet you did, Eddie, I bet you did. Well, let's get on out there. Wait till I get Earl from the filling station to help."

"I'll get the reward, won't I, Purs? Seems I should. I'm the one found her."

"How do I know, Eddie? I suppose so. Mrs. Wright's the one who put up the reward, so I guess she'll decide."

"I'll take you out there in my boat, Purs. And Purs—"

"Yes?"

"You think the town will pay for the gas? All three trips, that is?"

Laura watched him file through the arrivals gate at the island airport, the suitbag containing his one suit slung over his shoulder and in his hand the plastic shopping bag that contained whatever

74

else he remembered would be needed for his visit. It was unlikely that Alex would have been mistaken for any of the other men arriving with him, trim casual men from Boston law firms and austere Philadelphia banks. He was about to pass through a social examination, in an environment as different from his and Laura's September-to-June world at the Music Institute as a prehistoric Abenaki village on the Penobscot. She looked forward to his comments on the ways of the tribe that had been coming to Spruce Island for a hundred summers.

"Was it hot in the city?" she asked, and immediately wished she could withdraw the question. She knew it had been ninety-two degrees, and after waiting weeks to see him she wanted to talk endlessly and not about the weather.

"The big news in Spruce Harbor," she said as she edged the car into the highway traffic, "is that Mrs. Turner's body has been found."

"Who is Mrs. Turner?"

"She's a member of one of the old families who have been coming to Spruce Harbor since 1890. One grandfather was Vice President and another was one of the biggest vote buyers in Boston. She led a rather quiet life up here, with her friend Marion Blake. She was the president of the Plum Point Ladies Club this year but that was only because it was her turn. She was very fond of clothes and she dressed beautifully."

"I brought you a present but I left it on the plane. It was a Bartok score."

"I appreciate the thought—and considering how little I've played this summer, I appreciate your leaving it on the plane even more."

"Tell me more about Mrs. Turner."

Laura explained that her mother and Mrs. Turner had been children together at Spruce Harbor and that their houses were near each other on Sound Road. The *Harbor Times* reported that Mrs. Turner had excused herself during a picnic of the Plum Point Ladies Club and had not been seen again. Her car was found near the gate to the club property where everyone else had parked. Nothing was learned for two weeks until a lobsterman named Eddie Morse found her body in the sea. In the absence of local relatives, official identification was made by a friend, Mrs. C. Taylor Wright. Mrs. Wright had also offered a reward for information concerning Mrs. Turner's disappearance.

"Didn't anyone at the club see anything?"

"Apparently not," Laura said. "Sit back while I tell you about the ladies who belong."

The Plum Point Ladies Club, she went on, was a state of mind. There was no clubhouse, golf course, or swimming pool. Many years ago Mrs. Turner's grandmother and the other ladies who summered in Spruce Harbor got together for a yearly picnic. The picnics were always held on Plum Point, a low wooded bluff that jutted into the sea at the harbor's mouth. From these meetings the present club had evolved. At first there was only one requirement: a member must be a summer person who owned property in Spruce Harbor. Residence in the other three villages on the island, Gull Harbor, French Harbor, and Eastworth, was not recognized. Fifty years later another requirement had been added. To become a member, a person must be descended from one of the original Plum Point Ladies. Men might be invited for special picnics—on the Fourth of July, for example—but they were not normally included in the routine get-togethers. One member had purchased the entire point and given it to the club, and a fence was built from water's edge to water's edge, with gates that were kept locked. After years of discussion, a cottage was built on the property.

"The food at the picnics isn't exactly remarkable," Laura said. "Just sandwiches and tea and, of course, clam chowder."

"Ah, ritual consumption of sacred native food to ward off evil spells cast by day-trippers."

"Right," Laura said, and went on. "The only other structure on the property is a decaying summer house out at the edge of the rocks overlooking the sea. It was there long before the Plum Point Ladies organized themselves."

"And there in the long-ago dusks," Alex suggested, "girls in long white dresses and young men in white flannel boaters played mandolins and sang romantic songs. What else do the ladies do in this club except eat together?"

"Nothing."

"I wonder what an anthropologist would make of it. A social organization whose entrance requirements can only be satisfied by one's ancestors and which does nothing but meet occasionally on what has become highly desirable shorefront property and consume clam chowder."

"I suppose we maintain the organization," Laura said, "out of a half-humorous, half-serious sense of obligation to the past and to the people, many of them dearly loved people, who formed that past here in Spruce Harbor."

" 'We?' Are you a member?"

"No, but Mother is."

"When I was twelve," Alex said, "the greatest privilege of my life was to belong to the Rodney Street Rangers. We had a clubhouse over the garage of one of the members. I remember what pleasure it gave me to blackball applicants for memberships. Except one of the kids I voted against caught me alone on the street and gave me a black eye."

"On the way home we're supposed to drop in at a cocktail party the Mrs. Wright I mentioned is giving to mark the beginning of the Founders Day celebration. When I tell you that the celebration isn't going to occur until next year, Spruce Harbor's two hundredth anniversary, it will give you an idea of Mrs. Wright's dedication."

"Who is she anyway?"

"Only the prime mover and shaker-up of the island. She came here at a time when it showed signs of exhausting whatever social credit it had built in the early years of the century. The tourists were closing in, and with them all the establishments that cater to tourists—restaurants decorated with waterfront fakery, cheap bars, plastic motels. She bought the old Palmer place on Sound Road and set to work improving the community. She pushed the adoption of zoning ordinances and fought all the way to the state supreme court to make them stick. She headed a group that got the waterfront rebuilt to look the way it had a hundred years ago. She prevented the construction of a causeway from the mainland to the island. If it had been built, not even she could have saved Spruce Harbor."

"If they ever erect a statue to the person who has done the most for Spruce Harbor, that person should be Mrs. Wright," Laura said.

"I presume the Plum Point Ladies approach her on bended knee, bearing offerings of clam chowder."

"She isn't a member because her grandmother wasn't. Mother says this rankles Mrs. Wright more than she lets on because she wants so much to belong. She says Mrs. Wright is always trying to get the heritage rule changed so that she can become a member."

"It defies any reasonable explanation, doesn't it," said Alex, "that a competent powerful leader of the community like Mrs. Wright should want to belong to a little group of ladies who meet every now and then in a little cottage on a fenced-off reservation and eat clam chowder? Or that the ladies should refuse to change the rules and keep her out? From what you say, she has done more for the community than all the ladies put together."

"Oh, she has, but that's just the point. Keeping her out of their organization is the ladies' way of saying that even though Mrs. Wright gets things done that they are too ineffectual or too indifferent to do for themselves, there are still some aspects of life here that she can't dominate, some innerness that she can't invade."

"The Rodney Street Ranger syndrome," Alex said.

They passed a highway sign reading "Spruce Harbor." Fifty feet farther on where a propped-up sign suggested they "Stop At Paul's," the shoulder of the road was lined with crates displaying ears of corn, jars of jelly, crude containers of wild flowers, and plastic jars of a violent-purple liquid described as Spring Water Grape Drink. The proprietor was a boy in jeans, T-shirt, and a long-billed tan cap, whose eyes had a peering quality as though he were straining to see farther than anyone else was seeing.

"Come look at this," Laura said, stopping the car. "This kid is the island merchant. Last year he specialized in livestock, guinea pigs, hamsters, and, as he called it, a genuine, live stuffed python. He's a genuine con artist.

"How's business, Paul?" she asked as they stepped out of the car. "Where did you get corn this early in the season?"

"Oh, I get it around. Say," he said, "do you want to buy something special? Look at these."

He tilted a tall can toward them to show three lobsters sprawled on a fibrous mattress of seaweed, and poked them to demonstrate that they were still alive and edible.

"Where did you get them?"

"From my own traps. Me and Chokey—he's my partner but he had to go home and eat—we set some off Plum Point. We're going to put out some more and maybe go into lobstering and give up all this kid stuff."

"How much are you charging for them?"

When he told her, Laura laughed. "That's only about twenty-five cents more each than they would cost in the village."

"How about you, mister?" Paul asked. "Would you like to try a glass of genuine Spring Water Grape Drink? Fresh this afternoon."

"Only if the water came from the fountain of youth," Alex replied.

"Sorry, Paul," Laura said, "we have to push on. I hope you get rid of the lobsters while they're still fresh."

Back in the car Laura told Alex, "Paul is known as Paul the

Peddler. He's been selling one thing or another along this road since he was six years old. His grandfather has a chain of supermarkets hundreds of miles long. Apples don't fall far from the tree."

The cars ahead of them slowed down at a point where a man in civilian clothes wearing a policeman's cap separated the traffic between the main stream and those cars that were turning into a private driveway.

"Hi, Laura. How's the musically talented, rich city kid?"

"Fine, Purs, and how's the poor country cop? Making a dollar out of Mrs. Wright's cocktail party?"

"The more dollars, the less poor," he said.

"Is there anything new on the Turner case or are you sworn to official secrecy?" Laura asked.

"Official secrecy, hah! Any time I want to know what's going on on this island I only got to stop at two places. Earl Jenkins' filling station and Mrs. Barnes at the library—though my wife says the Elite Beauty Parlor is better than both. At the filling station they tell me the coroner's report says that Mrs. Turner was dead from a skull fracture before she was put into the water. Sorry, Laura, if you're going to turn into Mrs. Wright's driveway, you better do it. The natives behind you are restless."

"So instead of a missing-persons case," Laura persisted, "what you've got is—"

"Murder, seems like."

The house was wide-windowed, with numerous dormers in steeply pitched roofs that seemed unable to agree on a common level, its shingles faded from brown to streaked grayish tan. Rhododendrons reached to the roof of the deep porch that ran across the front, accentuating the depth and coolness of the house. Set into the base of one of the stone pillars at the foot of the steps was a masonry slab with "Limberlost" carved on it. To the right of the house a wide lawn ran down to a grassy point where a flagpole stood silhouetted against the water. The wide double doors were thrown back, the decibel level of the voices within indicating that the party was well under way.

A young maid with a serious face directed them across the gloomy entrance hall.

" 'My heart leaps up when I behold—' " Alex quoted.

Mrs. Wright greeted them before a tall fieldstone fireplace. Her tanned face bore an expression of impassivity that was augmented by her high-bridged nose and intense dark eyes that looked searchingly at those to whom she addressed herself as though focusing on them her entire strength and assurance. Her clothes, as Laura commented later, were obtained either from a men's tailor who had been requested to make them feminine or from a ladies' tailor who had been asked to make them masculine.

"Laura, how nice to see you." Alex had expected a booming voice to match the woman's powerful presence, but it was instead low and controlled. "I'm sorry you can't serve on the Founders Day committee. We could use some young people." She turned to Alex. "And how nice to meet you," she said with a lesser note of engagement.

"Weighed and found wanting, that's me, kid," he said to Laura as they moved on to the next room.

Laura guided Alex toward a woman who stood in the corner of the room inspecting a print, as though finding the picture more interesting than the people.

"Marion, this is a friend of mine from school, Alex Sartaine. Alex, this is Marion Blake. She is the Henry Moore of Spruce Harbor. When I was fourteen she immortalized my head in bronze. She is one of the reasons I studied music. I spent a lot of summers watching her break rock and I decided that, whatever I was going to be, it wasn't a sculptor." She turned serious. "I haven't been able to express my sympathy to you about what happened to Mrs. Turner," she said to Marion Blake.

The woman was square, with steel-rimmed glasses and the pudding-bowl haircut of a medieval serf. Her eyes were absorbed with some interior question and the expression on her face was both firm and uncertain. She laid a blunt, work-hardened hand on Laura's arm and after a pause in which she seemed to be dispelling a natural reticence said:

"All the talk here about poor Eleanor. I wish I hadn't come but I'm involved in this Founders Day business. I guess you know that I've got an entry in the contest for a suitable memorial. But I'm really in no state, Laura, in no condition to be out on my own."

Her left hand joined her right in its grasp upon Laura's arm as she addressed herself to Alex.

"As Laura knows, Eleanor Turner found me dying, literally dying, in the mental wing of a hospital in the city. I was desperately ill, and not just mentally. I had worked hard at my art for years. I was approaching middle age and had absolutely no recognition for it whatsoever. Eleanor changed all that. She brought me up here with her and nursed me back to health. She gave me a place to work and live and, most of all, she gave me back my confidence in myself and in my capacities."

"What motive would anyone have for killing Mrs. Turner?"

"The motive, in my opinion, was robbery. They didn't say anything about it in the news but Eleanor had stopped off at the bank on the way to that picnic and had taken out several thousand dollars in bearer bonds. That means that anybody who holds them can cash them. She was flying home the next day and was going to give them as a present to her niece's first baby. She went from the bank to the Plum Point Ladies' picnic, directly as far as anyone knows.

"But what I am saying to you, Laura," she went on, "is that I'm convinced they think I had something to do with her death. They will find out that I have a history of mental illness, they will learn that at times I was violent—"

"But you had everything to lose by the death of Mrs. Turner," Laura said. "She was your best friend. You lived in her home. You had nothing to gain."

"Not quite. There's something that nobody but me knows and it's certain to come out.

"I am due to inherit her entire estate."

The next morning, low swift-riding clouds covered the island and a steady gray rain fell.

"Let's go over to Rockhaven on the mainland," Laura suggested. "We can leave the car in the parking lot and take the ferry. There's a maritime museum, a couple of bookstores, some junk shops, and some second-hand stores that are putting on airs and calling themselves thrift shops. And on the pier there's a place called Squeamish's where we can get lobster rolls for lunch."

"Go over that part about lobster rolls again, leaving out the name of the restaurant, and I'm your man. And maybe in the thrift shops I can pick up material for my new article."

"What on?"

"Pre-electronic popular music in the United States between 1890 and 1920. Sheet music for piano is what I'm looking for."

"I know one place you should try," Laura said. "The Try Again Thrift Shop. We'll go there."

As they entered, a bell, activated by the opening of the door, jangled over their heads. A round rosy lady in a flowered smock beamed at them through jewelled glasses. "My, the weather has turned nasty, hasn't it?" she said.

"It has," Alex said and asked if the shop carried turn-of-the-century sheet music.

"We don't get that kind of thing," the woman said. "Mostly we take items that will sell fairly soon. We give the people who bring them in one-third of what we sell them for and the other two-thirds goes to the local hospital. We buy clothes, dishes, furniture—things like that."

As Laura and Alex turned back to the door Alex's elbow swept from the counter a wicker basket which held the outgoing mail awaiting pick-up. He scooped the half dozen envelopes together and replaced them in the basket.

"Look," Laura said, picking up the letter on top. The address read "Eleanor Turner, Sound Road, Spruce Harbor," and the return address was that of the thrift shop. She turned to the woman and asked her if she'd read of Mrs. Turner's death.

"Oh, I had no idea it was *that* Mrs. Turner," the woman said. "I never connected the two names when I addressed that envelope. That is a driver's license I found in a handbag that was left with us to sell. When the person who originally brought the bag in came back for her share of the sale money, we forgot to give her the driver's license."

"When was this?"

"About ten or twelve days ago, I should think. It sold quickly because it was an expensive bag. French manufacture. I think we got thirty-five dollars for it. It must have cost two hundred and fifty new."

"Do you know who brought the bag in?"

"No." A guarded note entered the woman's voice.

"You realize, I'm sure," Laura explained, "that you don't have to tell us anything. But a serious crime has been committed and the victim is someone I know. Can you tell us what she looked like? I assume it was a woman who brought it in."

"It was. She had an elaborate hairdo that was beginning to come apart. She was short and heavyset. Her hair was an unbelievable yellow and she wore a short skirt just above the knees and high white boots that almost dislocated her kneecaps. She said her boss had given her the bag and told her it was left behind by a customer who never came back for it. She said—and I couldn't agree with her more—that every time she carried the bag it made the rest of what she was wearing look crummy, so she figured she might as well get a few dollars for it. My guess is that she's a waitress."

"Did she sound like a local person?"

"Well, I've never seen her before but I'd guess she's from around here all right. She came in and left by the back door. There's a small parking lot in the back that the summer people don't know about but the locals do. She was driving a beat-up foreign car that had a piece of a bumper sticker that said 'Guns Don't—.' If it had had out-of-state plates, I think I would have noticed."

"Do you often find things in handbags that you get to sell?"

"It happens all the time. Once we found three hundred dollars tucked under a torn lining. This bag we're talking about now had at least eight or ten compartments so it would be easy for the girl to overlook one of them."

"Do you pay people by check?" Alex asked.

"We usually take their names and addresses and when the items are sold, we mail them a check for their share. But not everybody wants the money sent to their home. In that case we give them a numbered receipt and when they come in again, if the article has been sold, we give them cash."

"Do you remember to whom you *sold* the bag? Maybe if we could recover it—"

"There were two ladies in here from Boston. One of them bought it. I don't see much chance of tracing them, do you?"

After suggesting that the manager mail the license with a letter of explanation to the Spruce Harbor police, Alex and Laura moved on to Squeamish's. At their table by a window they sat looking down through the clear water at the pavement of beer cans on the bottom.

"What do we know?" Alex asked. "Or rather, what don't we know?"

"We don't know if Eleanor Turner left that bag behind her in a restaurant," said Laura. "We don't know if it was lost or stolen before she disappeared. We don't know if she had it with her the day she disappeared. But Marion Blake might know." Laura put her own bag on the floor. "I'll be right back."

Alex watched as she left the table and went to the phone booth on the pier. And we don't know, he thought, who it was that brought the bag into the thrift shop to be sold. But it's highly unlikely that, if the bag is in any way associated with the disappearance and murder of Mrs. Turner, it would have been brought in for sale. More than likely it would have joined the beer cans on the bottom of the harbor.

"Marion Blake checked through Eleanor's things and says the bag is missing," Laura reported. "She doesn't know if she was carrying it the day she disappeared. Marion says Eleanor bought it in Paris about a year ago and used it often. She's certain she didn't lose it in a local restaurant because she never ate in restaurants here. Marion also looked for the driver's license and couldn't find it."

"All we know then," Alex said, "is that the bag was brought to the thrift shop by a woman who might be a waitress, who drives a foreign car that carries a fragment of a gun propaganda sticker and has in-state plates. She is probably a native but is unlikely to live here in Rockhaven or the thrift-shop lady would know her."

"But we can't go up and down the coast looking for her in every restaurant we see," Laura said.

"Where is the biggest concentration of restaurants around here?" Alex asked.

"On the island, definitely. Let me get the telephone directory and we can count them."

The directory listed fifteen restaurants in the island's four communities—two each in Eastworth and Gull Harbor, three in Spruce Harbor, and eight in French Harbor.

"The ferry to the island leaves in five minutes," Laura said. "Should we catch it and check out the restaurants or stay and have lobster rolls?"

The restaurants in Eastworth, Gull Harbor, and Spruce Harbor revealed nothing. Laura drove across the island to French Harbor and parked in the town lot.

"Let's split up the restaurants," Alex suggested, consulting the list. "I'll take Windjammer, Santoro's, Anchor, and Mainsail. Huh, some names. Why don't they call themselves Deep Fat Fry or Fifty Frozen Foods? Or an Indian name which, when translated, means 'Would - You - Folks - Like - to - Wait - in - the - Bar - and - When - You - Have - Spent - Some - Money - There - a - Table - Will - Be - Available'? After we check the cars in their lots, we'll go in and take a look at the waitresses. If they try to seat you, just tell them you're looking for a friend, a certain James G. Blaine. I'm only trying to coach you as an innocent city kid, me being a wily musician full of guile."

"When I stop shaking with laughter I'm going to suggest that whoever gets back here first should check the cars here in the lot."

An hour and a half later they met at the car with nothing to report.

"Nothing in the restaurant parking lots," said Laura, "and every waitress I looked at resembled the woman Madame Le Thrift Shop described. And nothing in the town lot here, either."

"The restaurants I checked had nothing but fresh-faced pretty college girls working for the summer. It's in the eye of the beholder, they say."

What had seemed like a light-hearted digression, an essay at amateur sleuthing, was revealing itself to require what all detection is based on—patient routine slogging. In a subdued mood they drove home to Spruce Harbor.

"What about a place like that?" Alex asked, pointing to a cabinlike structure made of logs of an unreal irregular plastic perfection. In one window a beer sign flicked on and off, unsynchronized with the curly neon that crept along the ridge of the roof, flashing the name "Down East Bar."

"That's Chucky Logan's place. It's patronized mostly by locals but some summer people go there to stare at what they think are real live lobstermen. What they're really seeing are real live boozers. Pursell Small tells me that the police get two-thirds of their business from Chucky's place, winter and summer."

"Would it have cocktail waitresses?"

"I don't know. In the summer they might. I've only been in the place once and that was when I was in my teens and was demonstrating how free and independent I was. They don't serve much in the way of food. Let's just check the cars parked there anyway, as long as we're going by."

Laura swung the car into the parking lot and skirted the rear of the pickup trucks and panel vehicles whose drivers were able to bring their working day to an early conclusion. They found one foreign car of the type they were looking for but it bore out-of-state plates and a sticker authorizing the use of Harvard University parking facilities.

"Let me just take a look around the back," said Laura. "Maybe an employee would park so as to leave the front lot for the use of the customers."

She got out of the car and disappeared around the back of the building. Moments later she reappeared and motioned for Alex to join her. Parked before a rank of garbage cans was a small foreign car, its front end showing rusted dents and its bumper wearing a torn sticker reading "Guns Don't—." Alex wrote the license number down and said:

"This is the point where we should turn this over to your school chum, Pursell Small."

"Maybe so, but let's check inside. Think how patronizing I can be to Purs if we hand him a real hot lead."

At the far end of the bar where it turned at right angles, they saw a short, heavyset woman who waited while the bartender placed drinks on a tray. She wore a black dress of mid-thigh length, a patch of white apron, and high white boots with tassels at the top. Her face showed an aggrieved dissatisfaction and had the wary, surface-involvement-only look of one who dealt at length with the public and had found it not rewarding. Alex and Laura made their way through the beer-and-tobacco fumes to a dimly lit booth along the wall. They ordered beer and when the waitress had served them Alex asked:

"May we ask you a personal question?"

"In this job, mister, I get a lot of personal questions, but they're all the same one."

"We're trying to trace a handbag that belonged to a friend."

"Did she leave it here? You could ask Chucky if anything's showed up."

"We think it was last seen at the Try Again Thrift Shop in Rockhaven. Do you know the place?"

"Sure I know the place," she answered, her voice quick with resentment and suspicion. "Are you trying to say that maybe I know something about this bag?"

"That foreign car parked in the back. Is that yours?"

"Yeah. So what?"

"The bag we're looking for was left for sale at the thrift shop by someone who drove a car like that."

"There's a million cars like that, mister, so don't go trying to pin anything on me."

"We're not. It's only that you may not know that this bag belonged to somebody who was involved in a serious crime. It belonged to that lady whose body was found off Plum Point. Maybe you heard—"

"Well, don't come snooping around me," she said, "I don't know anything about it. You summer people make me sick. You don't *know* what it's like living up here! You don't know anything! You're a bunch of amateurs!"

She swept off with an unsteady gait, clutching her tray, her boot-top tassels flouncing. Laura and Alex stared at each other.

"She's right," said Alex, revolving his beer glass on the cigarette-scarred surface of the table. "We're playing at detection, knowing the responsibility for solving this belongs to someone else and that we can quit whenever we want. What right do we have to ask people questions?"

"But facts are facts," Laura said, "and they don't need official discovery to make them so. We did find out that Eleanor Turner's bag was sold."

"That doesn't mean it was connected to her murder," Alex said. "She may have lost the bag weeks before she died."

"And she may have had it with her the day she disappeared."

"But even if this waitress does know something about the bag," Alex said, "she won't tell us—and she probably won't tell the police. And we have put her on her guard for when the police do question her."

"Well, we've done everything we could," said Laura. "Let's get out of this depressing place and go and tell Purs what we've learned—or not learned."

When they returned to the parking lot they found the waitress waiting for them, pacing, her arms folded and shoulders hunched.

"Look," she began, a note of reluctant ingratiation in her voice, "maybe I was too quick in there. I been thinking. Why should I cover for that cheapskate and maybe get the cops on me when I haven't done anything?

"He promised me everything, sure, but when I asked for some money to make up the rent, you know how much he gave me? Six dollars! Six dollars! And a handbag that was found along the road, that fell out of somebody's car! He said I could get something for it, so I took it into that place in Rockhaven and they sold it and gave me twelve dollars. Now you tell me that it belonged to that dead lady.

"Now I hear he's running around with some floozy from French Harbor half his age who thinks she's going to get some of the reward money."

"Reward money?" Laura asked.

"The reward for finding the dead lady. I heard there was a reward."

"Who do you think is going to get it?"

"The guy I'm talking about. Mr. Eddie Tightwad Morse. Beer and hamburgers in some cheesy joint like this, that's what she'll get.

He's the one who give me the bag. It's a good thing the bag didn't look like it was ever wet or I'd wonder if Eddie didn't find it in the water when he found the body."

"Did this Eddie Morse act as if he'd come into any sudden money?" Alex asked.

"Him? He could pull up his lobster traps every day and pour diamonds out of them and you'd never know it. His mouth is just like the rest of him. Closed. That guy's still got his first blueberry-picking money.

"And that's all I know about it," she went on. "Look, you look like decent folks that would give a girl a break. Don't tell anybody where you learned what I told you. I don't want to get into any more mess with Eddie. I got enough trouble as it is. Today I heard that Chucky is looking for somebody younger."

The mailbox at the edge of the highway read "E. Morse." In the rutted driveway the tops of the weeds were grease-stained from brushing the engine pans of cars. The trailer-type dwelling rested on columns of gray cinder block and provided shelter beneath for nondescript items of rusting equipment. At the end of the driveway lobster traps were stacked in a neat wall, their precisely coiled lines and straight slatted sides giving an incongruous sense of order.

The man who answered Alex's knock on the aluminum door examined him unhurriedly through the glass, taking a pull from the beer can in his hand and staring at him with veined brown eyes. He pushed the door open a few inches with his beer-can hand. In the dim interior Alex could see the flickering heat lightning of a television set and hear the measured maniacal bursts of sound-track laughter.

"Something you want?"

"Mr. Morse, I wonder if we can talk with you about a handbag that you're supposed to have found?"

"Just a minute, let me turn that set off. No use it being on if nobody's watching."

When he returned he came outside, closing the door behind him, and stood looking at Laura and Alex with tight-lipped resentment.

"Ida Jean's been running off at the mouth about me again. She's a great one for bad-mouthing a guy. You give her a couple of drinks and she can go on all night, especially about her husband. I don't blame the guy for clearing out."

"But did you find that bag?"

"I found a bag. I don't know if it was Mrs. Turner's like you say or whose. I found it down at Plum Point, outside those chain-link gates where they park when they're using the grounds."

"When was this?"

"A Friday. It'll be three weeks this coming Friday, just before dark."

"That would be the day after the Plum Point Ladies had their picnic, the day after Mrs. Turner disappeared," Laura said.

"I had a couple of bags of garbage in the car," Eddie Morse went on, "and I stopped there to heave them into the bushes by the fence. Figured nobody would know, place is so overgrown."

Laura and Alex refrained from exchanging glances. Eddie Morse may or may not have been guilty of murder, but if he were to be convicted of defacing the landscape within Spruce Harbor, the sentence, if left to its citizens, might approach that for a capital crime.

"I saw this handbag lying in with the blueberry bushes at the edge of the parking space. There wasn't anything in it so I figured somebody had stolen it or found it, cleaned it out, and threw it away. So I give it to Ida Jean. I thought she might get a couple of bucks for it because it looked like it might have cost a lot new. I never connected it with Mrs. Turner and I don't see why I should have."

Eddie Morse dipped his head to the beer can and took a long swallow. "And you can tell Pursell Small that I'll tell him all about it, and the state detectives too if they're still around, when I come uptown tonight. Don't see what call you got to come messing in it anyway.

"Seems to me," he called after them, "that if you folks want to get mixed up in this business you might start by seeing when I'm going to get the reward for finding the body!"

"What about Mrs. Turner's car?" Alex asked.

"It was found in the parking area near the gate, where Eddie Morse says he found the bag. Marion Blake came out and drove it home."

"It's possible that the bag could have fallen out of the car when Mrs. Turner got out or when Marion Blake got in."

"But what happened to those bonds? Somebody got them."

"There is that. Rationally, though, it defies probability that one person should independently and by accident discover two separate facts relating to this murder. In the course of getting rid of garbage,

Eddie Morse finds the victim's purse. In the course of pulling up his lobster traps, he finds the victim's body."

"Logically, it's possible for both to happen to the same person."

"Another point in his favor," said Alex, "is that he talked to us. He wasn't exactly a fount of information but he could have told us nothing. Why did he talk to us at all?"

"Because he knows he is innocent, that would be my guess," said Laura. "We're passing the Plum Point property now. That fence is the boundary."

"Let's stop at the parking place and take a look."

The parking area, barely a car length in depth, was a cleared section between the edge of the highway and the dense undergrowth at the base of the fence.

"Show me the blueberry bushes Eddie Morse referred to."

"Most of the growth along the bottom of the fence is blueberry."

Alex left the car and walked through the undergrowth along the fence for fifty yards on either side of the clearing.

"What were you looking for?" Laura asked when he returned.

"Garbage. Why would somebody who could dump garbage a reasonable distance out at sea go to the trouble of driving down here and dumping it on club property?"

"What did you find?"

"When Leif Ericson or whoever it was who first discovered Spruce Harbor arrived, he couldn't have found it cleaner. I found nothing."

"I'm a coarse type. Instead of the apple tree, the singing, and the gold; give me sun, a bottle of wine, and a pretty girl," Alex said, leaning back against the rocks and turning his face to the sun. "Not in that order, of course."

"Dispensing with the required book of verse and loaf of bread, I see. Well, the first thing people in the arts must learn is to do without."

"Until this moment. Look how lovely it is here. Blue sea, white sails, dark green shores, old gray rocks to remind you of your mortality."

"It is a beautiful spot. You can see why the Plum Point Ladies let the summer house remain standing. Not only because of the view but as a reminder of a gentler day."

"It reminds me of the bandstands you sometimes see on the village greens in some old towns."

"They say that at least two generations of Plum Point Ladies have been proposed to in that summer house. Oh, we're going to have a visitor."

An outboard curved in toward the snaggled row of pilings that marked the remains of the old dock and bobbed alongside. A boy leaped out onto the decaying stringers, moored the boat, and picked his way along the dock.

"That's Paul the Peddler," Laura said, and waved for him to join them. "Who's watching the store, Paul?" she asked.

"My partner Chokey. I came out to see if there are any lobsters in our traps and maybe to set a couple more traps."

He pointed offshore where several orange and white buoys floated fifty yards off the rocks along with a dozen or so yellow plastic balls. "Oh, thanks, Miss Laura," he said, accepting a sandwich, "and thanks," he added, reaching for the lemonade that Laura held out.

"It won't be as good as Spring Water Grape Drink, but you ought to keep in touch with the competition," said Alex.

"That's right," agreed Paul, "but we don't make as much selling that as we do with the lobsters. So I'm going to put down some more traps. Mom bought a whole bunch of old traps and buoys to use in decorating for a party at the club. Afterwards, me and Chokey brought them out here and stashed them in that summer house there."

"Do you mind if I come up with you and see what it is you use?" Alex asked. "I'm a landlubber and I don't know anything about trapping lobsters."

They climbed the rocks to where the summer house stood between vegetation and rock. The structure was hexagonal, open-sided, its floors resting on masonry columns to which fragments of lattice clung, with elaborate scrimshaw scrolls and fretwork brackets on the posts and railings. Piled on the rickety bench that ran around the inside of the railing were a half dozen slatted lobster traps, semi-cylinders with concave ends. The buoys, which were designed to float above the ledges where the traps lay, were homemade and bullet-shaped, with short broomstick handles and heavy iron straps bent stirrup-like around the pointed ends. Twenty inches in length, and weighing six or seven pounds, the buoys resembled crudely whittled bullets with potato-masher handles.

"Now if you were doing a paper on how the machine has driven out the folk crafts, these would be an example," said Laura. "They don't use homemade buoys like this any more because the plastic balls are better. Some even use the plastic containers that cleaning compounds come in. The homemade ones were usually painted for identification and visibility."

"Yeah, we painted ours with orange handles and a white body," said Paul. "But I don't guess that anybody is going to mistake ours for those yellow balls out there. They belong to Mr. Morse. He's a pretty mean guy. We think he cuts our buoys loose."

"You mean that the lobster traps lying out there beneath the yellow buoys belong to Eddie Morse?" Alex asked. He looked speculatively at Paul, and asked:

"Would you take us out there? I'd like to look at some of Eddie Morse's lobster traps."

"Man, that's the worst thing you can do up here," said Paul, "fool around with some guy's traps."

"He's right, Alex," said Laura.

"All right, I'll tell you what. Paul, would you rent us your boat? For five dollars?"

"Well, yes, I guess so, though maybe I ought to get seven fifty."

"Seven fifty is a deal. Laura, can you run Paul's boat?"

"Yes, but we better have Paul start the engine. But why?"

"You'll see. Paul, here's your money. You come down and start her up and wait for us. That way, you won't be involved at all."

They climbed down the rocks to the dock where Paul started the engine and cast off the mooring line. Laura eased the boat away from the dock and headed it toward the buoys.

"Stop at that first yellow buoy, or whatever you do in a boat. Heave to or something."

At the first buoy Alex reached with the gaff and snagged the line leading from the buoy to the trap below. He hauled on the line, surprised at the weight of the trap, and slowly brought it up to the gunnel where he balanced it. He picked off streamers of kelp, looked briefly into the trap, and dropped it back into the water.

"Next buoy."

"I hope you know what you're doing."

"Of course I don't know what I'm doing. I just had a thought, that's all."

He pulled up three more traps, one of which held a lobster, examined them, and let them drop back over the side.

"Go to the farthest buoy out and we'll work our way back."

When he had examined the next trap, he swung it inboard and extracted from it a glass jar sealed with a rubber ring and a screw cap. He dried his hands on his shirt, twisted off the cap, and inserting two fingers into the jar, withdrew a stiff, official-looking document that had ornate numerals printed diagonally across its topmost corners. He handed the paper to Laura.

"This is a five-thousand-dollar Treasury bond!" she said. "But how did you know to look here?"

"Just a minute and I'll explain, but first, just in case Eddie Morse gets out here before we can take the proper steps, let's put the empty jar back in the lobster trap and drop it back where it came from."

"But what made you think of looking into the lobster traps?"

"An association of ideas based on something you said the other day after we had stopped at Paul's roadside stand. You pointed out that Paul's grandfather was the head of a vast mercantile organization and that Paul with his stand showed the truth of the old saying that the apple doesn't fall far from the tree."

"So?"

"Consider Eddie Morse. He found the body. He was in possession of the bag. This bond was in the bag when he found it, or when he took it. Since he can't cash it in for a long time, what would be a better hiding place than a lobster trap, especially one that nobody but Eddie Morse is ever going to haul up off the bottom? If you accept that this bond is the apple, it's likely that Eddie Morse is the tree it wouldn't fall far from. I know it's not rational, but we did find the bond."

"What do you propose we do now?"

"First, we don't say anything to Paul the Peddler. It might occur to him to sell the story to a newspaper. After he leaves, we make our way back across the Plum Point Ladies' property to where your car is. Then we look up your chum, Pursell Small, and present him with some hard evidence that makes it look very much as if Eddie Morse is guilty of the murder of Mrs. Turner."

"When I hear it expressed in those words," said Laura, "it makes me wish we had never gone to that thrift shop, that we had nothing to do with this. Up to now we were trying to solve a problem. Now someone is going to get hurt."

"Someone has already been hurt. And, anyway, what alternative do we have, Laura? If no man is an island, surely no man's death is an island."

It was not until the next morning that Laura and Alex were able to track down Pursell Small and present him with their findings.

"Let's go down and talk to Eddie before we do anything official," Pursell said.

Eddie appeared at the door of his trailer in answer to Pursell's knock, giving a snort when he saw Laura and Alex.

"I see you brought some Junior G-men, Purs."

"Eddie, I want to talk to you off the record but since I don't know at what point this might get to be official I got to tell you that you don't have to—"

"Yeah, yeah, Purs, I don't need no lawyer. You want to hassle me about that handbag. Like I already told these two-bit sleuths, I found it. I can't help it if I found it, can I? There ain't no law against finding things that I know of."

"Eddie, those lobster traps with the yellow buoys off Plum Point, are they yours?"

"Purs, you know they're mine. What about them?"

Without crediting its discovery by Laura and Alex, Pursell told Eddie about finding the bond.

"You don't know what you're talking about, Purs!" Eddie cried. "Those traps are passed by fifty boats a day! Everybody knows I use yellow buoys—you can't prove that I put the bond there! For all you know, they—" he jerked his head toward Alex and Laura "—planted it there themselves!"

"Look, Eddie, this is worse than finding Mrs. Turner's bag with the bond in it, or even stealing the bag. Here's a guy who finds the victim's body, a guy who admits that he had the victim's bag in his possession but didn't know whose it was. And then a five-thousand-dollar bond the victim was carrying when she disappeared suddenly turns up in this guy's lobster trap. I don't know about you, but if I was on a grand jury and that was all that was presented, I might vote an indictment. For murder, Eddie."

"Now, Purs, I've known you ever since you were born. Your dad and I served in the navy together. You don't think that I'd be mixed up in anything like murder?"

"Eddie, one of the advantages of knowing somebody all your life is that you get a pretty good idea of what they would and wouldn't do. In your case, I'd say no, you wouldn't have anything to do with murder." He paused. "But if you thought you could make a buck—"

"Look, Purs, I know you want to make a good showing in front of these summer people here, but why don't we let them get back to their yachts or something, and you and I can talk this out like good neighbors. Just the way your dad and I might have talked about it if he was alive."

When Pursell replied, there was no change in his voice nor in his expression, but Laura knew from the slight withdrawing movement of his head that, maybe soon, maybe late, Pursell Small would make Eddie Morse pay for having equated himself with Pursell Small's father.

"Let me point out something that maybe you haven't thought of, Eddie," Pursell went on. "If you admit you did what I think you did, and plead guilty, there won't be any long expensive trial. Now I'm not suggesting plea bargaining—that's up to the district attorney—but if you decide to fight this, then they'll try for an indictment and conviction on what's been turned up so far. If you *are* indicted, which seems likely, and go to trial, you're going to need some awfully high-priced lawyers to get you out of this. Even if they don't get you out of it you'll go to jail a mighty poor man."

Eddie gave them a startled look and walked away from them through the grease-stained grass to the end of the driveway where he stood with his back to them, studying the wall of lobster traps. When he returned he spoke in the aggrieved tone of a man subjected to unreasonable demands.

"All right. All right. I can't afford no high-priced lawyers. Here is how it was."

They listened without interruption and when he had finished Pursell sniffed and uttered a rude word. Indicating by a glance that Laura and Alex were to precede him in their car, he said: "Okay, Eddie, let's get out there right away and make another unofficial visit. But I can tell you right now, I think you're lying."

They heard running footsteps within the house and the door was violently snatched open. Mrs. Wright's maid was panting, her face frightened and her voice tense and trembling with fear.

"Oh, come in, come in, you're just in time! There's a terrible row going on! Miss Blake is here! I think she's crazy!"

As the maid led the way across the entrance hall to the closed door of Mrs. Wright's study, Laura and Alex heard Marion Blake's voice pitched high in hysterical indignation.

"How can you do this? You promised me! You said there was no entry that even approached mine. You told me to turn down that other commission in order to be free for this one!"

Mrs. Wright's reply showed a controlled irritation, the stern but kind parent whose patience is being tested. "Come, Marion, get a grip on yourself, you're losing control."

"It's all very well for you to talk. But I need that commission!"

"Of course, Marion, but there will be other opportunities. And haven't you always been provided for up here?"

"But they're saying you gave the commission to that man from Boston because he's a friend or relative of Eleanor Turner's and she gave a lot of money to your Founders Day fund."

"Nonsense, Marion, he's not a relative of poor Eleanor's nor of anybody else up here. She probably never heard of him. You're nursing an illusion to cover up your disappointment. You're fantasizing. The model you entered in the competition, indeed all your recent work, though admirable in every other respect, was thought by some, not by me, mind you, to be somewhat dated, whereas his is in a more modern idiom. So the committee decided against you."

"But what you tell the committee to do, they do, everybody knows that. *You're* the Founders Day committee."

"Oh, Marion, come now, that's not true. I have a vote like everyone else. They thought that your concept, and the model you submitted for the memorial, were not in keeping with the times."

"But you must know the work and the pure agony it took for me to come up with my entry. The promises you made to me were what kept me going. Oh, I'd like to hammer and smash until I can be myself again, until I can be clean again!"

"Marion! Put that down!"

Laura threw open the door and they saw Marion Blake leaning across Mrs. Wright's desk, her face contorted and tearstained, in her eyes the fixed gaze of one who is in the grip of committing an act she is fearful of carrying out but is powerless to refrain from. In her hand was a stone she had picked up from Mrs. Wright's desk, a grapefruit-sized piece of granite rolled by countless tides into a nearly perfect sphere. When she saw Laura and Alex she let the stone fall with a crash upon the desk and covered her face with her hands. Laura and the maid guided her to a chair where she sat, clasping and unclasping her hands, her head bowed. A long silence prevailed until finally Mrs. Wright spoke, her voice calm with a certain detachment.

"Your arrival was certainly providential," she said.

"Mrs. Wright, we came out here to tell you a strange story that a man named Eddie Morse is telling. He and Pursell Small are following behind but they must have been delayed. While we're waiting, I could give you the message that Mother gave me to give you at the cocktail party the other day. She asked me to tell you that the Plum Point Ladies felt rather embarrassed about not informing you sooner."

"You needn't be so hesitant about telling me, Laura. The Ladies were going to vote on a change of rules governing admission, primarily so that I could be admitted, which was very handsome of them."

"Mother was delegated by the others to tell you what happened. She finds it a bit awkward at this late—"

"No need to be diplomatic, Laura. The motion to change the rules was defeated eleven to ten, wasn't it? Was that your mother's message to me?" A weary note of exasperation crept into her precise speech.

Alex saw the flash of recognition sweep across Laura's face, to be replaced by a familiar expression, the absorbed watchfulness of a musician counting the beats until it is time for him to resume. Before she could speak, Alex broke in:

"Mrs. Wright, we think you should hear Eddie Morse's story. He's going to face some serious charges and maybe you could clear up some things right now."

"But I don't understand what possible connection I could have with anything this Morse man may be charged with. He's the man who found Eleanor's body, isn't he?"

They heard the slam of two cardoors, followed by a knocking at the main door of the house. In a few moments the maid brought Pursell and Eddie Morse into the study and, at a nod from Mrs. Wright, left the room. After Laura had introduced them, Mrs. Wright waved them all toward chairs.

"I am due at a committee meeting in half an hour," she said. "I should appreciate it if you would be brief. Now, how can I help you?"

"Okay, Eddie, give us your story," said Pursell, "again."

Eddie bent forward in his chair, squeezing his wrists between his knees, his eyes fixed on the floor a few inches away from Mrs. Wright's gleaming feet.

"I was in my boat off Plum Point tending to my traps when I saw these two kids climbing down the rocks from that rundown old summer house that sits on the rocks there. They had a couple of lobster traps and buoys that they took out in their outboard and baited and dropped over. It made me kind of mad to see kids, more than likely summer kids, messing with lobsters, so I went over after the kids had gone up harbor and snagged their lines. I cut their buoys loose and tied on my own buoys. Then I got thinking, wait a minute, maybe they got more gear in that old summer house and better I should bust it up right now. So I tied up at the old dock and went up to the summer house and, sure enough, there were three, four more traps and buoys. I figured maybe I could use the traps and had just picked one of them up when I saw this lady coming down that path through the trees. I remembered that this was private and posted land and I didn't want to explain anything to anybody—not that I had done anything wrong."

"Don't get too pure, Eddie," said Pursell. "On you it don't set right. The charge against you isn't likely to be trespassing."

"Well, I didn't want her to see me so I jumped down on the other side of that summer house and crawled underneath. I figured she was just taking a walk and would look around for a couple of minutes and then go. The floor was high enough off the ground so I could sit there behind the latticework without anyone likely to see me. I heard her come up the stone steps and walk across the floor just over my head. She walked back and forth a couple of times and then I guess she sat on the bench that ran around the place, then got up and walked some more. After about maybe five minutes, I heard her call to someone. I heard another person come up the steps and walk across the floor.

"This second person said she didn't see any reason why they had to meet there, that they could just as well have talked over the phone.

"The first lady said that she had had a special reason, that she had wanted the second lady to be the first to know about the plans she had for the club, and that she wanted the second lady to take her back to the picnic where she, the first lady, would tell all the others about her plan now that they had voted to change the rules on getting in and she was already as good as a member.

"The second lady said something about not doing anything yet but the first lady went on saying how in honor of her becoming a member she wanted to tell how she was going to build a regular clubhouse and get rid of that ridiculous little shack they had there now. The second lady said something about how the cottage had worked out Okay all these years and the first lady stopped her again. This time she seemed to be getting mad.

"But, the second lady said, they hadn't elected her a member yet because they hadn't changed the rules about admission yet.

"The first lady kind of snorted and said something about all she had done for the people up here and that all she had ever asked in return was to belong to a little group of women who had never really done anything, just happened to have grandmothers who summered here. She was getting pretty excited by now and I could hear her walking back and forth. How had they voted, she asked?

"The second lady sounded scared but she said the ladies at the picnic voted by writing yes or no on little squares of paper. She said she took them off to count because it made her nervous to count votes in front of that many people. She said that she had counted the ballots three times and the vote was ten to ten.

"Well, the first lady told her, you were president, why didn't you vote and break the tie?

"I did, the second lady said—I voted against changing the rules.

"The first lady screeched. I heard feet stomping and about half a dozen thuds. It stopped for a second and then, just like the last wave is sometimes the biggest and highest of all, I heard one solid whack, just like an axe hitting wood. Then nothing moved.

"Later I heard footsteps going down the steps. Through the lattice I saw the first lady hurrying back toward that path in the woods. I sat where I was until she was gone and then I crawled out and looked through the railing. The other lady was sitting sort of sideways on the bench and leaning against the railing as if she was looking at something on the ground just below the railing. And while I was looking at her she leaned sideways some more and kind of slid to the floor. Right near her head was one of them homemade buoys. It was easy to see what it had been used for. The lady was dead."

"Why didn't you go for a doctor?" Laura asked.

"Because I got a record, that's why. Purs knows that. Once you got a record the cops try and hang everything on you. I did two years in Thomaston for fencing stolen cars. Those two years taught me one thing: I was never going to be inside again. So I just walked down to the dock, took my boat, and went up harbor."

"Now, who do you say the first lady was?" asked Pursell.

"Purs, I already told you. It was that lady there."

Mrs. Wright stood motionless, her dark eyes cold and purposeful. So might a French aristocrat, Alex thought, have regarded a hostile peasant witness in the Revolutionary courts.

"That night," Eddie went on, "I was sitting at the bar in Chucky Logan's place having a couple of beers and I got thinking. I got a chance for real money, steady money, because I could put the bite on that lady for the rest of her life. And then I parlayed that into an even better idea. Suppose this second lady didn't turn up for a couple of weeks. There was sure to be a reward. What could be more likely than for me to find her body floating in the harbor, then go collect?

"So I had a lot more drinks that night and just before dawn I took the boat down to Plum Point and took the body out to where I had my traps and secured it to one of the buoys, fixing it so it would stay underwater. I had searched all around that summer house to be sure there wasn't anything left and that's when I found the bag. I took it along in the boat and was going to drown it but it seemed a shame to do that because it looked kind of new and expensive. I threw all the stuff that was in it in the water and that was when I found that bond. I had a screw-cap jar in the boat, so I put the bond in that and pulled up one of my traps and hid the jar there. I thought nobody but me would ever haul up those traps. A couple of days later when Ida Jean was after me for some dough I give the bag to her and told her I found it along the road. I figured she could get maybe a couple of bucks for it in one of them second-hand stores."

"This is nonsense," Mrs. Wright broke in. "If any of this is repeated beyond this room, be assured that my lawyers will file suit. It will cost someone a great deal of money over a considerable period of years."

"But I didn't! I didn't!" Eddie repeated. "I did all that other stuff but I never killed her!"

"Doesn't it come down to the word of someone with the highest standing in the community against the word of someone with a prison record?" Mrs. Wright asked.

"I think Eddie is telling the truth," Laura said, "because one thing he says he overheard ties in. When we first came in here, you said that you knew the motion to change the rules of admission had been defeated by an eleven-to-ten vote. Eddie says he heard Mrs. Turner tell you how the vote came out. My mother was present at the picnic when the voting took place. She said that everybody marked her vote on a scrap of paper and gave it to Mrs. Turner. She took them all outside the cottage to count them. And that was the message I was supposed to convey from my mother but which I forgot. None of the members ever knew the result of the voting. Mrs. Turner never came back."

Mrs. Wright stood with her back to the door, her hands clasped loosely behind her, chin up, lips parted as if waiting for the noise in the committee room to die before beginning her report. Then she whirled, opened the door, slammed it, and turned the key in the lock.

Pursell slowly hoisted himself from his chair and went to the telephone. After dialing and giving instructions he hung up and turned back to them. "Where can she go?" he asked. "This is an island. There's only the ferry and the airport."

He looked at Eddie Morse. "I don't know, Eddie," he said. "You would have been home free if you had been satisfied with what you had. The five-thousand-dollar bond, the reward, and maybe the blackmail payments for the rest of your life. But you blew it all for the sake of ten or fifteen bucks from a thrift shop for that handbag. Ten or fifteen bucks you didn't even collect for yourself.

"Let's go, Eddie," he said. "It looks like pretty soon you're going to have a reunion with your old buddies at Thomaston. But don't worry, the town will pay for the gas this time, too. . . ."

Laura and Alex drove Marion Blake to Mrs. Turner's house and when Laura had seen that she was taken care of, they returned to the car.

"The shock wave that is going to hit the Plum Point Ladies will go right off the Richter scale," Laura said.

"There *is* a consolation that will occur to them, though," Alex said.

"Consolation?"

"Well, justification then. I mean how right they were all along in refusing membership to Mrs. Wright. It's obvious that she just wouldn't do."

"Speaking of consolation, let's take the first step in putting all this behind us. Let's drive down to the village, get some sandwiches and a bottle of wine, and then go find a rock in the sun somewhere directly above the sea."

"Wonderful," Alex said. "And if you continue to deserve it, I may introduce you to the initiation rites of the Rodney Street Rangers."

"Do you think I could ever be admitted?" she asked, switching on the ignition. "My grandmother wasn't a Rodney Street Ranger."

The Wells Plan

by Thomasina Weber

The night air was still and frosty, numbing his cheekbones. To some it was stimulating, but to Percy Wells it was harsh, bitter, and miserable. He sighed with relief as he unlocked the office door.

He switched on his desk lamp and closed the blinds so no one would think the small loan office was open for business. Then, opening the safe, he removed all the cash and stacked it in equal piles on his desk.

It was two weeks before Christmas, the busiest season of the year for loans, with vacation time running a close second. Every other day Percy's employer, Mr. Cole, got additional money from the bank and dispensed it just about as fast. Tomorrow was Saturday and since the banks would be closed, the office was prepared for the onslaught to the tune of nine thousand dollars, counting the cash on hand when Percy had closed the books this afternoon.

Moving quickly, he carried his coat into one of the loan cubicles and spread it on the desk. Then he brought the cash in and distributed it inside the lining of the coat in the special pockets he had laboriously made so that it would lie flat and unnoticeable. Hanging the coat on its hanger, he looked at it critically. *Good. Perfectly natural looking.*

He pulled checks and papers out of the safe and scattered them on the floor. Then he unlocked the back door, which opened on the alley, and left it slightly ajar. Now came the worst part. Covering his hand with his handkerchief, he picked up the heavy glass ashtray from his desk. He was not sure that he could hit himself hard enough to make the police think he had been unconscious, and yet not actually knock himself out, but it was imperative that he do so. He would have only one chance. He could not afford to be unconscious with the door open; he had to know what was going on every minute. Sweat broke out on his forehead. He had always thought of himself as a calm man, the strong silent type, not afraid of anything. Maybe he had held this belief because he had never been called upon to prove himself. Well, now was the time.

Closing his eyes, he brought the ashtray hard against his temple. The room blurred and tipped and the pain screamed in his head. His hand lowered itself to the desk and his breath came fast. His entire body throbbed with the beat of his heart. *Just relax,* he told himself. *You did a fine job. The hard part is done.* Reaching for the phone, he dialed the police station.

Percy could not remember his father. With his mother away every day cleaning other people's houses, Percy was left to bring himself up. He became a reader, a thinker, and a planner, but the ideals he created had little connection with reality. As he grew older he modified them accordingly, but one remained unchanged: a son's duty to his mother. It was his responsibility to see that she was cared for as long as she lived.

As soon as he was old enough, he took over as breadwinner, feeling great pride that he was now able to take care of his mother. His mother grew more fractious as the years went by, however, and Percy began to think in terms of finding someone else to care for her. If he could pass her on, he would be free to live his own life. His various attempts to match her up with available gentlemen all ended in disaster. Then he thought of Florida. He had heard it had an abundance of unattached males. Equally as important was its sunny warmth. Winters were becoming increasingly unbearable, and Percy suffered through the aching cold. Florida seemed the ideal solution.

"Florida!" Mother had shrieked when he suggested moving. "You're crazy if you think I'd ever move to *that* place!"

"You could sit out in the sun—"

"And rub shoulders with all those bugs and snakes. Me, who can't even swim."

"Florida isn't under water, Mother." But she had already slammed into the kitchen.

Soon after that, Mr. Wilson entered their lives and Percy realized something drastic would have to be done. Rather than taking Mother off Percy's hands, Mr. Wilson had added himself to the menage. Applying himself with his usual thoroughness. Percy devised the Wells Plan.

Finally the day arrived to put it into operation. He had thought five o'clock would never come, but at last he was walking home through the early darkness, feeling the threat of snow in the air. He drew a searing breath into his lungs. Oh, how he hated the cold weather, the shivering ahd huffing through almost half the year waiting for three sweltering months flanked on either side by week after week of unpredictable climate.

Apparently Mother had been waiting for him; she opened the door before he reached it. "It's about time!" she said as Percy stamped into the house, blowing on his reddened fingers. "I've been holding supper for fifteen minutes."

"Ruthie had trouble balancing her cash drawer, so I stayed to help her."

"She's after your money, that one, and don't you forget it!"

Percy looked at his little bit of a mother. Her height was five foot two, one of the many insults life had heaped upon her, the most unforgivable being the husband who had so inconsiderately died young.

"Well, sit down, sit down, before the soup congeals." He took his place at the table. "Seems to me we could afford a pot roast once in a while," she muttered, stirring her soup violently and slopping it onto the metal tabletop. "We're not that poor, surely."

"I give you enough money to run the house, Mother. If you prefer to spend it on horses and liquor and Mr. Wilson, then you will have to be satisfied with soup."

"Who says I spend money on horses and liquor and Mr. Wilson? Who says so? I ask you!"

"The liquor is obvious, both from your condition and the contents of our garbage can."

"So you've sunk to rooting in the garbage can to discredit your poor old mother!"

"And Ruthie saw you and Mr. Wilson at the races."

"And what was a young girl like Ruthie doing at the races?"

"The same thing a poor old mother was doing, I imagine."

"Well, there isn't anybody who can say I give money to Mr. Wilson!"

"Mr. Wilson does not earn enough to afford gambling and drinking. Why do you think he comes over here so often?"

"Because he enjoys my company, that's why! One of these days we're going to be married."

Percy sighed. Mother's knight in shining armor was a free-lance janitor who had lost his wife some years ago. He was about ten years younger than Mother and slightly deaf, which explained how he was able to put up with her. No great spender, he lived in a small house at the edge of town and passed his evenings at the Wells house, sitting in their parlor with his feet up on the hassock and responding at proper intervals during Mother's monologues. Occasionally Mother would steer the subject toward marriage, at which times Mr. Wilson's hearing became noticeably poorer.

"I found your missing brown tie today," Mrs. Wells said.

"Oh? Where was it?" Percy asked.

"In the back of your closet."

He looked up, his spoon halfway to his mouth. "I have asked you repeatedly to stop snooping in my closet."

"Snooping! That's gratitude for you! You know I clean every Friday—"

"You snoop every Friday."

"I said I clean the house, and that includes your closet. Your guilty conscience just proves that you hide money around here, because whenever I find anything you say I was hunting for your money. Imagine, accusing your poor old mother of such a thing!"

Percy pushed back his chair. "I'm going to the office for an hour or two. I have some bookwork to do." He took out his wallet. "Here's your house money for the week, Mother. Try to save some of it for food, will you?"

His mother began to stack the dishes noisily in the sink. "Oh, what I wouldn't give to be able to stay inside, and not have to slosh to the market day after day in all kinds of weather, and to sit around the house and talk with friends of my own. But one of these days Mr. Wilson will ask me to marry him and you can part with some of your moldy money and hire somebody else to be your slave! Oh, yes, my day is coming."

Percy shut the door on her voice and walked down the street to the office.

"Now, you say you heard this gasping and crying at the back door and when you opened it, somebody shoved a gun in your stomach?"

"Yes, sir." Percy was holding his wet handkerchief against his head. The pain was almost gone, just a steady thumping left. Detective Lane was fat and red-faced and there was a deep purplish indentation across his forehead where his hatband had rested. A gold-plated tie clasp lay on the desk between them. It belonged to Mr. Wilson, and Percy had managed to palm it one hot night when Mr. Wilson removed his tie and opened his collar.

"You didn't recognize him?" asked the detective.

"His face was covered with a stocking."

"How about his voice?"

"Gruff. It was disguised, I'd say."

"Then it was probably someone known to you."

Percy said nothing.

"Did you get a look at the car?"

"It was quite dark in the alley. I had only a second to glance beyond him before he pushed me inside. All I saw were the whitewall tires."

"You say there was about nine thousand dollars?"

"Nine thousand, one hundred and thirty-four. Some of the bills were marked."

The detective leaned forward. "Did you say *marked?*"

"There seem to be so many break-ins during the holiday season. At the end of the work week I pencil in a tiny letter above the picture. I had just started doing this when the robber arrived."

"What letter did you use?"

Percy smiled. "I used an X this time. For Christmas, you know."

"Marked bills," repeated the detective as if unable to believe it. "Mr. Wells, you're the kind of man I admire. A good honest citizen with a brain."

"Thank you. Now, if you don't mind, I think I'd like to go home. My head . . . "

"Sure, sure. I'll have Smith drop you. You get some rest. I'll be in touch."

Percy walked to the back of the office to get his coat. "Here, let me help you with that," said Lane, taking it out of his hands. He weighed it speculatively. "Pretty heavy coat you got here."

"Yes, sir," said Percy, putting his arms into the sleeves. "There's nothing like a good lining to keep out the cold."

Back home again, Percy was alone as he'd expected. Friday nights, it was Mr. Wilson's custom to take Mother for a ride in his car. Percy looked at his watch: eight o'clock. They would be back at nine sharp, as usual. The hour was just enough time for Percy to make little bundles of the money. He hid one in his closet. Then he spread the rest evenly inside his zippered mattress cover. Since it was his job to turn the mattresses—"You know they're too heavy for me!"—there was no chance of Mother's finding it there.

He was hanging his empty coat in the closet when he heard Mr. Wilson's car pull into the drive. He was sitting in the armchair with the evening paper when they entered the parlor.

"Now what did you do to yourself?" Mrs. Wells said, frowning at Percy's head.

"The office was burglarized tonight, Mother."

"You mean *robbed?* Did they get away?"

"I'm afraid so." He got to his feet. "If you'll excuse me, I think I'll go to bed. My head is bothering me."

"Yes, you'd better," said Mother. "No sense in aggravating it and running up doctor bills. Goodness knows it's hard enough now to make ends meet."

"Good night, Mr. Wilson," said Percy.

Mr. Wilson, a smile on his bland face, nodded. "Very nice," he replied.

Percy did not feel his customary annoyance as he went to his room and closed the door. The Wells Plan was under way, and all he had to do now was wait.

It was ten A.M. the following Friday when Detective Lane came into the office. Mr. Cole was out, but Percy and Ruthie were there.

"I'd like to talk to you, Wells."

"Of course. Come with me." He led the detective into one of the loan cubicles. "Has something turned up?"

"I'll say. One of the marked bills."

"Well, now," said Percy. "That's fine. That's great." He gave the detective a broad smile. "This must be our lucky day."

"My lucky day, Wells, not yours."

"Oh?"

"A man would have to be pretty stupid to steal marked money if he knew it was marked."

Percy frowned. "But Ruthie and Mr. Cole are the only ones who know I mark the bills."

"Yeah."

"You don't think Mr. Cole stole his own money!"

"No, I don't."

Percy's eyes widened. "Surely you don't think *I* stole it?"

"How else would your mother get hold of the money?"

"My—my *mother?*"

"An hour ago, Estelle at the Dresse Shoppe called and reported that your mother had bought a dress—not off the sale rack as she usually does—and paid for it with a marked twenty-dollar bill."

"Well—I—I just don't know what to say."

"Why don't we go and find out what your mother has to say?"

Telling Ruthie he would be back as soon as possible, Percy rode home with the detective, thankful that it was an unmarked car.

Mother was wearing a bright new print dress when Percy ushered Detective Lane into the house. She acknowledged the introduction with suspicion.

"Detective Lane would like to ask you a few questions, Mother."

"What about?" She nudged a half-empty bottle on the end table behind the lamp.

"About a twenty-dollar bill you cashed at the Dresse Shoppe this morning."

Mother seated herself on the couch, crossing her arms in front of her new dress. She seemed to be having difficulty focusing her eyes. "What about it?"

"We'd like to know where you got it, Mrs. Wells."

Mother looked from the detective to her son and back again. "Why?"

"You tell me first."

"You think it's stolen money!" She jumped up to face her son. "So you actually turned me in! For eighteen years you've been hiding money from me and now, when I finally find some, you go running to the police and accuse me of stealing it!"

Percy opened his mouth to speak but nothing came out.

"That money was your son's?" asked the detective.

"What?" she said, turning back to him. "Oh, no," she added hastily, patting her hair. "It didn't belong to Percy at all."

"But you just said—"

"I didn't mean that! What I meant was, that's what he *thinks* happened." She tossed her head and placed her hands on her hips. "It just so happens I have a gentleman friend who gives me money regularly to save for him so we can get married. He's one of those men who can't save, you know. Well, he saw me in my old gray dress the other day and he told me to take some of his money and go out and buy myself a new one, so that's just what I did!"

"Are you sure that money didn't belong to your son?"

"Of course it didn't! Do you think I'd steal from my own son?"

"Where were you and your friend on the night of the robbery, Mrs. Wells?"

"Why, we went out for a little ride in his car, like we do every Friday night."

"Did you go anyplace special?"

"No, just for a ride."

He took a handkerchief out of his pocket and unwrapped it. "Have you ever seen this tie clasp before?"

"It belongs to Mr. Wilson."

"Are you sure?"

"Sure I'm sure. I bought it for him." She glanced at Percy. "It was his birthday," she said defiantly.

Percy stared ahead, said nothing.

"When is the last time you saw Mr. Wilson, ma'am?"

"Last night—oh, no. He didn't show up last night."

"Really? Well, maybe I'd better go have a talk with Mr. Wilson. Can you give me his address?"

She told him and he left.

"Well, Mother," said Percy, "you seem to have opened a barrel of snakes."

"*Me?* You're the one who squealed to the cops! I can't believe my own son would go running to the police just because his poor old mother borrowed a few dollars from him."

"I always told you you'd get in trouble because of your snooping."

"I refuse to discuss it," she said, and stalked from the room.

Percy looked at his watch; it was nearly noon. He would have time to make a sandwich and a cup of coffee.

He had two cups and then the doorbell rang. It was Detective Lane and a sergeant. "Where's your mother, Wells?"

"In her room."

"Good. You're the one I want to talk to."

"Come in. Did you find Mr. Wilson?"

"We did."

"What did he have to say?"

"Nothing much." He moved to the end table and picked up the bottle Mrs. Wells had tried to conceal behind the lamp. "You're drinkers?"

Percy shook his head. "Only Mother. She may run short of bread or sugar, but she never runs short of liquor."

The detective was examining the label while the sergeant stood, bored, by the door. "Looks like your mother doesn't trust you."

Percy smiled. "You're referring to her measurement scale, of course." Every time his mother opened a new bottle, she affixed a strip of masking tape over its full length and marked the liquid level each time she satisfied her thirst.

"You're a great family for marking things." Lane took the bottle across the room and handed it to the sergeant. "Don't mind if I take this along, do you?"

"I most certainly do!" Mrs. Wells was standing in the doorway of her bedroom, crackling with indignation.

Lane looked at her sadly. "Don't worry, Mrs. Wells, we're taking you along with it." He motioned to the sergeant who moved toward her.

"Just a moment," said Percy.

"We have a search warrant," said Lane. Percy watched the officer enter his mother's bedroom. The minutes ticked by in awkward silence and then he emerged, a full grocery bag under his arm. He nodded to the detective.

"All right," said Lane, "let's go."

The next few hours were the kind Percy would not care to live through again. Detective Lane droned out the required statement about rights, but Mother, her eye on the bottle in the sergeant's hand, ranted and raved, drowning out Lane's words. She was not at police headquarters five minutes before she had the entire place in an uproar. She managed to smash a few ashtrays, bouncing one off the head of an astonished desk sergeant. She also kicked over a wastebasket or two before anyone could believe what he was seeing and take steps to halt it. From what Percy could gather, it all stemmed from Mother's impression that she was being arrested for drinking in her own home.

Mother was sixty-five, though, and eventually she ran down. Percy had no idea how much time passed before she was finally seated, sweating and panting, in the detective's office next to Percy.

"Would you like to tell me why you killed him, Mrs. Wells?"

"Killed who?"

"Mr. Wilson."

"Mr. Wilson? *Somebody killed Mr. Wilson?*"

"We'll save a lot of time if you just tell the truth, ma'am. Now, where were you last night?"

"Home! I was home."

"That right, Mr. Wells?"

"I wish I could confirm that, but I had a headache. I went to bed early, so I really don't know where Mother was."

"What is everybody talking about?" shouted Mother.

Detective Lane sighed and looked at Percy. "Maybe if you ask her?"

"I can't believe this!" said Percy. "The fact that Mr. Wilson is dead is shocking enough, but murdered? And by my mother?"

Mrs. Wells seemed to have finally grasped what had been said. "Why would anybody kill my Mr. Wilson?" she wailed.

"Mother, Detective Lane says you killed him. Did you?"

She looked at him blankly. "We were going to be married someday."

Percy turned to the detective. "How was he killed? Where did you find him?"

"In his house. He was struck at the base of the skull by a full bottle of your mother's personally marked whisky."

"But Mother would have no reason to kill Mr. Wilson! They were constant companions."

"I guess you're in a state of shock yourself, Wells; otherwise you'd be able to figure it out. Your mother and Wilson decided to hold up the loan office. She knew you were working that night and that the safe would be open. So Wilson, with a stocking over his face, grabbed the money and conked you while she waited in the car—a car with whitewall tires, by the way. They agreed that he hold on to the money until things cooled down. Not because some of the bills were marked, though, for they didn't know this. They had to wait because neither one could become suddenly rich.

"When Wilson didn't show up as usual on Thursday night, your mother began to worry about him. Taking along a bottle of cheer in case they had to spend the evening at his house, she went there. She caught him in the act of packing his suitcase. The money was the first thing he had packed. She used the whisky, but not the way she had planned. Then she gathered up the money and went home."

Percy's mouth tightened. "That sounds like pure fiction."

"It isn't, Mr. Wells. Your mother's bottle was the murder weapon, and as she has just shown us, she has quite a temper."

"She could have given him that bottle as a gift."

"Then there was the matter of the stolen money. It was in that grocery bag in the back of your mother's closet."

Percy shook his head. "That is something I can't understand. Assuming that she did, somehow, manage to get her hands on that money," Percy went on, "that still does not prove she killed Mr. Wilson. I don't see how you can say she was even at his house."

"Because, Mr. Wells, your mother was in such a hurry to leave that she missed one packet of bills. It was underneath Wilson's body."

Mrs. Wells had been sitting like someone in a trance, but all at once she came to life. Some of the flying objects found their marks and others thudded and shattered against walls. It took three of them to subdue her.

Ordinarily, Percy felt relief when February was nearly over, but this year he was filled with joyous anticipation. He had his plane ticket for Miami and by this time tomorrow he would be flying high. Mother had never known about his regular raises and Christmas bonuses. His steady savings program had fattened his account, and it held more than enough to take him to Florida and support him in style until he could find a suitable job.

Mother had been found guilty, of course, but the jurors recommended mercy as he had known they would. It could so easily have been one of their own mothers on trial for her life.

It had worked out perfectly. Mother cleaned—snooped—only on Friday mornings, so he knew exactly when she would find the packet of marked money he had planted in his closet. That was why he could safely go to Mr. Wilson's house on Thursday night, dispose of him and set the scene, and, finally, leave the grocery bag of money in her own closet. Mr. Cole got all his money back, with the exception of the twenty dollars Mother had spent on her dress. As for Mother, she would be happy in prison. Now she would be able to stay inside and not have to brave the weather to shop for groceries. She would also have friends of her own, people to talk to. She would be taken care of for the rest of her life.

And Percy? Ah, Miami! He snapped his suitcase closed. The Wells Plan had been an overwhelming success.

A Debt to Doc

by Carl Henry Rathjen

Doc Hanrahan had been one of those oldtime general practitioners, whom some of the younger, country club specialists today refer to as Generally Poor. They're right, if you add it up financially, but if you balance it up with earned human regard, then these modern medics, some of them, are paupers compared to Doc Hanrahan.

Now Doc was dead, murdered. Someone had stopped his life with a heavy bronze clock, built into the belly of a prancing horse.

I remember that, as a kid who didn't want to have his sore throat painted with silver nitrate, I would intently watch that clock to hear the horse whinny when the second hand swept across XII. I was always skeptical, but Doc would smile and tell me to watch, and just about when the second hand was nearing its vertical, Doc's strong gentle fingers would grasp my lower jaw.

"Watch it, Eddie. He's taking a breath for it now."

I'd have to lift my head to watch the clock, and that meant my mouth would open wide because Doc held my jaw down. Then the swab would touch first one side of my throat, then the other, and somehow I couldn't see the clock but I'd hear the whinny. I was sure it came from Doc, and would accuse him of it. He never denied it, nor would he admit it. And come the next winter and another sore throat and we'd do it again. I always fell for it. Nobody else could pull something on me more than once, but Doc had a way with him. Or maybe he was the kind you didn't want to give a bad time, even though it meant you'd do something you didn't want to do.

Now somebody had given Doc a bad time. I felt sick in a way that Doc couldn't have fixed. The squad, looking for fingerprints and such, weren't making the usual remarks that would shock the average citizen who has never had to learn to take these things in stride, and not take too many of them home to the wife and kids. None of them had really known Doc, but they'd heard me speak of him.

The exception was Lieutenant Cheek. He must have known something about Doc after marrying Sylvia Kane, the girl who had been my steady in sixth grade until she "jilted" me for Whitey Hexheimer. Later, when we were older, Sylvia and I had taken up again until, while I was doing my stint in the army, she sent me a Dear John letter and I came home to find her married to a newcomer in town, a policeman named Cheek. Though it had worked out for the best and I was now happily married, there was always a restraint between me and Cheek after I joined the force.

Now, as I stood in the shambles of Doc's office, Lieutenant Cheek, tough, gray before his time, finally offered me a cigarette. I shook my head. He put the pack away without lighting one himself.

"I'll listen," he said. I didn't say anything. Cheek's voice got sort of challenging. "Guess it's obvious then. A hophead did it."

"Sure," spoke up Freidenberg, the precinct dick, behind us. He was always ready to agree if it would help him move down to headquarters. "With all the known peddlers locked up, the hopheads began the rounds of doctors' offices, trying to get what they needed, either by purchase or theft. I'd say it started as purchase here. There's no sign of breaking in. Dr. Hanrahan obviously wouldn't sell, and so—"

Somehow words squeezed through my throat and came out, sounding mangled. "I can't and won't buy it."

"I'll listen," Cheek repeated.

I shrugged. "I don't know yet. But I still won't buy it."

I did know, partly, but I didn't know the lieutenant well enough to be sure of anything. So I didn't tell him about the winter night when I'd been on the force two years and had dropped in after my tour because . . . yes, I had another sore throat . . . and Doc, smirking, was telling me to watch the clock and listen for the whinny when the guy came in with a gun in his fist. It was right after one of those narcotic roundups downtown. The guy was in a bad way, and it would have been nothing at all for me to take him. Doc prevented it.

Afterwards, after Doc had given him a fix and we had taken him, in Doc's old car, to a sanatorium, Doc had talked to me.

"He's sick, Eddie, and I'm a doctor."

"This has happened before," I said. "And with others, too," I charged. "I'll bet I could name—"

"And it will happen again," Doc came back. "I'll admit that not all of them want to be helped. I've tried to keep it ethical, though I suppose you'd prefer the term 'legal.' "

"I'm a police officer," I reminded Doc.

"So you are," Doc said. "Funny, you're still Little Eddie to me." Then he became serious. He wasn't blaming me, and neither could the addicts be blamed. "Blame the cause," Doc said sharply. "Don't take it out on the result. That's where you and I are alike, Eddie. We're forced to deal with results, but we should look past them to the causes, however obscure they may be."

So I didn't tell the lieutenant that Doc had compassion for hopheads.

"Let me look around a little first," I muttered to stall Cheek off.

I moved away, filled with dull, heavy, helpless anger. The squad tried to help. They only made me feel worse. They're a thorough bunch, and I knew I wouldn't find anything that they might have missed, even with the office the shambles that it was. The lock had been forced on the cabinet. Bottles and boxes had been pawed out to break open on the floor, spilling out a multi-colored confusion of pills, capsules, powders, liquids. I was staring at it when Cheek murmured beside me that most of the real stuff was missing.

"I still won't buy it," I said, moving away again past the locked safe to Doc's oaken rolltop desk. As a kid I used to be fascinated the way the slotted pieces of wood would follow the sweeping curves as the top was raised or lowered. As a man, I used to tease Doc that he was old fashioned, hanging onto this desk. He should modernize, keep up with the times. Doc's clear blue eyes, which never needed glasses, twinkled.

"Old fashioned! What's old fashioned about human illness? Call it strep throat or some other fancy name, but I'm still saying watch the clock and listen." Then, while I grimaced with the bitter taste of silver nitrate, he went on. "I am keeping up with the times. The times I've had with my patients, from birth to death. The times are all here in the case histories, up here and stacked in the cellar. I can re-live thousands of lives, and frequently project into the future. Suppose we start reading yours."

"No!" I'd laughed. "Not unless you promise to skip certain parts."

"I always do," he said, "because you learned your lessons from them. I can't say that for some of my patients."

I had a debt of memories I owed Doc. It was time to pay up, and I was going to welsh on the debt. The desk drawers had been yanked out and dumped, the same as the shoeboxes that served as Doc's files. Everything had been disarrayed and scattered. It looked like a cover-up of some kind to me, but a cover-up for what?

Cheek was watching me. If hands can lie, then my right hand did, the way I moved it to hold him off as though I didn't want to be interrupted while on the track of something. Pretending to be doing something, I knelt by the clutter of case histories. My eye saw names that meant nothing to me, until I saw Hexheimer.

I looked closer at the card. Whitey Hexheimer. A towhead kid and me, playing cowboys and Indians around his father's barn. Rainy days up in the hayloft, sometimes with girls. I turned the card over quickly. The last notation was dated two years ago. Doc's handwriting was as bad as on a prescription, but I knew that illegible technical stuff concerned a bullet wound, police-inflicted on the heels of a liquor store holdup. Whitey had dragged himself to Doc's office and Doc hadn't sent for me until Whitey was gone, for good. The bullet had been from my gun and I'd wanted to quit the force. Doc had talked to me.

"I could have told you when you were back in grammar school that it would end this way. But maybe I would have been reading wrong. After all, he might have just been curious when I caught him trying to open my medicine cabinet. And perhaps I'd better read up on you again. I must have missed something about your being a quitter."

"Doc, he and I used to pal together. If I'd known it was him tonight—"

Doc had gone right on talking as though I hadn't spoken. "When I wrote the character reference to accompany your application, I said you would never violate your oath. You didn't make a liar out of me tonight, Eddie. Not so far, anyway."

Curiously, still stalling under Cheek's watching gaze, I looked for my card. Keller, Edward. Or had Doc written it, "Keller, Eddie." I couldn't find it. In fact, I couldn't find any K's.

"That's funny," I said aloud, and I didn't sound at all funny. I began looking, sorting cards, but there were no K's or C's.

Doc always kept certain files locked in the safe, away from prying eyes. So his killer, probably thinking the card had been misfiled, had taken two stacks from the shoebox files.

I should have remembered the special file in the safe earlier, I thought, rising. Then, turning around, I got a jolt when I saw Cheek standing behind me. I put the old restraint on my voice.

"I'll buy your hophead story," I said slowly with some reluctance.

He let me have a long look before he spoke. "Do you think I offered it to you as an out?"

"Well," I began, "if Freidenberg hadn't filled it in that way—"

"Maybe I shouldn't have let him do that," Cheek cut in. "But you know how it is, Keller. You get a suspicion, knock it down because you can't believe it. Each time it comes up again, stronger. By then you figure you've kept silent too long and no one will understand. So you go on keeping silent. It becomes a habit, a bad habit of just watching, covering up. The kind of habit you find it hard to break, so when an out is offered—"

"You don't have to tell me how tough it's been to cover up," I said.

Again he offered me a cigarette. This time I took it. We stood there, measuring each other through the smoke.

"I didn't think it would go as far as it did tonight," he said.

"Same here," I agreed. "The card that will help tie this up is probably in Doc's safe." I lifted my hand, then let it drop helplessly. "Whenever you're ready to go to headquarters, I'll say my part of it, all the way back to the time when Whitey Hexheimer was used as a cat's-paw to try to steal dope from Doc."

"I knew about that, too," said Cheek. He hesitated. "On our way downtown, Keller . . . or can I call you Eddie? You won't mind?"

"Not at all," I said. "It might have helped if we'd gotten friendlier a long time ago, when we first met. But what could I have said, and how would you have taken it?"

"I wouldn't have," he said. "Now about that favor on our way downtown."

"I know," I said. "I was hoping you'd ask me. It will give me a chance to make up my debt to Doc, especially for sort of putting part of my oath on the shelf all these years."

"I figured it that way." Cheek held out his hand. "No hard feelings, Eddie."

"Thanks," I said, matching his grip, and knowing it wasn't going to be too difficult after all for me to take the brunt of clearing up Doc's murder, by arresting Cheek's hophead wife, née Sylvia Kane.

Footprints in a Ghost Town

by Donald Martin

Somehow he had got the notion that a ghost town would be a very peaceful place. It seemed like a very sound idea, for, after all, what were there in ghost towns except ghosts? And no matter how ghostly they were, still they never were as disturbing as people.

"Silence and solitude, those are the things I'm after," Alan said to the man with the martini, whom he did not know. "I want to get away from this sort of thing," he said, waving at the chattery party around them.

"That sounds like a splendid idea," the man with the martini said. "Ghost towns are intriguing places. Genuine Americana. Are you going to do a novel with a Western background?"

"That's still a state secret," Alan said.

There, that was still another pet annoyance of his. In New York you were forced to run up against these perfect strangers at these inevitable cocktail parties, strangers who pried blandly into your innermost secrets.

"Have you decided upon your ghost town as yet?"

"Yes," Alan said. "And please don't ask me where it is," he said grimly. "I want privacy, solitude, aloneness. For a year I hope to sit there amid the rotting boards of the past and write my book."

"Splendid idea," the man with the martini said. "Go West, young man!" he cried with alcoholic exuberance.

And when, a week later, Alan finally arrived in the place of his choice, he was certain his idea was a splendid one. Such a spot! Beauty, atmosphere, and solitude. The cherished solitude. The brooding quiet—measured from the hot dry earth, within a horizon of purple mountains, up to the hot white sky—was vast, intense.

The town itself had been called Cabin Creek. He had found it mentioned in one of the numerous Western histories he had pored over. Up to date maps did not carry its name. To history, to the mapmakers, to the world at large, Cabin Creek had vanished from the face of the earth. It had never existed, its people never lived. A dead place. Baked and bleached by decades of relentless sun. The nearest community was more than fifty miles away, New Cabin Creek. He would have to go there to buy his provisions, not more than once a week.

He parked his jeep in the middle of the main street and got out. Looking around at the crumbling buildings, he was delighted. Stepping up onto the elevated board sidewalk, he promptly crashed through, the rotted boards caving beneath him. He plunged forward, giving himself a nasty scrape. Restoring his balance, he laughed. This was not Park Avenue. He would have to remember the condition of the town. It wouldn't do to smoke in any of the buildings. A single match could annihilate his ghost town in a matter of minutes.

The word HOTEL struck his eye. It was written in faded black, perhaps charcoal, across a plank nailed sideways to a post in front of what had probably been the most elegant building in the old boom town.

Regarding himself as a guest in Cabin Creek, he laughed and decided he would put himself up in the hotel. Going back to his jeep, he took his few pieces of luggage and his typewriter, and, stepping carefully on the board walk, entered the hotel.

Inside it was very sad. The place was cloudy with spider webs, with dust. Pieces of sagebrush, whipped from afar by the desert wind, lay scattered about. Weeds grew through the floor in many places.

Playing his silly little game to the hilt, he strode to the desk, with his palm struck a phantom bell (sending aloft a flurry of dust), and said aloud to a phantom clerk who had clocked to dutiful attention: "Mr. Alan Arnold of New York. I believe I have a reservation."

Alan chose a downstairs room, not trusting the staircases. With a piece of sagebrush, he swept and cleaned the room as best he could. One piece of furniture remained, an old bureau. In it he placed his things. From the lobby he took a desk and chair (the chair received his weight with surprising strength) and placed them in his room. His bed was a pillow and several blankets, arranged upon the floor.

Later, he left the hotel and decided to have a look around his town. It had not been very big to begin with—it had surged to life on the crest of a silver strike in the mountains—and now there was very little left of it. There was the dusty main street, the buildings stretching along it in two weary, sullen rows, each clapboard structure sloping upon the next. A few small buildings had been built about the outskirts. These had largely crumbled back to earth now.

He passed the ruins, staring curiously at them, as at some American Pompeii. A warm breeze mixed the untrod sand, heaved a creaking board, fluttered a diaphanous spider web. Everywhere was the dead slant of shadows, mounds of dust and sand. Could he ever become a part of this place? he asked himself. Well, he was going to have to, if he was going to work here effectively.

At the edge of town, beyond the last house, he noticed a slight rise. Curious, he went toward it. Coming closer, he saw the remains of a wooden fence that had long ago fallen back. Something strange and eerie about the place held him there. And then he realized what it was, what it had been: a cemetery. It had the uncanny *waiting* stillness of a burial place. But there was an odd thing—there were no headboards.

Intrigued, he walked through where the gate had been. In some places the grass grew very tall. He could see places where graves had been dug and shaped. But no headboards. There were none standing and none lying in the grass. Did they bury nameless people here? He walked to the summit of the brief knoll and stood there, feeling the warm breeze, squinting in the bright, still, dry heat. From this elevation he stared down at the town. For a moment, the dead town looked rather hostile. He had an uneasy feeling.

Walking back from the old, forgotten cemetery, he made a mental note about the curious absence of headboards. Next time he drove to town, he would inquire about it.

As he neared the start of the main street, he thought he saw something move on a ridge a few hundred yards away. It made him stop and whirl, a wild surprise that was almost fear seizing him. He peered for almost a minute, but could see nothing. He brought out his handkerchief and mopped his face.

"Nothing," he said, aloud. "Probably my imagination. Or maybe the shadow of a passing bird." Then he smiled uneasily. His first day there and already he was talking to himself. But then, once he got to working, the novel would make him concentrate, would fully occupy his mind; then he would be able to take advantage of his solitude instead of its taking advantage of him.

That night, by candlelight, he began his work. It was a risk, he realized, to light a candle in all that dry rot, but he had no other choice, if he wanted to work nights.

He had been writing for more than two hours. He was making

notes in his notebook, writing with a pencil. So it was very quiet. He had become so intense in his work, was concentrating so deeply, that he had forgotten where he was. He was leaning over the desk, the yellow light flickering tiredly over the white page, bobbing shadows across his white shirt.

Then he heard the sound. He was caught up by it almost instantly. His pencil stopped in the middle of a word. His eyes looked up, a sharp fright coming into them. They roved warily about the dark, shadow-hung room. He waited.

The minutes passed. What had the sound been? He began to make himself hear it over and over in his mind, trying to recapture and identify it. It had been a quiet, surreptitious sound. Surely it couldn't have been made by a human. Perhaps some desert animal, a coyote. Some animal that had become aware of a new presence in Cabin Creek's decaying buildings and had come down to investigate. Perhaps a mountain lion. He wished he had brought a gun.

He waited. For almost a minute he sat without drawing a breath, his pencil poised above the half-written word. But the sound did not repeat itself.

The wind. That was what it must have been. Self-consciously, he forced a grin. He laid down his pencil and sat back, rubbing his hand across the back of his neck. He was going to have to get used to this sort of thing.

A few minutes later, he blew out the candle and went to sleep.

Dawn came, vast, solemn, empty. The light filtered mistily through the dirt-smeared windows. Alan sat up in his blankets. He stretched his arms, taking a deep, expansive breath. Then he got up and dressed. He took his water pail and went out. There was a creek just outside of town. This was his source of water.

As he was walking away from the town, whistling, swinging the pail, he suddenly stopped short. There before him in the sand were footprints, shaped out in the sand, empty, mysterious. They couldn't have been his; he hadn't walked this way. He followed them. They led down from the foothills, through the town, and up towards the cemetery. There they stopped, just outside the cemetery. Another set led back.

He looked around. So he *had* heard something during the night! Someone had been wandering about. And now the town, the same old assemblage of crumbling buildings, seemed almost to transform before his gazing eyes into something sinister, mysterious, not just something standing in ancient abandon and disuse, but standing with old and solemn purpose, guarding some inhabitant secret.

He did not get the water. He did not make himself breakfast. He was more disturbed than afraid. There was some logical explanation, he was sure. And he was going to find out just what it was. He went directly to his jeep, leaving his water pail in the middle of the street.

It was more than an hour's drive to New Cabin Creek. Driving out of the ghost town, he encountered several miles of rugged, unpaved road. Once he reached the highway, however, he was able to make good time.

New Cabin Creek had been built on the crest of a hill. It was not a large town, but it was modern, with some small industry. Alan followed the highway's endless streak of white line into town and pulled into a parking area.

Yesterday, he had made the acquaintance here of a rather old man who had been sitting on a bench across the street from New Cabin Creek's gas station. The old man—his name was Bill Dodge—had evinced some interest when Alan told of planning to live in Cabin Creek for a year. But then their conversation had drifted away from the ghost town into other channels. Now Alan would seek out the old man and ask him some questions. Crossing the street, he saw the old man. And Bill Dodge was quite an old man, close to eighty, small and stooped, with an unkempt thatch of white hair. The old man wore a string tie and a vest over his white shirt. He saw Alan crossing toward him and waved a friendly hand.

"Hello," Dodge said as Alan stepped onto the curb.

"I'm glad I caught you," Alan said. "I'd like to talk to you."

The old man gave him a look of shrewd appraisal, his blue eyes, almost hidden beneath thick white eyebrows, kindling a lively interest.

"Can we sit somewhere?" Alan asked.

They went to the bench. The old man, although no longer spry, had nevertheless retained a sharp, tough mind.

"Want to talk about Cabin Creek, do you?" he said.

"How did you know?" Alan asked, smiling.

"You've got a look about you. As if there's something you don't understand. A ghost town can give a man that look, if he's sensitive enough."

"Did you ever live in Cabin Creek?"

"Of course. I was a young man during its tail-end years. It only had about a six year boom, though that's a lot longer than most of them. I came down from Wyoming. I missed out in the silver strike, but I stayed on. The town didn't die that quick. After the strike it was a nice place. It died slow. In fact I was one of the last to leave Cabin Creek. I went to California for a while, then moved back here because this was the place where I was a young man."

"You say there's no one at all living out there now?"

"No."

"How about in the mountains? Any ranchers or prospectors or hermits or anybody like that?"

"No. There's no ranchers there, and nothing to prospect any more. As for hermits, there's none that I know of." The old man fixed an amused look on Alan. "There's no ghosts, either."

"But there's somebody there. Last night I heard something. This morning I saw footprints. They came down from the foothills, right across town, stopped at the cemetery, then went back."

"The cemetery you say?" the old man asked, his highly expressive eyes changing from amusement to sharp interest.

"Yes. And I want to ask you about that cemetery, too."

"Never mind that for a moment. What else'd you see? Did you go into the cemetery?"

"No."

"The footprints didn't go in there, either?"

"No. And one other thing. On this I could be mistaken. But yesterday afternoon I was sure I saw something move out on a ridge. Do you think it could have just been an animal?"

"No, no animal," Dodge said. "I know what you saw. The Indians."

"Indians?" Alan exclaimed, excited for a moment, but then certain the old man was laughing at him. But the old man's face remained completely serious.

"Yes. Two Indians. There's always two Indians over on that ridge You saw them. They generally don't like to let themselves be seen, though everybody knows they're there."

"But I thought you said . . . "

"Never mind that. I know what I said. It's these footprints of yours that interest me. Right up to the cemetery they went but not into it, you say?"

"That's right. But just a second. What about these Indians?"

"They won't bother you. They know what they're doing there. They come from a place in the mountains, from a small but very proud and religious tribe. A long time ago one of their chiefs was shot in the mountains just outside Cabin Creek. Because he was a great chief they brought his body in for everybody to look at. Then they buried it in the cemetery there. He was their greatest chief, Fire Heart. With the Indians he's still a legend, a god. There's always two of them, even now, in this day and age, sitting there watching his grave. They don't want nobody digging in it."

"Then it must have been one of the Indians I heard, going to the cemetery," Alan said.

"No," Dodge said. "They never come off that ridge, except on the anniversary of Fire Heart's death. Then they come down and put a stone on the grave. That time is close now, too. But it hasn't come yet. You heard somebody else last night, and I'll bet a ten dollar hat I know who it was."

"I wish you'd tell me," Alan said.

"You stay in Cabin Creek and you'll know soon enough."

"That's not a very steadying thought. What's it all about?"

"Well, it's a long story, and it happened a long time ago. I guess I'm the last one who still knows all of it. I knew the people, too. They're all gone now."

"Can you tell me the story?" Alan asked.

"I can, if you're interested."

"Of course I'm interested. Look, I want to stay in Cabin Creek for at least a year. I want to know what's going on."

"It happened right in the middle of the boom," Dodge began. He was not looking at Alan now, nor was he looking at the gas station upon which his eyes were fixed. He was looking back through the mists of time, back across countless summers and winters into that deep, lonely past which he cherished. "There was a lady named Diamond Annie, and there were two men who loved her, Adam Buzas and Tom Cartwright. Annie was queen of the Gallery, which was Cabin Creek's gaudiest night spot. Annie was quite a gal. Tall and beautiful, with a pompadour of the blondest hair you ever saw. Tom Cartwright was part owner of the Gallery. This made him think he was full owner of Annie. He did give her her nickname. He covered her with diamonds. Hardly a week would go by without Tom giving her another diamond. He insisted she wear them, too. She had them on her fingers, around her throat, in her hair. And never did a woman do them fuller justice." The old man paused for a moment, having a long look at Diamond Annie, his eyes musing appreciatively. Alan did not press him. In a few moments the old man began again.

"But Annie loved Adam Buzas. Adam was a young one who'd come up from Texas. He owned a small ranch outside of town, but he sold it so he could move into town and be close to Annie. She liked him. She liked him a real lot, and Cartwright knew it, and there was nothing he could do about it. Adam used to tell Annie that he would take her away from Cabin Creek. He told her he'd homestead out in Oregon. But she was afraid of Cartwright. Tom was slick and tough. But finally one day she told Adam she'd go with him. Tom heard of it and set out to stop them. He went to Adam, but Adam wouldn't scare. Then he went to Annie. She had just finished her packing. She was going, she told him. He told her different. Then he told her he wanted the diamonds back. She wouldn't give them. Then something happened. Nobody ever knew for sure just what. Some say that Annie tried to walk out. Tom shot her. She died there in the room.

"There was hell to pay for that. Tom had a lot of power in Cabin Creek, but not that much. Annie was a mighty popular girl. She had lots of friends, most of whom were all for stringing Tom up to the nearest rafter. Luckily for Tom there was a U.S. marshal in Fathersville, 'bout twenty miles east, and he got here and took over. They had to tie Adam Buzas down—and I mean literally tie him down—to keep him from busting the jail to get Tom. There was a quick trial. You never saw so many men sitting with guns in their laps in a courtroom. Tom pleaded guilty and got life. That seemed to satisfy most everybody. Tom's friends figured he'd get out in short time, but he never did. He died in prison, about ten years ago.

"Then things began to cool off. I mean maybe a year later—that's how high the temperature of the hotheads was around here. Folks began to ask what ever became of all of Annie's diamonds. The day she'd been killed, she'd just finished packing. Later they went through all her things—and Adam Buzas was standing right there—and they never found a trace of the stones. Some folks figured maybe she'd given them back to Tom. But she never did that. Then folks realized what must've happened. Those were different days. The roads weren't always so safe to travel. Annie knew that. She was a cagey girl. What she did was sew all the diamonds into her dress—the one she was wearing the day Tom Cartwright killed her, the same one she was buried in in the Cabin Creek cemetery.

"But just in case anybody took any notions about desecrating the grave, there was Adam Buzas. He'd taken rooms in a house on the edge of town. The house is still standing, I think; least it was two years ago, the last time I visited the place. Adam well knew where those diamonds were, and he knew what some people would do to get them. From his porch he could see the cemetery. And from the cemetery you could see Adam Buzas sitting on that porch with a rifle across his lap. It seemed that he was there day and night, that he never slept. He'd just sit there and watch the cemetery, him and that rifle, which he could well use, as they knew; just sit there and get old and old and old, till folks began to say that he probably forgot himself why he was there.

"But there was getting to be less and less folks to say it. Cabin Creek was all played out. Gradually, people there were dying out, or were packing up and leaving. No fresh faces came in. And then Adam Buzas was the last man living in Cabin Creek. I'd go down there once in a while to see him. He'd still be sitting on the porch with the rifle in his lap. I doubted whether that rifle could fire any more, but nobody was going to do anything to find out. He was the loneliest man in the world, sitting there grieving with all those ghosts around him. Then one day he went and took away all the headboards. There's probably two hundred graves in that cemetery. He was getting old then, and he figured that if folks still remembered the story and came to digging he would make it as hard for them as he could.

"Then Adam died. Not too long ago, either. Somebody went there to visit the place and they found him lying on the porch, the rifle on the floor. They buried him here in New Cabin Creek. Some sentimental folks thought it would have been a nice touch if they buried him in the old town near Annie, but that was the way they did it. So Cabin Creek was empty. But if anybody began to speculate on digging for the diamonds—not that anybody's sure any more where they're at—they changed their minds in a hurry. The Indians had heard the story. They knew all about it. Their chief was still buried there. When they heard that Adam had died, they expected folks would come out and start digging. They didn't want their chief disturbed. So one day they appeared there. Two of them. Always two. They sit for a week and then two more come, winter and summer, day and night. Nobody's ever tried them out yet. No more than anybody ever tried out old Adam when he was sitting on that porch. By now, though, the whole thing is almost forgotten."

"Except," Alan said, "by the person who was there last night."

"Yes," Dodge said. "God, I wish I were a younger man."

"You would try out the Indians?"

"Dig up Annie's grave? Me?" The old man passed him a rather

harsh look. "No, I would never do that. Anyway, nobody will as long as those Indians are there. This fellow last night found that out. He was probably heading for the cemetery for a look around; then the Indians let him know they were there. He tried them out. He'll have to try something better."

"Who do you think it was?"

"There's only one man that I can think of. Only a man who knew just where the grave was would be cocksure enough to go to the cemetery at night. And there is a man who knows. His name is Glenn Short. He came into New Cabin Creek on a bus about ten years ago. He started asking around about things, about Cabin Creek. Naturally folks referred him to me, being the unofficial historian of the place. He asked me a whole lot of questions about Adam Buzas and Tom Cartwright and Diamond Annie and about the grave and the diamonds. Well, I made sure I asked a few questions myself. I got it out of him that he'd been in the penitentiary and had known Tom Cartwright there. Then he said he'd come around as a favor to Tom, to look up some of his old friends. Well, Tom's old friends had been gone for more years than you can remember, so it was pretty obvious to me what Short was after, and he was fishing around to find out if it was still there. And if it was still there, then he knew where it was. Because Tom Cartwright had known. Tom had suspected that Annie had the diamonds buried with her and he took pains to find out which grave it was. Said it was because he wanted to have flowers placed on it the whole time he was in prison. Well, the flowers never showed up, just as Tom didn't. I guess when Tom began to realize that he was never getting out, he told the story to Short, told him just where to dig.

"So Short went there. But it was his misfortune to find Adam Buzas still there, still with the rifle. Tom hadn't told Short about Adam, so when Adam put a shot across Short's bow, Short took off and came back here. He hung around town for a few days. I suspected that he'd taken it into his head to go back to Cabin Creek and kill old Adam, Adam was the last one living there then. But he went to Salt Lake City first, maybe to get some money. Anyway, the next we heard was that he'd got into a scrape there and had got put away again. But now I suspect he's back, and that it was him you heard last night."

"Can you describe him to me?" Alan asked.

"Well, it's been a number of years now, but I don't reckon a fellow like him is going to change very much. He's not a very friendly looking fellow, and his name doesn't fit him. He's tall, half bald on top, with a sort of craggy face, with eyes that don't ever quite seem to look straight at you—I reckon they got that way from looking through bars too long."

"Do you think he'd be dangerous?"

"What would you think about a man who suspects there's an uncounted fortune in diamonds a few feet down?"

"What do you think I ought to do?" Alan asked.

Dodge looked at him. "It ain't my place to tell you, son," he said, "But if I were a young man, I know what I would do."

Alan Arnold was hardly a hero. He was the first to tell himself that. And he was hardly fearless. But he did have pride, as occasionally a writer has. If old Bill Dodge had said that he would have left Cabin Creek if in Alan's place, then Alan would have taken the advice. But Alan had felt the old man's wild, swaggering spirit surge once more in his tired old body. Alan envied that spirit.

And anyway, staying *was* the thing to do, if only to find out what happened, for the story intrigued him deeply. And neither was he in any grave danger, he felt. Glenn Short would have no reason to harm him—unless Alan objected to Short's digging for the diamonds. But Alan would have no reason to object. It was none of his business. Besides, the Indians would be there. They could take care of that.

He thought of the diamonds. How much could they be worth? Thousands? It excited him—just the thought of it.

He drove back to Cabin Creek. It was late in the afternoon. The shadows were beginning to lengthen across the empty main street. The peculiar, alienating air of mystery still pervaded the dead buildings.

He parked the jeep in front of the hotel. Before going into the hotel, however, he walked up to the little knoll where the cemetery was. He stood there, gazing wistfully. Diamond Annie. He wished he could have known her. From the soft, sad way Bill Dodge had spoken of her, he wished very much he could have known her. But even if he had, it would have done no good. He sensed that. They differed too much, one from the other.

The retreating sun was casting a soft copper light over the neglected, weed-grown cemetery. He looked out at it. It was poised over the mountains, bidding another of its infinite guardian farewells to Diamond Annie.

Then he turned around. There was Adam Buzas' house. The porch which had so faithfully supported his devoted, implacable figure for so many years had collapsed. It was a pile of rotted, eaten wood. Adam Buzas he knew. That kind of man he understood. He felt kinship with him and his long, lonely vigil. He and Adam Buzas would have been friends. But *such* devotion! It made him shudder now. It seemed somehow mysterious and inexplicable, like something told from a legend.

Having thus communed, ineffectively, with the veiled ghosts of an elusive past, he walked back to the hotel knowing, uncomfortably, that the Indians were watching him from their secret place, resenting him doubtlessly, not trusting him.

He entered the hotel. Walking towards his room he saw smoke. The first thing that rang in his mind was *fire!* He dashed into the room, then stopped short in the doorway.

A man was sitting there, looking at him, smoking a cigarette. Here was Glenn Short, just as the old man had described him, half-bald, tough-faced, his long legs extended before him. He was looking up at Alan, cynical, self-assured.

"Glenn Short," Alan said.

"That's right," Short said. He squashed out the cigarette on the desktop. On the floor, next to the chair, lay a spade. Alan glanced at it.

"You're going after those diamonds, aren't you?" he asked.

"That's right."

"You were poking around here last night."

"You've got good ears," Short said with a slow grin.

Short's hands had been folded over his middle. Now he opened them and Alan could see the handle of a pistol protruding.

Short looked out the window. "Sun's going down," he said. "I've got to start soon."

"What about the Indians?"

"I've got a theory about them. My theory is that they won't do a thing. Do they really care about the grave of that chief that died all those years ago? I don't think so. They're just sitting there because it's become a tradition, a tribal custom. I'll bet they'll even be glad once somebody takes those diamonds; it'll get them off the hook."

"How about last night? Didn't you try last night?"

"I just went for a look at the layout, just to see if the grave was still intact, and they didn't do anything."

"But you didn't have your spade with you?"

"No."

"What about me?" Alan asked.

"What about you?" Short said right back to him. "That's up to you. I'm taking those diamonds. It can be over your dead body or not. It's up to you. And if you don't think I'm up to it, mister, you just try me out."

Alan pondered this for a moment. Then he shook his head, his eyes falling. "I won't try you out," he said quietly. "It makes no difference to me."

Short stood up, spade in hand.

"During the day it's too hot; at night it's too dark. This is the time," he said. He tucked the gun more comfortably into his belt. He was quite a tall man, towering over Alan. He held out his palm. Alan looked at him.

"The key," Short said.

"The key?"

"To the jeep."

Alan gave it to him. It would be folly to resist this man who was not only much bigger but armed as well.

Short left. Alan sat down by the window. He watched Short stride up the street, the spade swinging rhythmically at his side. Short passed the house with the collapsed porch and strode up the knoll.

He knows just where it is, Alan thought bitterly.

Short paused, looking around, standing quite tall against the copper sky. Then he plunged the spade into the earth, defiantly, exclaiming his purpose to the watching Indians. For a few moments he dug, his long back curved, tiny streams of earth flying up.

Then, suddenly, a rifle crackled. Then another. The earth spurted at Short's feet. Quickly he flung down the shovel and went to one knee, his revolver drawn.

Feeling a hot constriction in his heart, Alan wheeled. From the window he could see them, the two Indians coming across the prairie, not at all like the Indians in a movie; there were no feathers, no warpaint, no war-whoops. They were dressed like other men, in plaid shirts and work pants. They were coming boldly, their rifles at their shoulders.

And just as bold, as fearless, was Short. He looked like some lone Custer, kneeling on the knoll amid the desolate headstoneless graves, firing his pistol. One of the Indians fell. The other was hit, falling for a moment into the grass, but then rising, coming up with a blazing rifle, advancing with a fierce and furious slowness, wounded, staggering, but inevitable. His rifle blazed again. Short screamed. Alan watched Short rise, stand full against the sky, then break and fall. The Indian's rifle dropped. His hands came up to his face. For a moment he plunged through the chest-high grass like that, blind, dying. And then he fell.

The silence resumed with a sudden, uncanny completeness.

Then Alan was running to the cemetery, a hot excitement teeming in his heart. He ran up to the knoll. He stopped. Glenn Short was dead. Next to him was the place where his shovel had so desperately scraped.

Alan stood above the grave. So here was where the diamonds were. Dig down a few feet with Short's spade and scoop them up. He pictured them there, the glittering stones clinging to the ragged remains of a dress, sewn there by the woman's trembling fingers as she was about to run off with her lover. And he thought of Adam Buzas who had sat away his life, in bitterness, in grief, in loneliness, and in mysterious love to guard the place where his heart lay buried. And of the Indians and their chief, of whom they were so proud and so jealous, who lay here somewhere close by.

And he thought of Cabin Creek, upon whose dying boards he had foisted himself: Cabin Creek, which would probably crumble to-morrow because now it had all happened, it was all done.

Had it been meant for Alan Arnold to come to this spot and dig into the grave of buried love and devotion and take the reward which had colored the dreams of dead men?

He lifted the spade and began pushing the dirt back into the hole Glenn Short had begun to open, covering it again, making it look exactly as it had before, like all the others.

No Small Problem

by John Lutz

The plain block lettering on the frosted glass read: WINKLER, M. D., PSYCHOANALYST. The frosted glass was in a door at the end of a hall on the seventh floor of the Preston Building, which was in one of the newer, wealthier areas of the city.

Winkler, a man of about thirty-five with a lean, scholarly countenance, sat in the soft leather chair and glanced at his desk clock. It was past three o'clock. His next patient was already fifteen minutes late. Winkler was still recovering from his last patient, a nervous, twittering dowager who started every interview with, "Doctor, the most revealing thing has happened!" Then she would proceed to tell him about some trivia that she expected to have deep psychic significance, and he played her game, right up to the final, shrill, "Until next week, doctor." The underbrained, overmoneyed idiot, how was she to know that the M.D. on Winkler's door stood for Marion Dwayne, not medical doctor. Winkler would have been the last to correct her.

A buzzer sounded, and Winkler stood and buttoned his tweed sportcoat, lit his pipe. His next patient, Virgil Sprang, had arrived.

Since Winkler used a confidential answering service instead of a receptionist, he opened the door to the anteroom and greeted his patient.

"Mr. Sprang?" Winkler asked, for it was Sprang's first visit.

The short, rather plump man nodded nervously, and Winkler ushered him into the office. He motioned Sprang into the semi-reclined lounger alongside the desk, and then sat in his leather swivel chair behind the desk, angled so that he could see Sprang much easier than Sprang could see him.

"Now, who was it who referred you to my services, Mr. Sprang?"

"I chose your name from the phone book," Sprang said in a high, nervous voice. "I, uh, didn't know any psychoanalysts, and you're located in a good section of town, so I knew you'd be reliable . . ." His voice trailed off self-consciously.

"Well, that's not the usual way I obtain my patients," Winkler lied, "but under the circumstances it was probably a wise thing for you to do." He opened a notebook and pursed his lips professionally. "Now, what seems to be your specific problem, Mr. Sprang?"

"Midgets."

"Ah, midgets," Winkler said, making a note of that. He looked up to see that Virgil Sprang had twisted his neck awkwardly and was watching him. Sprang had amazingly fish-like blue eyes behind thick glasses, and Winkler could see that he was waiting for some incredulous reaction to his statement.

"Any particular type of midget?" Winkler asked.

"Small ones," Sprang said, turning and lying back again in the lounger, "and redheaded."

"And just how do these redheaded midgets concern you, Mr. Sprang?"

"Why, they concern me by turning up everywhere I go and pointing those tiny silver guns at me."

"Silver guns?"

Sprang nodded. "They carry them in shoulder holsters, and they're very quick on the draw."

Winkler's pen moved over the paper smoothly, drawing absent-minded doodles of little fish. It really didn't matter because the tape recorder was spinning silently inside the desk.

"Just why do these midgets bother you in particular?" he asked Sprang. "Have you done anything to provoke them?"

Sprang thought and shook his head. "I haven't done anything to provoke anybody, but almost everybody is out to get me. Only the midgets are out to get me even harder. *They're* out to kill me, no matter what!"

A paranoiac, Winkler decided. He'd had a few before and found that he could sell their files quite easily at a good price. The various confidence men with whom he did business could think of a thousand ways to make money out of a man like Sprang, just as Winkler was making thirty dollars an hour out of him. The difference was that Winkler wasn't taking any risks by doing anything illegal. Anybody could hang up a psychoanalyst's shingle in this state. No medical degree was necessary, as it was to be a psychiatrist, and it wasn't Winkler's fault that his name was Marion Dwayne.

"Tell me," Winkler asked, "have you ever seen two of these midgets at the same time?"

"Well . . . no," Sprang admitted. "But they don't look exactly alike. I think there are at least three of them."

"But it *is* possible, isn't it, Mr. Sprang, that there is only *one* redheaded midget?"

"Oh, sure, it's possible, but it isn't likely. I've seen them too frequently, and sometimes they're dressed differently."

"But why would they be after *you?*"

"Why is everybody after me?"

Momentarily stumped, Winkler puffed on his pipe and turned to his notes. "That's what we intend to find out, Mr. Sprang," he said at last.

Sprang was remarkably at ease for a patient on his first visit, and Winkler had no trouble getting him to talk freely. While the patient was rambling on, Winkler thought of different things and doodled on his notepaper, letting the tape recorder do its job.

"It's been very interesting, and possibly very informative," Winkler said when an hour was up. He closed the notebook with a quick little snap as Sprang stood.

"If you could just tell me what I'm doing that makes them want to get me," Sprang implored. "I went to the police but they laughed and said—"

"Yes, yes," Winkler cut him off gently. He handed Sprang some white forms and a pen. The forms requested information about Sprang's personal life, everything from his marital status to his bank account. "If you'll just fill these out at the table in the reception room on your way out ..."

"Certainly, doctor," Sprang said, and Winkler knew that he had his confidence.

He accompanied Sprang to the office door with a patronizing hand on his shoulder.

"Is next week at this time agreeable to you as your next appointment?" he asked, puffing loudly on his smoldering pipe.

"Just fine," Sprang said, "and thank you, Dr. Winkler."

Winkler had examined Virgil Sprang's forms carefully before filing them. He was interested to find that Sprang was married, childless, and had no outstanding hobbies or weaknesses. He was even more interested to see that Sprang had some time ago inherited a good deal of very lucrative income property and was not wanting for money. Now, when he answered the waiting room buzzer and the well-heeled blonde identified herself as Mrs. Virgil Sprang, Winkler saw where most of that money no doubt went.

"The purpose of my visit, Dr. Winkler, is to find out whether or not my husband is a patient of yours," Virginia Sprang said as she sat opposite Winkler on the other side of the wide desk.

"You mean he came to see me without confiding in you?" Winkler asked. "Highly unusual."

"Virgil is a highly unusual man," Mrs. Sprang said with a smile. She was a beautifully built woman, expensively groomed, but there was something vaguely predatory about her lipsticked mouth, with the fine, even teeth and the slightly underslung chin. When she smiled, Winkler was reminded of a shark about to turn for the fatal snap of jaws.

"How long," Winkler asked, "has he been afraid of these midgets that he sees?"

"Then he *has* told you about that," Virginia Sprang said, crossing her long legs with a swish of nylon. She put a forefinger to the corner of her mouth and closed her eyes momentarily in thought. "He's been on the midget kick for a little over a month," she said after a pause, "but before that it was somebody else out to get him. He's got this idea that everyone's out to get him."

Winkler placed his pipe between his teeth. "A not uncommon ailment," he said professionally to Mrs. Sprang. "Tell me, has your husband sought treatment before?"

She nodded. "He's been to several doctors. He gets better for a while, then in a few months he's back to his old ways, like buying shutters and padlocks for all the windows in the house."

Winkler tore his eyes away from the expensive diamond on Mrs. Sprang's finger. "I assume the main purpose of your visit is to find out how you can help your husband in the psychoanalytic process."

"Sure," Virginia Sprang said. "But like I told you, it never does much good."

"I've studied your husband's case, Mrs. Sprang, and I'm sure that eventually he can be cured by professional help." Winkler smiled and stood. "Of course this will demand your cooperation also, occasional appointments for us to talk about your husband."

"Of course," Virginia Sprang said.

Winkler walked to the office door and opened it. "And now if you'll excuse me, Mrs. Sprang . . . I'd like to talk to you longer but I have an appointment with a patient in five minutes." He shrugged. "A friend of the mayor's who can't be kept waiting."

"I understand, doctor." She walked to the door and gave him her slyly eager smile.

"I'll be in touch," Winkler said.

* * *

Virgil Sprang was obviously more upset than he'd been on his previous appointment. He almost fell into the lounger beside Winkler's desk, and even in the air-conditioned office he was perspiring heavily.

"You look as if you ran all the way here," Winkler observed.

"Ran for my life, doctor!"

Winkler opened his notebook and tapped his pencil point lightly on the desk. "The, uh, midgets?"

Sprang nodded and rested his head against the back of the lounger. "One of them followed me all the way here in one of those little foreign cars. Every time I turned a corner he turned, too. It was terrible." Winkler drew a smiling fish and said nothing.

"When I finally got rid of him I drove straight here," Sprang went on, "and there was one of them right there in the lobby, by the elevators. I ran all the way up the stairs."

"Have you had any other experiences with them during the past week?" Winkler asked.

"All the time. And once the one who makes nasty jokes even shot at me."

Winkler raised an eyebrow. "Shot at you?"

"In the garden behind our house," Sprang said. "He stepped out from behind a tree and grinned at me. Then he aimed and fired."

Winkler thought about that for a long time. "Did you look for the bullet, Mr. Sprang?"

Sprang sighed. "I thought you'd ask that. I looked in the side of the house but I couldn't find anything that looked like a bullethole." His voice took on hope. "But it might have hit a tree limb!"

"Might have," Winkler admitted. "You mentioned that one of these midgets cracks jokes?"

"Nasty jokes," Sprang said, shaking his head in disapproval. "He yells things at me you wouldn't believe, Dr. Winkler. Things I wouldn't repeat."

"I see no reason to repeat them," Winkler said. Not wanting to lose Sprang as a patient, he let Sprang rant on while he sat and pretended to take notes, waiting for the monotonous hour to come to an end.

Winkler thought no more about Sprang until three days later when he read in the morning paper that the poor man had leaped from the roof of a ten story building. He had left no note, but suicide was assumed. Winkler cursed at having lost such a promising patient and dismissed the matter from his mind.

Then a week or so later he chanced across Virgil Sprang's file and a thought occurred to him. Certainly the bereaved and now even wealthier Mrs. Sprang deserved consoling; and if Winkler was any judge, she would be very consolable widow.

That afternoon he parked his car in front of the Sprang residence and walked up the winding sidewalk to the front door. Virginia Sprang herself answered his ring. She was very pale, and visibly surprised to see him. He detected a certain reluctance as she invited him inside.

"I dropped by to say that I was sorry about Mr. Sprang," Winkler said. "I had no idea from our interviews that he was considering such a drastic thing."

"Virgil could get very depressed," she said, staring at the carpet. She seemed to have no intention of inviting Winkler to sit down, so he walked past her and helped himself to a chair.

"I suppose it was quite an ordeal for you, too," he said.

She followed him to the living room but did not sit. Winkler noticed that her black dress fit her very snugly.

"I do appreciate your concern, Dr. Winkler," Virginia Sprang said, glancing at a sunburst clock over the stone fireplace, "but I really have to be somewhere in less than a half hour . . ."

"Can I drive you?" Winkler asked.

"Oh, no, I've called a cab."

"Well, in that case . . ." Winkler stood and walked slowly to the front door, which she already had open for him. "I'll drop by some other time," he said with a smile. "That is, if you don't mind."

Her return smile was quick and apprehensive. "Not at all. But do call first to make sure I'm home."

Winkler patted her cool hand consolingly and left.

He was halfway to where his car was parked, his head bowed thoughtfully, when he became aware of someone walking toward him up the long, winding sidewalk. He raised his head to look, and his step faltered with surprise. Approaching him, strutting jauntily, was a redheaded midget.

"Afternoon," the midget said as he passed, and Winkler made it to his car fast.

He reasoned the whole thing out as he drove to his office. The midget and Virginia Sprang were obviously in cahoots for Virgil Sprang's money. They had taken advantage of his acute persecution complex and hounded him to death, turning up everywhere he went, firing blanks at him. It was no wonder the fool was so agitated the last time he'd been in Winkler's office.

Winkler parked in the Preston Building lot, stopped in the lobby cocktail lounge for a drink, then went up to his office to consider the possibility of blackmailing the midget and Virginia Sprang.

As soon as he opened his office door he gave himself a mental kick and recalled with certainty that he'd had only one drink downstairs in the lounge. Standing on the square-tiled floor like so many strategically placed chessmen were three redheaded midgets, all wearing identical well-pressed dark suits. As Winkler instinctively walked around behind his desk and sat down they moved in front of him to form a small barrier between him and the door.

"I assume you gentlemen are in the employ of Virginia Sprang," Winkler said, regaining some of his composure. He noticed that one of them had Virgil Sprang's file folder tucked beneath his arm.

"Virginia Jones," the midget in the middle corrected. "She's married to me now. I'm Stubby Jones."

Winkler cleared his throat of fear and swallowed. "Congratulations," he said, for lack of anything else to say.

The midget waved a short arm. "My brothers, Spike and Louis." They nodded. "We sort of stick together to get along in this world."

"Then all of you—"

"Oh, we didn't murder him," they said almost in unison. "He ran up on the roof and we just walked toward him and he jumped."

"Still," the midget in the middle shrugged, "the police might not see it that way."

"And one of you *did* shoot at him in his garden."

Stubby Jones grinned. "Only blanks. We wanted him to be a suicide, not a murder victim."

Winkler looked at the small men and decided not to be cowed. He gathered his courage for a bold front. "I take it you want to buy my silence," he said.

"I don't think we can afford that," one of the midgets said, and three small hands darted inside three small dark suitcoats and three small caliber chrome pistols were aimed at Winkler; tiny guns, to be concealed beneath tiny clothes and fit tiny fingers.

"These guns are untraceable," the midget on the left said. "We bought them in Europe when we were with a circus. From a tattooed lady who—"

"Now see here!" Winkler began.

"Now, now, doctor," Stubby Jones said with a nasty leer, "there's no need to be a Freud." High-pitched laughter sounded through the office.

"But I'm not even a real doctor!" Winkler tried desperately to explain as he started to stand.

There was a soft, staccato sound, like a miniature motorcycle engine turning over nine or ten times and failing to catch, and Winkler dropped back into his desk chair. Tiny holes appeared magically in his forehead and the tweed of his sportcoat, and he sat very still, his glazing eyes wide open in surprise.

Still smiling, one by one, the midgets left the office.

Water Witch

by William M. Stephens

The summer had been a scorcher in Miami, with that sultry humidity that breeds hurricanes, suicides, murders, and insurance claims. Our office was so swamped with claims, in fact, that I hadn't even taken a vacation.

Now things had slacked off a little, though, and I sat after lunch one Friday with my feet propped on the air conditioner, planning ten carefree days in the Bahamas, skindiving every day and swigging rum punches every night. On the street outside, the soft ocean breeze flirted with the girls' skirts, and inside the office the clatter of typewriters was pleasantly interspersed with the click of high heels.

The buzzer on my desk sounded, and the frog-like voice of McGinnis grated on my ear. "Jim, I want to see you." With a certain amount of apprehension, I sauntered into the boss's office.

Duke McGinnis, our district claim manager, is a grizzled veteran of twenty-five years with Trans-Ocean Marine and its affiliated life and accident companies. He's as conservative as a two-dollar bet at Hialeah, and he lies awake nights worrying about the validity of claims. I think if he ever found out he'd paid an undeserving claimant, he'd shoot himself.

He waved me to a chair and chewed his cigar around to the other side of his mouth. I saw two claim reports on the desk in front of him. "We got two doozies here, Jim," he growled happily. For Duke the claim business is a constant game of wits; and the bigger the claim, the bigger the challenge.

"Maybe you forgot," I said. "I'm going on vacation Monday."

"Two doozies, Jim," he repeated as he squinted over the reports. "Together they may involve a hundred thousand clams. One's a sunken yacht and the other's a missing woman—a Latin beauty." He grinned wolfishly. "Yachts and dolls. Both suit your tastes. Which one do you want?"

"Who's the woman?" I asked. I was going on vacation come hell or high water, but it didn't hurt to express a polite interest.

"Carlotta Villegas, wife of the Cuban sugar millionaire. Villegas

140

was a big politico before the revolution—remember? He barely got out alive and brought his wife to Miami. She was a show girl in one of those fancy Havana clubs before he married her."

I raised my eyebrows. "I like beautiful women, but I prefer the ones who haven't disappeared. You need Jackson on this case, Duke. He speaks Spanish. Anyway, I'm leaving for the Bahamas in a couple of days."

"Then I guess you want the yacht loss." He grunted. "By an odd coincidence this tub was sunk in the Bahamas. You can stop at Bimini, give the boat the once-over, and cable me a report. Shouldn't take you more than a few hours."

He was a cagey one, all right; led me right into that one. "I'm taking a pleasure trip, Duke, not a business trip," I said.

He shrugged. "Some guys would get a lot of pleasure out of going over there on the expense account."

He had a point there. And maybe the job wouldn't take long. "Where is this yacht?" I asked.

"Near Bimini. Garbord Rake, the owner, just called me on the radio-telephone to report the loss. Said his boat hit a reef this morning and sank in a hundred feet of water. He and his mate were picked up off South Bimini. You can get the whole story from Rake at dinner tonight—on the expense account."

"Tonight?" I said, standing up. "Wait a minute, Duke. I can't go to Bimini today. I don't have air in my diving tanks. I haven't packed. I've got a date with a gal—and—"

"You've got time to break it," he interrupted. "The plane doesn't leave till four thirty-five. That gives you over an hour. Your ticket's at Chalk's Flying Service. Don't worry about diving gear. Harry Horne's *Reef Raider* is at Bimini now with a party of skin divers. You can rent some of Harry's equipment. Take your bathing trunks and underwater camera. I want to see some pictures of that tub before I pay out fifty grand." He waved his hand in a gesture of dismissal and pressed a buzzer. "I've got to find somebody to handle this missing woman case."

"Sorry I can't take that one, too," I said dryly and turned to leave.

"One more thing, Jim," he said. "Don't rush this investigation. Check it out thoroughly. I don't trust this Garbord Rake."

I stopped. "What's the matter with Rake?"

"I've just got a hunch. I didn't like his voice." His eyes narrowed. "For one thing, he doesn't want you over there before Monday. Says the weather's too rough to find the wreck."

I shrugged. "Could be. What's suspicious about that?"

"Two things. the Coast Guard says the whole Bahama Bank is as flat as a millpond. Also, I just called the *Reef Raider* through the Marine Operator, and Harry Horne says Garbord Rake has chartered him to go diving tomorrow." His eyes glinted. "Seems funny for a man who nearly drowned a few hours ago to want to go diving."

"Sounds like he wants to beat me to the wreck. Wonder why?"

"Ask him," said Duke. "Good luck, Jim. Don't take any wooden shillings."

The two-engined amphibian took off from the seaplane base in Biscayne Bay, rose over Millionaire's Row, and flew parallel to the rock jetties guarding Government Cut. A few miles offshore the greenish-brown water changed abruptly to a rich indigo. Along this ragged line marking the edge of the Gulf Stream, a dozen charter boats trolled for sailfish. Ahead was a monotony of blue, broken only by a southbound freighter trailing a shimmering wake that reached to the horizon.

In twenty minutes, the low islands of the western Bahamas appeared on the horizon. Bimini was dead ahead, and I could see the Marlin & Tuna Club at the tip of the island. Across a narrow channel was South Bimini. Farther south, the deserted lighthouse at Gun Cay was barely visible. As we drew near, I studied a row of brown rocks off South Bimini that stuck out of the sea like Indian arrowheads. These fossil growths of sharp coral could rip out a ship's bottom in seconds. Rake could have hit one of these, but he'd almost have to be dead drunk, or running at night.

As we passed over the deep outer reef, the velvet of the Gulf Stream changed to the pale green of the Bahama Bank. The water was as clear as mint julep. The pilot set the amphibian down in the harbor near a row of plush charter boats, then gunned the engines and taxied up the ramp. I crawled out, showed my papers to the British customs officer, then walked through the Marlin & Tuna Club grounds to the hotel.

Bimini is only fifty miles from Miami, but it's like a different world. Stateside tensions have a way of disappearing, and a kind of island magic takes over. The palms rustle lazily, and the natives laugh and sing and stroll along as though they had nowhere to go and all day to get there. It's hard to realize the traffic jams of Miami are only thirty minutes away.

As I checked in at the desk, the clerk nodded toward the cocktail lounge at the other end of the lobby. "A gentleman wants to see you, sir." Through the open door I saw a heavy-jowled man staring at me. I asked a native boy to take my luggage to my room, then walked over.

I realized suddenly that I knew Garbord Rake. Not personally, but by reputation. I'd seen his picture in the sport and society pages of the Miami papers. He'd been a well-known playboy in Miami Beach, married to an older woman with enough money to support his hobbies of ocean-racing and big-game fishing. When his hobbies grew to include affairs with younger women, his wife had divorced him. He had a look of dissipation now, and a bit of a paunch, but his neck and shoulders were powerful and his face deeply tanned. He wore a loud Hawaiian shirt and baggy slacks.

"Mr. Reddy?" he said. "We've been expecting you. I'm Garbord Rake." He shook my hand and measured me with a slight smile. "And meet Seth Withers, my mate. Excuse our appearance. We had to borrow these clothes. Took a swim in the ones we had on."

The second man was hunch-shouldered and thin, with sallow features and a nose like a hawk. There were scratches on his face, and one of his eyes was puffy. "Pleased to meetcha," he said, extending a limp hand.

"What happened to you?" I said. "Have a fight?"

He looked away, flushing darkly. Rake said, "Seth got knocked down when we hit the reef. Banged his head on something or other."

"Oh? Any serious injuries?"

"No. We were fortunate in that regard. We could have been killed. Waitress!" he called in a loud voice. "Get a move on, girl. Two more here, and the same for Mr. Reddy." He glowered at the girl. "These natives don't know the meaning of efficiency. You have to build a fire under them." He tapped a cigarette nervously, looked at me and twisted his lips into another smile. "My insurance company provides fast service, Reddy."

"You're just lucky." I grinned. "I'm on my way to Nassau on a vacation. Thought I'd stop over as long as I was in the neighborhood."

He laughed and visibly relaxed. "Well, this shouldn't delay you much. There's no question about the value of the *Water Witch*. Had an appraisal by a marine surveyor a month ago. She sank in deep water, though, and I doubt if she can be raised. Say the word and I'll get a salvage man from Miami to take a look. Now let's get the necessary papers filled out so you can be on your way. You can stop off on your way back from Nassau and see how the possibilities for salvage look."

"Thanks," I said, "but I'll have to dive down and see the wreck before I go. My boss wants some underwater pictures." I waved my hand deprecatingly. "Can't really blame him. When you ask a man to pay out fifty thousand dollars, he wants to have a few things in the file besides the accident report. I'll have to take some statements and—"

"Hold on," he said. "I realize you've got to justify the payment. But you don't mean you're going down a hundred feet or more and try to get pictures of the boat? That's ridiculous! There won't be enough light for pictures. Do you have a camera that'll stand the pressure?"

"Oh, it'll stand the pressure," I said, "and I've got a whole bag full of flashbulbs."

He looked into his drink. "It sounds stupid to me. But it's your funeral."

I didn't like the way he put that, but I managed to grin. "I'm just a working man, Mr. Rake. I follow orders." I pulled some papers from my pocket. "Let's get this report filled out." I turned to the mate. "Where were you, Mr. Withers, when the boat hit the reef?"

Before Withers could answer, Rake said gruffly, "He doesn't know anything, Reddy. He was down below. I'll tell you what happened."

"All right," I said, feeling my ears get red, "you tell it, Mr. Rake."

He lit another cigarette. "Well, we'd just installed two new engines in the *Water Witch*. I figured on running in the Miami-Nassau race, so wanted to check her performance. We left Miami early this morning, planning to clear customs at Bimini and go on south to do some spearfishing. I thought we were in open water, when suddenly we hit something solid and I felt the whole bottom rip open." He passed his hand over his face. "My beautiful *Witch*. It was horrible. She started settling immediately. I didn't have time to do anything—find my cash box, get my clothes, anything. Barely got our life jackets before she went under. We didn't have sixty seconds, did we, Seth?"

The mate nodded grimly. "About sixty seconds, I'd say."

"Did you send out a distress signal on your radio?" I asked.

Rake glanced quickly at Withers, then said, "There wasn't time. The radio was underwater before I got to it. We were helpless, Reddy. It happened so fast."

I nodded. "You didn't find your cash box?"

He shook his head. "Luckily, my credit is good on the island. All the money I brought—about five hundred dollars—was in that cash box."

That was reason enough, I figured, for a man to want to get to his boat in a hurry. There was nothing suspicious about that. Still, maybe because I just didn't like Garbord Rake, I felt there was something phony about his story.

I filled out the preliminary report and had Rake sign it. "Now," I said, "can you tell me where the boat went down?"

"There's a chart on the wall in the lobby. I can point out the approximate spot."

"Fine," I said, standing up. As I turned to follow the two men, something impelled me to turn around. At the next table a dark-haired beauty watched me intently. I hadn't seen her when I came in, but I had the feeling she had heard the entire conversation. As my eyes met hers, she gave a slight turn to her head. Clearly she wanted to talk to me. Whether it had anything to do with the case, I didn't know. Frankly, I didn't care. She looked like a very interesting conversationalist.

Rake led me to the chart in the lobby. "It was right about here," he said, pointing. "Probably one of these rocks."

"Why, man," I said, "those rocks stick up several feet. Did you have your eyes closed?"

"Don't be nasty, Reddy," he said, flushing angrily. "I've crossed the Gulf Stream a hundred times and never scraped the paint on a boat before. I just didn't see the reef. It was in my blind spot, dead ahead."

I studied the chart. The boat sank a mile or more south of the channel. Why would a good yachtsman like Rake be so far off course?

He was watching me intently. I shrugged. "The boat shouldn't be too hard to find, Mr. Rake. I understand you're going out on the *Reef Raider* tomorrow. I'll come along and help you look, if it's okay. What time are you leaving?"

He hesitated. "About nine."

"Fine. I'll see you at the dock."

He shrugged. "Anything you say." He smiled suddenly and slapped my shoulder. "Sorry I jumped down your throat, Reddy. I'm under a bit of a strain. Will you be my guest at dinner?"

I hated to turn down a free meal, but that beautiful brunette was still in the lounge. "Guess not, thanks," I said. "I want to look up a friend. Don't worry about the outburst. I asked for it." We shook hands again, and he and Withers walked away.

I deliberated over whether I should go to my room to change and shave. It took me a good half-second to make up my mind. Then I beelined into the bar. The girl was still there. Her eyes were green. "May I?" I said, pulling back a chair. "My name's Jim Reddy."

She nodded. "Please don't think I'm being forward, Mr. Reddy, but—well, I saw that yacht hit the reef today."

"You did!" I exclaimed. "Where were you?"

"Upstairs—in my Bonanza. I flew over from Fort Lauderdale this morning. I'm Linda Falcara—a fashion photographer—over here to take pictures of native costumes."

"So all fashion photographers buzz around in Bonanzas? I guess I'm in the wrong racket."

She smiled and gave me a level look. "My father is head of Falcara & Mohr, the advertising agency. Otherwise, I wouldn't have the job or the plane. I like flying and I sometimes get pictures the agency can use."

That was being candid. She looked the candid sort. "Well, about this yacht," I said. "What did you see?"

She leaned forward and those green, beautiful eyes grew serious. "I was some distance out, approaching the island, when I noticed the yacht. It was headed for the Bimini channel, but it suddenly swung around and started the other way. It turned so suddenly I thought something was wrong. Maybe somebody had fallen overboard. So I circled South Bimini without landing and turned back over the ocean. They were headed southwest now and I saw the rocks ahead of them. I flipped to the International Distress frequency to try to warn them."

"Did you reach them by radio?"

"No. The frequency was tied up. A woman's voice was shouting in Spanish—one of those Mexican shrimp boats, I guess. So I dived straight at the reef to try to attract their attention, then pulled out just above the water and flew by the yacht." She looked at me steadily. "This is the funny part. There wasn't a soul at the wheel."

"What? Are you sure? They probably had two wheels—one in the cockpit and one on the flying bridge."

"Of course they did. There was nobody at either one. There was nobody in sight anywhere." She paused. "Then, while I was circling back, they hit the reef and started sinking. I gave Bimini Radio a mayday call. And just before the boat went under, I saw two men appear and jump overboard. I circled over them until a boat came out and picked them up."

I was thinking a number of things, all at once. "Have you told anybody else about this?"

She shook her head. "Not about nobody being at the wheel. I was going to ask Mr. Rake about it. That's why I came into the lounge. I saw he was busy, though, so I sat down here. When I heard him lie to you, I decided to tell you what really happened. Mr. Rake said he was headed into Bimini harbor when he sank. That isn't true. He had swung around and started southwest before he hit the reef."

I bit my lip in concentration. "At the time thc boat turned around," I said slowly, "there had to be somebody steering. Did you see anybody then?"

"Yes. A big man. It must have been Mr. Rake."

"Did he know you were up there?"

"I doubt it. Not then. I was at a thousand feet. Of course, he saw me circling later—after they sank. And he must have heard me when I buzzed the boat."

"Maybe not, if he wasn't in the cockpit then. Those two engines could make a lot of noise." I thought for a moment. "Maybe they were having engine trouble. They weren't adrift, were they?"

"Adrift? Why, they were cutting through the water like a speedboat."

"In that case, they may not know you'd been watching them earlier—before they hit the reef. Let's keep that a secret between the two of us."

She nodded, wide-eyed. "What's it mean?"

"Beats me," I said. It was a puzzler, all right, and I didn't want to go to Rake and lay my cards on the table. Not until I had a few more cards.

I decided that an evening of dining and dancing with Linda might bring out some more interesting facts. Not even McGinnis could complain about my entertaining such an important witness—on the expense account.

We went to the Angler's Club and feasted on conch salad, broiled lobster, and rum punches; then to a native place where the rums were punchier and the dancing wild. By midnight I was feeling a little wild myself, and when I fell on my back showing Linda how to do the limbo, she thought we should call it a night.

I woke in the morning feeling like a dehydrated cactus, but I knew that a quart of ice water, a good breakfast and a few minutes in the water would cure what I had. The ice water and the breakfast didn't do it, and when I got to the dock at nine o'clock to go aboard the *Reef Raider,* I felt even worse. The boat was gone. A native boy said the boat had left an hour earlier. Rake had tricked me. They had left at eight o'clock instead of nine.

I walked by the pool and there was Linda, looking perfectly fresh, untouched by the night before. She swam several lengths of the pool and climbed out. She wasn't even breathing hard.

I returned her cheery "good morning" with a weak wave of my hand and sank into a deck chair. "Are you sure," I said, "you weren't hired by Garbord Rake to make me miss the boat?"

She took a chair beside me, saying, "I told you a dozen times last night you should go back to the hotel and get some sleep."

I had to agree she was right. "Well," I sighed, "Rake wanted to get to the wreck ahead of me, and it looks like he succeeded."

"You could hire a boat to take you out to the *Reef Raider,*" she said.

"That's an idea."

"I've a better one. They may spend hours looking for the wreck, and they may not know where to look. Dragging a diver behind a boat at two miles an hour is no way at all to find the *Water Witch.*"

"You sound like an expert. What's a better way?"

She smiled at me with pity. "Have you ever watched birds over the ocean? They spot fish you can't even see when you're sitting in a boat in the middle of a school."

I sat up. "Your plane! That's a terrific idea! Will you take me up?"

"On one condition," she said. "That you'll take me skin diving." Then, seeing the look on my face, she went on quickly, "I've dived before, Jim. I won't be in the way."

I groaned. She drove a hard bargain. I don't like female skin divers. Either they're squeamish and feminine, or they turn out to be Amazons who show up the men by diving deeper and staying down longer. It just doesn't work out. But I needed that airplane. This girl could swim—I'd seen that. She didn't look like an Amazon, either—more like a mermaid with legs. I just hoped she wouldn't mistake me for a shark and shoot me in the back with a speargun.

After she changed into a blouse and shorts. I hired a native to scull us across the channel to the landing strip at South Bimini. The Bonanza was a beautiful machine, sleek and streamlined and painted a sparkling green.

I said, "You do have a pilot's license?"

She turned, and I decided that her eyes were a little greener than the airplane. "Do you want to go with me or not?" she said. "I've been flying since I was nineteen."

"That long, huh?"

She wasn't going to be needled by me; she lifted her legs and got into the cockpit.

I climbed in the other side, latched the door, and examined the instrument panel critically. I had three hours of solo time myself, but mentioning it right then didn't seem like a good idea. "Here, let me help you fasten your seat belt," I said, trying to make amends.

"No, thank you," she said firmly. "Better fasten your own. I might get confused and fly upside down."

"Okay, okay," I said.

She took off smoothly, banked over the water, and flew parallel to the shore at an altitude of five hundred feet. I saw the *Reef Raider* below, towing two divers.

"They're way off," Linda said. "It's farther south." She pointed. "See the three rocks in a row? It's near them, I think."

And there it was, like a long shadow on the bottom, only a short distance to seaward of the middle rock.

She smiled. "Shall I buzz the *Reef Raider* and show them where to look?"

"No. I should say not. I want to be along when they find it."

We landed and took a swim. When the *Reef Raider* came through the channel, I left Linda at the pool and went to the dock. Captain Harry Horne brought the bow into the tide, and his mate Al Suggs threw me a line. I dropped a clove hitch around a piling and Horne reversed the engines, easing the stern against the wharf. "Hi, Jim," said Harry. "Meet Chuck and Suzy Murphy. They're diving with us all week. I think you already know Mr. Rake and Mr. Withers."

Chuck Murphy was a muscled Irishman who gave my hand a firm shake. His wife was small and blonde. They were both deeply tanned. "How's the diving?" I asked.

"Pretty good," said Chuck. "Visibility's been good all week. Lots of big fish, too."

"We've been looking for the *Water Witch,*" said his wife. "But no luck."

I turned to Rake. "You told me you were leaving at nine. What happened? You change your plans?"

"You must be mistaken," he said blandly. "We'd figured on leaving at eight o'clock all along."

"Well, it doesn't matter," said Captain Horne. "We're going out again after lunch. We'll shove off about one o'clock, Jim."

I nodded. "I'll be here. And I'd like to bring a friend."

Harry lent me some diving gear and I looked up Linda. I didn't doubt her statement that she had dived before, but I wanted to be sure of her ability before we went overboard in a hundred feet of water.

We went to a rocky beach near the hotel and I helped her put on the lung and a weight belt. After she pulled on her flippers and mask and waded into the water, I followed, using a snorkel. A short distance out, the bottom dropped away to twenty feet, and she sank without effort, breathing easily and regularly. When I "accidentally" dislodged her mask by kicking it with my foot, she didn't panic but replaced it immediately and, like an expert, blew hard through her nose to clear it. Finally, I motioned her to the surface and said, "Now, go down to the bottom and wait. When I come down, take your mouthpiece out and hand it to me. I'll take a breath and hand it back. Got me?"

She nodded, and then did the routine without a hitch. The inexperienced diver is usually terrified at the idea of giving up the air hose while underwater. After that, I didn't worry about Linda. And so with no qualms, I sank the lung on the bottom and told her to dive down, put it on, and swim back to the surface. For her, it was as easy as flying a Bonanza.

After lunch we boarded the *Reef Raider* and I performed introductions. "Oh, I know who you are," said Suzy Murphy to Linda. "You're the girl with the airplane."

Garbord Rake was very interested. "I want to thank you for circling us after the *Witch* went down," he said. "I wondered who our guardian angel was. Quite a coincidence—your being there at just the right time."

Linda smiled. "I was about to land when I saw you hit the reef."

Rake looked at her steadily. "Too bad you weren't a little earlier. You might have been able to warn me."

Linda didn't bat an eye. "It is too bad," she agreed.

I went up on the bridge where Harry was steering and asked him to try the area near the three rocks. When we reached the spot, Harry cut back the throttles and Al let towing lines out. Chuck and I took first trick, hanging to the ropes and breathing through snorkels as Harry ran the boat ahead slowly.

Visibility was exceptional—well over a hundred feet. To my left, the rocks jutted up like pillars from a ledge fifty feet down where parrotfish and snappers moved through branches of staghorn coral. The seaward side of the ledge dropped sharply to the smoky depths.

Chuck and I spotted the dark form at the same instant. He looked at me, then pointed down. I nodded and raised a hand to signal Harry to stop. The thing we saw was dark and indistinct, like an odd patch of coral. But it wasn't coral. Nature creates some strange formations in the sea, but never one with straight lines and sharp angles. This object came to a definite point.

I breathed deeply for a full minute, then jackknifed my body and kicked downward. At thirty feet, the mask cut into my face and my ears hurt. I blew through my nose, and the discomfort disappeared.

The object I saw was definitely a boat. On the edge of the drop-off, pieces of coral were freshly broken, and sea fans had been uprooted. The yacht had sunk to the ledge, then slid over, stern first.

She was deeper than I had figured. On reaching my safe limit—about fifty feet—there was still fifty or sixty feet of water between me and the bow of the wreck.

I shot to the surface and gulped the delicious air. "She's directly below," I called. "Drop a buoy right here."

I climbed the ladder into the boat and began strapping on a lung. Rake had his gear on and was peering over the side. I said, "How long is the *Water Witch*, Mr. Rake?"

"Sixty-two feet overall," he said.

"Then she's in a deep hole. The stern must be a hundred and fifty feet down. I wouldn't advise any of you to go that deep unles you've had a lot of experience."

"I've been down a hundred," Chuck said. "I'll take it easy and stick with you, Jim."

"A hundred and fifty feet isn't deep," said Rake disdainfully as he picked up a speargun. "Come on, Seth. I need that cash box." He rolled backward off the gunwale.

Withers turned to me quickly. "Mr. Reddy," he said in a low voice, "I'd like to talk to you when we get back. There's a couple of things—" He stopped as Rake stuck his head up, treading water.

"Save the chitchat, Seth," he called. "Let's get down there."

Seth looked at me meaningfully and I nodded. He climbed down the ladder, looking more than a little nervous.

"Wait up," I said to Rake. "We'll go down together."

He waved a hand and sank from sight. I buckled my harness in a hurry, then turned to Linda. "You stay up here. This is deep water and there may be a current. Why don't you and Suzy snorkel on the surface?"

"We'll keep an eye on them," said Harry.

"Sure will," said Al. "It'll be a pleasure."

"Let's go, Chuck," I said.

I picked up the metal housing containing my camera, tied a bag holding flashbulbs to my weight belt, and rolled over the side. In a moment, Chuck joined me. Way down, a stream of bubbles indicated where Rake and Withers had gone below the drop-off.

Chuck was in good diving condition and went fast, without hesitating, while I had to stop twice and rise a few feet to equalize the pressure in my ears.

The yacht lay on its side on a steep slope, with its bow tilted upward. My depth gauge showed a hundred and fifteen feet. The handsome teak foredeck showed no damage, and the brightwork still had its luster.

Chuck sank next to a porthole and flashed his waterproof light inside. The two bunks appeared freshly made. In a corner of the cabin I saw an object that seemed out of place—a lady's white purse. I decided I'd take a look at it before going up.

But first, I tapped Chuck's shoulder and sank down to examine the bottom of the hull. There was a gaping hole in the bow, just below the water line, and a jagged tear that extended back for about twenty feet through the mahogany planking. The frames were splintered, the stringers twisted out of shape.

I inserted a flashbulb and took a picture of the stove-in bow. When the bulb flashed, it sizzled like a cigarette dipped in water. I released the bulb and it floated upward. After several more close-ups I backed off, opened up the lens, and took several shots of the entire gash in the hull with Chuck hovering within it. That should satisfy McGinnis that the yacht was a total loss.

I wondered where Rake and Withers had gone. They might have been only twenty or thirty feet away, for all I knew, since the diffusion of light at that depth gave everything more than a few feet away a blurred, ghostly look.

We swam back to the foredeck and saw a hatch cover hanging open. I went through the opening and Chuck followed with the light. We were in the galley. Above our heads, opened cupboard doors hung down. Below us, other cupboards were closed. On the almost vertical deck, the chairs, table, and stove, bolted in place, appeared to be defying the law of gravity.

Leaving the galley, we dropped down into the passageway. Two doors were on each side. The first door on the lower, or port, side was locked. An insulated wire came up through the wall, its end dangling. A similar wire was hanging from the base of the radio antenna. Rake couldn't have sent a distress signal. The wire had been cut.

The other door on that side opened easily. This was the head. Opposite this door we found a stateroom containing fishing and diving gear, two bunks, several rolled-up charts, and a few magazines lying in soggy heaps.

I remembered the handbag and worked back up to the forward stateroom on the starboard side. Opening the door, I looked in the corner. The handbag wasn't there. Chuck came into the room and shone the light in the corner. The bag was definitely gone. Chuck looked at me, and I shrugged my shoulders. We left the room and swam down the passageway to the cockpit.

My depth gauge showed a hundred and forty-five feet. We had been down twelve minutes. Since we were using almost six times as much air at that depth as on the surface, we didn't have much time left. I pointed upward and Chuck nodded in assent. We followed the rail up to the bow, then went slowly to the surface.

I unbuckled my lung, handed it up to Al, and climbed aboard. Everybody was looking worried. Garbord Rake sat on the deck smoking a cigarette. "Where's Seth?" he asked.

I stopped. "I thought he was with you."

"He disappeared. I was feeling dizzy and had to come up. I looked for Seth and he was gone." He stared at me and took a long drag on his cigarette. "I can't understand why you didn't see him."

His attitude made me come to a sudden boil. "He went down with you," I said. "You should have stayed with him. Why didn't you wait for us?"

Harry Horne looked at his watch. "Nineteen minutes. He can't have much air left."

I reached for a new tank. "I'll take a look."

"Better not," said Harry. "If you go down again, you're asking for trouble. The bends are no joke, and there's not a decompression chamber closer than Key West. Al and I can go."

They put on their gear quickly and went over the side. The rest of us sat silently on the deck. After a while I said to Rake, "By the way, has a woman been on your yacht recently?"

"No," he said, his face expressionless. "Why do you ask?"

I shrugged. "Just wondering."

I would have left it at that, but Chuck had to open his big yap. "We saw a handbag in the boat," he said.

"Really?" said Rake. "That's strange. Where was it?"

"In the forward cabin on the starboard side," said Chuck.

"That's Seth's cabin. I'll bet he had a girl aboard in Miami. He stays on the boat, you know. We'll ask him when he comes up." He lit another cigarette. "Next trip down," he said casually, "we'll take a look at that handbag."

"Afraid not," I said. "It's gone. Somebody took it." I looked over the side and saw Harry and Al rising to the surface with a limp form between them. "What's more, I'm afraid Seth won't be answering any questions. It looks like he's had it."

Everybody rushed to the rail as the divers surfaced and pushed Withers out of the water. His mouthpiece was hanging on his chest and his head lolled lifelessly. We laid him on the deck and his body made a sloshing sound like a watersoaked pillow. Water trickled from his blue lips.

"He was lying on the rocks a few feet from the port rail," said Harry.

A pool of blood was forming on the deck. "Where's the bleeding from?" I asked.

"He's not bleeding—I am," said Harry, holding up a slashed arm. "I crawled under the stern and cut myself on the propeller." He turned to Al. "Lock this lung in my cabin. I want to see if it's working right."

"Shouldn't we do something?" cried Suzy. "Shouldn't we give him artificial respiration?"

"Sure," said Harry. "Sure. But there's not a chance in a million. He's full of water—wasn't even buoyant after we removed his weight belt. We had to haul him up."

Garbord Rake shook his head. "Poor Seth. He must have had an attack of nitrogen narcosis."

"Maybe," I said grimly.

He looked at me. "What else could have happened?"

"I don't know what could've happened," I said. "It could've been a lot of things." Narcosis was a definite possibility, I knew, although few divers have severe attacks at less than a hundred and seventy-five feet. Air embolism was another possibility—but extremely unlikely. Maybe his tank had not been properly filled—mistakes happen on the best of boats—and he had run out of air. Maybe the air had been bad. Maybe something was wrong with his regulator. There are dozens of ways a diver can have a fatal accident.

We took turns giving artificial respiration all the way back. Harry called Bimini on the ship-to-shore, and a British doctor was waiting when we docked. It was hopeless, just as Harry had figured. After a cursory examination, the doctor shrugged. "He's quite dead. Obviously drowned. He was probably dead before you brought him up."

Nobody had much to say at dinner that night. Later, Linda and I went back aboard the *Reef Raider*. Harry had the gear Withers had worn spread out on the deck of the cockpit.

"Jim," Harry said, "we got a funny situation. This bottle's holding fifteen hundred pounds of air. He couldn't have been down ten minutes when he died. There's nothing wrong with the air, and I can't find anything wrong with this regulator."

"Maybe he got narcosis and fainted," I said. "Then the mouthpiece fell out of his mouth."

"Maybe, but I don't think so." He picked up the tank. "Did anybody touch this air valve after we brought the body aboard?"

"I didn't see anybody," Linda said.

Harry frowned. "The valve was closed. The air was shut off."

His words hung in the air like heavy smoke while the three of us looked at one another. I felt a shiver go down my back. "My God, what a perfect way to kill somebody."

"That's right," said Harry. "A perfect murder—or a fatal accident. We'll never know. Anybody could have closed that valve after we brought the body aboard. It's a thing you do without thinking when a diver comes aboard. You have to close it, in fact, in order to take the regulator off the tank."

Linda looked thoughtful as she fingered the valve. "But it's so simple to turn. If Rake had shut the air off, couldn't Withers have reached behind his neck and turned it on again?"

"Maybe," said Harry, *"if he had known.* Some people can reach their valve and, then again, some can't. But who would ever think of it? Imagine for a moment: you're swimming along; you take a deep breath, hold it as long as you can, and exhale; then take another deep breath. Somebody shuts off your air just after you've inhaled. You don't know anything's wrong and start to inhale again, there's no more air. What do you do? You panic, that's what. You don't think of the possibility your air's been shut off. You think something's wrong with your lung. In shallow water, you might make it to the surface. Deeper than fifty feet, you don't have much chance.

At a hundred feet you're dead. You panic, swallow water, and drown."

He was right—and it was frightening to think about. A murder like that could be committed with divers all around. It would take only a second to shut a man's air off; then the murderer could swim away casually. Ten or fifteen seconds might go by before the victim emptied his lungs and tried to inhale.

I placed a call to McGinnis's home through the Marine Operator. He answered right away and I gave him a rundown. Since too many other people might be listening to their radios, I didn't mention that we had a possible murder on our hands.

"Okay," came his clipped voice. "Be careful, Jim. Now, what's the story on the yacht? Are we liable?"

"Damned if I know. The boat hit the reef and sank, no question about that. It looks like Rake was negligent—and maybe worse—but that's beside the point unless we can show he violated some condition of his policy. So far we can't. So we're stuck—I guess."

"Okay," said McGinnis. "Don't waste too much time on the case. Get to the heart of it."

"Sure, sure, boss. I'll keep you informed."

I put down the mike and the three of us sat in silence. I lit a cigarette. "By the way," I said, "did Rake find his cash box?"

Harry shook his head. "When he came up, he said he couldn't get to it."

"Maybe there wasn't any cash box," Linda said. "Maybe that was an excuse to get down there and dispose of Withers."

"Could be," I said. "I know Withers had something to tell me. He hinted at it just before he dived. It could've been something Rake couldn't afford to let me find out."

"Maybe he wanted to tell you that nobody was steering the boat," said Linda.

"That's not enough to commit murder over. That's no ground for my company to refuse to pay. I'd like to know *why* nobody was steering."

"What's this all about?" said Harry.

Linda explained what she had seen from the airplane and Harry asked, "Could they have jumped off earlier?"

"No," she said. "They were still aboard. They came on deck after they hit."

"That handbag is another strange thing," I said. "Rake must have taken it from the cabin. But why?"

"Jim!" Linda said. "I just thought of something. You know those scratches on Withers' face. They looked like fingernail scratches." She turned to Harry. "Was your radio on yesterday, at the time the *Water Witch* sank?"

He rubbed his chin. "I don't know. We were at the north end of Bimini, skin diving. Why?"

"When I first saw the boat below me, I switched to the distress frequency to try to call them. A woman's voice was talking away in Spanish. She sounded excited, real excited, and awful close."

"She might have sounded close," Harry said, "even if she'd been all of five hundred miles away."

"Anyhow, it gave me an eerie feeling. At first it didn't seem to tie in. But I've got a strong feeling now that a woman was on that boat."

I thought about the cut wire coming from the locked stateroom. The radio was in the room. I jumped to my feet. "Harry, have you got any full tanks of air?"

"They're all full," he said. "I turned on the compressor when we came in."

"Will you take me out there—to the wreck?"

"Now?" he said. "Are you crazy? I wouldn't go in that water at night, man."

"Will you take me? Yes or no?"

"You ever heard of sharks? Wait till tomorrow."

"I'm afraid to wait," I said. "If Rake killed Withers, he's desperate. He'll go to any lengths to keep me from finding out whatever it is he's hiding. I'd rather chance the sharks than dive on that wreck with Rake tomorrow. He just might get careless with his speargun."

Harry stood up. "All right. I'm not letting you go down there alone."

I looked at the raw gash in his arm. "You can't dive, Harry. Why, if that cut started bleeding, we'd be shark-bait for sure. Where's Al?"

Harry grabbed his cap. "Let's find him."

"And quick," I said.

"You get a bike and start at the other end of the island. We'll check the hotel bar, the Angler's, and Brown's. See you back here in thirty minutes."

We checked every club on the island without success.

"I think he's got a girl," Harry said, "but I don't know where she lives."

"Just forget about Al," I said. "Let's shove off." Harry was staring at his diving racks. "What's the matter?"

"My double-block tank!" he said in rage. "It's gone! Somebody must've swiped it!"

"Could be it was just borrowed," I said. But I had the feeling you have when you're whistling in the dark.

The sea was calm as we hit open water. Linda touched my arm and pointed. The full moon was blood-red as it rose over South Bimini. "What a beautiful night to be out on the water," she said.

"But not *in* the water," Harry said. "The fish are active on the full moon. I hope you know that, Jim."

"I want a vacation." I laughed nervously. "And I don't get one till I finish this job."

Harry's spotlight soon picked up the buoy we had left to mark the spot. An empty outboard skiff was tied to the buoy.

"Rake's down there," said Harry. "He probably went off and stole the boat like he did my tanks."

He eased the bow of the *Reef Raider* into the wind, and I lowered the anchor next to the buoy.

Linda's eyes were wide and anxious. "Jim," she pleaded, "why don't you wait until he comes up?"

My mouth felt dry. "Look, honey, I've just got to find out what he's up to."

"He's probably got a speargun."

"Probably has," I said. "He'd be crazy to dive at night without one."

She looked at me without speaking. Then she put her hands to her side, unbuttoned her skirt and stepped out of it. Underneath she wore shorts. "All right," she said. "If you're fool enough to go, so am I."

"Oh, no, you don't."

I said no a few times, in various ways, but she ignored me and calmly selected a mask and tried it on, then looked at the row of tanks. "Give me a hand, Harry," she said. "How do you fix this regulator doo-hickey?"

"Listen," I said, grabbing Linda's arm, "you're not going down there. This is dangerous business. You don't seem to understand that."

She pulled her arm free, looking angry—at me—and worried—about me—at one and the same time.

I looked at Harry, one man asking help from another. But I didn't get it from him. He said: "I don't think anybody ought to go, Jim. But if you're set on going, as you plainly are, you'd be better off to take her. You know you'll have to leave the anchor rope to go to the wreck, and you might have trouble finding your way back. If you come up a long way from the boat, you might be a goner. With Linda along, you can leave her holding onto the rope and with a flashlight burning. Another thing: if there are the two of you, Rake's less apt to try something."

I sighed and looked at Linda. Then I finally said, "Okay. But listen to me. We'll go down slow. If your ears hurt, stop. If you feel dizzy, start back up the rope. I'll stop every now and then to shine the light in your face. If you don't feel right, point upward. If you feel all right, nod your head."

"You'd better take guns," Harry said.

"Oh, sure. Let Linda have the gas gun and the short spear. Don't use it," I cautioned her, "unless you can see the whites of a shark's eyes. When I leave you, hold tight to the rope. Don't move until I come back." I turned to Harry. "If Rake comes up, signal me by gunning your engines."

"Right," he said. "Good luck, kids."

We went over the side and swam to the bow. I let the anchor rope slide through my hand as we sank. My other hand held the speargun, and the flashlight was tied to my belt. Linda held to my arm.

I was surprised to see that the darkness was not total. The moon was so bright that I could see Linda's eyes through the face plate of her mask. But forty feet down, the darkness closed in. I looked toward the surface and saw the *Reef Raider's* lights winking blearily as the boat rocked in the gentle swells. Where we were, the water was still, and there was no sound except the tinkle of our regulators and the bubbling of released air.

Below the drop-off, little flashes of phosphorescence, like lightning bugs, swarmed about us. Occasionally a bright flash appeared—like a silent green explosion—as large fish struck at their prey. Barracudas, I guessed.

As we sank along the steep coral slope, I turned on my light, illuminating sea fans, starfish, and sea anemones. My shoulder brushed against a bed of fire coral, and I grimaced in pain. I knew I'd have large welts on my skin in an hour.

We passed a maze of crevices and tiny eyes glowed as lobsters, shrimps, and crabs observed our passing. In one black hole I saw the green head of a moray eel, seeming to gasp in open-mouthed agony as it sucked water through its pulsing gills. I glanced at Linda. Her eyes were round and frightened, and she tightened her grip on my arm.

I slowed our descent and flashed the light against my depth gauge. One hundred feet. The wreck should be directly below, unless we had drifted while lowering the anchor. I heard a dull, clanking sound. It could have been caused by a current dislodging a hatch or door, or it could have been the creaking of watersoaked planking. But it sounded to me more like a diver's tank striking a solid object.

I put my face plate next to Linda's and shone the light between our faces. She crinkled her eyes. I placed her hand on the rope, indicating that she was to remain there, then showed her how to point the light so I could see it from below. I squeezed her arm and continued downward alone, keeping my light turned off.

I expected at any moment to feel my foot strike some part of the wreck. Finally, it seemed to me that I was an awful long distance below Linda's light. I flashed my light on briefly to read my depth gauge. One hundred forty feet. I felt a prickle of fear. I'd missed the wreck.

I peered about, trying to penetrate the inky void that enveloped me. The fireflies still winked all around, but one area to the side appeared darker than the rest. That would be the wreck. Having no algae growth or lime encrustation, it did not attract the luminescent creatures that swarmed elsewhere.

I released the rope and moved toward the black splotch, kicking my feet slowly. My head touched a solid object, and I jerked my speargun upward. It hit something with a metallic bang that vibrated for several seconds. I moved my hand over the object and realized it was a ventilator. To orient myself I clung to the ventilator for a moment, not daring to turn on my light. Was it my imagination, or did I hear another diver's bubbles? Was the sound coming from behind me, or from the ventilator?

I took a chance and flashed the light on for a second. The lower rail of the deck was within a foot of my flippers. Below was rock and sand. I was on the lower side of the foredeck, within a few feet of the locked stateroom.

I sank below the rail and onto the rocky slope where the wreck lay. Now out of sight of both the forward hatch and the cockpit, I turned on my flashlight and peered under the wreck. There was a foot of space between the gunwale and the sand.

I stuck my hand under the wreck and felt my way along until I reached the brass ring around the porthole of the first stateroom. There wasn't enough space for me to wriggle under the ship, so I laid down my speargun and fanned the sand to clear a tunnel. Then I eased myself underneath, cursing silently as my metal tank hit the hull with a bang. I turned onto my side and lay still for a full minute; then I eased forward and pushed my hand inside the porthole. I touched something soft and yielding. I pushed at it, and it moved away, then came back. My skin crawled as I touched a wristwatch and swollen fingers. Reluctantly, I moved my face to the opening and shone the light inside. A woman's body turned slowly. She wore a white dress, and her long dark hair floated lifelike in the water.

The body moved aside suddenly, and I saw a glint of moving metal. In panic, reflexively, my head jerked back. There was the whoosh of a gas gun and my flashlight came apart in my hand. I clutched at the spear—which had dug lightly into the sand after hitting my flashlight—and drew it out. I kicked my flippers hard. Then, too late, I remembered my speargun lying on the sand. Without a light, I couldn't hope to find it. I had Rake's spear, but no way to propel it. I wondered if he had another spear.

There was a scraping sound. I twisted in a circular motion, trying to determine the source of the sound. There it was again. Was it below or to the side? Rake was coming out of the wreck after me. But where was the wreck? Without a point of reference, I was completely disoriented. I couldn't find Linda's light, and wondered if some part of the wreck was between her and me.

I had the sensation of sinking slowly into a bottomless inkwell. I kicked my feet frantically. Was I going toward the surface, off at an angle, or driving myself deeper? Breathing in great deep gulps, I fought the panic that closed in, the fear that my air would soon be gone.

Then, miraculously, there was the light, bright and clear, no more than twenty feet away. I moved toward it, my fear subsiding.

The light was directed at my face, blinding me. There was nothing else in my vision, but that beautiful light. Then the light went out. I groped blindly, reaching for where the light had been, realizing—finally—that the light had been held by Rake. In the middle of a deep breath, my air stopped coming.

I kicked my feet hard and reached behind my head to turn the valve back on. Then my air hose was yanked from my mouth. I fumbled for the mouthpiece and felt the torn end of my intake hose. My hose was ripped. Like a blind man in a sea of mud, I flailed my hands, striking out at something I could not see or reach. Green lights danced in my eyes as my burning lungs begged me to open my mouth and swallow the cool clean water. Blurred, scarcely visibly, I saw Rake's flashlight as he hovered out of my reach, waiting for me to die.

In the deathlike silence before oblivion, I heard the whoosh of a gas gun and a thump, and Rake's light moved in a funny, circular motion as it went away, growing smaller and smaller as it sank, sank . . .

A mouthpiece was pressed between my lips and I grew dizzy as fresh air flooded my lungs and reason returned to my oxygen-starved brain. I took two more deep breaths, then handed the mouthpiece back to Linda and looked below where a tiny stationary light glinted.

We clung together, taking turns breathing from her regulator as we went to the surface. Harry helped us into the boat, and I sank to the deck, my head throbbing. Linda was shivering convulsively, and Harry handed her a towel. "What happened?" he said, leaning over me. "How'd your hose get torn?"

"Rake," I said, still gasping for air. "He tore it loose."

"Where is Rake?"

I looked at Linda and she looked away. "He had an accident," I said.

The radio crackled. "Miami Marine calling the yacht *Reef Raider*. Come in, *Reef Raider*."

Harry picked up the mike. "This is the *Reef Raider*."

"This is Miami Marine. I have a call for Mr. Jim Reddy."

I took the mike and McGinnis's voice croaked, "Jim, is Garbord Rake around?"

I glanced at Linda and Harry. "No, he isn't, Duke."

"All right, get this. The police picked up a thug who says he kidnapped Carlotta Villegas, the Cuban millionaire's wife. She's the woman who was missing, you know. This thug says he drugged the lady and put her on Rake's yacht Thursday night. Rake was to turn her over to some bandits on an island off Cuba. This crook says Villegas took several million in gold certificates out of Cuba when he skipped the country, and somebody down there wants them back. Villegas was on the wrong side during the revolution, so I guess they kidnapped his wife for revenge as well as ransom."

"And how was this lady dressed, Duke?"

"White dress, white shoes. She's small, dark, long hair—"

"All right," I said. "You lose on that claim, Duke. The lady's in the *Water Witch*."

Duke grunted, "Dead, huh? I was afraid of that."

"I think she was murdered," I said.

He was silent for a couple of seconds. "Well, we'll have to pay off on the death claim, but we're clean on the yacht loss. Rake used his yacht in the perpetration of a crime—either kidnapping or murder, or both—and that's a violation of the terms of his policy. Tell Rake we're denying liability."

"I can't tell him, boss," I said. "He's down there with the lady. He had another accident."

I could hear him take in his breath. "Okay, okay, send me a complete report and we'll close the file. Are you coming back on the next plane? You know, we need you at the office."

"Aren't you forgetting my vacation?"

"You still wanta go skin diving, huh?"

I looked at Linda. Her soaked blouse and shorts clung to her body and her hair was like a stringy mop. She looked terrific. "No, I'm tired of skin diving," I told McGinnis. "Be that as it may, I'll see you in a week or two—unless I decide to change my racket."

I laid the mike down and said, "I could do with a rum punch."

"Me, too," Linda said in a small voice. Standing by the rail, she looked at the dark water and shivered. "So there was a woman on the boat? She must have been the one I heard on the radio."

I nodded. "Maybe they did a bum job drugging her, and she came out of it while they approached Bimini. I guess that's how Withers got his face clawed up."

The rest of what must have happened wasn't too hard to figure out now. Rake couldn't enter the harbor with the girl screaming and fighting, so he'd swung the boat around and left the wheel to help subdue her. Maybe she'd locked herself in the cabin—trying to get help on the radio. But somebody had quite obviously cut the antenna wire to keep her from getting through. And they'd been so busy handling her they hadn't seen the reef.

"I wonder," said Linda, breaking into my thoughts, "could they have saved her?"

"It's hard to say," I said. "But one thing's sure, when the boat started sinking, Rake knew he'd face a kidnapping rap if he did save her. He must have had a key to the room she was in, because when I looked through the porthole, he was in there with the body."

Harry said, "So it must've been the body he was after, not that cash box of his."

I nodded. "I'm sure it was. He was probably out to weight it down, somehow, so the fish would have a chance to get at it, and get rid of the evidence."

Linda leaned against me, and I put an arm around her. She was still shivering. I said, "Let's get back, Harry. We need those rum punches."

He hesitated. "You don't think Rake'll come up?"

I shook my head. I had to restrain myself to keep from looking at Linda.

"Okay." Harry started the engines. "I hate to mention it at a time like this, Jim, but what about my tanks? Rake was wearing my best double-tank unit."

"Trans-Ocean will pay for it. That's the least we can do for the help you've given us. I'm certainly not going down there after it. And let's tow that skiff back for its owner and take in the buoy."

I didn't say so, but I didn't want the spot marked for fear skin divers might run across Rake's body—impaled on Linda's spear—before the sharks had a chance to dispose of it.

My report said that Rake had disappeared, cause unknown. After all, that was true to the best of my knowledge. Linda hadn't volunteered any information and I hadn't asked her for any. My motto is: when a girl saves your life, don't ask questions.

You Can't Win 'Em (at) All

by Ed Lacy

The municipal casino in Nice, France, is one of those clumsy old buildings like something out of a creepy movie. What I mean is, maybe a hundred years ago it held a couple of concert halls and was probably called "grand." Today, the upstairs part is jazzy with the real casino, a fancy nightclub, and an expensive restaurant, but the big hallway downstairs is dim and drab, divided by thick old dark curtains hanging from the high ceiling. The *boule* room is in the rear. *Boule* is the poor man's roulette. The numbers run from one to nine, an ordinary rubber ball is used, and the payoff odds are seven to one. You can walk in without a tie, even in shorts.

To give you a hint of how badly my luck was going, I'd started for the *boule* room, made a turn into a darker and smaller hallway, and was lost. True, I was juiced on French booze, but not that drunk. Lighting a match, I saw I was in this dusty, curtained passageway. I heard sounds ahead of me and, parting a curtain, burning my fingers before I got another match working, I saw a small door. Opening this, I was on top of the *boule* room chatter, with only another old curtain between me and the room. Peeking through a slit in this, I saw the *boule* room okay, but it wasn't an entrance. Somehow I'd ended up behind the change desk, the cashier.

Cussing silently, I turned around, stumbled out to the main hallway, and finally made the entrance to the *boule* tables. I paid my franc to get in and didn't see Frankie, nor did I expect to. I played a handful of francs and lost, as usual. The crazy drinks I'd had were making me a trifle sick, so I went to our hotel room. Frankie wasn't there, either, which didn't help my mood.

On Nice's rocky beach that afternoon we'd been making a play for a large Dutch blonde in a skimpy bikini. I knew I was going to win because Frankie's a bag of bones in trunks, while my two hundred and thirty pounds of solid muscle cuts that well known figure. Of course, neither Frankie nor I spoke Dutch, but when the big babe started walking gingerly across the pebbles toward the blue Mediterranean, obviously needing help, we both jumped up. Skinny Frankie ran across the damn rocks like a native and reached her first.

Those big pebbles were killing my feet, and as I neared her I took a pratfall. She turned, along with all the others on the *plage,* and laughed at me, while Frankie put his arm around her waist, helped her down the rocky slope and into the water.

I don't like being laughed at; in fact, I wanted to belt Blondie. Instead, I eased to my feet like a punchy fighter and finally reached our dressing room. I left the *plage* to tie one on, leaving the lush bikinied blonde to lucky Frankie.

It must have been about two A.M. when Frankie came into our hotel room and turned on the john light to undress, whistling softly. When I sat up in bed, Frankie asked, "Where've you been, Mike? We looked all over for you. She had a friend, another fine blonde and so lonely. Man, a couple of sexboats. Shame, they're leaving in the morning, part of a tour."

See the way my luck has been? All lousy.

My being in France seemed like a break at first, and maybe I've no right to beef. I'm living good over here. It started a month ago, back in the States. I was at the track and by the fourth race I'd taken a bath, was broke. I was hanging around the ten dollar WIN window, hoping to see anybody I knew, to make a touch. This skinny guy, who looked like I'd seen him before, came along followed by a big slob giving him a fast sales pitch. When Skinny shook his head, the goon tried to grab a ticket from Skinny's mitt. Glancing at me, the thin guy called, "Mike, help me!"

I flattened the slob with a gut belt and as the guards started toward us, this thin guy said, "Mike, let's cut!"

The races were over and we lost ourselves in the crowd. Once we were outside, this guy said, "Thanks, Mike. Don't you remember me, Frankie Dill?"

"Sure," I said, although the name didn't ring any bells.

"When you were bossing the Turbans, I used to hang around with the gang."

He came into focus then. All that was eleven years ago, when I was sixteen and the Turbans were the roughest bopping gang in town. Frankie Dill had been a runty kid I used to send to the store for sodas or butts, an errand boy nobody paid any attention to.

"What are you doing these days, Mike?" he asked.

"Nothing much. Working the docks, a bouncer in a bar over the weekends. You holding a winning ticket on the last race, Frankie?"

He grinned. "I got the Twin Double, worth $2,194! That punk back there was trying to fast-talk me into letting him cash it, said he had a phony social security card, so I'd save the tax bite. I told him no dice and he—"

"Frankie, *you're holding a $2,194 ticket?*"

"Yeah, I've been lucky the last year or two, winning five or six hundred bucks a week—cards, to the track office in the morning Double last month for a grand," Frankie said calmly. "Let's take a cab back to the city. I'll go down to the track office in the morning to cash my ticket."

"Then you'll have to pay the income tax bite?"

Frankie shrugged narrow shoulders. "I don't mind giving Uncle Sam his cut. I got a fifty-dollar gambler's stamp, play it legit, including my taxes. Keep out of trouble that way."

In the taxi Frankie suddenly asked, "How much time did you get for that stolen car, years ago?"

"Six months. Why?"

"Ever been in stir again, Mike?"

I shook my head. "What you bringing up all this old stuff for, Frankie?"

"I been thinking I ought to take a vacation. That guy you slugged might be looking for me. I'm pretty well loaded and I've always wanted to see Europe, but I don't like traveling alone. I've no record and if you only did six months, you can get a passport. I speak high school French, let's see what's cooking in Paris, Mike. I'll pay your way."

Six days later we were on an Air France jet. Frankie isn't tight with his loot; he bought me a couple of suits and in Paris we put up at a swank hotel. Frankie slipped me two hundred bucks. "Spending money, Mike. When you need more, shout."

Let me tell you, Paris was a drag. We got there in a cold rain on a Thursday and it was still raining on Sunday when Frankie said, "We seen the nightclubs and striptease joints, the hell with this rain. Let's head south to the Côte d'Azur. They say it's a sunny ball."

Five hours later we were taking the sun on a *plage* in Nice, watching the bikini babes. Nice is great, and you'd think with a setup like this going for me I'd be content. But I wasn't. Frankie took care of the bills, but it annoyed me to be dependent upon him. When I was bossing the Turbans, Frankie would have been delighted to shine my sneakers. Now I felt like his flunky. I mean, I've always stood on my own two big feet. I wanted to show Frankie I could make out without him.

Nothing broke for me, though. Like we played *boule* a couple of times, neither of us winning, but Frankie liked the game and said he was working on a system to beat it. Monday night we went to the trotters in a city outside Nice named after Jimmy Cagney, although they spell it Cagnes. Horses are horses in any language, but I dropped sixty bucks' worth of francs while lucky Frankie, who kept telling me to follow his picks, won himself eight hundred francs for the night, which is about a hundred and sixty dollars.

In Paris I'd bought a couple of lottery tickets at three francs each. Each Wednesday they pick the national lottery winners in France. On Thursday morning I stumbled through a French newspaper while we were eating the rolls and coffee the hotel called a breakfast. I didn't see my numbers and was about to tear up my slips when Frankie said, "Let me see them. Here, you big dope, you won a hundred francs. They also pay off on the last number and you got a 'five' in the 'O' series."

A hundred francs is only twenty bucks but it gave me a lift, as if my luck was finally changing. I asked, "How do I collect? Do we have to go back to Paris?"

Frankie tried reading the news item, then he said, "No. I'll show you where to collect here in Nice."

After breakfast we left the hotel and I stopped for my usual ham and eggs at a sidewalk cafe. Then Frankie took me to a tobacco shop where they sold lottery tickets. I gave them my ticket and got a hundred-franc bill. The good feeling left me when Frankie handed in a lottery ticket of his own. He had the last three numbers and had won a thousand francs!

Holding up the bills as we left, he asked, "Need more spending money, Mike? I'd be glad to—"

"No!" I only had about fifty bucks left, but I was damned if I'd ask him for any more money. We bought a couple of lottery tickets for the next week and then went down to the *plage,* where lucky Frankie also won the big blonde.

Lying in my bed, staring at the darkness, listening to Frankie breathing evenly in the next bed, I started thinking about how I'd got lost in the casino, ending up behind the change desk. At that desk you get chips for your money and money for your chips, if you win. I figured at least a couple of grand was lost in the casino every night and it was all at that little change desk.

It would be a cinch to come up behind the desk again, clout the one guy there, grab all the paper money, and scram the way I'd come. They had three floor men working the *boule* room but they were always watching the tables. Nobody kept an eye on the change desk. I kept twisting the idea in my mind, sweating a lot, a little hung over. I hadn't pulled a job in a lot of years and I sure didn't want to do time in a French can. But with two grand of *my own,* I'd feel like a man again, instead of Frankie's pet ape. Although he never said anything, I knew he enjoyed giving me a handout, making up for being a bag of bones and for the brush-off I'd given him back in the teen gang days. Yeah! I'd flash the two grand and say I'd gone to Monaco, won at the Monte Carlo casino. Still, I knew it was risky. In a strange city it would be iffy, but in a strange country it's stupid. In fact, the only reason Frankie and I didn't gamble upstairs at the real casino was, we didn't understand this *chemin de fer* and the rest of the card games.

I slept on the holdup idea and awoke in the morning with a headache. It was another sunny day and Frankie suggested we take the bus to Cannes, which has a sandy beach.

I enjoyed the sand, showed off my swimming, and was feeling great. I told myself the holdup bit was a wrong move. When we were dressing in our *cabine,* I said something about why didn't they clean up the place, and kicked some old newspapers under the bench. Frankie, who was sitting on the one chair putting on his shoes, asked, "What was that yellow thing, Mike?"

"Just some dirty cardboard."

Frankie reached under the bench and damn if he doesn't pick up a dirty pigskin wallet. It belonged to some cat from Lincoln, Nebraska, and held a thousand dollars in travelers' checks, about seven hundred francs, and fifteen very green U.S. ten-buck bills!

Handing me a couple of tens and some francs, Frankie said smugly, "I told you to look at it. The traveler's checks are no good to us, so we'll toss them and the wallet into a mailbox."

That tore it! I was fed up with being a jerk—I knew I was going to rob the casino, purely for my own self-respect!

We returned to Nice and had a good steak and a *salade niçoise* in one of those little non-tourist restaurants Frankie was always finding. He suggested we take in a movie, that he'd translate for me. I told him to go it alone; French movies left me all mixed up and feeling dumb. Like in Paris we saw a U.S. western, but with the talking dubbed in French.

Going to the casino, I found the curtained passageway. It was less than two hundred feet long. Gently opening the door, I stared through a slit in the curtain at the back of the change guy's head.

He was a plump little guy in a blue tux. On a shelf under the desk he had piles of ten-, twenty-, one-hundred-, and five-hundred-franc notes, with trays of chips stacked at one side. I studied the *boule* room, everybody standing two or three deep around the tables, including the floor men. There was a small bar across from the change booth, but the bartender was busy washing glasses. Two hundred feet. I'd cover that in a few seconds, another second to sap the change guy, catch him by the collar so he'd fall without any noise. With my reach, it'd be no trouble reaching through the curtain and scooping up the paper francs. I'd wear a coat, stuff the dough inside my shirt. The only real risk was somebody coming to the desk for chips, or my being seen after leaving the main hallway, meeting somebody on his way in to play *boule*. He'd remember a clown my size.

That was the chance, but I'd stroll in casually and stop to light a cigar if anybody was around. Then, less than three minutes later, I'd casually stroll out, stuffed with francs.

It sure would be a bang to dump the dough on my bed, bull Frankie how lucky I'd been at the Monte Carlo casino, which is only about a half hour bus ride from Nice. I was tempted to pull the job there and then, but I decided on the next night. I like to figure all the angles, never pull a job too fast.

The next afternoon we met a couple of U.S. college girls on the *plage*. I knew nothing would come of it, but Frankie said it was a pleasure to talk to them, suggested we buy 'em supper.

I told him, "You take 'em to supper, since you all speak this amateur French. I think I'll see what this Monte Carlo's all about."

"You'll lose your shirt there, Mike, stick to *boule*. Hey, tomorrow night we'll go to the trotters again."

"I at least want to say I been in the Monte Carlo casino. I'll take it easy. Maybe I'll see Princess Grace."

Frankie gave me a sad look. "Citizens of Monaco aren't allowed in the casino, they're too smart to gamble. Okay, enjoy yourself. Need money?"

"No."

I ate alone in some tourist trap, got nicked twenty-five francs for a meal not half as good as the eight-franc ones Frankie found in his restaurants. I bought a heavy cake of soap and put it in a sock, and a small flashlight. Then I sat on the promenade, watching the waves, and figured by midnight the change desk would have its top money.

At five after twelve I had a fast drink and walked into the Nice casino. It seemed too quiet downstairs, although the good jazz band was playing upstairs in the nightclub. I walked into the curtained passageway without being seen. When I opened the door back of the last curtain, it was so quiet that at first I thought the *boule* room was shut. But looking through the slit in the curtain I saw the usual crowd around the tables. The bartender opposite the change desk was reading a paper. Nobody seemed to be talking much. I took a deep breath and put my left hand through the slit in the curtain, grabbed the change guy's collar, and pulled him back. His head and my soap sap, in my right hand, hit the curtain at exactly the same time. With my left hand, I lowered him gently to the floor. Not a soul had noticed anything.

When I put my left hand through the curtain for the money, I got a bad shock. There were only a few paper bills on the shelf! Not knowing what to do, I grabbed them and ran back along the passageway. Shoving the bills in my pocket, along with the flash and sock, I cased the main hallway. It was empty. Walking out, I crossed the street to the neat park, tossed the crumpled cake of soap in a trash can. Then I walked to the promenade, wiped any possible prints off the flash, put it into the sock, and hurled that into the sea. Sweating like a bull, I stopped at a sidewalk cafe for a beer.

I counted the bills in my pocket—eleven ten-franc notes, three twenty-franc bills, and one fifty-franc note: two hundred and twenty francs. I started sweating more. I'd risked a foreign jail for a lousy forty-four bucks! Maybe the prints of my left hand were on the change guy's collar? No, he'd start sweating when he came to, mess up any possible prints, and nobody had seen me reaching through the curtain or leaving.

It took another few beers to brace my nerves and at one A.M. I went to our hotel room. Frankie was reading a magazine in bed. He asked, "How was the Monte Carlo casino?"

"Aw, I never went in, just walked around the town and took a bus back to Nice. You get anyplace with the college broads?"

Frankie waved a slim hand in the air. "Stop it; I didn't expect to. A couple of nice kids." He pulled back the cover at the foot of his bed, revealing stacks and stacks of French bills. "But my system scored in *boule!* It was a gasser, Mike. I went to the casino at eleven P.M. and I could do no wrong. By midnight I'd broken the bank there and left. I won $1,763 in francs! I never was so lucky. Help yourself to all the francs you . . . Hey, what's the matter, Mike, you look like you're going to bawl or something!"

My Escaped Convict

by Donald Honig

At fourteen I had all the glory and admiration a boy could possibly ask. The chief of police came across on the ferry from his office in Manhattan to shake my hand, right in the middle of town. The volunteer firemen let me drive their wagon up Grant Avenue, let me ring the old brass bell and lay the whip to St. Brown, the mightiest horse in Capstone. They held a clambake in my honor on the first Saturday, and all the men drank to my health from out of big-handled steins.

But I didn't deserve any of it; they never knew. But I was undeserving, and I was ashamed. They said that I had been brave and courageous and that Capstone should be proud of me, but they never knew everything that I had done, that I had been doing those two days before it happened, because there are some things a fourteen-year-old boy cannot ever tell; and then when he is old enough to want to disburden himself, it is too late because people—the ones he would want to tell—would no longer have the same interest and sympathy and understanding.

So I never told anyone, and it's been my secret, my haunting companion, for sixty years now, one part of boyhood that never stopped being, that remains, like a piece of bright enduring cloth in an old faded fabric.

In those years there was a wide bloomy marsh in the back of town. It was not far from our house and often I would walk there with Chip, my terrier, even though we—all the children in town—were forbidden to go there because of the marsh's foreboding aspect. It was a silent, solitary place, not deep, with wet spongy underfooting in the places where you could walk, and tall gray-looking grass. I often went there when I wanted to be alone. I would take off my shoes and walk through the water, feeling the soft mud ooze through my toes. Sometimes a mist would lie over it and then the marsh would close up and I could hear the bullfrogs bellow, but could not see anything, and that was when I loved it best, and feared it most, when it seemed mine alone.

I was going there with Chip one evening, heading across the old

172

abandoned Vandermeer farm, when I heard my named called. I turned and saw Paul Farmer running out of the wood toward me.

"Danny!" he yelled again. "Where are you going?"

I waited for him to catch up. He was a thin, sickly youth, always a bit short of breath, even when he wasn't running, with wide pale eyes that always appeared startled. Paul was always following me—not that he was my best friend, but it seemed that he was always waiting for somebody to pass by and I was always passing.

"What do you want?" I asked.

"Where are you going?"

"To the marsh."

"You've got a secret place there, haven't you?" he said.

I didn't say anything. I wanted to let him keep thinking that.

"Well, you'd better not go today," he said.

"Why not?" I asked as Chip, impatient, wound about my legs.

"Because—" Paul paused, leaving the word hang, poised, like an incompleted thrust, his eyes growing larger, more startled than ever, the color of a dusty mirror. "Didn't you hear?"

"Hear what?" I asked, bending and patting Chip's head for a moment to quiet him.

"About the man who escaped. A killer. His name is Jim Baily."

"Escaped from where?"

"From a prison out on the Island. He's a killer, and he was said to be heading in this direction. Some of the men are outside Dooley's now with rifles." He paused to catch his breath. Then he began again. "They say he's very dangerous, that he'd kill again rather than go back to prison. So you'd better not go near that marsh. For all you know he might be hiding in it."

"He might be," I said, turning and walking. Chip gave a little yelp of joy and began to dart through the grass, his forelegs striking forward.

"Where are you going?" Paul asked.

He asked it again. Not that he didn't know. He knew. But he was so taken aback that he asked it several more times, and maybe even more than that, because once I got into the wood I was out of earshot.

The marsh began a few feet beyond the wood. I walked around the water, walking where the ground always pushed forward when it was stepped on, through the tall grass. Chip had gone on ahead. I could see the grass stirring where he was running. It was starting to get dark now and I knew that I couldn't stay there very long. I stood still, listening to the long, patient, timeless sound of the quiet, staring out at the gray sky which showed neither day nor night, as if time had stopped.

Then I heard him. I heard first the sound of water—he was rising in it, had been lying in it. Then I saw him, rising through the grass, the water running off him, having blackened his shirt and trousers; the biggest man I had ever seen, thickly built, with a large, close-shaven head, with sharp little eyes, a large thick nose squared fiercely in the middle of his face. He watched me. We watched each other, waiting for the other to say or do that which might begin it.

I knew who he was. He knew I knew.

"Why, you're just a lad," he said, his voice harsh but surprised. He was standing knee high in water, the grass risen thinly in front of him.

I was not afraid. I hadn't been afraid from the first. He probably saw this and perhaps was impressed, was grateful.

"What's your name, lad?"

"Daniel Bright."

"Bright, eh? And are you a bright lad?"

"I don't know," I said.

"We'll see, then." He came through the grass, parting it with his hand, his feet dragging in the water, making it rock, the grass waving. He came up to where I stood, continuing to look down at me, warily, the corners of his eyes twitching as if to get into me, through me.

"You gave me a fright," he said. "You made me lie in the water."

"I'm sorry," I said.

"Well, maybe you can make up for it."

Chip showed himself then, bounding through the grass. At the sight of Jim Baily he stopped, poising himself on his forelegs, his ears perking.

"You've a nice pup there," Jim Baily said. "He said hello to me without making a sound. You live near here, boy?"

"Just the other side of the wood."

"That's very good. Now, you've got nothing against Jim Baily, have you?"

"No, sir. I don't think so."

"That's good." He stared down at me. The squinting in his eye-corners had stopped and now I couldn't tell what his eyes were doing. I sensed his appraisal. I looked at his huge work-toughened hands, at his torn water-blackened clothes; then back up to his eyes where I noticed now a tiny scar on the ridge of the cheek just under his eye, and up to his large close-cropped head that looked like a gray cannonball, and I thought to myself that he was the most terrible man I had ever seen.

"Who comes here?" he asked.

"To the marsh? No one. Except me and Chip. Just me and him."

"You like it here, eh?"

"It's quiet."

"Can you keep a secret, lad?"

I thought for a moment, looking at him, perhaps pitying him, unafraid—strangely, calmly unafraid.

"Yes," I said and now he smiled, slowly, and nodded his huge head and I felt as if I had entered into some terrible pact with him.

"Good lad. Are you alert enough to pull a little wool over your mother's eyes?"

"I can get you some cornbread and milk," I said.

He sighed. "Ah, rye whisky would be the tonic, but I'll not put a lad to stealing whisky. Milk and cornbread. Well, it's better than what they gave me there."

"In prison?"

"Yes."

"Will you tell me about prison?"

"When can you come back?"

"Tonight."

"Run then, lad. I'll be here. And make sure to see who's behind you."

I ran home, Chip at my heels. When I came into the kitchen Ma was there, just clearing the table, putting the dishes in the wooden sink. She looked at me. I was sure she saw Jim Bailey in my face. I tried not to look straight back at her. But she didn't say anything. I went inside where Pa was. He was sitting comfortably in his chair, like he was set for a long conversation.

"Where've you been?" he asked.

"Walking with Chip."

"Have you heard about the convict?"

"Yes."

"You'd better be careful in your wanderings. They say this man is a killer."

"Who did he kill?"

"His wife."

"Why?"

"I don't know. You'll have to ask him that."

"Do you think he'd tell?"

Pa laughed.

"Suppose I met him," I said. "What do you think he'd do to me?"

Pa laughed again. "The best thing is not to meet him," he said.

I got the cornbread and the milk and I ran back, Chip following, barking in his soft little excited voice.

It was full dark now. I'd never been in the marsh at night and it looked different, dark and still, like a place outcast from all other places, brooding and lusting in its own dark solitude.

I walked where I knew it was dry. Then I saw him, or rather he was there, tall and thick, there almost before I saw him, like someone upon whom you simply open your eyes.

"You've got it," he said. He took the bag from me. He sat down and began eating, tearing chunks of bread off with his teeth, gulping the milk from the jar. I watched him, watched his cheeks bulge and his throat gulp. He ate desperately, angrily, panting.

Then the bread was gone and the jar was empty and Jim was sitting there, shivering in the chill, his arms crossed over his chest.

"There's a smell in this marsh," he said. "A damned smell."

"You said you'd tell me about prison," I said.

"Never mind prison. I want to get prison off my mind."

But that was all right. I waited for a moment, holding the tip of my tongue between my lips, watching him shiver. Then I asked, "Why did you kill your wife?"

He looked at me, his eyes thin, curious.

"She was a bad woman, Daniel," he said, saying it as if he expected me to challenge him.

"Bad?"

"Very bad."

"They why did they put you in prison?"

"I've often wondered about it myself."

"How long were you in prison?"

"Seventeen years. That's a long time, eh, Daniel? It's longer than you're old, eh? And I think it's enough. I'll not go back, ever."

"What will you do?"

"I don't know, Daniel. You're my only friend."

"Yes," I said.

"What are they doing in town?"

"The men are looking for you with rifles."

"Are they?"

He was still shivering. It was getting chilly.

"You'll catch cold here," I said.

He laughed. "Ah, Daniel," he said. He slapped my leg. "You're my friend."

I could still feel it that night, lying in bed, where his hand had struck. I thought of him sitting in the marsh all night, shivering, alone. I wished there could have been some way to have gotten him into the house, to share with him our warmth. Never had the night seemed so long and cold and dark and empty, and I thought of how he would rather be out there in the marsh instead of in prison. And I thought of the injustice, sending him to prison for killing his wife who had been a bad woman, and I thought of waking up Pa and kneeling by his bed to tell him about Jim and about the injustice. And then I fell asleep.

I had put some cheese and ham in a bag the night before, with a jar for water, so when the morning came I had no trouble. I rose at sunup, before Ma and Pa, and filled the jar from the pump and left. Chip ran on ahead, knowing just where we were going.

The mist was still clouded over the marsh, looking quite mysterious, ghostly, like a cloud that had come down to earth to leave some fallen angel there. I couldn't see anything. I called his name. Then I saw him, half saw him in the mist, getting up, looking like he was afloat. He looked like a ghost. He stood there and looked at me and he looked like he was dead, but just the same standing there looking at me. Then, waving his hand, he brought me forward.

I went into the water, wading toward him. He was standing in the water, the grass all around him.

"You shouldn't call my name out like that," he said.

He took the bag from me and went and sat on the soft, spongy ground. He ate slowly this time, but he ate it all, the bread and the cheese and the ham, and he drank the water. Then he put the jar down and looked at me. His beard was beginning to show now, gray and sharp on his face. I noticed, too, a long dark scratch down his cheek which hadn't been there before.

"What are you going to do?" I asked.

"I don't know, Daniel."

"I'll bring you something to eat every day."

"You're my first friend, Daniel. But I won't stay here long. They'll be looking for me here soon."

"No one knows you're here."

"They know I'm close. I left last night."

"You did?"

"But I didn't get far. I was crossing somebody's yard when a dog came at me. He wasn't a nice pup like yours. I had to kill him."

"You killed a dog?"

"They'll find him this morning and they'll reason out the rest for themselves."

"Do you know whose dog it was?"

"No."

I was silent. I looked down into the water. It lay very still. I could see the clouds in it, the thick gray overcast that wasn't letting the morning begin.

"I had to kill him, Daniel," he said. "He came at me. And he was making too much noise."

"Whenever I hear of a dog dying I think of my dog," I said.

He looked at Chip. "What would you do if it had been yours?"

Still looking at the water, I said, "I'd shoot you."

He thought for a while, sitting quietly. Then, "What would you shoot me with, Daniel?"

My father had a pistol. He kept it in a drawer in his room. I had seen it several times, but I never thought much about it because I wanted a rifle. Jim said if he had that pistol he could get away, that he wouldn't have to spend any more nights shivering in the marsh.

It wasn't that I was tired of helping him. I would have gone on helping him as long as he wanted. But he said this would give him his chance. He said if men knew he had a pistol they would be afraid to come near him, and he could get away without harming anyone.

So I went and got the pistol. As I was coming back the clouds were breaking and the day was beginning, a sharp brightness spearing across the sky. The mist had lifted and a covey of small birds was just rising, sailing off in widening circles. This time I saw him right away. He was sitting in the grass, looking like he was in a cage. He stood up when he saw me. The sun was on him, the grass making thin broken shadows on his chest, up to where his shirt lay open at his throat.

Then I heard Paul call my name. At first it sounded far away. And then—even before he yelled again—very near. Jim looked at me and the twitching came back into the corners of his eyes.

"He'll see you!" I whispered. But he just stood there, big and stolid, and I knew then why he was not being concerned about being seen and why Paul hadn't yelled that second time. When I looked, I saw Paul standing on the little rise at the edge of the marsh, thin and startled, his arms hanging straight down at his sides, looking like he had been mesmerized. I thought he would run. But he didn't. Probably because I was there. And Jim seemed to know he wouldn't run.

Jim said, quietly, talking to me, but watching Paul, "Bring him here."

"It's all right, Paul," I said.

Paul came down into the marsh, carefully, putting his feet into the yielding ground with great care.

"What did you follow me for?" I asked.

But he was not looking at me. His startled eyes were fixed upon Jim. Then he edged close to me. I thought he had understood right along, but he said to me, "Danny. It's him."

"Who is it, lad?" Jim asked, his voice pleasant, but dangerous, like something in it was gathering.

"Danny," Paul whispered. Then he tried to get away. He started to run, and he might have, too, if I hadn't grabbed him for a moment. I didn't want him to run. I just wanted to explain that Jim was my friend, that an injustice had been done to him. But I didn't get the chance to say it. Jim came smashing through the grass and threw both his huge hands around Paul's throat, and it looked for a moment as if he had lifted Paul's head clear off because as his hands went up Paul's head with bulging eyes and gaping mouth went up with them, until I saw Paul's stiff legs and his shoes not touching the ground and his arms out straight like a scarecrow's.

Jim kept lifting him like that and Paul's mouth was open shouting nothing, and then Jim threw him down into the marsh. Paul's board-like body smashed a trench into the marsh, hurling up twin flanks of water. Then Jim was over him, his hands hidden in the water where Paul's head had gone.

"Jim!" I cried.

Paul's feet were kicking furiously, thrashing the shallow water.

I leaped forward and pulled at Jim's shoulder, but he was like a rock. I looked down. I couldn't see Paul's face, but the water continued to swirl and bubble around Jim's thrusting wrists. Paul's arm rose from the water, thin and feeble, hung like that for a moment and then collapsed.

I had the pistol in my hand then and Jim was just turning toward me, his huge head wheeling on his shoulders, his eyes furious and amazed. And that was the worst part of it, pulling the trigger just as our eyes locked. The shot was loud, like an explosion. From the other side of the marsh a covey of birds flushed and scattered into the sky.

So Paul was dead. And Jim Baily was dead. And that Saturday they were singing my name at the clambake, and how could I tell them they shouldn't be doing it?

A Husband Is Missing

by Fletcher Flora

I spent a quiet afternoon breaking the tenth commandment. This commandment, as you may recall, is comprehensive. It starts out naming a number of things you are not supposed to covet if they happen to belong to your neighbor, and then, just to plug up all loopholes, it ends by saying you are not supposed to covet anything of your neighbor's whatever. One of the items specifically mentioned is your neighbor's wife, and that was my specific trouble.

By neighbor is not meant merely the guy who happens to live next door, or across the street, or in the general vicinity. By neighbor is meant anyone you care to mention. This, it seems to me, makes the whole regulation extremely difficult, if not impossible. I can see how you can reasonably be expected to resist taking any action in the way of *appropriating* whatever it is you covet, but I can't see how you can resist *wanting* to appropriate it, which is what coveting means, even if it happens to be a wife, and especially if it happens to be a wife named Ann Christopher.

What this is leading up to is a coincidence and the beginning of quite a situation. I was spending this quiet afternoon coveting, and the phone rang, and it was Ann on the wire, and that was the coincidence. It made me feel very queer. I felt as if she'd called to tell me to quit thinking like that, and maybe to slap my face.

"Hello, Mick," she said. "This is Ann."

"Hello, Ann," I said. "Did you call to slap my face?"

"Don't be absurd. How could I slap your face over the telephone?"

"I don't know. It's my guilty conscience, I guess. Anyone with a guilty conscience is always expecting unnatural things to happen to him."

"Are you drunk, Mick?"

"No."

"Why should I want to slap your face in any event?"

"Never mind. I'm not admitting a thing. Do you want something in particular?"

"Yes. I was wondering if you could tell me where Cal is."

Cal was her husband. He was also my friend. And neighbor. I was constantly reminding myself of these facts.

"I haven't seen Cal for five, six days," I said. "Why?"

"He didn't come home last night."

"Is that unusual?"

"Well, no. Not exactly. Frequently he gets into a poker game and plays all night, but he always comes home early the next morning at the latest, and here it is almost four o'clock in the afternoon, and he still hasn't come."

"Cal's all right, Ann. I've known him to trot along in one of those games for twenty-four hours."

"That was before we were married. When we were married, he promised never to stay away so long, and he hasn't."

"Until now. Now he has. Ann, honey, Cal could break that promise as easily as I can break the tenth commandment."

"What's the tenth commandment?"

"No matter. What do you want me to do?"

"I'm nervous and worried and inclined to drink too much gin, and I wondered if you'd be willing to come over and hold my hand or something."

"It'll be a pleasure," I said.

And that was the beginning of the situation that turned out to be quite something. I went downstairs and got into my Olds and drove to the apartment building in which Ann and Cal Christopher lived. Between my place and theirs, after thinking part of the way about Ann, I thought the rest of the way about Cal. I had known Cal for a long time, since college, and I liked him. He was a slim six-footer with devastating charm and flexible ethics and educated hands that could do remarkable things with fifty-two cards. He was the kind of guy a girl would want to marry, and shouldn't. I wondered what shenanigan he was up to now, and where he was likely to be in case I was compelled by neighborliness to go looking for him. I sincerely hoped, wherever he was and whatever he was doing, that nothing worse than a divorce happened to him as a consequence.

At the apartment building, which was impressive, I went up in the elevator to the seventh floor and down the hall to a blond door with a button to push for chimes. I pushed the button and listened to the chimes, and Ann opened the door promptly. She was wearing a white blouse and a pair of black velveteen fancy pants, and I could smell her hair, which was about the same pale color as the door, and the sight of her was certainly nothing to diminish my covetousness and put me in a more compatible position with my conscience. She tipped up her chin and smiled and held out her hand that I had been summoned to hold, and I began holding it immediately.

I held the hand into the middle of the room, where I released it reluctantly out of deference to the other man present. I hadn't expected him, and I didn't want him, and the truth is, I resented him. In my opinion, anyone ought to know when to be a certain place and when to be somewhere else.

"Do you know Wade Hacket?" Ann asked.

"I don't think we've met," I said.

Wade Hacket stood up and extended a hand. I took it less enthusiastically than I had taken Ann's, and I released it much sooner. When it was gone, I didn't miss it. But Hacket, I had to admit, was a personable sort of guy. He was about my height, slightly short of six feet, with the blocky body of a 1947 tackle going slowly to postgraduate fat. As far as I could judge from the expression on his handsome, swarthy face, he did not regard me as a nuisance to be tolerated as a matter of courtesy.

"Mick is an old friend, Wade," Ann said. "Mick Mahony. That's actually his name, incredible as it seems."

"My parents were peculiar," I said.

Hacket smiled politely and said he was glad to know me, and Ann said, "Wade's our medico, Mick. He was making a call in the building and stopped in for a drink."

I didn't know if this was simply a matter of identification or an attempt to explain Hacket's presence, which was unnecessary. I'm always suspicious of unnecessary explanations. As if to substantiate part of what Ann had said, Hacket reached down to a table beside the chair in which he'd been sitting and lifted a glass filled with something that looked like quite a lot of bourbon and a little water.

"I didn't know you and Cal were ever sick," I said.

Ann gave me a queer look, which did not seem justified by the remark, and Hacket said, "Not frequently enough, I'm afraid," which was a joke that didn't make anyone laugh.

"It's fortunate, nevertheless, that he stopped," Ann said. "He's going to leave me something to take the place of the gin."

"She's upset because Cal's strayed off the reservation." This time Hacket laughed at his own joke, in order to show clearly that he certainly didn't consider for a moment that there was anything seriously extra-marital in Cal's defection. "A mild sedative won't do her any harm."

I didn't share Hacket's certainty about Cal's behavior by any means, having known Cal from some time back and being a firm believer in Kipling's theory of the leopard and his spots. It was true that Cal had been an admirable example of fidelity since marrying Ann about nine months ago, but this was, in my opinion, a condition which could last only so long under the most favorable circumstances. I didn't say this, of course. I smiled at Ann and tried to look reassuring and wished that Hacket would go away so I could start holding her hand again.

"Are you actually worried about Cal?" I said.

"Well," Ann said, "I would be greatly relieved if I knew where he is and what he's doing."

"He's in a game somewhere," I said. "Pretty soon he'll come home with his pockets full of money and his arms full of flowers. You ought to learn how to exploit your advantages, honey. A situation like this could be worked by a clever girl for a diamond bracelet or a mink stole at least."

She missed the humor and shook her head. "No. He promised he'd never stay away this long. I knew he gambled when we were married, of course, and I was willing to accept it, and so we talked about it honestly and made a compromise agreement. I promised never to complain so long as he kept the agreement, and he promised to keep the agreement so long as I didn't complain, and the agreement was that he would never be gone longer than twelve hours at a time."

"All right." I sighed and sat down. "I am also prepared to reach an agreement with you. If you agree to fix me a drink about the same size and color as the one Dr. Hacket has in his hand, I agree to go looking for Cal. I'll probably get my ears pinned back for my trouble, but I realize that this is merely part of being a good neighbor."

While Ann was mixing my drink, Hacket finished his and stood up. He said he had another call to make and had to be getting along. Ann said thanks very much for everything and to drop in any time, and he said he would, thanks, and left the mild sedative on the table and went out carrying his black bag. Ann looked at the sedative and decided on a gin and tonic instead, and we sat together on a sofa holding hands with the hands that weren't holding glasses. This is known as innocent contact and is acceptable between friends. It was a pleasure and an aggravation.

"When did you see Cal last?" I said.

"Last night. He left the apartment early. About seven o'clock."

"Where did he go?"

"He didn't say. He said he might look up a game, but he didn't say where. I didn't ask. It's part of the agreement not to insist on knowing such things."

"Okay. I know places to look. Did he say when he'd be back?"

"No. It was understood that he'd be home within a certain time."

"I know. Twelve hours. Terms of the agreement. I believe I'll have another drink, if you don't mind."

I had the second drink and held her hand some more for comfort, and then I went away and started looking for Cal.

I went to half a dozen places I knew, but he hadn't been at any of them, and then I went to a place called the Number Ten Club, and that's where he'd been. I didn't learn that right away, however. The bar was open, but the club proper wasn't, and neither were the game rooms upstairs. I had a drink at the bar and listened to some faint conversation going on among a marimba, a drum, a bass fiddle, and a clarinet behind the closed doors of the main room. It was pretty good conversation, and I liked especially what the clarinet had to say to the marimba, though the marimba came up with some remarks that were pretty fine, too, and what they were all saying with improvisations, the marimba and the drum and the bass and the clarinet, was "Baby, Won't You Please Come Home?" This was appropriate to my errand, to say the least, and it got me to thinking that maybe baby had already come home while I was prowling the places where he hadn't been. I got off the stool at the bar and went back to a phone booth outside the door to the gentlemen's room. In the booth, I dropped a dime and dialed Ann's number.

"Is that you, Mick?" she said, after I'd said hello.

"Yeah. Has Cal showed up yet?"

"Not yet. Have you found out anything?"

"I've found out that he wasn't at six places last night. I guess this is something in a negative sort of way."

"Where are you now?"

"In the bar of the Number Ten Club. I don't know yet if he was here. I've been having a drink and listening to some conversation. I'll ask someone pretty soon."

"Thanks, Mick. I'm truly grateful."

"It's all right, honey. Consider it good works to expiate my sins."

"What?"

"Nothing, honey. I'll call again later."

I hung up and left the booth and tried the closed doors to the main room. They were unlocked, and I slipped through and pulled them shut behind me. The only ones in there besides me were the marimba, the drum, the bass, and the clarinet. They didn't pay any attention to me, didn't even know I was around, just kept talking and talking to each other. At first I couldn't understand the language they were now using, but after a minute I thought I recognized "Potato Head Blues," which is, I think, a very, very old language that must have come up from New Orleans around the first of the century with Jelly Roll Morton or someone like that. I walked the length of the room, picking my way through a litter of small tables, and went through a door at the end into a short hall and upstairs into a longer hall, a gauntlet of closed doors. I ran the gauntlet of doors to the door of an office, so marked, and on this I knocked.

The office belonged to a man named Duane Holland. The whole Number Ten Club belonged to him, as a matter of fact. Among other things he owned were a distillery, a chain of candy stores, a female musical comedy star, two councilmen, and majority stock in the mayor. He had accumulated all this before the age of forty, which he was still barely before, and this was a striking commentary on his natural accumulative ability, when you stopped to consider that he'd started with nothing but an alcoholic mother he had since lost. He was smooth as silk, hard as agate, sharp as a tack. These are all deliberately trite phrases, applied to a trite type. Life has done him over and over again, and you always have to respect him, but after a while you get a little tired of admiring him. Right now, after I'd knocked, he invited me in, and I went.

He was sitting behind a mahogany desk with a napkin tucked under his chin. With his cropped brown hair and small hard face, he might have been a professional athlete or a junior executive or a scoutmaster or anything successful you cared to guess, including exactly what he was. Spread on the desk before him was an early dinner brought up from the kitchen below—rock lobster tail, baked potato with sour cream and chives, asparagus tips, tossed salad loaded with crisp slices of radish and cucumber. Conscious suddenly of an enormous, aching cavity below my diaphram, I became aware that it was after six and a long, long way from a light lunch. Looking across the desk at me with no surprise and no discernible animosity, Holland dug a bit of lobster tail out of its red shell, dipped it in a little pot of drawn butter, put it in his mouth. I could taste it all the way over to where I stood.

"Hello, Mick," he said.

I nodded. "I hope I'm not intruding," I said.

"Not at all. Come in and sit down."

He indicated a chair at a corner of his desk, and I walked across and sat in it. It was upholstered with foam rubber under tan leather and was comfortable. I could smell the lobster tail and drawn butter and also coffee keeping hot in a Pyrex carafe.

"Hungry?" he said.

"I am," I said, "rather."

"There's another tail here. More than I want. Use my salad fork."

I pulled my chair closer and ate the second lobster tail. We took turns dipping into the little pot of drawn butter. He ate all the baked potato himself, but I got about half of the salad and a cup of coffee afterward. Everything was very good, and we didn't spoil it by talking about anything more important than who the hell was going to beat the Yanks.

"Anything special I can do for you, Mick?" he said finally.

"Maybe," I said. "I'm looking for Cal Christopher."

"For Cal? Why?"

"His wife's upset. Cal hasn't been home since yesterday about this time."

Holland laughed and started to say something, but just then a waiter knocked on the door and came in for the dinner service, and Holland sat quietly and waited, just laughing softly all the while, until the waiter was gone.

"Something's funny?" I said when the door had closed.

"I was just thinking that Cal's wife is going to be upset most of her life if she gets upset every time Cal takes off for a while. She better get used to it."

"She probably will eventually. Meanwhile, they've got an agreement."

"What kind of agreement?"

"Nothing important. Just something between them for convenience. You seen Cal in the last twenty-four hours?"

He shrugged and inspected the nails of his left hand. Taking a little gold penknife from a pocket, be began to trim carefully the nail of the index finger.

"I have to know how this figures, Mick. Do I look like someone who'd help a wife pin something on a husband? Let her hire a detective if she wants to keep herself informed."

"It's not like that. She's worried, that's all. She thinks something may have happened to him."

"Like what?"

"She didn't say, and I didn't ask her, and she couldn't have told me if I had. Just upset. Just worried. You know how it is."

"No, I don't. If anyone ever worried about what might happen to me, they kept it secret."

"Look. As far as I'm concerned, it's this way. Wherever Cal is or's been, whoever he's with or's been with, all I want is to tell him please to go home and to hell."

"In that case, I saw him last night, and I wish I hadn't."

"Why?"

"He walked out of here with about thirty grand that he didn't come in with."

I whistled inadequately. "That's a big haul for poker. A game in one of the private rooms?"

"Not poker." Holland shook his head. "He won it in a hurry at the craps table. Took him less than an hour. The guy had the devil's own run of luck."

"I didn't know Cal went in for craps."

"Last night he did. He shot craps and walked away with about thirty grand."

"What time did he leave?"

"I don't know. He didn't take off immediately, anyhow. He played blackjack with Gail Sullivan for a while, maybe an hour, and then I saw him later down in the bar. As I recall, it was after eleven when I saw him there. He was tying on a pretty good one. Celebrating, I guess."

"Was he alone?"

"There were people around. I wouldn't know if he was *with* any of them."

"Did he leave alone?"

"I didn't see. I said that, didn't I?" He folded the blade of the penknife into the gold handle and returned it to his pocket. "You might ask the bartender."

"Thanks," I said. "I'll ask him, but he probably won't remember a thing."

"Bartenders usually don't," he said.

I got up and walked over to the door and turned. "Thanks again," I said. "For everything. The lobster tail and all."

"Don't mention it," he said.

I went downstairs, and I was no longer easy in my mind. Take a guy with too much alcohol in his blood and thirty grand in his pockets, I thought, and it is entirely possible that something unfortunate could happen to the guy or the dough or to both.

In the main club room, the marimba, the drum, the bass, and the clarinet had quit talking to each other. They sat in silence having a drink and a smoke.

The bartender listened politely to my question, but he couldn't remember a thing for sure. He did have a foggy recollection of serving Cal at the bar, but he didn't know if it was early or late, and as a matter of fact he didn't even know for certain if it was last night or maybe the night before.

"Sorry," he said.

"That's okay," I said.

"Well," he said, "you know how it gets in a place like this. Everyone in a hurry. Everyone with a great big thirst that can't wait. It's all a guy can do to remember what day it is."

"It's Saturday," I said.

"Thanks. I'll try to keep it in mind in case anyone asks."

"Do that. In the meanwhile, if you can remember the recipe, I'll have a twenty dollar bourbon-and-water highball."

"Did you say twenty dollars?"

"That's what I said. If you can remember the recipe, I said. A guy with all your mental problems might have trouble."

He mixed the highball and set it on the bar in front of me and took my twenty between two fingers. He took seventy cents out of his own pocket and rang it up and put the twenty in the pocket where the seventy cents had been.

"Now that I'm concentrating," he said, "things are getting a little clearer."

"Take your time," I said. "No hurry at all."

"Well," he said, "it was about eleven. A little after. It's all coming back to me very clearly now. He'd made a killing upstairs at the craps table and he came down here to celebrate. He was by himself then, but later, around a quarter to twelve, Gail Sullivan came down and joined him. You know Gail?"

I did. Tall redhead who dealt blackjack upstairs. The one Cal had played with for an hour, according to Duane Holland, after leaving the craps table. Even for a guy with a steady schedule with someone like Ann, Gail would have made a very interesting diversion, and

I was beginning to get an idea, which did not by any means leave me incredulous, of where Cal might have gone, and perhaps still was.

"I know her," I said. "Goodlooking redhead. Deals blackjack."

The bartender nodded. "She is and does. Well, as I said, she came down around a quarter to twelve. Had her coat on. Dark fur of some kind. Must have got relieved from her game upstairs because it was long before quitting time. She and Cal had a couple of drinks together and left and that's the last I saw of them."

"You're sharp now. You're remembering real good."

"As I said, things are clearing up. I even remember thinking what a lucky son of a gun he was. In addition to all that cash, the redhead. Yuh know what I mean?"

"Sure. Some guys have all the luck. Craps, cards, love. Anything you can think of. Well, I've got to get along. Thanks for concentrating."

"Don't give it a second thought."

I finished the twenty dollar highball, which was no better than a lot of others I'd had for seventy cents, and went out of the bar and out of the club and down the street to my waiting Olds. Twenty minutes later, in front of the apartment building in which Gail Sullivan lived, I left it waiting again. I knew the apartment building was the one in which Gail Sullivan lived because I had been there before, and I had been there before because I am also a fellow who has occasionally been diverted. I contend, however, in spite of her being a very tough competitor, that Gail could never have diverted me from Ann, as she had apparently diverted Cal, but I had to admit that this was no more than an academic point that would have interested Ann very little and Cal even less.

At Gail's door, I knocked and waited. After a while, I knocked again and waited again. I had about decided that the apartment was empty or occupied by people who didn't want to be disturbed, but then the door opened suddenly with no prelude of sound, and I could see that what I had done was interrupt the essential business of dressing for work, which explained my having to wait. Gail was wearing a pale gold cocktail-type sheath that was calculated to make blackjack a privilege and losing a pleasure, or at least acceptable as a fair fee for the show. Her red hair was a little disordered from having gone through the dress, and she was approximately three inches shorter than full-dress height from having come to the door in her bare nylons. She didn't look definitely hostile, but neither did she looked particularly pleased.

"Hello, Mick," she said. "What's on your mind?"

"May I come in?" I said.

"Not if it can be prevented," she said. "Damn it, Mick, I work nights. You know that. I'm just dressing to leave."

"I won't delay you," I said. "I'll talk with you through a crack in the door."

"Oh, come on in," she said, very inhospitably.

She stepped aside, and I went past her and stopped and waited while she in turn came past me and went into the bedroom. I went after her and sat on the edge of the bed while she sat on a little bench in front of a dressing table and picked up a brush and began to stroke her hair. Her hair was deep, deep red. Under the strokes of the brush, it began to glow like the heart of a coal, but more deeply and darkly than any coal could glow. We watched each other in the mirror.

"What do you want, Mick?" she said.

"Information," I said. "I'm looking for a friend for a friend."

"Do I know any of your friends?"

"I think so."

"Well, it's a small world. Am I supposed to know something about this particular friend?"

"That's what I'd like to find out. Shall I be subtle, or shall I ask you directly?"

"Ask me directly."

"All right. Was Cal Christopher here last night?"

"Shall I be subtle, or shall I answer you directly?"

"Answer me directly."

"None of your damn business."

"You're right. I admit it. But the only reason I want to know is to satisfy myself and someone else that he's all right."

"Cal's a fairly competent guy. Why shouldn't he be all right?"

"Probably he is. But he hasn't been home for twenty-four hours, and he hasn't been seen for about eighteen by anyone I've seen, and he was carrying thirty grand that he won in Duane Holland's crap game."

She stopped brushing, the brush poised over her glowing hair, and turned her head to look at me over her left shoulder.

"That much? I knew he won a bundle, but I didn't dream it was so much."

"The statistics were furnished by Holland. He wouldn't be likely to exaggerate."

"That's true. He wouldn't." She laid the brush down and stood up abruptly and walked across the room to a closet. She returned to the dressing table with a pair of gold sandals and sat down and put them on. "All right, Mick, just between you and me and not for casual conversation, he was here. He was here until about eleven o'clock this morning, and he left in perfectly good condition with everything he had when he came. Is that satisfactory, or do you insist on details?"

"No details necessary. Maybe you could tell me, however, if he mentioned where he was going from here."

"He didn't say. At the time, it didn't strike me as being important."

"Sure. I can see it wouldn't." I stood up and walked over to her and put a hand on her head for a second. I had an idea I could feel the fire in her hair, but it felt no different from other hair I'd felt on other heads. "Thanks for the confession, honey."

"My pleasure. They tell me it's good for the soul."

"See you again?"

"Could be. Come around when there's more time."

"I'll do it. Goodbye, now." I went back down to the Olds and sat in it for a while. It was then around eight, and I didn't know where to go or whom to see or what, in general, to do. After a while I decided I had better check with Ann again, so I drove to a drugstore and did that by phone, but Cal hadn't come in or reported or been reported on. Ann said she thought she'd start calling hospitals and maybe the police, and I said it was all right about the hospitals, if she wanted to, but that I'd hold off on the police until the very end because she didn't have anything, in the first place, that would do more than bore them, and it was something, in the second place, that would infuriate Cal if he turned up okay. I hung up without telling her about Cal and Gail, or about Cal and the thirty grand.

After that, lacking a better plan, or any real plan at all, I made a long round of all the places I could imagine Cal's turning up in, including the seven places I'd already been, and by the time I'd finished it was after one A.M. At the last place, I called Ann again to tell her I was going home to bed and would see her later in the morning, but the phone rang and rang at her end without ever getting an answer, and so I went home to bed without telling her.

The next morning I got up about eight and had a cup of coffee and a roll at a drugstore and got to Ann's about nine. She let me in and turned immediately without speaking and walked across the room and sat down on a straight chair. She walked with odd rigidity, as if it required the utmost effort and caution to control the movements of her body, and she sat on the chair with the same rigidity, poised on the edge with her knees together and her hands clasped on her knees.

She was wearing a plain dark suit, and her face looked tightly drawn and very tired with dark smudges under her eyes. She looked, I thought, as if she had tried, with soap and water and meticulous grooming, to hide the ravishments of a week's binge.

"What's the matter with you?" I said.

I went over and took one of her hands, and it lay like ice in mine. She did not look at me, but sat staring with wide, dry eyes at a small charred place in the pile of the carpet where someone, sometime, had dropped the coal of a cigarette.

"They've found a body," she said.

"Body? Whose body?"

"It's Cal's."

"How do you know? Did they tell you that?"

"No. It's just something I feel."

"Just something you imagine, maybe. It's probably not Cal's at all."

She shook her head and went on, staring at the small charred spot.

"Who found the body?" I said.

"Someone. Out in the county. The sheriff or someone."

"How do you know this?"

"I called the police this morning, and they told me about it. Someone named Sergeant Durham did. Last night I took the sedative that Wade Hacket left, and it apparently did me some good, for I was able to go to sleep, but not good enough, for I kept dreaming and had a bad time altogether. This morning I knew I couldn't stand it any longer, and so I called the police and was told that they'd found the body, and this Sergeant Durham said it would be a good idea if I came down and looked at it."

"They haven't been able to identify it definitely themselves?"

"I don't think so. Something happened to it, I think. Something that prevents them from knowing."

"You see? You call about a missing husband, they've got a strange body. Naturally they want you to look at it. That's just routine, honey."

"You are trying to be comforting, Mick, and I'm grateful, but I have this feeling. I have this terrible feeling."

"Are you going down there?"

"I have to go. I have to find out, of course. Sergeant Durham's coming for me."

"Would you like me to go along?"

"If you don't mind. It would be very kind of you to come."

I tried to rub a little warmth into her hand, but it was no use. Her flesh was cold and stiff. It felt embalmed. I wanted to say something sensible and reassuring, but I couldn't think of anything she would be likely to accept as either, and I was still trying to think of something when someone outside the door set off the chimes. I went to the door and opened it, and there stood a small, thin man wearing a blue suit and a gray hat and black shoes. He took off his hat and stood on one leg while he rubbed the toe of a shoe up and down the calf of the leg he was standing on. He didn't seem to be conscious that he was doing this.

"I'm looking for Mrs. Christopher," he said.

"This is her apartment," I said. "Come on in."

He came inside and saw Ann and walked over and stopped about four feet from her.

"Mrs. Christopher?" he said.

"Yes." She turned her head and looked at him, but I had the impression she didn't see him clearly at all. "You're Sergeant Durham, I suppose."

"That's right. We talked on the telephone."

"I know. I remember. This is Mr. Mahony. A friend. I want him to come with me."

"That's all right." He looked at me briefly. The irises of his eyes were pale and streaked, like faded blue calcimine on old plaster. "It's always nice to have a friend around."

"Do you want to go now?" she said.

"Not just yet. I'd like to talk with you first, if you don't mind."

"I don't mind. Won't you sit down, please?"

"Thank you."

He looked around for a chair, but he made no move in the direction of one; so I got a mate to the one Ann was using and carried it over to him, and he nodded his head and sat down on the chair and placed his hat carefully in his lap.

"It might be a shock," he said. "Seeing the body, I mean. I ought to tell you what to expect."

"Is it necessary?"

"It's advisable."

"Tell me, then."

"Well, it's this way. The body was found on the bank of Indian River, out in the county. Where it was found is a place where the river is shallow with flat gravel banks and rock bluffs on both sides. The bluffs are about thirty, forty feet high. The body was on the bank on the east side, at the foot of the bluff. It's a pretty secluded place, and all around is a lot of underbrush and scrub timber, and it was just plain luck the body was found as soon as it was. The way it happened to be found, this old fellow who lives in a shack out that way—a river rat, they call him—was out in the river noodling catfish. That's a way of catching them with your hands. Anyhow, he was doing this when he came around a bend and saw this light up the river, a fire, and he went up there out of curiosity to see what it was, and it was the body. Burning I mean. Someone had carried it there and soaked it with gasoline and set it on fire."

Durham stopped talking and watched Ann carefully for signs of disintegration, and so did I, but she didn't even sway, didn't move in the slightest, seemed only by a kind of deadly chemistry to shrink and grow terribly small on the edge of the chair.

"This old river rat," Durham continued, "was pretty scared, I guess. Naturally. For all he knew, of course, whoever did it might still be around in the dark watching. He did what almost anyone would have done, which was to get out of there as fast as he could. He got to a place with a phone and called the sheriff, and when the sheriff got there with a deputy about thirty minutes later, the three of them went back to where the body was, but by that time there wasn't anything left that wasn't too badly charred to be recognized by anyone for what it had been. Not right off, that is. But you can't destroy a body entirely that way, of course. Bones are left. Teeth are left. Sometimes you can tell a lot from teeth and bones. Was there anything unusual about your husband's teeth or bones, Mrs. Christopher?"

He stopped again, watching and waiting while I cursed him in my thoughts, and pretty soon Ann answered him in a small, thin voice that seemed, somehow, detached from any physical source.

"The middle toe of his right foot was half gone," she said. "He lost it when he was a boy, he told me. He never said exactly how."

"All right." Durham held out his own right foot and stared at it as if he were looking through shoe and sock to reassure himself of his own middle toe's normality, and then he stood up and said abruptly with an effect of casual brutality, "Well, let's get on downtown. You ready, Mrs. Christopher?"

She said she was in her small detached voice, and we drove down in the police car with Durham. In the morgue, we looked at the charred body, and it was easier in the end than might have been expected, for it was surely nothing that had anything to do in any real way with anyone we had ever known. It was about the right height, however, and looked as if it had been about the right build and weight, and the middle toe of its right foot was half gone. While we were there, Ann stood a little apart and seemed so frail and precariously balanced that I was afraid to touch her in the fear that she would dissolve in dust, and when we were finished and gone, in the police car with Durham on the way home again, she sat in a corner of the seat and closed her eyes and looked dead. Back in the apartment, she went into the bedroom and lay down on the bed, and I followed and stood looking at her, and I thought that she was far too quiet, and that it was a bad sign. Pretty soon, if nothing was done, the break would come, and it was surely something it would be wise to prevent.

Turning, I went into the living room where Durham was sitting.

"I'm going to call her doctor," I said.

"You better," he said.

I looked up Hacket's office number in the directory and dialed it. His answering service said he wasn't there at the moment, but had called in to say he was on the way, and I told her where to send him, and to do it just as soon as he arrived. Then I sat down and watched Durham, and he watched me. We sat there for a minute or two watching each other.

"What's your position in this?" he said at last.

"She told you," I said. "A friend. His first, then hers. A friend to both."

"I see. When did she say he was home last? About seven o'clock night before last, wasn't it?"

"That's right."

"Did she make any effort to locate him before she called us this morning?"

"Yes. She began to get disturbed yesterday afternoon. At least that's when she called me. I prowled all over town trying to find out where he was, but all I found out was where he'd been for part of the time the night before."

"Where was that?"

"The Number Ten Club."

"Oh. Duane Holland's place. Anything happen there that might explain anything?"

I told him about the thirty grand. I thought about telling him about Gail Sullivan, how Cal had spent the rest of the night with her, but I decided that I wouldn't do it yet, not quite yet. Durham was interested in the thirty grand, and was plainly thinking hard about it.

"That's a lot of money," he said. "That's more money than I ever hope to see. It could explain a lot of killing, all right, but there's a lot about this particular killing that it doesn't explain at all. A strong-arm guy who kills for dough doesn't go in for any elaborate disposition of the body. He just leaves it lying somewhere."

This was something that even I could see, and it had been bothering me, as it was bothering Durham, gnawing away at the edge of my mind.

"Maybe the thirty grand wasn't the motive at all," I said. "Maybe he was killed for another reason entirely."

"Yeah," he said. "That occurs to me."

His pale calcimine eyes moved over me slowly, with a kind of ocular sneer. At first I didn't get the implication, but then I did, and I was shocked and scared and sore in turn.

"Look," I said. "I said I was a friend. His and hers. That's what I was, and all I was, so don't go getting any clever ideas otherwise."

"Me? I'm not clever. I got all I can do to get any ideas at all, let alone clever ones. What the hell are you talking about?"

"You know what I'm talking about. I may play fast and loose with the tenth sometimes, but I never fool around with the sixth."

"What's this? You've left me way out in left field, brother."

"Ahhh, you were thinking I might've done it because of Ann. Fine tabloid-type love stuff. If you don't want to waste a lot of time, you'd better forget it."

"Is that what I was thinking? I don't remember saying anything like that."

"You implied it."

"Did I actually do that? I didn't know I had any talent at all for indirection. Most of the time I have trouble finding the words to say what I mean straight out." He stood up suddenly and grinned at me.

"Well, don't let it worry you. From what you said about the thirty grand maybe not being the motive, I can tell you're thinking pretty good about this, and I imagine we'll need all the help we can get before we're through. You get any more ideas, you let me know, will you?"

He said this in perfectly good humor and with apparent sincerity, and there was no way to measure the extent of his sarcasm, or if there was any sarcasm intended at all. He put on his hat and went out, and I walked over to the door of the bedroom and looked at Ann on the bed. She hadn't moved in the slightest and still looked dead. I spoke her name softly, but she didn't answer or open her eyes, and I went back to my chair in the living room and sat down and waited for Hacket to arrive, which he did about fifteen minutes later.

"What's the matter?" he said. "Has Cal turned up?"

"He's turned up," I said, "but there's nothing you can do for him. Ann's the one you need to see. She's having a pretty bad time."

"Is something wrong? Tell me!"

"Cal's dead. Someone killed him and hauled his body out into the country and set fire to it. They found it last night."

"Good God!"

His mouth dropped open after the exclamation, and his face was all at once loose and gray and very ugly. Then, after a few seconds that seemed much longer, he jerked into motion and went swiftly past me into the bedroom. I heard him speak, but I could hear no answer from Ann, and then I heard him moving around a little, a few small sounds in the execution of whatever was necessary, and it was ten to fifteen minutes, I judged, before he returned. He had recovered his assurance and his color, and his voice sounded almost casual.

"You're right," he said. "She's in a bad way."

"No wonder," I said.

"Of course. I gave her something that will knock her out for quite a long time. An injection."

"I was afraid she'd crack up if something wasn't done."

"So she would have. Certainly. You were wise to call me."

"Will she be all right when she comes to?"

"At least she'll be a little better able to bear the pressure. What a horrible thing to happen!"

"Yeah," I said, and sighed.

"Why? Can there be any reason for it?"

"Since it happened, there was apparently a reason."

"Yes. Naturally. Does anyone have an idea what the reason was?"

"He won thirty grand in a crap game night before last."

"He was killed for the money?"

"Maybe. It's a reasonable theory."

"I suppose so." He dropped into a chair and held his head for a moment. Straightening, he said, "I wonder if I could have a drink. Just a short one."

"Of course. I'll have one with you."

We had the drinks, which were not so short after all, and afterwards he arose and picked up his bag, which he had placed on the floor beside his chair. Carrying the bag, he went to the bedroom door and looked into the room.

"She'll be all right now," he said. "Are you going to stay?"

"No. I'll have to be going soon."

"She shouldn't be left alone now, and someone should be here when she comes around, I think. For a day or two, anyhow. She should be undressed and put into bed properly. Could you wait here a little longer until I send a nurse? I'll have one come as quickly as possible."

"All right," I said. "I'll wait."

He nodded and left. When the nurse came, I left, too.

I should have quit then, for the whole thing was in the hands of the police, which was where it belonged. But I didn't quit, for the simple reason that it was impossible to start suddenly doing nothing. I got into the Olds and drove out to the county seat and found the sheriff in his office on the first floor of the county jail. He was an enormously fat man who moved with remarkable agility and talked too much in a high, thin voice. I told him who I was, which didn't impress him, and told him who the burning body had been, which did. It also filled him with a kind of hot, ebullient indignation. It was a damn shame, he said, when a regularly elected law officer of the county had to get that kind of information from strangers. The snotty city cops were obligated to let him know what was developing because the body was found in the county, and the county therefore had original jurisdiction, and if those city cops ever wanted any more cooperation from his office, they better start treating him right. I agreed that they hadn't treated him right.

"However," I said, "it hasn't been long since the identification was made. I know because I helped make it. His wife and I. Probably the police just haven't got around to notifying you yet."

"Maybe." He looked at me speculatively, blowing his lips out in the shape of a wet and nauseous kiss. "You say you were a friend of his? This Cal Christopher, I mean."

"Yes."

"You got any idea who did this thing?"

"No."

"Damnedest thing I ever saw. Body burning there at the foot of the bluff, I mean. Hope I never see anything like it again."

"I can imagine."

"The stink was bad. By God, it was bad!"

"I wonder if I could see the place," I said.

"What for?"

"I don't know, really. It's just something I'd like to do. As I said, he was my friend. The best friend I ever had. I'd feel better somehow if I could see where it happened."

"That makes no sense to me, son. Seems to me it'd make you feel worse."

"A man isn't always reasonable, I guess. Sometimes he feels a kind of need he can't explain."

He watched me for a few seconds, making up his mind, blowing his lips out and sucking them in.

"Well," he said, finally, shrugging his massive shoulders, "I can't see why not. It's a crazy thing to want to do, if you want my opinion, but otherwise I can't see anything wrong with it. I'll drive you out there myself."

We went out in the county Ford, and it required about twenty-five minutes. Most of the way we were on a narrow concrete county highway that climbed, after a while, into flinty hills covered sparsely with scrub oak, and then we turned off onto a narrow dirt road, hard as iron, that ran back through high grass and brush to the bluff above the flat gravel bank of the river, a kind of shelf between the water and the bluff, where the body had been found burning. The bluff was pretty steep, but not even close to perpendicular, and a path angled down the face of it to the gravel bank below. It would not have been difficult to drag a body down the path, and the fire it made burning might have burned itself out unseen if it had not been for the unpredictable noodling of a river rat.

We went down the path and looked around, but there was nothing much to see—nothing but the river and rocks and the face of the bluff, and on the rocks near the bluff the smoked site of a fire. The murderer, whoever he was, must have descended and climbed the bluff at least twice and maybe more. Down with the body, then up alone and down again with fuel. Gasoline, Durham had said. It might be possible to learn who had bought a quantity of gasoline recently. Many people, no doubt. All of them innocent, but one. Well, that was the kind of job the police would do. I turned away and climbed back up the bluff with the sheriff following, and we drove back to the county seat in the Ford. I got out of the Ford and into the Olds, and the sheriff stood for a minute by the door.

"Satisfied, son?" he said.

"I guess you could call it that," I said. "Thanks."

"Don't mention it. You see those snotty city cops, you tell them I said where they could go."

"I'll do that," I said.

I drove back to town, and it was six o'clock when I got there. I thought I would stop somewhere to eat, but the thought sickened me, so I drove directly to Gail Sullivan's apartment building. It was getting pretty late, almost time for Gail to be dressing for work, and I didn't anticipate a warm welcome. It wasn't.

"Mick," she said, blocking the doorway, "you're a very nice guy, and I like you, but you're getting to be something of a nuisance."

"Sorry," I said. "I know this isn't the right time, and even if it was, there isn't enough of it. I've just come to tell you that I may be compelled to put the finger on you. I'm sorry for that, too."

"What do you mean?"

"I mean that I'll go along with a peccadillo, but not with murder."

The only signs of shock were a sucking sound of indrawn breath and a sudden stillness in her eyes. After a moment, she released her breath in a long sigh and stepped out of my way.

"You'd better come in," she said.

I walked in and sat down, and she followed a few steps and stood looking down at me. She was wearing a white terry cloth robe over nothing, and her feet were bare, and it crossed my mind that she was one of the few women I'd ever known who didn't have to worry a bit about getting caught in whatever she was or wasn't wearing.

"I was about to take a bath," she said.

"Sorry. I think I said that before."

"It's all right. You look beat. Would you like a drink?"

"No, thanks. My stomach's empty, and I don't think it would be a good idea."

"There's no food in the place."

I shook my head. "Food doesn't seem like a good idea, either."

"Where was he?"

"Cal?"

"You know I mean Cal."

"Up to about eleven yesterday morning he was here. You said that."

"After eleven?"

"I don't know. Up until sometime last night, that is. Sometime last night he was lying out in the county beside the river. Burning like a torch. Someone took him there and soaked him with gasoline and set him on fire. Now he's downtown in the morgue."

"Oh no," she said, and pressed a hand to her face, fingers spread wide.

I wondered what might go on in the mind of a woman who remembered intimacy with mutilated flesh. It wasn't the pleasantest of speculations.

"So you may have to tell the police he was here," I said.

"All right, if necessary. I won't consider myself ruined."

"Is it also all right if you become what is known as a logical suspect? He was here. He had thirty grand, and no one has been found who has seen him since. It will be a fair assumption that you could use the money. You can see, honey, that you're not in a good position."

"Damn it, Mick, are you trying to scare me?"

I shook my head. "No."

"What I told you is true. He came here with me, and everything was fine between us, and he went away about eleven the next morning."

"I remember what you said. How well do you know Duane Holland?"

"I work for him. How much can you know about your boss? Or about anyone?"

"How far do you think he'd go to recover thirty grand?"

"Don't be silly, Mick. Duane's lost more'n that before, and he'll lose more again, and in between he'll win far more than he'll ever lose all times together. Besides, assuming he'd be capable of killing for reasons of his own, he'd hire it done—I know that much about him—and there wouldn't be any tricks with the body afterward. What's more, it would have happened the same night Cal won the money. Right afterward. When they were sure he had it on him."

"That sounds reasonable. That's what the cops will figure."

"But it didn't happen that night. Cal was here with me all the time."

"That's what you say. Over and over. But you work for Holland, honey. The cops may take that into consideration."

She took a deep, ragged breath that shook her body. Her mouth twisted with bitterness. "Thanks for your confidence, Mick. Now get out of here. I need that bath more than ever."

"Don't get excited. I'm not accusing you, honey. I'm just trying to—What bothers me, you see, is the business with the body. Why didn't it just turn up in the river, or in a dark corner of a dark alley, or anyplace a body might naturally turn up after being killed and robbed? You see what I mean? Cal was a natural for robbery, carrying all that money the way he was, but the fancy business with the body obscures the motive. It gets everyone thinking along other lines. Maybe it was an attempt to prevent identification, or maybe it was an attempt to hide the method of murder, and neither of these fits a robbery pattern at all. It's very confusing, isn't it?"

"Why don't you let the police get confused? It's their job."

"I know. I got no business meddling. I wonder if Cal actually had the money when he was here."

"He must have. He didn't mention it, and I didn't see it, but he could have had it in his pockets if it was in large denomination bills."

"Sure. Which it probably was. The point is, where did he go from here? And it's a big point, honey. Especially for you. You can see that."

"I don't know where he went. He didn't say. It seems I have to keep repeating things."

"Nothing that would even give you a faint idea?"

"Not that I—Now wait a minute . . ."

She stood there stiffly, a big redhead with a sudden big thought, something remembered all at once. Her eyes strained for complete concentration, and a thumb and finger came up unconsciously to pinch her lower lip.

"He had these marks on his left arm," she said.

"What?"

"These marks. A lot of tiny punctures. I thought at first he was a mainliner."

"Cal? That's crazy."

"I know. But he had the marks, and it was the first thing I thought of. I don't like dope addicts, and I asked him about the marks, and he just laughed. He said he used a needle, but not for that. Insulin, he said. He said he was a diabetic."

Suddenly, like an electric shock, I remembered the odd look Ann had given me when I'd made the remark about not knowing that she or Cal was ever sick.

"Are you sure?"

"Of course I'm sure. He said he had an injection once every twenty-four hours. Did it himself. He said that reminded him that he'd used the last of his supply of insulin, and he had to get more."

"All right," I said, "all right. It's getting late. If you'll get dressed, I'll drive you around to the club."

"You don't have to bother."

"It's no bother. I want to make up for being a nuisance. Just get dressed."

She went into the bedroom. I could hear her moving around in there. From the bedroom, she went into the bathroom. I sat and listened to the sound of running water. It took her maybe twenty minutes to bathe and dress, and when she came out ready to go, she looked as if she had spent hours on it.

At the Number Ten Club, she went directly upstairs, and I went into the bar. Duane Holland was sitting there over a highball.

"Hello, Mick," he said. "Hear they've found your friend Cal."

"That's right," I said. "What was left of him."

"It's nuts," he said. "I can't understand it."

"I think I'm beginning to," I said. "Maybe."

He swallowed some of the highball and looked at me from the corners of his eyes. "Is that so? Well, Cal was a nice guy. He didn't deserve this kind of finish."

"He didn't," I said. "He surely didn't. I wonder if you'd be willing to help me sort of square things away. Post-mortemly. Not that it'll do Cal any good, of course."

"Suppose you just tell me what's on your mind."

"You run a gambling house. Lots of people gamble in it, and most of them lose money in it, and some of them lose more money than they have. I'd like to know whose paper you're holding currently."

"Not many. No one owes money to Duane Holland very long. You could count the current total on the fingers of one hand."

"I'm only interested in one finger."

"Okay. You name the finger, and I'll tell you if you're right."

I told him, and I was right, and then I had a sandwich and a drink and went home. There, I dialed Operator and asked for police headquarters. I'd never phoned headquarters before, and I didn't know whether to ask for a person or a department or what. I settled for a person, Sergeant Durham, and I was surprised when he was put on promptly. Late as it was, I thought he'd probably gone home, or wherever he went after work, but I guess cops work all hours.

"Hello," I said. "This is Mick Mahony."

"Mick Mahony? Oh. Oh, yeah. Mick Mahony. What's on your mind?"

"Did they do a post-mortem on Cal Christopher?"

There was an interim of silence, except for the humming wire, and then he came back. "Funny you should ask that. Why do you want to know?"

"Why shouldn't I want to know? Is it so odd for a man to want to know what killed his friend?"

"Come to think of it, I guess not. Cops develop blind spots in these things. The truth is, nothing happened to him that you might have suspected. No fractured skull. No bullet hole. No knife wound. He was poisoned. In spite of the fire, there were traces of it. Cyanide."

"Thanks," I said.

"Wait a minute," he said. "Don't try to hang up with just a thank-you and a goodbye."

"I'm tired," I said, "and I'm going to bed. In order to do that, I've got to hang up. I'll come around in the morning and tell you about an idea I've got."

I hung up then. Before I went to bed, I called Ann's number. The nurse said she was still asleep and resting quietly.

Between eleven thirty and noon of the next day, in Wade Hacket's reception room, the receptionist was not present. No one was waiting in any of the silver fox finished oak chairs. From the consultation rooms beyond the reception room there was no sound, no sign or feeling of life or motion. I walked past the receptionist's desk and opened a door and looked into the room behind it. Wade Hacket, in a white linen coat, sat at another desk with his head in his hands. He lifted his head at the sound of the opening door, and the flesh of his face was soggy and gray.

"Mahony," he said, as if he were uncertain of the name and trying it for effect. "I'm not having office hours now."

"I know," I said. I went over and sat down in a chair across the desk from him. "Are your receptionist and nurse always gone at this time?"

"Yes. Yes, they are. It's their lunch hour, as a matter of fact. Why?"

"In that case, they must have been gone when Cal Christopher was here day before yesterday."

"Cal? Was Cal here then? Possibly he was. I've forgotten."

"Had you already forgotten the afternoon of the same day when you stopped at his apartment and talked with Ann? Even though she was disturbed because he hadn't come home? It seems to me that would have been enough to remind you."

"It does, doesn't it. He must not have been here that day, then. I'm sure I'd have remembered."

"Oh, he was here, all right. He was out of insulin and had to stop for more. Something like that can't be neglected. How long have you been treating Cal for diabetes?"

"I don't know exactly. I could look it up if it's important. Ever since he became my patient, whenever that was."

"I'm curious about that. How did Cal happen to become your patient?"

"It seems to me that you're asking a great many questions, Mahony. Do I owe you some kind of accounting?"

"Never mind. I think I know how it happened. He met you in one of the places he was always going. Maybe the Number Ten Club. Once you became friends, it was natural for Cal to adopt you professionally. That was the way Cal operated. He always went all the way with his friends. It's interesting that you and Cal both had the fever."

"Fever? I don't understand you."

"Gambling fever, I mean. Do you think they'll ever discover a miracle drug to cure it? In my opinion, it's not likely."

"Don't be ridiculous. I like to play games of chance on occasion, and I can afford it."

"Really? Why don't you pay your debts, then? The twenty grand to Duane Holland. Whatever else to whoever else."

He made a desperate effort to assume an attitude of defensive dignity, but the effect was pathetic. His gray face sagged and looked sick. In his eyes there seemed to be no sign of fear or anger, but only, instead, an expression of dumb wonder at the strange and deadly vulnerability that was his as a consequence of what he had done and become.

"You're out of your mind," he said. "What makes you think you can come into my office and talk to me this way? Please leave at once."

"Sure," I said. "I didn't come because I wanted to, and I don't want to stay any longer than I have to, and I wish to God that I could forget you entirely the moment I leave, which will not be possible. Before I go, however, I'd like to know one thing. I'd like to know why you fouled it up by getting fancy. Why didn't you just hit him over the head with something? It would have been so much easier that way. Easier afterward, I mean. You could have locked his body in a room or closet, just as you did anyhow, and then you could simply have taken him out at night and dumped him in a dark corner somewhere. With the thirty grand on everyone's mind, it would have passed as robbery, and no one would ever in the world have thought of Dr. Wade Hacket.

"But you didn't do it that way, and I guess, after all, that you don't have to tell me why you didn't, because I think I know. It was a kind of compulsion. It was a murder that practically committed itself, and you were merely, in a way, its agent. Here he was in your office, and nobody was here but the two of you, and he made the fatal mistake of boasting about the thirty grand in his pockets, as one guy with the fever to another, and maybe he even showed it to you. Thirty beautiful grand with no strings or claims or taxes attached, and you needed it desperately, and everything seemed as perfectly right and ready as the devil himself could have arranged it, and so you killed him for the money, and it was done almost before you knew it. He needed an injection of insulin, and you gave him cyanide, and it was that quick and that easy."

He looked up at me, and his mouth worked, but no sound came out of it, and I knew that there was no way at all that he could have gotten away with what he'd done. Even if he had escaped suspicion entirely he would have been trapped in his own guilt and destroyed in time by his own mind. He had been seduced to murder by weakness and need and rare opportunity, and he could never have survived it long. It had been his guilt, I thought, which had compelled him, no more than four hours after the murder, to visit the apartment in which Cal had lived, to talk with the woman who had been Cal's wife.

"So you had the body on your hands," I said, "and you began to think, and you must have known that you had made a bad mistake. With the cyanide in him he would never pass as a plain robbery victim, and the poison would plainly point to you if he was ever traced as far as your office and no farther. It was clear that the body had to be destroyed. As a doctor, you could have cut it up and disposed of the pieces, but I guess you didn't have the stomach for that. There were other alternatives, too, and probably you chose the way you did simply because, in the end, it had to be one way instead of another. There's no way of knowing exactly why these things are done, I understand. To me it seemed pretty crazy, burning a body that way, but Sergeant Durham of the police says it's happened lots of times in various places. He says it isn't really unusual at all. Have you met Sergeant Durham? He's waiting out in the reception room right now, and if you haven't met him I think it's high time you did."

He stood up all at once behind the desk, rising with what seemed a single convulsive jerk of his whole body, and I thought for an instant that he was coming over the desk at me, but he didn't. Very slowly he sat down again and put his head in his hands, and Durham walked into the room, and I walked out.

"Thanks," Durham said. "You did fine."

I didn't answer. In the street, I stood on the curb and wondered where to go. I thought of Ann, about seeing her and talking with her and holding her hands for comfort, but there was now no pleasure in it, or expectation of pleasure, for it had somehow been made impossible by what had happened, and I thought of Gail Sullivan, but there was no pleasure in that, either, and seeing her didn't seem appropriate under the circumstances. Finally I thought of home as a place to go that was probably as good as any other place, and so that's where I went, and what I did after getting there was have a great many solitary drinks over a period of a great many hours.

Sam's Conscience

by Douglas Farr

The chief leaned far back in his leather chair, planted his heels on the top of his mahogany desk. "So tell me, lieutenant," he said. "The Morgan case . . ."

The lieutenant hesitated uncertainly. "There are curious coincidences," he began.

"Coincidences, uh-huh."

"So I've been trying to deduce . . ."

"Deduce!" The chief's body remained placid, but a thundercloud in the shape of a frown passed over and darkened his broad, flat face. "What are you, Nero Wolfe or a cop? Deduce! Easier to sit around and deduce than to get out and do the legwork, is that it?"

The lieutenant was not thin-skinned, not after having dealt with the chief for so many years. Now he deemed it practical to show humility and respect for a greater mind than his own. "Would you please let me explain, sir? Frankly, I need guidance on this, sir. And I'd like you to decide what I should do next on this case, sir."

Mollified, pacified, the chief nodded. "Go on, lieutenant."

"Well, to begin with, sir, this Sam Morgan is a burglar."

"Burglar? I thought he was . . ."

"I mean, *was* a burglar. I was deducing, you see, sir. Sam Morgan actually has a record, I found out. One conviction for burglary in 1946. Served two and a half years. Time off for good behavior. Very good behavior. Sam was a model prisoner. Warden was really sorry to lose him. All right, late in 1948, Sam is released from prison. Is never picked up again. Fact Number One. Fact Number Two, Sam can give only a very vague account of how he made his living in the past ten years. Odd job here and there, of course. But they are only cover-ups probably. Sam's first love is burglary. He remains a burglar by profession."

"You deduce that, lieutenant?"

"Yes, sir. Based on my experience with all types of criminals. Of course, Sam is not the usual type burglar. Sam is what you might call a burglar of the old school. He is a small man, nimble, wiry, quick. Like a cat. And like a cat, he can get in almost anywhere. He is a mild-mannered man, with no visible bad habits. He does not burglarize to buy dope, or to support fancy women, or anything like that. He is a burglar because he has a natural talent for it. He likes it. He prefers to do it more than doing other things. In a way, he does not really look upon himself as a criminal. A gentle burglar. In a small, unassuming way, a gentleman burglar. Unfortunately a vanishing type."

The chief sighed nostalgically. "Unfortunately . . ."

The lieutenant took courage from the other's mellow mood. "Now, I am deducing here again, sir, as I reconstruct the history of Sam. If you'll be patient, I'll bring in other facts, other coincidences, sir. But for the moment I deduce. Sam, I think, has a partner in crime, another character with a known burglary record. Sidney Tepper . . ."

"Tepper! You mean . . . ?"

"I see, sir, you're beginning to make your own deductions," the lieutenant interrupted hastily. "But allow me to go on, sir. Now I'll admit I have no proof—and can't possibly get any proof—that Sam Morgan and Sidney Tepper are associated any time in this period 1948 to the present. But I deduce. You see, their talents are in a way complementary. They make a natural team. Sam, who is very good at getting into places, and Sidney who has the contacts with the fences and can dispose of the loot. Sam the artist, and Sidney the businessman. You admit this makes a good team, sir?"

"Oh, sure . . ."

"Now I bring in another case, sir, the Garman case. You remember the name Max Garman. Let me speculate on what possibly—I say possibly—happened to Max Garman. In this particular year—last year, 1958—our friend Sam Morgan is working as a shoe salesman. Now this I checked. Sam Morgan is not very interested in his shoe selling job. He shows up for work only about half the time, and when he does show up, he doesn't sell many shoes. The owner of the shoe store told me he kept Sam around only because Sam seemed to be such a nice guy. So it's just a cover-up job, maybe?"

"Yes, maybe."

"All right. Now let's suppose Sam and Sidney are working together in 1958. The Garman job is a typical one calling for Sam's and Sidney's special talents. Furs and jewelry lying around the house because Max Garman likes to buy pretty things for his wife Leona, but there's not much cash around. The house has good locks, but that's all right with Sam. Now, chief, let's suppose it was Sam and Sidney who were at the Garman house in 1958 . . ."

The chief took his feet off the desk top and sat up straight. The thundercloud was on his face again. "You're theorizing, lieutenant . . ."

The lieutenant wasn't to be stopped, though. And he had a bit of the blarney in him. "No, chief, I'm presenting you a combination of facts, coincidences, and possibilities. Then I'm going to ask you to theorize."

For a moment the chief continued to eye his underling suspiciously. But then he seemed to catch the implication and admission of his superior authority and brain power. He subsided again, leaned back, bestowed his heavy heels once more on the patient desk top.

"Proceed, lieutenant."

"Let's say then that Sam and Sidney did the Garman job. We don't know they did, of course, but for the moment let's assume. Sam probably is the one who goes into the house first. Maybe Sidney doesn't get a chance to go in at all, because the whole thing happens so fast. But Sam gets the surprise of his life. I checked this on Leona Garman's old testimony. That night, of all nights, she and Max had a fight. Max decided to sleep downstairs on the sofa. Now what burglar would expect to find the man of the house sleeping on the sofa? Sam is no strong-arm boy. He never hit anybody in his life. He's not looking for trouble. He wants to get in quietly, get out quietly. But there's Max Garman on the sofa. Maybe he wakes up, or maybe he's not even asleep. He hears Sam come in. Max has a gun—remember, the gun checked out as Max's gun, all right. He gets the gun and takes a shot in the dark at Sam. Misses. Then there's a scuffle. Sam is wiry and quick. Max Garman is slow and fat. Sam doesn't want to kill anybody. All he wants to do is get away. But that fool Max won't let well enough alone. There's a scuffle. Max gets shot with his own gun. And all Sam was trying to do was defend himself; so Max is killed in self-defense."

"Homicide," the chief intoned judicially, "while committing a felony is first-degree murder, not self-defense."

"Yes, sir. But you can't blame Sam for trying not to get shot."

"Assuming it was Sam who was in the Garman house that night."

"That's right, sir. Assuming. Now let me go on, sir. If you'll remember, chief, we never solved the Garman case. And if you'll remember also, the case got an awful lot of newspaper publicity. Man murdered while defending his home. That kind of thing. Pictures of the widow and her two orphaned children. Real good sob stuff. The papers played it up big. Now I go on deducing, sir. Would it be strange if Sam Morgan followed the story in the papers and was awfully bothered by it? Remember, sir, our gentle burglar type. A man with a conscience."

"Assuming it was Sam who shot Max Garman?"

"Oh yes, sir. Assuming."

The chief stared at the ceiling. His mood wasn't easy to guess. His tone of voice had been flat, unemotional, unrevealing. He could be going along. Or he could be waiting to pounce.

"Proceed with your fabrications, lieutenant," he said.

The lieutenant swallowed. He had fifteen years on the force that he was laying on the line. He'd said Sam Morgan had a conscience. Well, he had one, too. Therefore he had to continue. Probably the chief wouldn't let him stop now even if he wanted to. Fifteen years on the force . . .

"Yes, sir," he said. "It was hard to check with the shoe store owner, because he doesn't have good records of that kind of thing. But he seems to remember that about the time of the Garman murder, Sam doesn't come to work for about two or three weeks. What's he doing all this time? Maybe, I say, maybe he's having an attack of conscience. A gentle man, who never hurt a fly, suddenly he's a killer. And there's those stories and pictures in the papers, torturing him. Sam has a soft heart for widows and orphans. He is going crazy. A nice woman doesn't have a husband any more and two nice kids don't have a father any more on account of him. Confessing the crime won't do these people any good. What will? Only one thing, Sam finally figures. Max Garman has to be replaced."

The chief glanced across the desk through slitted eyes. "Sam Morgan married the Widow Garman, that we know," he said sagely.

"Yes, sir, that we know. I tried some subtle questioning on this angle, you see. I tried not to let on what I had in mind. But I questioned Sam and I questioned his new wife, the former Mrs. Garman. I tried to get the picture—how they met, why they got married. I didn't get much. Only this. Sam seems to have shown up in Leona Garman's life for the first time about a month after Max Garman was killed. He gives her some vague story of having known Max and wants to know if he can help out in any way. The kids take to him from the beginning. Which gives him the excuse to come back. This goes on for months. Now what is Sam doing? Maybe he has marriage in mind from the beginning, maybe not. Maybe at first he tries to serve as a temporary companion, and then one thing leads to another. In any case, when the proper year has passed, the Widow

Garman becomes Mrs. Sam Morgan. Does Sam actually like this marriage arrangement? Frankly I don't know. He doesn't talk any more than he has to. The new Mrs. Morgan ain't no beauty and she ain't no spring chicken, either. But maybe Sam is happy because he's doing his duty. He's paying his debt to society."

"Assuming," said the chief, "that Sam shot Max Garman?"

"Assuming, naturally. There is this unexplained fact, though. We have no record, no way of knowing that Sam actually knew Max, as he told the widow he did. Where or how did Sam know Max? We have only Sam's word, very vague. And Max is dead. And why, all of a sudden, out of the blue, did Sam come to the Garman house and start playing with the orphans? This is a strange coincidence, chief."

"Uh-huh."

"Now we come to the final piece of the puzzle," the lieutenant said. "Where is Sidney Tepper all this time?"

"Assuming that Sidney was Sam's old partner?"

"Assuming, yes."

"Did you check for stoolies? Anybody that could link Sam and Sidney as partners? Or that they even knew each other?"

The lieutenant swallowed in embarrassment. This was the weak part of his case, and he knew it. But he couldn't lie, even if he wanted to.

"I ran a pretty thorough check on that," he said. "Didn't turn up anything."

"But wouldn't you think . . . ?"

"Yes, sir, you'd think that if Sam and Sidney had been partners, somebody would have known about it. Unless . . . unless Sam and Sidney were very clever and secretive. Which I think they were. And which is why they never served second sentences, either of them. They were smart. They profited from their first mistakes."

"Uh-huh."

"Well then, let's take Sidney now. He is with Sam the night Sam has to shoot Max. So he is technically guilty of first-degree murder also. But he does not have the conscience Sam has. And maybe also he is less disturbed because he didn't actually pull the trigger on Max. He lays low. Maybe the partnership is permanently dissolved. But Sidney also reads the papers. Every good burglar does. He reads about the widow and the orphans, but he doesn't cry. Then a year later, he reads a marriage license notice or something. Sam Morgan marrying Leona Garman. Here are two familiar names. But two people he certainly didn't expect would get married. Obviously

Leona doesn't know who Sam really is. But Sam certainly knows who Leona is. Why in the hell, Sidney asks himself, is Sam marrying the widow of the man he shot? And Sidney comes up with an answer completely different from Sam's."

"Which is?"

"Which is this. That Sam's motives are not humanitarian. Maybe Sidney does the same checking that I did. And he finds out that Max Garman did indeed have quite a little bundle of life insurance. Slightly over a hundred grand, in fact. Enough to make Sam overlook the fact Leona ain't no spring chicken, and also to keep him from having silly ideas about a man shouldn't marry the widow of a man he has killed."

The chief had pressed the finger-ends of his two hands together in a kind of praying gesture. "So Sidney thinks of blackmail?"

"Exactly, chief!" The lieutenant said it with unnecessarily warm enthusiasm. The chief needed to be encouraged in this deduction business.

"What then?" the chief asked.

"Sidney contacts his old friend Sam. Very bluntly he asks the question which is bothering him. And when he hears Sam's answer, he laughs. Conscience? Sidney doesn't know what it is. He is a cynic. Also, as you point out, chief, he is a blackmailer. He asks Sam for his cut. Sam maybe gets mad, but he also sees that Sidney can make trouble for him. All right, he tells Sidney, so you think I married Leona for her money. But how can I give you a cut? All right, even if I control the money myself, how can I explain giving a wad of it away? I can't tell her why I had to give it to you, can I? On this point, I think, Sidney, being a smart lad, agrees. In fact, he has probably thought of the difficulty already. You can't explain giving it away, Sam, he says. But you can see to it that a certain amount of cash is lying around the house on a certain night. And you can also see to it that the house is not too hard to get into."

The chief pursed his mouth thoughtfully. "Not a bad idea for Sidney to think of," he said. "Assuming . . . "

"Sure, chief. Assuming. Okay, the night is arranged. The setup is agreed on. Sidney, plying his old trade, enters the old Garman house, now the Morgan house. Kind of history repeating itself, in a way. Only this time it turns out much differently. Sam has not had a fight with Leona, but he is waiting in the dark living room anyway. And he has a gun like old Max had. But he's cleverer than Max was. And he shoots straighter. Knowing that the first payoff to a blackmailer is seldom the last one, he shoots Sidney right in the heart."

The chief dragged his heels off the desk top and sat up ponderously. "Which is what happened, of course," he said. "Sam Morgan shot an intruder entering his house illegally, which he had every right to do. Defense of property. Self-defense."

"Right, chief. We can't touch Sam as long as his self-defense story holds up."

The chief's eyes bored into the lieutenant's own. "Well, does it hold up or doesn't it?"

"On the surface, yes. But there are these coincidences I mentioned. Sam's burglary record, one known offense. His curious job record after prison. The curious fact of an old burglar's marrying the widow of a man who was shot by a burglar. And the whole odd business of two burglaries in the same house, both ending in homicide."

"You're a numbskull, lieutenant. You can't arrest Sam Morgan on evidence like that, much less convict him."

"Yes, sir, I realize that."

"Then what are you telling me this story for?" The chief heaved his vast bulk out of his squeaking chair. He towered over the lieutenant. "What in hell am I supposed to do?"

The lieutenant put on his best air of humility. "You're supposed to deduce now, sir. You're supposed to tell me what to do next. I could check some more. I could doublecheck. I could grill Sam. I could ask Leona some very personal questions which I haven't asked yet . . ."

"Lieutenant, the police department doesn't exist to annoy honest citizens like Leona Morgan."

"What shall I do then, sir? Call the case closed, or shall I go on assuming . . . ?"

The chief exploded at that. He was rather famous for megaton-force explosions. This was one of them. He talked for about ten minutes. He didn't throw the lieutenant off the force. Didn't even demote him. Possibly he didn't think of it. His tirade, briefly, added up to something like this: "You'll assume nothing further, lieutenant. You'll stop being an armchair detective and start being a cop. You can call the Morgan case closed."

The lieutenant's reply, oft-repeated, consisted of: "Yes, sir."

And after that ten minutes of vituperation, he walked out gratefully into the fresh air. He felt good. He still had an instinct, an intuition, that the story he'd told the chief, how Max Garman and

Sidney Tepper had been shot by the same man at the same address, was essentially true, give or take a detail here and there. But he'd received an order. The case was closed. And a really decent burglar wouldn't be bothered.

Sam's conscience was clear. And so was the lieutenant's.

Sweet Smell of Murder

by Allen Lang

Sergeant Read Fowler claims that the cop who makes good on
Saloon Beat is the sort of man who'd also make a great playground supervisor. It takes rare tact, on C-Shift or on the
playground, for the man in authority to keep his charges from building fires on the merry-go-round, fencing with carving knives, or
burying their sisters in the sandbox. The man responsible for a half-
pint ballgame, like the man on the beat, has to umpire so skillfully
that the diamond never explodes into a battlefield.

Not that Three Rivers is a rough town. Actually, visiting salesmen
up from Indianapolis and truckdrivers en route to Chicago find it
absurdly quiet. Keeping the peace in Three Rivers isn't too big a
problem. Counting Sergeant Fowler and the man who answers the
phone at the station, eight men are plenty to keep the traffic flowing
on Main Street and the civic atmosphere clear of violence during
C-Shift's third of the day. Three Rivers is bigger than the crossroads
burg a sheriff can handle with a part-time deputy, and it's smaller
than the city where the cops have to walk their beats in pairs,
phoning the station every half hour as evidence that they haven't
yet been ambushed. For most normal things, Three Rivers is the
ideal size for a town.

At eight P.M., when Fowler's shift comes on duty, the fun and
games are just getting under way. Except for Sundays, holidays, and
election day, when the bars are closed, the main business of the
Saloon Beat is to serve as a sort of friendly Shore Patrol. C-Shift
keeps an eye out for the citizen who follows a quart of martinis with
one cup of coffee—black for the road—then hurries out to the parking
lot to grab up the reins of his two-twenty horsepower. In Three
Rivers, that citizen will be met at the tavern door by a Saloon Beat
cop, who will coax the car keys out of his hand, seat him in the front
seat of a squad car, and chauffeur him home to bed. The teenage
roadrunner, test-flighting his hotrod on deserted streets just before
dawn, may be called to a halt by the same cop. Here the rules are
a little different: after the kid has seen his driver's license confettied
on the pavement, he'll walk home with a traffic summons in his

jeans. In the season when the corn is standing finger-high in the fields outside of town, the C-Shift policeman is called upon to referee the greatest game of them all. He may be found, flashlight in hand, an "I-hate-to-ruin-the-party-but" expression on his face, informing a side-road Romeo that carrying through his celebration of the traditional rites of spring with the Juliet beside him in the car (she's eager, too, but she's only seventeen) could cost him five years more than shooting up a bank.

If the work of Sergeant Read Fowler's C-Shift seems petty, that's because Three Rivers is, after all, a moderately quiet town. Most mornings, the sergeant can write up his log for C-Shift in two lines. However, the Sunday morning that the town lost its only pharmacist, Sergeant Fowler filled three pages of the report book.

Saturday night at nine thirty, Sergeant Fowler made his first stop at Ollie's Oasis. Ollie's place is the town's busiest tavern, a prime checkpoint on the Saloon Beat. As Fowler stepped into the cool, beer-tinted atmosphere of the Oasis, Ollie's radio was blasting out a play-by-play on the state basketball finals, while net fans listened across the bar as raptly as though the radio were reporting the repeal of income tax. Sid Caesar, buffooning an opera, competed from the twenty-one-inch color set that hung from the ceiling in the corner. Below the TV set, the pinball machine was busy making its unique racket. And nearby, some enemy of music had fed the jukebox, and a hog-caller with guitar accompaniment started paying out his five cents' worth of stomp and shout.

Fowler seated himself at the bar and dropped a dime on the counter. He shouted over the din toward Ollie, who was intently mopping the end of the bar nearest the radio. "Everything quiet here?" Fowler demanded.

Ollie, untouched by Fowler's irony, sighed and left the basketball game. He dumped a Coke over a glassful of ice chips and brought it to the policeman, scooping up the dime in the manner of a man unaccustomed to such small change. "Any new developments in the Three Rivers crimewave?" he asked.

Fowler smiled and shook his head.

A drunken tenor solo rose abruptly from one of the parties boothed along the wall. "Hey, Sue! Where's the eight beers I asked you for a week ago? We ain't had enough hops in this corner to wet our feet." Sue Putrament, Ollie's waitress, waved "okay, okay," and swung her tray onto the service section of the bar, a place marked off by a couple of arching pipes like a stanchion. Ollie left Sergeant Fowler to get Sue's beers from the cooler. He flicked them open, cupped glasses over the bottlenecks, and rang up Sue's two dollars. As Sue carried the tray of beers over to the table that had demanded them, Fowler saw that her right eye, in spite of her attempts at cosmetic disguise, was still ringed by a gray bruise.

Fowler looked down the bar toward Chet Putrament, Sue's husband. Chet was nursing a beer and watching his wife, watching to see that none of the wise guys in the barroom reached for her, or whispered to one another with their eyes on her back and laughed male laughter, watching to see whether his wife smiled at any of the malty nonsense her customers offered her. Chet shouldn't be here, Fowler thought. For one thing, he was an obvious focus for trouble. A drunk, clipping his hand across Sue's thigh, could cause an explosion it would take a hundred sutures and a lot of bandages and time to cure. Chet would save more money toward that truck he wanted if he drank less beer. It wasn't fair of him to spy on his wife while she worked to help earn the truck. Fowler shook his head, thinking that he himself was much too lucky, having the fine family that he did, to be moralizing about the troubles of others.

Chet Putrament looked down the bar toward Fowler, saw the sergeant's frowning gaze, and, misinterpreting it, looked quickly away. He knew how the policeman felt about him, about a man whose wife had frequent "accidents" that left her with a black eye or a cut across the face. Chet signaled Ollie for a fresh beer, and sat watching his wife move among the tables.

A big man, his shirt smelling of yesterday's sweat and spilled drinks, banged himself down on the bar stool beside Sergeant Fowler. "Well, bless my bonnie brown eyes!" he said, grabbing hold of Fowler's left biceps. "I get to sit right up next to Three Rivers' celebrated young psychologist. Do you suppose, Sergeant Fowler, that a bit of your erudition might rub off on me?"

Fowler shook his arm free from the man's grip and glanced at his wristwatch. "You're right on schedule, Vanbuskirk," he said. Roger Vanbuskirk ran the drugstore down the street. Evenings, he practiced his second profession, town drunk. This gag about psychology was wearing pretty thin, Fowler thought. His brother cops kidded him about taking extension courses from State, but Vanbuskirk laughed up the notion of a policeman's studying psychology as being wildly ridiculous, something like fitting tap shoes to an elephant.

Vanbuskirk nodded toward Fowler's Coke. "Drinking on duty, Dr. Pavlov? Who's watching your couch?"

"May I buy you one of the same?" Fowler asked him.

"Thank you, but no. I have little taste for such innocuous extracts. What I crave right now are the spirits of peat-smoke, compounded in Glasgow."

Fowler looked down at Vanbuskirk's hands, gripping the beaded bar edge to control their trembling. It was as criminal as murder to allow this man to step behind his prescription counter, he thought. Last winter, when the doctor had prescribed a cough mixture for Fowler's twin boys, Vanbuskirk, still a little buzzed from the night before, had mixed up a compound so heavy on codeine that a dose of it had knocked the kids out for sixteen hours. Now, of course, most of the Three Rivers' doctors carried their medicines with them.

Ollie, not waiting for Vanbuskirk's instructions, was dispensing a double shot of Black Label over ice, adding a squirt from the bottle as a special lagniappe for a volume customer. He set the scotch before the druggist with the reverence due a dollar's worth of whisky. "Soda?" Ollie asked.

"Ollie, I congratulate you on your memory," Vanbuskirk said. "Yes, soda." He reached into his pocket for what Fowler always thought of as the Great Vanbuskirk Fortune, a roll of bills the size of a modest cabbage, its leaves held in place by a broad rubber band. Vanbuskirk worked a twenty out from under the band and slipped it on the bar. "Let me know when that melts away," he said. "There's more where it came from, publican." He sat holding the whisky glass in his left hand, the roll of bills in his right, like a king holding the symbols of his royalty.

Ollie stared at the roll as though trying to determine the denominations of the bills from their exposed edges. "Good take at your drugstore today, Mr. Vanbuskirk?" he asked.

Vanbuskirk shook his head. "If I depended on today's take, I'd be drinking aspirin and water instead of scotch and soda," he said. "And, Ollie, I much prefer this delightful juice." Vanbuskirk raised the glass to his lips and drank very slowly, closing his eyes to savor his favorite anesthetic.

The barroom had become almost quiet the moment Vanbuskirk had exposed his famous bankroll. This, too, was part of Van's nightly ceremony. The noise rose again, but Chet Putrament's gaze still centered on the packet in Vanbuskirk's right hand. Fowler didn't like the look of hunger on Chet's face as he looked at the money. He spoke to Vanbuskirk. "Someday," he said, "somebody's going to accept your invitation to take that roll away from you. You might get hurt."

"Not with you around, sergeant," Vanbuskirk said. "I'm safe, and my money is safe, guarded by your fine little police department. I'd offer up a toast to the Three Rivers police, sergeant, if you were drinking a fluid worthy to the drinking of toasts, rather than that tonic for ailing infants you've got." He finished his scotch, sucking his teeth to make sure he had it all, and raised a finger for another drink.

Sue Putrament, walking past Vanbuskirk's perch on her way to her station at the bar, kept her distance from him like a bird reconnoitering a tethered tomcat. The druggist had pinched or propositioned Sue every time his drunkenness coincided with her propinquity. As she sidled past him, Sue gave Vanbuskirk the look she'd give something spoiled and found in her lunch.

Ollie measured out another double scotch. "No one should carry a bundle of bills that could choke a horse," he announced.

"Don't worry," Vanbuskirk said. "I never congregate with hungry horses. You just tend to your trade, Ollie; I'll manage my finances."

Ollie glowered, and slammed the Black Label back among the other bottles behind the bar.

Vanbuskirk was off. From now on, Fowler thought, Van's course from gaiety to stupor could be charted in any handbook of toxicology, under the heading, "Alcohol." Fowler got up. "I appreciate your testimonial to the Three Rivers cops, Van," he said, "but I still wish you'd check your loot with a bank. They pay interest, you know."

"I heard," Vanbuskirk said. "I'll keep my money close, though. It consoles me."

Fowler turned away. When Ollie switched off the lights at one A.M., Vanbuskirk would still be here, sprawled over the bar, dug in deep toward numbness. He'd been drinking like this for two years, ever since his wife was killed by a drunken driver out in front of the Vanbuskirk Pharmacy. An odd, inverted sort of poetic justice, Fowler thought. Vanbuskirk, like a tooth gone rotten under a crust of clean enamel, had collapsed with his wife's death. He was a hollow man now, trying to fill his emptiness with whisky and the pomp of his bankroll. The Vanbuskirk Pharmacy wasn't likely to be in business much longer. People don't care to have their prescriptions filled by a lush.

He took his time leaving Ollie's Oasis, talking to everyone who wanted to talk, saying hello to the two or three men he hadn't seen here before, identifying them as salesmen visiting the Three Rivers Household Electric plant, or semi-drivers on a night's furlough from the freeway.

When he glanced at Chet Putrament, Chet nodded back, then turned to lift his empty beer bottle to signal for another replacement. He'd be soused by the time his wife got off duty. Maybe by tomorrow, Sue would have a matching set of shiners. If she did, Fowler resolved, he'd arrange a fatherly talk with young Chet Putrament—a fatherly talk in the woodshed tradition, from which Chet might emerge with similar decorations. Sure, the guy had his troubles, but Sue wasn't the cause of them. She had to work, helping him buy the semi-tractor that would establish him as a free-lance trucker, a small business-man in his own right. Then he could get out of the Household Electric shipping room, and Sue could fold up her waitress's apron and put it away for good, and the two of them could begin living the way Chet had promised her they would.

Everybody has troubles, Sergeant Fowler thought as he stepped out into the gray, green-smelling night. He thought of his wife and the boys, smiled, and corrected himself. Everybody had troubles but him.

He made the rounds of the bars as he did six nights a week, drinking spikeless Cokes, refusing testimonial shots of whisky, say-ing hello to all the friendly faces and nodding to all the sullen ones.

Not every call Sergeant Fowler made during his eight hours on duty was to a bar. He talked with his subordinates when he spotted their cars, tested a random selection of Main Street shop doors to make sure that their owners had locked them, talked to the boys at the firehouse. He checked the darker country roads, trying not to embarrass the kids more than necessary, just prowling the squad car past the couples in the parked cars with the red light flashing on top as a go-slow warning.

After half a dozen Cokes in noisy taverns, Fowler was glad to see both hands on his watch pointing up. Lunch time. He drove out toward the country club for a steak sandwich and coffee. Even though he'd forced the club to scrap its three slot machines, most of the members liked to see Fowler show up out there.

Twelve thirty. In half an hour the taverns closed, a condition of one of the statutes of the Sovereign State of Indiana. The twenty-three hours remaining to Sunday were always anticlimactic, Fowler thought. Everything closed down for the day but the churches and, in the afternoon, the YMCA swimming pool. Closing time was the critical time, when the members of the drinking classes sometimes protested the sudden damming-up of the flow of fluids. Fowler phoned Max, the desk man at the station. No squeals, Max reported, using a word he'd picked up off television. No prisoners in the city jail. (This was merely part of Max's routine of reporting. There hadn't been a customer for that jail in the past three months.) "Everything's rosy, sergeant," Max summed up his report.

Fowler parked in front of the Oasis and went in to see whether Ollie needed the moral support of the law to make his customers concede that their revels were ended, that the dry Sabbath had indeed begun. Not tonight. Nearly everyone had departed. Vanbuskirk was clutching his empty glass, sprawling, all-elbows, growling half-words at Ollie. "That's all, Van," Ollie said, speaking slowly with the hopeless patience bartenders show at closing time. "Go on home now. You've got to open your store in less than eight hours."

Vanbuskirk answered with the exaggerated care of drunks. "Won't sell me any more? Well, then! I got a US *Pharmacopoeia,* I'll have you know, and a million bottles of tinctures and extracts back at my store; and any one of them will taste better than this expectorant you've been foisting off on me for the last hour. Perjury, it is, a travesty on the noble name of scotch." Hiccups ended his monologue. Vanbuskirk rotated the whisky glass between his palms, then looked into the soda glass, squinting shrewdly at the ice chips to see whether he could spot the drain his liquor had run out. He brought the roll of money from his pocket and peeled off another twenty, tearing the bill half through in getting it out from under the fat rubber band. Trying to slap the twenty on the bar top with a commanding gesture, he flipped it over onto the duckboards at Ollie's feet.

Ollie picked up the bill and tucked it back into Vanbuskirk's pocket. "Good thing you live near a good supply of aspirin," he said. "Sergeant Fowler?" he asked, spreading his hands in a gesture of defeat.

"You should fix Van a bar stool on wheels," Fowler suggested. "Often as I have to carry this cargo home, I'll have to be joining the longshoreman's union."

"I'd just as soon he didn't come in here in the first place," Ollie said. "Save us both a mess of bother. Bigshot!" he snorted. "Comes in here flashing a queen's ransom, but he's just another wino at heart." Ollie looked at Fowler. "Yeh, I know what you're thinking, sergeant. I sell him his poison at a profit, so who am I to gripe. The thing is I don't like a man drinking up in a week of evenings the money it takes men like me and you a month to make. Will you tell Vanbuskirk that, sergeant? Will you tell him to stay clear of my place?"

"Tell him yourself, Ollie, when he brings his thirst in here on Monday," Fowler snapped. "Come on, Van." He hoisted the druggist from the stool, aimed him at the door, and half-carried, half-dragged the man out to his squad car.

Fowler draped Vanbuskirk over the front seat of the police car, got in, and drove the four blocks to the Vanbuskirk Pharmacy, across the street from Osborn's Grocery. He fireman-carried him to the back door, tugged his burden's keychain free to open the door, and sprawled him onto the cot in the cubicle at the back of the store. Undoing Vanbuskirk's shoelaces and tugging off his shoes and stockings, Fowler tried to make the man comfortable. A false and temporary comfort, he thought, with the hangover Van would have in the morning and with kids on their way to Sunday School rattling the front door, demanding comic books and Cokes to lighten their journey. He tried to work the bundle of money out of Vanbuskirk's pocket, meaning to lock it up in the open desk drawer. Vanbuskirk, feeling hands on his money, sat up straight, opened his unfocused eyes, and lashed out with his fists like a drowning man. Sergeant Fowler pushed him back onto the cot. "Okay, bruise yourself on the Vanbuskirk Treasure, I don't care." He draped a cotton blanket across him, saw that the flashlight stood beside the head of the cot in case Vanbuskirk had to answer his phone on an emergency call (pity the patient whose prescription would be compounded here tonight! Fowler thought), and set the alarm clock for opening time, eight thirty.

His duties as valet over for the night, Fowler left the drugstore by the back door, trying it after him to make sure it was locked. He wasn't really much bothered by this nightly duty of carting the druggist home and tucking him in. What was bad was that the man was killing himself. That, Fowler thought with grim humor, was a felony.

Fowler got back into his car. Two and a half hours to go, then three days off. He generally took his wife and the twins up to Blue Lake on his off-days. The kids would spend their time screaming on the aquaplane behind the ancient outboard, piloted by their mother, while he sat on the porch of their cottage, writing up his latest lesson in the correspondence course in psychology, or working toward the Civil Service exams for police lieutenant. The Three Rivers department needed a police lieutenant like Monaco needs a generalissimo, or Nebraska an admiral of the fleet; but it never hurt a man to know his trade. Maybe a bigger town? Chicago? Don't worry about that yet, Fowler thought, parking in front of the station. Think instead of this afternoon, hot sunlight on his naked back, the noise of the kids tearing up the beach, and that pneumatic woman of his toting a couple of chilled beers out to the porch to quench his studious thirst. Yeh.

He walked up the sandstone steps into the Three Rivers police station. Max looked up, grinning, from his desk. "Get all the lubritoriums padlocked?" he asked.

"They were really jumping tonight, Maxie," Fowler said. "There'll be many a red eye in church this morning." He sat down, his fingers together, reached up, arching his back and yawning. "Long week," he observed. "Every night, I had to carry Roger Vanbuskirk home. His way of life may be ruining Van, but it furnishes me with a great course of calisthenics."

"What do you suppose will come of Vanbuskirk, sergeant?" Max asked.

"What's going to come of all of us?" Fowler asked. "Same thing with Van, only sooner for him. Wish we could do something about him. He invites grand larceny every time he flashes that General Motors' payroll he carries. Maybe the possession of untold riches builds his self-esteem; but some night, Max, that man is going to get himself rolled."

"Don't see what you're worried about, Sergeant Fowler," Max said. "Vanbuskirk gets so drunk you could snatch out his appendix without his noticing it. If someone does roll him, he won't know it."

"You're wrong about that," Fowler said. "Van's got this plutocrat-reflex. Touching his bankroll is like offering profane love to a virgin: he automatically protects what he most prizes. He'll get hurt if anyone goes for that roll seriously." Fowler stood, frowning, his hands thrust deep into his pockets. "Max, you know maybe I'd be better off in Chicago, where I could be strictly cop, listening to the complaints of strangers, arresting anonymous people."

"You might be better off," Max agreed, "but Three Rivers wouldn't." The phone went off, giving the desk man immediate occasion to cover his embarrassment by rattling off the formula of his name, rank, and duty. Max listened, tugged the report book straight before him, uncapped his pen, glanced at the clock across the room, and took rapid notes in his handwriting that looked so much like italic type. "We'll take care of it right away, Mrs. Osborn," he said into the phone.

Sergeant Fowler watched Max hang up. "What's she phoning for, at two o'clock in the morning?" he asked. "Mice in her cracker barrel?" Mrs. Osborn ran the grocery store across the street from Vanbuskirk's Pharmacy.

"She glanced out her bedroom window and saw a small light in Van's place," Max said. "Says she's worried. Fire, maybe."

"More likely, reflected headlights on the plate glass window," Fowler said. "Why the devil didn't she wake up those sleeping beauties over at the firehouse, if she's got fire on the brain?" He shrugged. "I'll run on over to make sure Vanbuskirk's sleeping sound, though. See you later, Maxie."

Three Rivers was deep in its Sunday sleep as Fowler drove past the gray hulk of the county courthouse. Way off on the horizon of his hearing was the burp of the transcontinental trucks, flatulent giants, booming over the freeway. He parked the police car in front of Vanbuskirk's Pharmacy and got out. There was a flicker of light and a silhouette in the second story window of Osborn's Grocery. Fowler waved toward the half-visible Mrs. Osborn, assuring her that the situation was now well in hand. He picked up his flashlight and looked through the front window into Van's store. Everything looked all right from there, everything but that dim light coming around the partition behind which Vanbuskirk slept. Probably, Fowler thought, after getting up to ease some gastrointestinal crisis incident upon drinking all that Black Label, Van had fallen back onto his cot and left his flashlight burning.

He went to the back door of the drugstore and tried the knob. Locked as tight as he'd left it, an hour ago. He pounded on the door with the side of his fist, then listened. Quiet inside. He pressed his ear to the panel of the door. There were not even the snuffling noises of Vanbuskirk's drugged sleep. Giving up here, he walked around the building, flashing his light at the lower windows.

On the darkest side of the store, his flashlight beam disappeared into a black rectangle. The half window leading down to the basement had been pried open and ripped from its hinges. Fowler crouched and played his light over the furnace, the cartons of hair tonic and soap. Everything was furred with coal dust. He dropped his legs through the opening and dropped down to the basement floor. What the hell, he thought, his uniform was due for cleaning anyway.

He walked to the right of the dim footprints that led from the window. Either the man who'd come in before him had left by the back door, with the night-latch set to lock behind him, or he was still in the building, adequately warned by now of Fowler's presence by the pounding on the door. He snapped open the flap of his holster and tucked it back out of the way. At the stairway he paused to memorize the cartons he'd have to avoid on the way up, and the number of steps to the stairs. Then he snapped off the flashlight and went up a step at a time, transferring his weight from one tread to the next cautiously. At the top, Fowler found the doorknob and silently twisted it open.

Chewing gum. The air at the back of the drugstore was sticky with the sweet smell of chewing gum. Mint? Wintergreen, that was it. Sergeant Fowler stood silently in the basement doorway, inspecting the silhouettes of the drug and cosmetic counters, the amber glass from the bottles lit up by Vanbuskirk's flashlight, lying on the floor and tilted toward the front of the store. There was no sound of human breath.

The light switch was beside the back door. Fowler walked slowly toward it, his left thumb poised over the cut-on of his own flashlight, his right hand hovering over his gun butt. The heel of his boot struck an oily spot on the linoleum floor. Fowler dropped his flashlight, banged against the wall on the palms of his hands, scrambled back to his feet, and slammed on the lights; all in the almost-instantaneous response to his reflexive reaction to falling.

In the cubby at the back of the store, Vanbuskirk lay half under his cot, his throat cut, a puddle of blood gluing his hair to the linoleum. Fowler glanced down at the heel of his boot. No, he hadn't slipped in blood. It had been the oily fluid pooled around a broken bottle. He knelt and dipped his fingertips into the puddle. He sniffed them. This was the chewing gum odor he'd noticed when he first opened the basement door. He unfolded the label from the broken bottle. "Oil of Wintergreen (Methyl Salicylate), USP. Synthetic."

Fowler picked up the phone the way they'd taught him to at the academy so that his prints wouldn't obliterate any already on the instrument. He dialed the station. "Max, this is Fowler. Get the chief out of the sack and over to Vanbuskirk's Pharmacy. Tell him to use the front door. Van's been murdered. And Maxie, you'd better call the sheriff, ask if we can borrow his lab men."

Hanging up, Fowler went to the front door and unlocked it for the chief. Then he rejoined Vanbuskirk. He patted the body. Still warm. The roll of bills was gone, of course, together with that torn twenty Ollie had stuffed into Van's pocket. Fowler brought his hand away from the dead man's chest with a grunt of surprise. Not only had Van's throat been cut, but he'd been stabbed several times. And his face was marked, Fowler noticed, the sort of marks a man might have if someone had slapped stiff fingers across his eyes a dozen times or so. So Vanbuskirk had put up a fight to guard his money. Then he'd been knifed. Not a clean butchering job, either; but a violent catharsis for rage, worked out on a dying man.

The chief came in the front door, walking soft in slippers. The sergeant in charge of A-Shift, wakened two hours early, waited outside in the chief's car. At first, Fowler thought the chief had switched from khaki to the sort of shirt Mr. Truman was accustomed to wear in Florida; then he realized that what he was looking at was the chief's pajama top. The chief spoke with exaggerated softness, the way some men do when they're holding tight to their self-control. "Where is he, Sergeant Fowler?"

Sergeant Fowler showed him.

"Who would want to do a thing like this, Read?" the chief asked, swallowing hard.

"Whoever wanted a fat chunk of tax-free income for five minutes' work," Fowler said.

He then gave his boss a rapid rundown on Mrs. Osborn's call, on the open basement window, the tracks in the coal dust downstairs, and the shattered bottle of wintergreen.

"You must have somebody to suspect more than you do others," the chief insisted. "We can't use that cliche, 'an unidentified prowler.'"

"Yeh, I've got some people in mind," Fowler said, "but we can't call them suspects yet. Interviewees, maybe. I'll want to talk to Ollie the bartender, for one." Fowler paused. "What is Ollie's last name, chief?" he asked.

The chief shrugged. "Never thought of his having one, Read. Just Ollie-the-Bartender, for the last thirty years. Do you think he did it?"

"Maybe," Fowler said. "No special reason he should have, though. None that I know of." He leafed through the phone book. "Ollie Jones," he reported. "Soon's I came to the J's, by association I remembered his name was Jones."

"Ollie maybe have a grudge against Vanbuskirk?" the chief asked.

"A grudge? Not exactly," Fowler said. "More a bunch of gripes. Ollie told me at closing time this morning that he didn't want any more of Vanbuskirk's trade, not if he commissioned to buy all the whisky in Scotland."

"You didn't care much for the late Roger Vanbuskirk yourself, did you, Read?" the chief asked.

"He nearly poisoned my sons with a concoction he blended during a hangover, when he couldn't quite make out the doctor's writing. If they'd died . . ."

"But your boys didn't die," the chief said. "So we'll cross you off our little black list. Who else?"

"Sue Putrament. Vanbuskirk has been known to offer Sue the supreme demonstration of his affection, which she refused violently. The time I saw this happen, Vanbuskirk was so drunk he didn't seem to feel the side of Sue's hand hit his mouth."

"And that brings in her husband."

"Chet Putrament has an evil temper," Fowler said. "Yes, Chet and Sue Putrament will have to be interviewed. Maybe all the people who were in Ollie's Oasis tonight will have to make statements and establish alibis. Must have been fifty, sixty people saw that bankroll tonight. A man spending his last quarter on his twelfth beer is likely to notice another man flashing a roll that could buy a truckload of the stuff. But besides all the witnesses to Van's demonstration last night, every social drinker this side of the Wabash has heard of the Vanbuskirk Fortune. It won't be easy picking a killer out of that crowd."

"We have those footprints downstairs to work from," the chief suggested.

"Sure. But all our potential suspects have feet." Fowler glanced into the phone book again, getting Ollie's address, and that of the Putraments. "I'll get to work waking up the populace."

"I'd best phone the paper, or we'll never hear the last of it," the chief said. "They can make enough off their space rates to the AP to pay off the mortgage on their press. Won't get another chance like this soon."

"Hope not," Fowler said. "We need every taxpayer we've got. Watch the prints on the phone, chief. We may need even those."

"What did you say that stuff is that smells like after-shave lotion?" the chief asked, looking down at the pool around the broken bottle.

"Wintergreen," Fowler said. "You know, chief, that sweet smelling stuff might just help us find the man who did this." He read the labels on the stock shelves, and found what he wanted on the shelf just above Vanbuskirk's cot. He took the bottle down and showed it to his boss. "The killer must have knocked that other bottle of this off the shelf while he was fighting Vanbuskirk. Van put up quite a struggle when he thought his money was threatened; I found that out myself." Sergeant Fowler tucked the second bottle of wintergreen into his back pocket, like a hip flask.

"What are you going to do with that?" the chief asked.

"Whoever knifed Vanbuskirk will never admit it unless we prove it so tightly that he's got no way out, or unless he's emotionally off balance while I'm questioning him," Fowler explained. "This bottle of wintergreen could be the psychological lever I can use to tip the murderer over. If it doesn't work out that way, we've still got those footprints downstairs, and there may be prints around. What I'm going to try will only take an hour or so, anyway."

"Okay, Read. If this lever of yours doesn't pry anything loose, we'll fall back on footwork and the sheriff's laboratory man. But I wish you luck."

"Thanks, chief."

Fowler went out to his car, conscious of the bottle bulging his back pocket, a lump about the size of a hand grenade. With luck, that bottle might blast the mystery of Vanbuskirk's death wide open.

Driving south toward Ollie Jones's home, Fowler added up what he knew about the man. Ollie had a reputation for being a fast man to pick up a nickel, a slow man to lay one down. Since he supported his greed with hard work and sound business sense, though, no one felt bitter about Ollie's success. He'd built the Oasis from a neighborhood beer-bar to the most popular tavern in town. The Oasis had paid for his home out on the South Crescent, where Ollie's neighbors were doctors and lawyers and corner-office executives at Household Electric. Ollie Jones was no Macbeth, Fowler thought. If he'd knifed Vanbuskirk, it had been in a fit of rage, not as part of a shrewd plan to add a couple of hundred dollars to his bank account. Ollie would have picked up the money afterwards, of course, because Ollie wasn't the sort to leave money lying around. The question was, had Ollie hated Roger Vanbuskirk enough to slash his throat open, then drive the knife blade into his chest and belly half a dozen times to boot? That was a lot of hate for a little bartender to hold, Fowler thought.

He parked in the Jones driveway and pushed the doorbell. It chimed rather than rang, an effect typical of Ollie's South Crescent gentility. There were footsteps after a while, the light flashed on outside the front door, and the door opened six inches, checked by a chain. "Ollie Jones?" Fowler asked, unable to see him, dazzled by the light.

The chain rattled and banged down. "Come in, Sergeant Fowler," Ollie said, opening the door. "What's the matter? Something at the Oasis? Fire?" He looked anxiously at Fowler.

"Nothing like that. Something Freudian, the way everybody's worried about fire tonight," Fowler said. "I just want to ask you a few questions, Mr. Jones."

"Hey, now! What's this 'Mr. Jones' line leading up to? Don't get official with me, Sergeant Fowler. Me and the Alcoholic Beverage Commission get along just fine, my city liquor license is paid up and in-dated, and me and the mayor . . ." Ollie squeezed two fingers together " . . . are like that. Don't start—"

"Okay, Ollie," Fowler interrupted. "This is something we can sit down and discuss." He went into the dark living room and sat on the sofa, shifting his weight so that he wasn't sitting on the bottle. Ollie sat down across from him, looking worried, but not, Fowler thought, with a worry of murder-suspect proportions. Ollie's anxiety seemed more the sort a man shows in the anteroom of the Internal Revenue Service. Well, if he was cutting corners, that didn't matter right now; cutting throats was the business of the evening. "Ollie, did you notice anything peculiar after I'd driven off with Vanbuskirk this morning?" Fowler asked.

"Peculiar? I noticed that I was tired. Still am. But that's not peculiar."

"Nobody followed us, or made especial comment about us?" Fowler asked.

"I didn't see anyone behaving funny," Ollie said. "Of course some of the crowd had had a few, and I was pretty busy."

"Of course," Fowler agreed. "Ollie, will you do me one more favor? Just close your eyes for a minute?"

Ollie leaned forward, staring at Fowler in the darkness. "I'd have sworn those were pure Cokes you were drinking," he said. "What's with this runaround, Sergeant Fowler?"

"Humor me, please," Fowler asked. "Close your eyes."

"Okay." Ollie closed his eyes and leaned back in his chair, sighing. "You may not be able to persuade me to open them before noon, though."

Fowler took the bottle of wintergreen from his back pocket, uncapped it, and shoved the open bottle under Ollie's nose. "What is this, Ollie?" he demanded.

Ollie opened his eyes and looked down at the open bottle. "So that's what you been drinking!" he said. "No, thanks. I wouldn't care for any."

"I wasn't offering you a drink," Fowler said, feeling that his theory had worked him into a ridiculous sort of situation. "I just want to know whether you recognize this smell."

"Yeh," Ollie said. "Creme de menthe, isn't it? Or maybe that kind of foreign lady's-drink that comes in a skinny bottle with a twig inside. Why all this nonsense about sniffing at liquor on a Sunday morning, sergeant?"

Fowler capped the wintergreen bottle and returned it to his hip pocket. "Okay, Ollie, we'll abandon the subject. Do you carry a pocket knife?"

Ollie pushed himself out of his chair and plodded over to the stairway. "Bring it right down," he said. "I'll tell my wife that you and me are gonna play mumblety-peg, till sunup."

After a minute or so, Ollie plodded back down the stairs with a knife in his hand. Wearily, he presented it to Sergeant Fowler. "Wife's asleep," he said, his tone indicating that she'd betrayed him by sleeping while he was forced to remain awake.

Fowler looked at Ollie's knife. A switchblade. He touched the button and eight inches of blade flashed out, quick as a magician's trick. "You can get ninety days in jail for carrying this thing," he remarked. "Five hundred dollars' fine, too, if you stand in front of a rough judge."

"Are you shaking down everyone in town for switchblades, or just me?" Ollie asked. "Okay, I broke the law; so give me ninety days. But make it in a cell that's got a bed in it."

Fowler held the open knife up to the hall light. "What's this stuff back in the groove?" he asked. "Rust?"

"Let me see," Ollie said, reaching for the knife. Unthinking, Fowler handed it back to him, then stepped back, remembering the punctures in Vanbuskirk's chest. "That ain't rust, Sergeant Fowler," Ollie said. "That's blood."

Fowler rested his hand on his pistol butt.

"Yeh, blood," Ollie said. "I docked the tails of my brother-in-law's new boxer puppies Saturday. He didn't have the heart to do it himself. He was afraid the pups'd grow up hating him if he cut them. He didn't care if they grew up hating me."

Fowler let his hand drop away from his pistol. "Sorry I bothered you, Ollie," he said. "I'll have to take this knife along with me, though, now that I've seen it. That new law, you know."

"All right," Ollie agreed. "But you can tell the State Legislature that I'm going to bill them five bucks for it. I bought that knife a year before they passed the law that said I couldn't have one." He opened the front door. "Can I ask you what this is really about, Sergeant Fowler?"

"Roger Vanbuskirk was knifed to death this morning," Fowler said.

"God!" Ollie exploded. "And me with a bloody knife in my pocket. Now I'll never get to sleep."

Fowler put Ollie's switchblade in the glove compartment of his car. If necessary, he'd send it down to Indianapolis to have those bloodstains analyzed. Indianapolis could tell whether that blood was Vanbuskirk's, or whether it belonged to a set of bob-tailed boxer puppies.

Three thirty A.M. Sergeant Fowler looked in his notebook for the address of the Putraments' walk-up apartment. After he got there, he spent five minutes thumbing the doorbell. Finally, the stairwell light flicked on, and someone ran down the steps, unlocked the door, and opened it. It was Sue Putrament, wearing a flannel bathrobe over her pajamas. The reason for her delay in answering the bell was apparent in the damp hair over her forehead. But the cold water she'd splashed over her face had failed to clear the marks of weeping from her eyes or to chill pinkness into the slate-colored, side-of-the-hand bruise over her left cheekbone.

Fowler reached up to run his finger gently along the bruise. "What was his excuse this time, Sue?" he asked.

"It was nothing, Sergeant Fowler," Sue insisted. "Chet had maybe a beer or two too many. Did the neighbors complain about the noise? I'm sorry about the noise, but Chet's asleep now and everything's fine."

"I want to talk to him."

"He's asleep," Sue repeated. "Can't you skip it this time, Sergeant Fowler? Chet didn't mean to hurt me, and it won't happen again. He's just so worried because we can't seem to get money in the bank for that truck of his."

"May I come in, Mrs. Putrament?" Fowler asked.

Sue glanced up the stairs, toward her sleeping husband. "All right.

But he didn't hurt me, sergeant. You won't arrest him, will you? It would only be worse, if we had to pay a fine."

"There's no danger of Chet's being fined," Fowler promised her. He followed Sue up the stairs into the three-room apartment. The front room—living-room-plus-kitchen—smelled of onions, fried potatoes, and sleeping drunk, with a faint undertone of wintergreen. Fowler lifted his fingers to his nose. Maybe the only wintergreen in here was the bottle in his back pocket, and the stuff he'd picked up on his fingertips back in the drugstore. But maybe Chet Putrament had brought some of that smell up here on Roger Vanbuskirk's bankroll. "May I see your bathroom, Sue?" Fowler asked.

Sue looked startled at his request; then, her hostess-instinct taking over, she pointed to the bathroom door. Fowler went in, switched on the light, and looked into the shower stall. The tile floor was puddled. He went back out to Sue. "Did Chet take a shower when he came home?"

"I made him take one," Sue said. "I was trying to sober him up with cold water. That's when he hit me. You see, you can't really blame him."

Fowler took the bottle from his pocket and unscrewed the cap. "Have you smelled anything like this earlier this evening, Sue?" he asked.

She turned away from the bottle. "No," she said. "I don't like that smell."

Fowler capped the bottle and nested it back in his pocket. "Most people find it very pleasant," he said. "I'm going to have to take Chet down to the station for a while, Sue."

"He didn't really hurt me, sergeant," Sue protested.

Fowler went over to the bedroom doorway and switched on the light. Chet Putrament, sprawled over the middle of the double bed, growled at the light and threw his forearm over his eyes. "Get up, Chet," Fowler said. He picked up Chet's clothing, draped over the back of a chair beside the open window. Carrying the things to the bed, he patted them for the roll of bills, or a knife. The bills weren't there, and neither was the murder weapon.

Chet came awake suddenly, threw the clothes off his chest onto the floor, and belched gigantically. "What the hell?" he demanded of the universe. "Can't a man even sleep any more?"

"Get dressed, Chet," Fowler snapped. "You're coming with me to the police station."

"I won't sign a complaint, Sergeant Fowler," Sue said, standing in the doorway. "Why take him in, if I won't sign a complaint?"

Fowler didn't answer. He picked up Chet's shoes from under the bed, four feet apart, and looked at their soles. He couldn't see coal dust there, but maybe the lab man's microscope could. "Will you bring your husband another pair of shoes, Sue?" he asked.

"He can wear those," Sue insisted. She held the bathrobe tight around her, drawn defensively close at the collar.

"I'd rather Chet wore another pair of shoes, Sue," Fowler said gently.

Sue bit her lip, then went to the tiny closet and brought out a pair of tennis shoes. Chet was silently dressing himself, in an automatic way that showed that he didn't yet realize that this wasn't an ordinary getting-up in the morning.

"May I come along with Chet to the station?" Sue asked.

"By all means."

She disappeared into the bathroom with her waitress's uniform in her hand. In the moment she took to change, Sue also laid pancake makeup heavily over the bruises on her face. On a girl Sue's age, the effect of the thick makeup was ludicrous. Poor kid, Fowler thought. He carried Chet's shoes with him down to the squad car, and the three of them rode to the station.

Max was still on the desk, though A-Shift's desk man had shown up. Max had his pen tip poised over the report book as Fowler came in between Chet and Sue Putrament. He looked at Sue's camouflaged wounds, then at Chet's puffy-eyed look of arrogance, and wrinkled his nose in a manner that showed that he'd formed a moral judgment. "Are you booking him, sergeant?"

"Yes, Max. Interrogation in the murder of Roger Vanbuskirk," Fowler said.

"Murder?" The bruised, drunken look on Chet's face broke away, replaced by panic; he twisted to get Fowler's hand off his upper arm.

Fowler let him go without a struggle. Chet fell against Max's desk, then stood, holding to the desk for support. "You were in Ollie's Oasis tonight till closing time, weren't you?" Fowler asked.

"You know I was!"

"I just want to ask what you saw there," Fowler said. He turned to Sue. "Please wait here, Mrs. Putrament. I'd better talk to your husband alone. Max will get you some coffee, if you like."

"I want a lawyer," Chet snapped.

Fowler took a dime from his pocket and handed it to Chet. "There's a pay phone in the men's room over there," he said. "Phone anyone you like. We'll wait till he gets here."

Sergeant Fowler's willingness to accept his demand left Chet undecided what to do. He looked at the dime in his palm, then suddenly flipped it back to the sergeant. "Hell, I don't need a lawyer to tell you what I saw at Ollie's," he said. "Come on, let's get this over with."

They went into the chief's office. Sergeant Fowler didn't switch on the lights. The furniture in the room was outlined in the light that came in over the transom. "Sit down, Chet," he said. Fowler sat behind the chief's desk, opened the drawer to make sure that the flashlight was there, and stared at Chet for a moment.

"Saving electricity?" Chet asked, his voice strained, but trying for the light touch. "Us taxpayers ought to be grateful to you for cutting the town's light bill."

"Where did you go after Ollie's Oasis closed, Chet?" Fowler asked.

"Where's to go at one thirty on an Indiana Sunday morning?" Chet demanded. "I went home, with Sue."

"While you were in Ollie's, did you see Vanbuskirk holding a large sum of money in his hands, from which he paid for his drinks?"

"Sure, I saw him; everybody saw Big-Deal Vanbuskirk and his bankroll. That's what he liked, for people to stare at that money of his, and think, What a big shot! That rotten phony!"

"Vanbuskirk a phony?" Fowler asked. "I thought he was a good man, an honest businessman—"

"He was a rotten phony!" Chet shouted. "Drinking up every cent he had, losing his business, fooling people." He nodded toward Fowler, half-visible across the desk. "You think I'm someone to talk, maybe. You think I shouldn't talk, when I drink myself. Well, listen, Fowler. I drink beer, and I can afford beer—not scotch. I drink because I've got to stay in Ollie's and keep an eye on Sue, so that the hoodlums that hang out there won't get fresh with her."

"Why did you hit Sue tonight, Chet?"

"Hit her? I never hit her. Is that woman lying about me again? Still trying to get me in trouble?"

"Why'd you hit her, Chet?" Fowler insisted.

"And you're helping her!" Chet shouted, jumping to his feet. "You're trying to break her up with me. You making a play for Sue yourself, sergeant? She's a pretty girl, and you've got a pretty uniform. What's it matter that you're both married? Is that why you're always hanging around Ollie's place when you're supposed to be on duty?" Chet was screaming. "Get dumb old Chet out of the way; then you and Sue . . . " Chet was leaning across the desk, the veins in his neck silhouetted against the light from the top of the door. "It won't work, Fowler! You're just as phony as Vanbuskirk, but you won't get away with it!"

"Putrament!" Fowler shouted back. He jumped to his feet, snapped on the flashlight, nailing the beam between Chet's eyes. He hurled the bottle of wintergreen across Putrament's shoulder. It smashed against the wall, and the candy smell of the stuff filled the air. "You knifed him, Chet."

"He was a damned phony, like all of you, with that Mickey Mouse money of his—" Chet leaped over the desk, fumbling in his pocket, searching wildly for something that wasn't there. Fowler lifted the flashlight and rapped it against the side of Chet's head. Chet went down to a kneeling position beside the desk, sobbing.

Sergeant Fowler switched on the lights and opened the door. "Max!" he called. "Bring in a pencil and some paper for Mr. Putrament. He's got something he wants to write for us."

And Chet Putrament did write down everything. He wrote that they'd find the knife and the money he'd taken from Vanbuskirk in the toilet tank in his apartment. The A-Shift sergeant left at once to pick them up. Chet wrote that Sue didn't know what he'd done. He wrote this several times. He'd hit her, sure, when she'd insisted on knowing what the minty smell was he came in with, and why there was blood on his hands, and why he'd insisted on taking a shower at two A.M. But Sue didn't know what he'd done.

The A-Shift sergeant came back from the Putrament apartment with the roll of bills, damp, still held by Vanbuskirk's broad rubber band. He handed the money to Sergeant Fowler, together with the knife that had killed Roger Vanbuskirk. This was a switchblade, almost exactly like the one Fowler had taken from Ollie Jones. "The knife was strapped under the rubber band to anchor the money in the tank," the day shift's sergeant said.

Fowler pushed the button and looked at the wicked blade that had snapped out. "Once the medical examiner's report was in, telling what sort of blade had made Vanbuskirk's wounds, Ollie would have been in big trouble," he said, "dog blood notwithstanding." He closed the knife and laid it on Max's desk to be labeled for the court. Then he flipped the rubber band off the Vanbuskirk Fortune. The outer bill was the twenty Van had torn that morning; evidently, Chet Putrament had added it to the roll. Under the twenty were a ten, a five, and two ones. "Thirty-seven dollars, genuine," he said. He stripped off a single bill from the inside. The paper was slimy, and the green ink had smeared.

The chief hurried in, freshly-shaved and with the pajama top replaced by a uniform shirt and tie. "Max told me what you found, Read," he said. He took the phony bill Sergeant Fowler was holding and held the wet paper under the light. He read aloud the printing on the bill, " 'Ten Rollars, United Snakes of Albania. STAGE MONEY: OF NO VALUE.' " The chief gave Fowler the bill and sighed. "Tough. Vanbuskirk was broker than we realized, and prouder, in his oddball way. He was so broke he had to dazzle the drinking peasants with a wad of stage money," the chief said. "It's kind of a shame his secret had to come out this way, post-mortem. I understand the whole story now, Read, but for one thing. Why did you have to perfume my office with a busted bottle of oil of wintergreen?"

"Chief, when Vanbuskirk felt Chet Putrament working his roll out of his pocket, he woke up and grabbed his flashlight, turning its light into Chet's eyes. I couldn't get that roll away from Van earlier because no matter how drunk he got, Vanbuskirk kept part of his mind guarding that bundle. He must have been afraid of having it stolen, and of the thief showing up his masquerade with stage money. Anyway, Chet grabbed both the light and the money, dropped the bills, and hit Vanbuskirk to shut him up. Then he looked at the money he'd dropped. You know Chet's temper, chief. When he found that nearly all the money he'd fought so hard to get was garbage, he went wild. While he was getting even with Vanbuskirk for making a fool of him, punching holes in Van with his switchblade, Chet knocked a bottle of oil of wintergreen off a shelf.

"In your office, I repeated the same stimuli. Made Chet get mad, which is easy enough to do. Dark room. A sudden flashlight beam in the eyes. Breaking glass, and the smell of wintergreen. Chet, having the sound and smell and anger and brilliant light of a couple of hours ago burst upon him all at once, lost control of himself, tried to kill me, forgetting that his knife was in the toilet tank with his worthless loot. His nervous system was just carrying through the program it had used before in this situation. Except that this time his intended victim was sober, and ready to club him on the side of the head with a flashlight."

The chief glanced up at the clock. "Breakfast time, sergeant. And you've got three days to get this mess out of your system."

"No relaxation for me," Fowler said. "I've got to fight Sunday traffic out to Blue Lake; then I've got to work on my correspondence course."

"What are you studying this week?"

"Conditioned response," Fowler said. He put on his cap. "Chief, do me a favor? Air out your office while I'm gone. Somehow, I can't stand the stink of wintergreen."

The Donor

by Dan J. Marlowe

When I took a trip west, I was picked up on a murder rap and was found guilty by a jury. The judge pronounced the death sentence. It didn't matter that for once I was innocent. It seemed that this was what I had unconsciously been preparing for nearly all of my life.

I had gone to reform school when I was twelve, prison when I was eighteen, and spent most of my life in one penitentiary or another. I've stolen cars, cashed bad checks, burglarized stores, and committed armed robberies. During any given ten-year period, I was seldom outside the walls of an institution for more than a few months at a time.

So, at forty-eight, with the handwriting on the wall, I decided to leave life with more style than I had lived it. I might not have lived well, but I could die well. When the automatic appeal had been denied, I told my court-appointed lawyer that I wouldn't need him any more. I settled down to the death-row routine of tearing pages from a calendar and waiting for the big day.

You'd think the warden would have been happy to have a prisoner who wasn't always bugging him for some special privilege or other, but he wasn't. For some reason my attitude seemed to bother him.

"It's not natural for a man in your position to show so little concern," Warden Raymond worried.

"How would you know what's natural, warden?" I asked. "All you know about prisons you got out of books. You've had your appointment for only a year, and you go home every night. You've got a lot to learn."

He didn't get mad. He just shook his head. He looked like a tired David Niven except that his hair was reddish-brown. He had dark circles under his eyes most of the time. There was a prison joke about those dark circles. Warden Raymond had a young wife, a tall, buxom, hippy girl who exuded a rare blend of sex and innocence.

Before I landed on death row, I'd seen her occasionally when she came inside the walls for prison activities. Most often she played the piano at some of the shows. She could walk between two lines of

240

silent men, nodding in friendly fashion from side to side, entirely unaware of the sparks thrown off by her healthy young body. There wasn't a man in the prison who didn't envy Warden Raymond the dark circles under his eyes.

The chaplain came to see me a few times, but I ran him off. "It's got to be better the second time around, Pilot," I said to him. The men called him the Sky Pilot. He wasn't able to cope with my theories on reincarnation, so he stopped coming.

My only other visitor was Warden Raymond. The death-row cell was a large one. It contained a cot, a small table with a pair of chairs, and a few shelves and bookcases plus the usual sanitary arrangements. The warden would have himself admitted by the always-present guard, stand in front of me for a moment shifting his weight from one foot to the other, then sit down. I'd roll onto my side and set the book I'd been reading on the floor beside the cot.

The warden made more frequent trips from his office to my cell as the big day grew closer. Each time I saw him he looked worse. It was going to be the first execution for each of us, but to look at him you'd think he was the one who was going to ride the lightning.

"You know the—uh—execution is only a few weeks away," he said to me one day, lighting up a cigarette in fumbling fashion.

"I know."

"Have you decided which—uh—which method you want us to use? There are two approved methods of execution in this state, hanging and the firing squad."

I tried to sound flippant. "Back east they have this cheap power, warden. I thought everyone went for electrocution nowadays."

"You have a choice," he answered. He didn't sound happy even telling me about it.

"Okay, I'll take the firing squad," I said.

I started to reach for my book, thinking the visit was ended, but the warden spoke urgently. "Doesn't this bother you? Don't you feel—uh—odd, having to choose the way you're going to die?"

"Why, no. If you've got to go, and I don't seem to have much choice about that, what's so hard about selecting the method?"

He grimaced and left the cell.

During the next couple of weeks I ate well and got plenty of rest. I gained five pounds and the warden lost ten. He obviously spent more time thinking about the execution than I did. The poor guy had too much empathy for his own good. He even tried to get the governor to commute my sentence to life imprisonment, and came to my cell almost in tears when he failed. He was getting on my nerves a little bit, although it's hard to dislike a man because he doesn't want to kill you.

Then, when the execution was a week away, the warden showed up in front of my cell with a stranger. Instead of his usual uneasiness, Warden Raymond's manner displayed embarrassment. "This is Dr. Sansom," he said to me. "He'd like to talk to you."

I sat up on my cot. This Dr. Sansom must have some kind of clout. Not every doctor, even, makes it onto death row. The guard came over and unlocked the door, but only the doctor entered the cell.

"I'll leave you two alone," Warden Raymond said quickly, and hurried away.

"Come to see if I'm healthy enough to kill, doc?" I asked as he sat down. His mouth smiled but his eyes didn't. He was young, but he had the coldest looking eyes I'd ever seen on a human being. "You don't want to mind him," I went on, nodding in the direction of the warden's departure. "He's taking all this pretty hard."

"And you're not?"

"That's right."

"That's what they told me, and that's why I'm here." He crossed his legs at the ankles. "I'm chief of neurosurgery at Mercy Hospital in town. I want you to donate your body to science. Specifically, I want you to donate it to me."

There was nothing bashful about the guy. Just like that, he wanted my body. "How come, doc?"

"You've read about the organ transplants performed recently —kidneys, livers, hearts?"

"I can read the big print in the newspapers."

Irony was wasted on him. "Techniques have been developed that would have seemed miraculous even six months ago. You might be able to save several lives."

"Several?" I said uneasily. I had a mental picture of myself being cut and dealt like a deck of cards. "Look, I'm not a kid any longer. I'm pushing fifty. I always thought you people wanted young meat. Besides—" and I drew a breath of relief "—when the bullets get through with me, my ticker won't be any good to me or anyone else."

He had an answer for everything. "The prison physician tells me that you're in remarkable condition for a man your age. You've led a life of regular hours and exercise, sheltered from the vices prevalent outside prison. I'm sure your organs are just what I want. As for the wasteful method of execution you've chosen, though, I wish you'd reconsider."

"Not a chance, doc."

"Well, what about the body?"

I still didn't care for the idea of being used for spare parts, but with my new image of myself, it was hard to be ungracious. "I'm not about to change my mind about the firing squad," I said, "but you're welcome to what's left."

"Fair enough," he said, and rose to his feet. He pulled a large envelope from his inside breast pocket and handed me a crackling legal paper to sign. He was taking no chances on my changing my mind. I signed the paper, and Dr. Sansom departed.

After that I was glad the execution date was so near. It was difficult enough some days to appear unconcerned, and the doctor had added a mental burden. When I had thought of myself as dead, I had pictured myself sleeping peacefully with my hands folded across my chest. Now I didn't care to dwell upon the final scene.

On the morning of the execution the warden was still more shook up about it all than I was. He looked as though he'd been up all night, and his breath made no secret how he'd spent his time. I followed him out into the prison yard with the preacher by my side. I watched the warden's legs quiver, and to tell you the truth I could have used a shot of whisky myself.

The prison guards I'd come to know waved or nodded as I passed, with a few murmured reassurances; the guards who weren't following me, that is, to make sure I didn't change my mind about going peaceably.

The prison yard was cool. The first rays of the sun were striking the top of the east wall. A heavy wooden chair with leather straps attached to it sat facing a small wood and canvas structure fifty yards away. I knew that the firing squad was already inside the structure, concealed from view by the canvas awning. When the time came, the awning would be raised and—*pow!*

Twenty yards to the left of the chair a large, white tractor-trailer was parked. Dr. Sansom stood beside it with a number of other men. They were all wearing light green hospital gowns. The only sound was the hum of a diesel generator mounted on top of the trailer. I figured it was needed to run the equipment needed to keep my body from spoiling during the run into town.

I went directly to the chair and sat down. I could hear the guards exhaling sighs of relief that they didn't have to wrestle me into it.

The warden read a paper—mumbled would be more accurate—to the official observers, and then a pair of guards fastened my arms and legs with the leather straps. The prison physician pinned a target to the front of my shirt, and a hood was dropped over my head.

In the dead silence nothing happened for a few seconds. I was trying to think of something clever to say when I felt as though I'd been struck in the chest with a sledgehammer. Immediately after that I heard the roar of the rifles. The echo rebounded from the stone walls. Blood gushed into my throat, and I remember thinking that Dr. Sansom wouldn't be able to use my lungs, either.

Then I couldn't think anything . . .

When I opened my eyes, I could see light and movement, but I had difficulty in focusing upon it. I felt weaker than I had ever felt in my life.

"Send for Dr. Sansom at once!" a female voice said urgently. "He's regained consciousness again and this time he seems rational!"

There was a flurry of movement around me. Shapes slowly became more distinct. Then I was looking into the cold-eyed features of Dr. Sansom. I felt a burst of indignation. To further his own bizarre experimentation, that frosty-orbed magician had taken me from the firing squad chair and given me a new heart. I raised a trembling hand as I tried to complain to him, but all I could utter was gibberish. Then I saw freckles on the back of my hand.

My hand? I'd never had a freckle in my life! I sank back upon the pillow, exhausted. That fiend hadn't given me a new heart. He'd put my brain into someone else's head. God only knew how many parts he'd divided me into.

"Don't try to talk yet," he said soothingly. "You've been in a coma for a long time. Lie quietly and get your bearings." I became conscious of bandages on my face. "You're making a fine recovery. We'll have you up and moving around in a few days now. When we remove the bandages, you'll look almost the same as you did before you went through the window of your car. Most of the scars will be hidden by your hair."

Not by a flicker of an eyelash did he indicate he realized—and none could know more surely—that he was speaking to a split personality, my brain in another man's body.

I hadn't noticed previously, but there were tubes connected to my other arm and my side. Dr. Sansom and the nurses disconnected them as my own life cycle took over the function of keeping me breathing. My own? I closed my eyes and stopped thinking about it. They took away the machinery that had kept me alive while I was in the coma.

I gained control over my new body in the days that followed. Speech was most difficult. At first I had to concentrate hard to form each word, but soon I was speaking sentences. Dr. Sansom let me get out of bed and move cautiously around the room. He watched me with a gleam in his eye. I found that it was like trying to drive a car after a long prison stretch. I had to develop new depth perception and judgment.

I gained strength every day. That was when I first became conscious that my new body was a young body. I felt better than I had for years. I felt a chill, though, when Dr. Sansom said something one day about getting me back on the job. Surely he realized I had no job to which to return? Mentally I was still a middle-aged convict who'd spent over thirty years behind bars. I had no skills, no training, no education that hadn't come from reading two or three books a week, no matter what prison I happened to be calling home. The only thing prison had prepared me for was more prison. There was no possible way I could merge with the life-style of the man into whose head my brain had been inserted, and I didn't try to fool myself into thinking that there was.

Then Dr. Sansom appeared at my bedside one day with an armful of clothing. "Get dressed," he said. "We're going to take a ride to your office. It will just be a short visit this time, but it's time you became reacquainted."

Reacquainted!

One of the nurses drove the car. I sat in the middle with Dr. Sansom beside me. I stared at the dashboard, trying to keep the blur of rapidly passing scenery from confusing me further. Then the car stopped, and I looked out through the window. I drew a long, unbelieving breath.

They helped me out of the car. The walk was lined with people. Smiling people. All the way to the office I accepted greetings from uniformed prison guards, many of whom I knew from my stay on death row.

"Welcome back, Warden Raymond," they greeted me.

Inside the office a young, buxom, hippy girl dashed to me. "Oh, darling," she cried out, "it was so difficult for me to stay away, as they said I must!"

I took her in my arms.

I didn't even mind Dr. Sansom's sardonic glance as I took my wife in my arms.

The only job in the world I fit perfectly.

The only job in which I could actually do some good.

I know life is better the second time around.

You Can Get Away with Murder

by Charles Boeckman

The Mardi Gras hysteria had faded slightly in the predawn hours. Now it was starting again. Merrymakers, looking slightly stunned, were groping their way out into the narrow streets that were littered with last night's confetti and streamers. Parade floats were assembling. Somewhere a musician blew a forlorn, cracking note on a trumpet. The whole city was gulping tomato juice and gin, shaking off last night's hangover and bracing itself for the madness about to erupt again in the streets of New Orleans.

"Hell, lieutenant, I've never seen so much blood in one room in my life." The uniformed officer was standing spraddle-legged on the bottom step of the courtyard stairway, like a bulldog guarding a bone.

Homicide Detective Lieutenant Mercer Basous, his long, homely face serious, cast a preliminary glance around the courtyard. The banana trees were dripping moisture. A night fog that had rolled in from the river, crossed Jackson Square, and enveloped the French Quarter had not entirely dissipated. Basous shivered. The town was chronically cold and damp—when it wasn't hot and damp. He sometimes wondered what had possessed those eighteenth century Frenchmen to pick a swamp hollow below sea level upon which to build a town.

His gaze took in the bloodstains splashed across the cobblestones to the courtyard gate in the west wall. The person or persons unknown who had shed blood in the room upstairs had enough left to splatter a trail on the stairs and courtyard.

Basous assumed that the small group of curious people huddled in the courtyard lived in the apartments surrounding the courtyard. They were in bathrobes and slippers.

"All you people live here?" he questioned.

A general murmur in the affirmative ran through the group.

"Anybody hear a disturbance up there last night?"

No response.

"Well, then, who called the police?"

A plump, middle-aged woman attired in a housecoat, her hair in curlers, moved slightly forward. "I did, Mr. Policeman. I am Mrs. Le Monnier, the landlady. I live there on the ground floor." She pointed across the courtyard to a door half hidden by vines and banana trees. "I came out this morning to get my paper, and the first thing I saw were those horrible bloodstains."

"Who lives up there?" Basous nodded at the apartment at the top of the stairs where the violence had taken place.

"Bubba Noss rents the place. Hardly ever seen him here, though. He often lets friends use the room."

Basous took out his notebook and jotted down the name of the landlady and the apartment tenant. "Was he here last night?"

"Don't know. I don't pry on my tenants."

Somebody in the crowd made a derisive sound. She turned and glared at them.

Basous' partner, Lieutenant Roy D'Aquin, entered the courtyard from the north gate. "I had the dispatcher check it out, Mercer. Nothing at the morgue last night, and none of the hospitals got anybody severely cut up or suffering from loss of blood."

Basous nodded. "Roy, would you get statements from these people? I'll go take a look at the room."

He motioned to the young patrolman, who turned and jogged up the stairs. Basous walked. He'd had a hard week.

The patrolman, opening the door for Basous, said, "I didn't enter the premises, sir. Just looked in. Didn't want to disturb any evidence or fingerprints."

"You're disturbing any fingerprints that might have been on that doorknob," Basous commented, nodding at the uniformed officer's freckled hand grasping the outer knob.

The patrolman's face turned red and he drew his palm back, self-consciously wiping it on his trouser leg. Stiffly, he said, "I observed blood and the appearance of a struggle, but no person, alive or dead, was in the room."

"Anything else?"

"The room had an odor of cigarette smoke, whisky, and perfume, sir."

Basous took pity on the kid. He was trying very hard and was obviously fresh out of the academy.

"Very good, officer. You did it all right by the book."

The patrolman beamed.

Basous took a single step into the room. A bed lamp had been left burning. He murmured an exclamation in his native Cajun French as he made his preliminary survey before moving farther into the room. The one-room efficiency had a kitchen alcove to the right. To the left, a door opened on a small bathroom. In the main room, a couch had been opened to make a bed. The sheets and pillows appeared to have been slept on. There was little blood on the bed except for a few splattered drops. Most of it was on the north wall, the floor, and the bathroom.

D'Aquin joined him. "Nobody down there had a thing to say. Must have been a quiet murder or we have a bunch of sleepers. *Mon dieu!*" He looked around the room. "Looks like a convention of hemophiliacs got into a knife fight."

Basous began moving in slow, careful steps about the room, his trained eyes inspecting everything. Then he came to the bed. He studied it for a minute, bent over and sniffed the pillows. He took envelopes and a pair of tweezers from his coat pocket and carefully plucked some fallen hairs from the pillows and bed, placing them in individual envelopes, afterward sealing and labeling them. Then he slipped the pillowcases from the pillows, folded them and stuffed them into his pockets.

Basous and D'Aquin got on their hands and knees and, placing their cheeks close to the floor, sighted across it for any small objects the preliminary search might have missed. With an exclamation, Basous picked up a bit of plastic. He examined it for a moment, passed it on to his partner. "What do you make of it?"

D'Aquin frowned at the object. "Looks like a contact lens that got dropped and stepped on."

"Yes, I think that's what it is." It went into an envelope.

Then Basous, who was a very careful, deliberate man, and a confirmed believer in the value of keeping notes, sat on the side of the bed, placed his notebook on his thigh, and began writing. Following the date and address of the investigation, he wrote:

"Investigating officer reported bloodstains around room and on stairs leading down to patio and across patio. He also reported the odor of cigarettes, whisky, and perfume in the room. This was all confirmed by our inspection. Further examination revealed no weapon. Table and chairs were overturned. General appearance of a struggle. Bed had been slept in, apparently by a man and woman. One pillow smelled of perfume, and pillowcase had powder, lipstick smears, and a few strands of long, dark hair. The other pillowcase was slightly stained by hair oil and contained strands of shorter dark hair. Found on the floor near the bed was a small object which appears to be a piece of a contact lens. Effort had been made to remove fingerprints and other objects which might identify room's occupants. There was no ashtray, whisky bottle, or glasses, which one would expect to find in the room. No articles of clothing."

He thought for a moment, then added: "Preliminary evaluation: possible rape-murder or lovers' quarrel. Woman might have been killed and the body carried away and disposed of."

D'Aquin, who sometimes grew impatient at Basous' slow, deliberate methods asked, "Shall I put in a call to have a fingerprint man sent over from the lab?"

"Yes. I have a feeling he won't find much, though. And of course we'll need the blood typed."

On the way down the winding iron stairway, D'Aquin observed, "Of course we don't *know* a crime was committed here."

"You think it was just a bad case of nosebleed?" Basous said dryly.

"Well, it could have been some kind of accident—"

"Then why did they go to the trouble to remove all traces of cigarettes, ashtrays, bottles, and glasses that must have been here, according to the odor in the air? No, an act of violence took place here last night," Basous said firmly.

When they reached the street, one of the early-morning Mardi Gras parades was passing by. A marching Dixieland band was playing "High Society" loudly. The sidewalks were already crowded.

D'Aquin took Basous' envelopes to the police laboratory while Basous spent an hour around the neighborhood asking questions. He made one call that proved fruitful. Directly across the narrow cobblestone street from the courtyard's north entrance was an artist's shop and private gallery. The artist was Benjamin Wyle, a thin man with a bushy red beard. He had been open until long past midnight, trying to sell some of his paintings to tourists. Around two A.M. he had seen a man and woman unlock the courtyard gate and go in. The couple appeared to have been drinking and were on very friendly terms. He did not get a clear look at the man, but did see the woman and was able to describe her in detail. "She was a remarkably beautiful woman," he said.

"You're an artist," Basous pointed out. "Could you draw a sketch of her in color?"

"Yes, I think so. An artist doesn't forget a face like that."

The artist went right to work on the sketch. Basous went in search of breakfast. He found a small coffee shop not too jammed with tourists where he had pancakes and several cups of *café au lait*.

When he returned to the artist's shop an hour later, Benjamin Wyle handed him the finished sketch. It was of a brunette woman about thirty years of age.

"I agree," said Basous. "A most beautiful woman—very striking."

He showed the sketch to the tenants of the courtyard apartments, but none had seen the woman. Then Basous battled his way through the Mardi Gras throngs now crowding the streets in ever-increasing numbers to police headquarters on South Broad, where he rejoined his partner, Lieutenant D'Aquin. He showed the sketch to D'Aquin, who whistled appreciatively. (D'Aquin was something of a ladies' man.) "What a shame to waste anything that looks like that." Then he asked, "What do you want to do now?"

"Well, I think we ought to go talk to this Bubba Noss who pays the rent on the apartment, *n'est-ce pas?*"

From the landlady he had obtained the information that Bubba Noss ran a "head shop" for the hippie crowd in another part of the city.

"We'll have to go the long way 'round," D'Aquin said, nodding at the crowded streets.

The day had turned overcast. A cold mist was in the air. Basous turned up his coat collar and trotted out to the car. D'Aquin drove. Mercer Basous was not fond of heavy traffic or crowds. Were it not for his job, which he liked, he would be happy to return to the small Arcadian village on the Bayou where he had been raised, and trap muskrats for a living.

Bubba Noss was six feet tall, weighed two hundred and fifty pounds, wore a full beard, beads, and sandals, and did not like the police.

"No, I don't know who she is," he said sourly, handing the sketch back to D'Aquin.

"Well, she was in your pad last night."

"Man, lots of chicks are in my pad every night."

"It looks very much like this one got herself murdered there," D'Aquin said.

Bubba gave him a sullen, hostile gaze. "Look, I don't know what you're talking about."

Basous glanced around the shop. It smelled of incense, which was probably used to cover up the pot that was smoked there. The goods on display included fringed leather jackets, floppy brimmed hats, books, and various other articles of clothing and paraphernalia favored by the hip subculture. Several bearded, sandaled youths were lounging about, giving the two detectives curious, unfriendly stares.

"Your apartment is covered with blood." D'Aquin pursued. "Somebody—we think this woman—got cut up pretty bad."

"Man, you've wigged out. There ain't no blood in my pad." Then he exclaimed. "Wait a minute! Do you mean my place over in the French Quarter?"

"You have more than one pad?"

"My living quarters are here, upstairs above the shop. I just keep that pad in the Quarter for kicks. You know, atmosphere. Sometimes when I or one of my friends want to impress an out-of-town chick, we take her there. Sometimes I let my customers and friends use it for a party. Man, all kinds of people have keys to that place."

"Where were you last night?"

"Here—upstairs. We had a big Mardi Gras party going on early in the evening."

"How about after midnight?"

Bubba's beard split into a toothy grin. "I was in jail. The cops come in and busted me and my friends for disturbing the peace. They thought we were smoking grass, but couldn't find any. I just got out of the slammer an hour ago."

"You have to admit," said D'Aquin, "that's a pretty good alibi."

"Yeah," Basous said, staring moodily at the Mardi Gras crowds as he and his partner drove back to headquarters. There, Basous went to the crime laboratory on the first floor.

"I've been going over this material you brought in, lieutenant," the laboratory criminologist told him. "I'm typing a report, but I'll tell you what we've found so far. There were face powder, lipstick stains, and perfume residue on one pillowcase. It was all easy to identify, but not of much value in tracing the person who used it. It's all of types widely used and distributed, though high quality, indicating expensive taste. The other pillowcase was slightly stained with hair oil of a type men use. The hair from that pillow was heavy with dark melanin pigment, indicating the man it came from had black hair. The longer hair picked from the pillowcase which had the lipstick stains was also heavily pigmented, but take a look at it through the microscope."

Basous bent over the instrument. He said, "No roots."

"Exactly. So we can be pretty certain it came from a human hair wig. Now look at this." He placed another slide containing a strand of hair under the microscope. "Notice the lack of pigment and the air spaces—the vacuoles. This is definitely from a blonde person. My educated guess is that the woman was wearing a brunette wig, but is actually quite fair—a natural blonde."

"Hmmm," Basous murmured. "I'll have an artist make another sketch of the woman as a blonde. How about that bit of plastic? My partner and I think it is a contact lens."

"It is. I sent a man to the optical shop and they were able to calibrate the prescription. Here it is." He handed Basous a piece of paper. "Oh, the blood in that room is type B negative."

"Thanks. Any fingerprints?"

"Not much luck there. Mostly smudges. Somebody went around wiping everything in sight."

"I figured as much because whoever it was carted off the bottle, glasses, and ashtray. Well, many thanks."

Basous left the sketch of the woman with an artist who did some work for the police department, asking him to sketch her as a blonde. He checked with Missing Persons, but so far no male or female had been reported missing. Then he and D'Aquin went out for lunch.

Basous ordered oysters Bienville with which he had a small bottle of Chablis. After the meal, both detectives had Louisiana coffee, black and heavy with chicory. During the meal, Basous acquainted D'Aquin with the information from the laboratory.

"So," D'Aquin summarized, "sometime between two A.M. and dawn, a blonde woman wearing a dark wig went to Bubba Noss's apartment in the French Quarter with a man who had dark hair. They had a party, drinks, and then the woman, who had type B negative blood, got cut up awfully bad, probably killed."

"I don't see how anyone could lose that much blood and survive," Basous agreed.

"But we know it wasn't Bubba Noss because he was in jail at the time."

"Yes. From what he's told us, it could have been one of many people. Apparently his whole crowd of swingers uses that place as a party room and shacking-up pad. Either the man or the woman—or both for that matter—could have had a key."

D'Aquin said, "I guess it's up to us now to find out the identity of the couple, starting with the woman, since we have a pretty good idea what she looks like."

"And we have the contact lens," Basous reminded him. "More than likely it belonged to the woman. She would be too vain to spoil her kind of looks with glasses. And with her obvious class, she could afford the best ophthalmologist in the city for the examination and contact lens prescription. We can make the rounds of the doctors this afternoon and see if one of them recognizes her from the sketch."

"That might work. Unless, of course, she was from out of town, and there are an awful lot of visitors at Mardi Gras time—and unless the lens belonged to the man; or it was dropped by somebody else at a previous time."

"That's what I like about you, D'Aquin. You're always so damned optimistic."

They spent the afternoon plowing through the Mardi Gras crowds that were growing denser and drunker by the hour.

They went to seven ophthalmologists, and at the eighth office they struck pay dirt. They didn't even have to take up the doctor's time. The receptionist recognized the sketch—the blonde one—at once. "Oh, I'm almost sure that's Mrs. Arthur Turner . . . Linda Turner. She was in just last month."

"Was this the prescription for her contact lenses?" Basous handed her the paper with the lens prescription.

"I can check her records." She went to a filing cabinet. In a few minutes she returned. "Yes. That's it."

Basous' homely face momentarily reflected his inner elation. "Could we have her address?"

She wrote the address on a slip of paper. "I do hope nothing has happened to her, officer?"

Basous did not reply. He and his partner returned to their car. Basous looked at the address and muttered a Bayou French exclamation under his breath. "She lived in the Garden District. Very posh address."

They drove to the address, parked in front of the house. Basous looked up at the sweeping lawn, the costly home with its plantation-style Ionic columns. "I don't look forward to this—telling the man that his wife shacked up with some dude in the Quarter last night and then got herself knifed and probably dumped in the river."

"Wonder why he hasn't reported her missing?"

"She probably gave him some story about going to visit friends or relatives, so he hasn't missed her yet."

They rang the bell. A maid ushered them into a parlor after Basous showed her his identification. He sat precariously on an antique chair and looked around at the grand piano and thick carpet and costly paintings, holding his hat between his hands.

Presently Arthur Turner, a man in his fifties, silver-haired, with a deep golfer's tan joined them. "Gentlemen—Mildred said you are from the police . . ."

"Yes." Basous looked uncomfortably at his partner. He was not very good at coping with things like this.

D'Aquin came to his rescue. "It's about your wife, sir," he said gently. "When did you see her last?"

Turner looked surprised. "About two minutes ago. We're having cocktails in the family room. Why are you asking about my wife?"

D'Aquin turned and stared rather foolishly at Basous, who thought his own expression must be pretty sheepish. Finally he cleared his throat and asked politely, "May we have a word with her, sir?"

"Well, I suppose so." Turner left the room, then came back immediately with his wife, a stunning blonde woman—Linda Turner.

The two detectives quickly rose. It was Basous' turn to clear his throat. "Pardon us for this intrusion, Mrs. Turner. Could you tell us where you were last night?"

She regarded him with a puzzled expression, looked at her husband, then again at Basous. "Right here at home with my husband. Why are you asking, officer?"

Turner had put an arm around his wife. "We had a quiet dinner at home and spent the evening watching television; keeping away from the Mardi Gras crowds, you know. Would you mind telling me what this is all about, sir?"

"Please excuse us for disturbing you. Perhaps it is a case of mistaken identity. We're just doing some routine checking . . ."

Out in the car, D'Aquin said, "She's lying."

"Of course she's lying. And her husband is covering for her. There is no question but that she is the woman in that sketch." Basous slapped his forehead. *"Mon dieu!* So it was the *man* who got his throat cut, and all the time we've been thinking it was the woman. But I simply cannot see how a woman could knife a man, then carry his body down the stairs and across the courtyard to the gate."

"Perhaps he staggered out of the room under his own power."

"Or the woman had help. Why would she kill him? Did he threaten to blackmail her? Or was it a matter of jealousy? Anyway, we can't arrest her yet. Everything is too slim and circumstantial. We don't even know who the man was. You know, I think we ought to check the list of everybody who got busted at Bubba's party last night. It looks very much to me like Linda Turner or the man she was with, or both of them, ran around with that crowd. Bubba's friends might be more willing to talk to us than Bubba was, especially if we lean on them just a bit."

Back at the police building, Basous and D'Aquin went over the records of the arrests made at Bubba Noss's apartment the night before. They ran a check to see if any of those booked had a police record. Several did, and Basous selected the most promising. "Nikki Lane. Female. Age twenty-one. Several arrests. One conviction for possession of marijuana. Served time as a juvenile offender. Was on probation a year."

Basous said, "Let us pay a visit to Miss Lane. I see she lives in a little town on the other side of the river. It just so happens I am acquainted with a family-operated restaurant in that same village which will not be overrun with tourists, and which serves some of the very best authentic homemade Creole gumbo you ever tasted. It will be about time for the evening meal when we get there."

D'Aquin laughed. "You do like your meals on time, Basous."

The Arcadian agreed.

They drove over the Huey Long Bridge and stopped at the small cafe in the village. They were served steaming bowls of Creole gumbo and when D'Aquin sampled his, tears filled his eyes. He quickly gulped a drink of wine. "This is really fiery!"

"It's real Louisiana Cajun cooking," Basous said happily, beads of perspiration popping out all over his long, homely face as he ate the spicy dish with relish. "This gives a man the spirit to pole a pirogue all day and dance the *fais-dodo* all night."

After two large bowls of gumbo and several cups of black chicory coffee, Basous was ready to call on Nikki Lane. They found her address to be one of a row of unpainted shacks just below the levee. In the weed-filled yard were parked several motorcycles. When the detective knocked, a young woman with stringy blonde hair, dressed in bluejeans, barefooted, carrying a baby on one hip, came to the door.

"We'd like to speak to Miss Nikki Lane," said Basous.

Her expression was wary. "That's me. What do you want?"

Basous showed her his badge. Her expression turned to fright. "Listen, I'm clean. What are you bugging me about?"

"You were arrested last night?"

"That was a mistake. They busted us for disturbing the peace. They thought they were going to find some grass or smack. But we were clean. They let us go this morning."

"The point is, you hang around with Bubba Noss and this crowd of swingers. Have you ever seen this woman? Does she come to Bubba's parties?" Basous showed her the two sketches of Linda Turner, both the brunette and the blonde version.

"Is that all you want to know?" she asked.

"Yes—unless, of course, you decide not to cooperate. Then we might think of a lot of other things to question you about."

Relief showed in her eyes. "Sure, I know her. Why shouldn't I tell you?" She shrugged. She pointed to the brunette sketch. "That's Helen Davis. I've seen her at several of Bubba's parties."

"Did she ever tell you her name was Linda Turner?"

"I don't know nothin' about that. I know her as Helen Davis."

"Was she at the party last night?"

"Yes. But she left early. Before the fuzz raided the place."

"Was she with somebody?"

"Sure. Same guy she always comes with. Ron Giampietro."

"Ron Giampietro," D'Aquin muttered as they drove back across the Huey Long Bridge.

The name was familiar to both detectives. Giampietro owned a small strip joint on Bourbon Street, but his main activity was being a bookie and small-time hoodlum.

"I wonder how a high-class dame like Linda Turner ever got involved with a shady character like Giampietro," Basous mused.

"His kind often attract women," said D'Aquin, who considered himself something of an expert on female psychology. "They get bored with their rich husbands and nice, safe routine at home. They go looking for adventure. A guy on the shady side, an outlaw, excites them."

"Well, if Giampietro took her to that French Quarter apartment last night, he either got himself killed or killed somebody else up there."

They parked as close as possible to the Quarter and got out and walked. The Vieux Carré was sealed off to automobiles during Mardi Gras. By now darkness had fallen, a cold, drizzling darkness, making the filigree ironwork on the balconies gleam and imparting a soft patina to the ancient, crumbling buildings; but the weather did not dampen the Mardi Gras spirit. The narrow streets—Bourbon, Chartres, St. Louis, Royal—were crowded from curb to curb with boisterous merrymakers, many of them carrying huge, drink-filled glasses. Jazz poured from every doorway, loud and brassy, and not too much melody.

Basous questioned the manager of Ron Giampietro's strip bar, The Blue Spot. No, he had not seen Mr. Giampietro since yesterday. No, he would not allow Mr. Giampietro's apartment to be searched without a warrant.

The two detectives went off in search of a judge who would issue a search warrant. It was nearly midnight when they returned with the warrant. Giampietro's apartment was across a walled courtyard behind the strip joint. His quarters were expensively furnished. Basous and D'Aquin spent an hour searching the premises with meticulous skill and patience. At last Basous found an item that was helpful. It was a notebook. He studied the names and figures entered in ledger-like style and uttered an exclamation when his eye fell on a particular entry.

"What is it?"

"Unless I am badly mistaken, I now know what happened. Ron Giampietro was indeed murdered last night and I know who had the motive and opportunity. Come on."

Basous hustled D'Aquin out into the streets again. The homely detective's long, lanky legs carried him plowing through the throngs. They had but a few blocks to walk to the artist shop of Benjamin Wyle, situated directly across the street from the courtyard apartments which had been visited last night by Linda Turner, alias Helen Davis, and Ron Giampietro.

"Ah, Mr. Wyle," said Basous. "Still open, I see."

"Just trying to pick up a few bucks from the tourists, lieutenant." He smiled, fingering his bushy red beard. "Did you find out who the woman was you were looking for?"

"Indeed we did. We also found out who the man was."

"Hey, that's good detective work. Who was he?"

"Ron Giampietro. You know him, Mr. Wyle?"

"Let me see . . . I think he owns a joint over on Bourbon Street."

"Come, you can do better than that, Mr. Wyle. In fact you placed a lot of bets with him. From the amount of money you owed him, I would say gambling is quite a passion with you."

The artist's face turned pale. "How did you know—"

"Mr. Giampietro kept a very good set of books. They show how much you'd lost and owed him. He has a reputation for leaning on people quite heavily when they can't pay their I.O.U.'s. What did he threaten to do, Mr. Wyle? Break both your arms? Put out a contract on you? And was that why you went over there, knowing you could catch him off guard when he was having a romantic interlude with Mrs. Turner? You killed him and carried his body out and dumped it, probably in the river. You knew, of course, that Mrs. Turner wouldn't dare turn you in without compromising herself and her sordid affair."

The artist's face was now the color of a dirty gray bedsheet. "Now wait a minute—"

"Read him his rights, D'Aquin."

D'Aquin recited, "You have the right to remain silent. Anything you say may be used against you. You have the right to an attorney. If you can't afford an attorney—"

"Wait a minute!" Wyle half-screamed. "You're not pinning this on me." He wiped his sweating face with a handkerchief. "You're right about the I.O.U.'s. You're right about the threats Giampietro was making to me. He really had me scared. But I didn't kill him. Arthur Turner did that."

"What?"

"I recognized Mrs. Turner even with that brunette wig. I've seen her before. In fact, she and her husband bought a painting from me for that mansion they live in. So, when I saw her go up to that room with Giampietro, I put in a telephone call to Arthur Turner. I told him if he'd come to the address I gave him, he would find his wife in bed with Ron Giampietro. I told him the west gate would be unlocked. The street on that side is not closed to automobiles. I have a key to the courtyard gates since I have an apartment there myself.

"This morning when you questioned me, I drew the sketch of Mrs. Turner, hoping you'd trace her and eventually charge her husband with the murder. Of course I had to draw her with the brunette wig in case another witness turned up. Still, anyone would recognize her if they really knew her."

Arthur Turner's car was searched the next morning. The trunk had been washed but careful inspection by the police laboratory turned up traces of type B negative blood. That evidence, along with the testimony of Benjamin Wyle—who had to be granted immunity from prosecution—plus others who knew of the affair between Mrs. Turner and Giampietro would have been sufficient *corpus delicti,* even if Giampietro's body had not been eventually found floating in a bayou where Turner had dumped him. There was enough circumstantial evidence to convict Arthur Turner.

Apparently Mrs. Turner had been contrite, begged forgiveness, and Turner, a man passionately in love with his beautiful young wife, had forgiven her after he dispatched Giampietro.

Basous should have been happy with a case successfully solved but his homely face wore an expression even more dour than usual. "You know what really bugs me?" he said to D'Aquin.

"What?"

"The real murderer is going scot-free. When Wyle picked up the phone that night and called Arthur Turner, he killed Ron Giampietro as surely as if he'd stuck the knife in him, and there isn't anything we can do to him. Do you realize Benjamin Wyle got away with murder?"

The Invisible Cat

by Betty Ren Wright

Most towns have a Miss Cassells who serves, self-appointed, as its guardian of morals. Our Miss Cassells was fortyish, and apparently always had been, was given to letter-writing, white collars, and pointed shoes, and was a great patron of repentant sinners. Her notes signed "An Anxious Friend" and "One Who Cares" are part of the town legend, and her murder—no matter what story you believe—was as neatly appropriate as the third-act curtain of a college student's first play.

The town misses the old girl. In her day she was credited with breaking up eleven marriages (including Katherine's and mine), being the direct cause of three suicides, and driving two ministers to request posts in other cities. She wasn't good, but she was interesting, and in a dull town like our town she was therefore important.

It was on the Fourth of July, seven years ago, that we lost her—a day hot enough to be remembered for that reason alone. The temperature had stayed in the upper nineties for a week, and on the morning of the Fourth you could feel the town bracing itself for the long haul ahead. In our town there are certain things that are always done on the holiday, and it takes a lot more than the weather to change the schedule. In this case, the heat just got things started earlier; by five thirty A.M., the kids were roaming the streets and firecrackers were popping like corn in a hot pan. Over on the south end the racket is always the worst, and it was there that the Travvers boys—scrounging in the dump for tin cans—found the first body.

Eddie Travvers called the police station. And right after his call, Miss Cassells phoned in to say that a man in a baggy white suit had jumped out at her neighbor, Caroline Smith, when Caroline opened the back door to let in the cat. Miss Cassells' voice was as chilly as ever, but in the background Caroline could be heard, all stops open.

You see, the state mental hospital is only a quarter mile from our city square and folks are likely to think of that first when there is trouble. Dick Repa, who is one-third of our police department, called the hospital; they made a quick check, and sure enough one of the

261

most violent patients was missing. The superintendent of the hospital was frantic and promised to send some men immediately to help with the search. But the terror had begun. It was a situation our town worries about, the way other places worry about earthquakes or floods.

The body the Travvers kids had found was that of Joe Diggs, a harmless old sponger who lived off a disability pension and anything the townspeople wanted to give him. There was no question but what the lunatic had done it; old Joe had been strangled with a sock of the kind issued by the hospital and carrying an identifying mark. Our switchboard operator, Mae Purtell, got busy and within half an hour every kid in town was back home and houses were locked up tight. Skittery old maids began hailing the police station faster than Mae could handle the calls, and a volunteer posse followed up each SOS, poking through attics and cellars that hadn't seen a man in twenty years. By eight thirty that morning, a tourist—driving through on his way north to one of the resorts—would have thought a plague had hit us. Except for the posse, there wasn't a soul in the streets, and every house had a withdrawn look, as though begging the lunatic not to notice it.

They couldn't find him. They combed garages, barns, and woodsheds, timidly at first, then with more courage as they were joined by state police. The morning passed, and the temperature rose. Miss Cassells finished a furious letter to the hospital superintendent (found on her desk later, by neighbors) and started one to the governor. The troopers distributed tear gas bombs.

By noon, folks were saying the crazy man must have left town, and some of the reckless ones were opening their second story windows a crack for a breath of air. Emmeline Loring, known far and wide for foolhardiness, even went out to feed the chickens she kept behind her garage. Tommy Parks and Ellis Townes found her there, the back of her head completely crushed in, and her fist closed tight over something. When the state troopers came they pried open her fingers, and a little stream of chicken corn poured out.

Right then and there, a certain percentage of the volunteer help disappeared. You could see why. Murder in the abstract—at the city dump, and done upon a nobody while Mr. Ordinary Man was asleep in his bed—was rather exciting. But murder at noon on the Fourth of July, when the parade ought to be breaking up at the city square and the kids getting their ice cream, murder done to a friendly, opinionated old lady who was reduced now to complete indifference, that was something else. At a time like that the bravest man is likely to start saving himself for his wife and children.

Of those who stayed, two took poor Emmeline down to the police station in a car while the rest continued searching on foot. More troopers arrived and threw a cordon around the town so that no one could come in or leave. We were like a lot of mice locked up with an invisible cat, wondering where the thing was and whether it was still hungry.

At four o'clock nothing had changed except the temperature, which had passed the all-time record. It was too hot to move away from the radio and its frequent bulletins, so few people saw Miss Cassells as she walked through town to the church. It would have been a sight to remember: dark blue cotton dress and broad white collar, white gloves, long white pointed shoes. With the temperature pushing 105°, and a homicidal maniac loose in the streets, Miss Cassells was all dressed up and going about her business.

It developed later that at least six of the posse met her on her way. Most of us were searching on the outskirts of town, but a few men were patrolling the square, and they all recalled their surprise and horror at seeing a woman alone on the street. After they identified her the feeling changed; it seemed pretty unlikely that even a lunatic would attack Miss Cassells, and besides—well, if you'd ever received one of the old witch's letters you'd know why the feeling changed. She had a real gift for sending vicious half-truths, where they would do the most harm.

Even so, all six men made it their job to warn her, and got condescending smiles for their trouble. She *always* practiced the organ at four thirty, and that was that. Gene Pierce followed her to the church and waited while she unlocked the door and let herself in. He said afterward that he would have gone in, too, and stayed, if it had been anyone else. Instead, he waited across the street in the shade for a while, then walked across the square with Binny Draper.

Miss Cassells told the state troopers the rest of the story that night—how she went straight to the organ in the choir loft without bothering to turn on the overhead lights. Under the particular circumstances of that afternoon, she was probably the only person in town who would have considered the lights a bother. But that was what she said. Many Sunday mornings, sitting alone in my pew, I've pictured her climbing one of the two staircases to the loft, her white collar disembodied in the darkness until she switched on the console lamp—for the last time.

She played a Bach Invention first, to loosen up her fingers, then started working on the offertory music for the following Sunday. While she played, she glanced once in a while into the little mirror fastened at the side of the organ. It's there so the organist can tell when the choir, or the bride, is ready to come down the aisle, but Miss Cassells always used it to check up on who had come to church and who hadn't. I suppose that even when the church was empty, it was hard to break the habit. She had been playing about fifteen minutes, glancing into the mirror occasionally, when she saw a man standing at the altar rail down in the church. He was wearing rumpled white pajamas.

They figured afterward that he must have gone to the church right after killing Emmeline Loring, and crawled in through an unlocked basement window. He stayed there all afternoon, maybe even slept in the church kitchen, until the sound of the organ got him moving again.

At first Miss Cassells, being herself, kept right on playing. The man's face was turned up toward the music; he had a placid, rather pathetic look, like a child disturbed in the middle of a dream, and she may have thought that if she kept on he would wander away. Then his arms moved and she saw that he had come prepared to play the critic. There was a knife in his hand.

What followed may have lasted only a few minutes, or much longer; Miss Cassells wasn't sure. She slid off the console bench and started toward the stairs on the left. When she reached them, he was waiting at the bottom. She turned back, and he turned, too. It was like a queer, pointless game that could go on forever. He did not look at her—his head had dropped when the music ended—but he seemed able to anticipate her every step. There was something terrifying in the way he moved; it was as if nothing could distract him.

"I thought of the men on whose conscience my death would lie," she told the troopers that night. "Those negligent doctors at the asylum. I hope they will be made to understand what it was like. I hope they'll have to pay. And the ones to blame for that hallway. They should suffer for it."

The hallway to which she referred so kindly is a narrow little passage leading up from the basement to the center of the loft. It hasn't been used by the choir for at least ten years, and at the last redecorating, paneling was laid across the door, with hidden hinges so that the hall behind the panel could still be used for storage. They had been playing their follow-the-leader game for quite a while when Miss Cassells thought of that hallway, and the memory must have seemed like a reprieve straight from heaven. If she could go through the panel without his looking up, she thought, he might not be able to find the opening for several minutes—long enough for her to go down the hallway, through the basement, and up again to the front door.

For the last time she started across the loft. This time she walked behind the choir benches instead of in front of them, and slid her hand lightly over the panels until she found the right one. It opened, and the man did not look up. She stepped inside.

There was no light. In the old days Miss Cassells had used the hallway a hundred times, and under any other circumstances she would have realized at once that it was unnaturally dark. But this time she believed the hall was heaven's answer to a deserving prayer, and she didn't begin to doubt the answer until her outstretched hands struck something hard in front of her. Then the darkness had to be explained, and, as clearly as if she had helped them, she remembered the day the choir members crated up all the old hymnals and little-used music and carried the boxes through the panel. From floor to ceiling the crates were piled, and they made a blind alley of the little hall.

"I began to pray," Miss Cassells told the troopers that night. "I prayed God to remember the life I had led and to reward me with a quick and easy death. And to punish those who were responsible. It was sinful ignorance to leave a hallway completely blocked that way."

She was nearly unconscious when the panel opened and the lunatic in his rumpled white suit stood in the light. "I fell down," she recalled. "I fell on my knees and tried to pray. But I couldn't look away from the knife. He was staring at it, too, and then he looked over his shoulder at something and the knife fell on the floor. It was right in front of me. He walked away, and I heard him go down the stairs and out through the chancel door. Then a man called hello from the rear of the church and I heard someone coming down the aisle. Everything got horribly dark, and that's all I remember."

They caught the lunatic as he was strolling across the square, and five minutes after that Ed Burns and Tom Nichols found Miss Cassells. She had been stabbed twice, and had bled a great deal, but they roused her at the hospital, and for a couple of hours it looked as if she was going to pull through. That was when the state troopers got her story.

"Now you find him," she said. "The devil who stabbed me. I've told you everything just as it happened. Now you find the devil who would stab an unconscious woman."

They tried. Some of us, who were known to have had dealings with her in the past, had to put up with quite a bit of questioning. But the knife had no fingerprints on it at all, and as for opportunity, every man in town had had a chance to slip away from home, or from the posse, if he wanted to. She was always in the church from four thirty to five thirty; with any kind of luck, the madman would have got the blame. And as for motive, there was plenty to go around. Miss Cassells summed it up well with her last words. "One spends one's life trying to help others, but the world is never grateful."

That was how we lost her. Or at least, that was how she said we lost her. There are a few cynics and parlor psychoanalysts in our town who believe it really was the maniac who stabbed Miss Cassells, and that the second man in her story was born of a guilty conscience, of just plain meanness.

I don't take part in the discussions; I find the speculation rather amusing. In any case, half this town is going to look with suspicion at the other half for as long as we all shall live, and Miss Cassells couldn't have wished herself a more appropriate memorial than that.

A Woman Is Missing

by Helen Nielsen

Einar Peterson's body was wearying of life. He slept at the touch of his silvered head on the pillow; but when his wife, Amelia, fastened her hands on his shoulders and shook with all her housewife strength, he awakened, trying to remember where he was, and why he was no longer the boy he'd been dreaming of, sailing his small boat on a bright Sunday on Lake Vatern. Without his glasses, Amelia's face bobbed above him like a pale balloon.

"Einar—Einar. Something's wrong in back!"

"What? Where?" Einar mumbled.

"In the tenant's house in back. I think it's Mrs. Tracy sick again."

Einar Peterson pulled himself up in the bed and groped on the night table until his slightly arthritic fingers located his eyeglasses. With them in place, the pale balloon now had gray hair and troubled eyes.

"Mrs. Tracy?" he repeated. "What is it, Mother? What's wrong?"

"I don't know. I woke up because of the lights in the driveway and the motor running."

"Maybe it's the mister."

"In the driveway? You know the mister always comes home up the alley. Anyway, it's only ten thirty. I looked at the clock when the lights woke me up. Get up, Einar. Go see. That poor little Mrs. Tracy—"

Amelia liked to worry about people, and the night air was damp and chilly outside the blankets. Einar didn't want to get up; but now he could see that the light reflected on his wife's face wasn't from the ceiling fixture—it was from a glaring beam outside the bedroom window, and the noise he heard wasn't from the old refrigerator in the kitchen—it was the sound of an automobile motor. Reluctantly, he parted himself from snug comfort and padded to the window to which Amelia had preceded him.

"Somebody went back to the tenant house," she whispered. "It was a man."

"Did you see him?" Einar asked.

"Hush, not so loud. No, I didn't see; but I heard the footsteps. I think it must be a doctor."

"A doctor! Why would a doctor leave the motor running?"

"I think it's an ambulance. There's a funny light on top."

The window was open two inches. Einar lifted the sash quietly and poked out his head. Amelia was right. The automobile he saw certainly did have a light on top.

"It's a taxi," he said.

"A taxi? Here?"

"Quiet!" Einar drew back inside. "Somebody's coming."

Einar Peterson watched the brightness in front of the headlights; but the heavy, man-like footsteps skirted the light and passed by the window in shadows. They stopped at the taxi. A door opened; then silence behind the idling motor, and darkness behind the lights except for the small, round glow of a cigarette.

"Look," Amelia whispered. "She's coming."

Linda Tracy was such a very young woman, it was difficult to realize that she was married to Mr. Tracy and would have been the mother of his child if it had been God's will. She looked more like one of Einar Peterson's teenage granddaughters except for something . . . Einar Peterson's mind always caught on that odd feeling when he thought of Mrs. Tracy. Something. She walked rapidly into the headlights, head down except for an instant when she turned and stared almost directly at the dark window behind which the two unseen watchers were hidden. She was wearing a light colored coat and very noisy heels, and, this they would remember to tell the police, a very fearful expression on her face. She passed the window and entered the cab. The glow of a burning cigarette spun into space and was lost in the darkness. The door of the taxi slammed shut. In a matter of seconds, the taxi was gone.

"Well," said Amelia. "What was that?"

Einar Peterson removed his glasses and padded back to the bed.

"Einar, I'm worried. Mrs. Tracy never goes out at night. Her lights always go off just after ten o'clock. Einar—"

Einar's answer was a snore. She lowered the window to within two inches of the sill and returned to bed; but she didn't sleep. There was something strange about Linda Tracy. Amelia had never mentioned her feelings to anyone, not even Einar; but there was something . . .

Chester Tracy was a slight, sandy-haired man with a peering face.

That was how he impressed Sergeant Mike Shelly. He had probably started peering when he was a kid, his nose pressed against the store windows full of Christmas toys he would never receive. Children who had done that never lost the look; it grew older with them. There was fear in his face, too; fear muted by shock. Shelly had to pry words out of him.

"When did you get home, Mr. Tracy?" he asked. "At what time—exactly."

Tracy was possibly forty. He wore suntan cotton pants and a brown leather zipper jacket with an I.D. badge from Flight Research pinned to the breast pocket. The photo on the badge would have embarrassed the Passport Bureau.

"The usual time," he said. "I work the five forty-five P.M. to two forty-five A.M. shift."

"What time?" Shelly persisted.

"It takes me eighteen minutes to drive home. I've clocked it a hundred times—just to keep awake. It may take eighteen and a half if I miss the green light at Slauson."

"Then you were home at a few minutes past three."

"At three minutes past—exactly. I looked at the kitchen clock when I came in."

"The light was on?" Shelly asked.

"It's always on when I come home. Linda leaves it for me when she goes to bed."

"And so everything seemed normal."

"Until I started down the hall to the bathroom," Tracy said. "I saw that the bedroom door was open. It's usually closed because of that light in the kitchen. I looked in to see if Linda was all right, and that's when I discovered—" Tracy's eyes were less glazed now. Emotion was breaking through the numbness. "Why are you asking all these dumb questions?" he demanded. "My wife's gone—don't you understand? I called you because Linda's gone!"

A missing wife can mean many things—Mike Shelly had carried a police badge in his pocket long enough to know that. He'd talked to the old people up front, but he had to question Tracy alone. Outside, Shelly's partner, Sergeant Keonig, was searching the grounds. Inside, Shelly stood in a living room just large enough for one small divan and two slipcovered chairs, pried away at Chester Tracy, and puzzled over the photographs he'd found in a double frame on the side table. One side of the frame showed Linda Tracy close up: blonde, smiling, lovely; the other held a full length Linda attired in an abbreviated bathing suit: blonde, smiling, lovely. She was nine-teen years old. The forty-year-old man with the peering face had told him that.

"I know that your wife's gone," Shelly answered quietly. "I'm looking for her. I've been looking for her ever since I got here. A photograph isn't enough, Mr. Tracy. I need to know what kind of woman your wife is."

Reactions could be startling, particularly in the pre-dawn hours of a torturous night. Color flooded to Chester Tracy's face.

"What kind of woman?" he echoed. "Is that any way to talk to a man in my position?"

"Mr. Tracy—"

"She's my wife. That's the kind of woman she is! She's my wife!"

If someone had bought the finest toy in the shop for that kid with his face pressed against the window, and then taken it away, the emotional response would have matched what was written on Chester Tracy's face.

"I was thinking more of her habits," Shelly explained. "Where she goes. Who she sees . . . "

"But she doesn't see anyone! She doesn't go anywhere—not without me! My wife lost a baby four months ago. Since that time, she hasn't been well. She never goes out unless I take her in the car."

"Where do you go?"

"To the market. Once in a while to a drive-in movie."

"Never to friends?"

"With me working the hours I work? I went on swing shift for the extra money after Linda got pregnant. Since then, we have no friends. Ask the Petersons up front. Linda walks up to get the mail every morning—the box is on Peterson's house. That's as much as she goes out without me. Every night I call home during the ten o'clock coffee break—"

"Ten o'clock," Shelly echoed. "Did you talk to your wife at ten o'clock tonight?"

"I did."

"Did she seem nervous or upset?"

"No more than usual. Linda's been nervous and upset ever since she lost the baby. That's why I call her every night. I catch her just before she takes her sleeping pills—"

Tracy's voice ceased as the front door opened. It was Keonig. He glanced at Tracy; then turned to Sergeant Shelly.

"I didn't find a single footprint," he said. "This house is built on a cement slab. It extends along the right side for the width of about ten feet, all the way to the alley. There's an old station wagon parked on that extension."

"That's mine," Tracy volunteered.

"In front," Keonig added, "the cement narrows to a walk leading to Peterson's driveway—the way we came. I'd hoped our man might have stepped off the walk and left a print in the soft flower bed under the Petersons' windows, but all I found was this—"

Cupped in the palm of Keonig's hand was a cigarette butt—standard brand, filter tip.

"Peterson said the man who came for Mrs. Tracy tossed a cigarette into the flower bed," Shelly reflected. "Keep it."

"It was all I could find," Keonig repeated.

"Try the bathroom," Shelly said. "Or does your wife keep those sleeping pills in her bedroom, Mr. Tracy?" Shelly set the double-framed photograph back on the table and turned toward the hall. "You take the bathroom," he told Keonig, "and I'll take the bedroom. You come with me, Tracy. I'll need you."

In a square cell with one window, curtained, shade drawn, the bed was turned down and a soft, pink nightgown laid out for its missing occupant. Shelly studied the display while Chester Tracy, at his request, took stock of his wife's closet.

"I think there's a blue dress missing," he reported.

"A blue dress," Shelly repeated.

"Sort of a suit. You know, a dress with a jacket over it."

"What else?" Shelly prodded. "Shoes?"

The shoe rack held, at quick glance, a good dozen pairs of slippers and pumps.

"I think she usually wore black pumps with the blue dress," Chester said. "I don't see them here."

"Black shoes," Shelly echoed. "What coat?"

"The Petersons said a light coat. That would be the one she called a cashmere. It was new. I got it for her with my last big overtime check."

Shelly picked up one of the pumps from the rack and examined it. Size 5A. It was clear plastic with a spike heel. He turned it over in his hands. The soles were badly worn, especially at the toe. The heels weren't.

"Are these new, too?" he asked.

"I got them for her for Christmas," Chester answered.

"Is anything else missing?"

The question kept Chester busy, while Shelly examined the rest of the rack. Most of the shoes were dress pumps or sandals, but there was one conspicuous pair of walking flats. When Keonig came in from the bathroom with the sleeping pills, Shelly still held one of the flats in his hand. A small crust of dried mud loosened at the prod of his fingernail and fell to the floor.

"I had to dig, but I found them in the medicine chest," Keonig said. "Now maybe you'll tell me why."

"Because Mrs. Tracy took sleeping pills every night after her husband's ten o'clock call."

"Not tonight," Keonig said.

"Obviously. That's interesting, isn't it? Let me see that bottle." It was nearly half full. Shelly read the prescription label and frowned. "Dr. Youngston," he read aloud. "Two pills before retiring. 10-7-59. Keonig, what's the date?"

"It was the twelfth of January at midnight," Keonig answered.

"Dr. Youngston," Shelly mused. "Your wife did see someone outside of this house, Tracy. Who else?"

The man still seemed to be in a state of shock. He groped for words. "I told you—no one."

"At any time—before your marriage."

"I didn't know Linda very long before our marriage. Leo talked me into going to this party—"

"Leo? Leo who?"

"Leo Manfred. We worked together at Flight Research. Look, why don't you stop asking these questions? Why don't you look for that cab?"

"Where can I find Leo Manfred?" Shelly persisted.

"I don't know! At home, I suppose. I lost track of Leo when I went on nights. I don't even know if he's with Flight Research now."

"But he did know your wife?"

"That was months ago—seven, eight months ago."

"Leo Manfred and Dr. Youngston." Shelly slipped the bottle of pills into his pocket. "Who else, Tracy? Who else knew that your wife would be here alone at ten thirty? Who might she have gone with without fear?"

"But she was afraid," Keonig protested. "The Petersons said—"

"Who else, Tracy?"

Chester Tracy sank down on the edge of the bed. The kid with his face pressed against the window wanted to cry; but the kid was a man of forty, and so, instead, he took a pack of cigarettes from his pocket, standard brand, no filter tip, pulled out one cigarette and held it between thumb and forefinger, until the thumb clenched white and the cigarette snapped in two. He looked up.

"I can't think!" he protested. "You're the police. Find my wife! Please, find my wife!"

Linda Tracy, white Caucasian, female. Age: 19. Height, 5'3". Weight, 110. Blonde hair, hazel eyes. Probably wearing a blue jacket dress, black pumps, and a light tan cashmere coat. Last seen entering a taxi at 1412 North . . .

A description of the missing woman was going out over the police radio before Shelly and Keonig left the Peterson property. Shelly took a turn about the premises, while Keonig used the telephone. It was still a good hour before dawn, and a light fog had wrapped the world in a close, damp blanket. At the side of the tenant house, Shelly found the station wagon, the windshield and windows curtained with moisture. Beyond it, the paved area terminated at an unpaved alleyway. He took a few steps into the alley and peered toward the street lamp at the nearest corner. It was at least four lots distant—darkness and fog prohibited a closer guess—and no back yard taxpayer units such as the Petersons had added were in evidence. This was the route by which Chester Tracy had arrived home—the only other access to the property except the front drive. Underfoot, the stubborn adobe had absorbed most of a none too recent gravel topping, and the pale light from the corner lamp caught in small, wet shallows of leftover rain. Shelly scraped his shoes clean on the parking slab and returned to the car and Keonig.

"It's a break—that cab business." Keonig said. "A cab can be traced."

"I know it can," Shelly mused. "That's what is bothering me."

A cab can be traced, but it takes time. Time to check each office of each company; run down each call sheet; pry out of bed a driver who had worked most of the night. Meanwhile, a sun rises, a city comes awake, the air begins to fill with the aromas of coffee, frying bacon, and, predominantly, carbon monoxide. Shelly couldn't wait. The Southern Area telephone directory listed a Dr. Carl Youngston on Manchester Boulevard; hours: nine to five.

At ten minutes before nine, Mike Shelly waited in the foyer of a handsome new medical building and watched a slender, blond young man in a gray topcoat unlock the slab door leading to Dr. Youngston's office. He stooped to retrieve an advertising folder that had been deposited in the mail slot and arose, pulling a pair of tortoise-rimmed glasses from an inner pocket. These he donned in time to bring the full width and height of Mike Shelly into focus.

Surprise didn't seem to unnerve the doctor.

"Do you have an appointment?" he asked.

Shelly's appointment was a badge that bridged all priorities. Inside the office, Dr. Youngston removed his topcoat, straightened a tie that caught the blue of his eyes behind the tortoise rims, and then scrutinized the bottle of sleeping pills Shelly now held in his hand. " 'Linda Tracy,' " he read aloud. " 'Two every night before retiring.' Yes, I remember Mrs. Tracy. Quite a young woman. Quite—" he hesitated "—attractive," he added.

"You *remember* Mrs. Tracy," Shelly echoed. "Isn't she your patient now?"

"I suppose she is. Her record is in my files. It's just that I haven't seen her for some time."

"Since she lost her baby?"

"Oh, yes. Certainly. Before, at the time, and after."

"She took it hard, then?"

"Every woman takes it hard. Some may seem indifferent, but that's superficial."

"But doesn't a miscarriage affect different women in different ways?"

Dr. Youngston wasn't over thirty-five. His blond hair was clipped close; his clean-shaven face had a military alertness about it.

"What's your problem, sergeant?" he queried. "Is Mrs. Tracy in trouble?"

"Why do you ask that question?"

"Why is a police officer at my door when I open the office in the morning?"

"It could be Mr. Tracy who's in trouble."

"Mr. Tracy was never my patient. Mrs. Tracy was."

"You're using the past tense again, doctor."

"All right, sergeant, I'll take your bait. Has Mrs. Tracy been murdered?"

It was early morning, but the fog had lifted and the sun was shining through the windows. The world was bright, and Dr. Youngston didn't seem a morbid-minded man.

"That's an interesting thought," Shelly mused, "but so far as the police know, Mrs. Tracy is only the victim of abduction."

"Abduction? What do you mean?"

"I'm not sure. That's why I came to you. A doctor does more than treat the body, doesn't he? You have to understand something of the psychological makeup of the patient."

"I'm merely an obstetrician," Youngston protested.

"Merely? Wouldn't an obstetrician need to know quite a bit about feminine psychology—not to mention family relationships? Now, consider this situation, doctor. Knowing Mrs. Tracy, and there you have me at an advantage, what would you make of it if I told you that some man, unidentified, had called for her in a taxi last night at ten thirty while her husband was at work on the night shift. The landlord and his wife, awakened by the sound of the motor outside the window, got out of bed and watched through the window. They saw the taxi waiting. Moments later, they heard a man—careful, apparently, not to step into the beam of the headlights—come from the Tracy house at the rear of the lot."

"I'm familiar with the Tracy house at the rear of the lot," Dr. Youngston said. "I was called there when Mrs. Tracy lost her child."

"Good. You see the picture, then. Shortly after the man reached the cab, Mrs. Tracy came from the house. She didn't avoid the lights. The landlord and his wife both insist that she looked frightened. She went to the cab, entered it, and the cab drove off."

Youngston had followed the story carefully.

"And hasn't been heard of since, I presume."

"Exactly," Shelly said. "By the way, could I trouble you for a cigarette, doctor?"

"Sorry," Youngston answered. "I never acquired the habit." He appeared thoughtful for a moment, then asked, "What does the cab driver have to say?"

"We're tracking him down now," Shelly replied. "What I'm interested in is your reaction. What do you think happened last night?"

It was a tough question to spring on a man so early in the morning. Youngston frowned, thoughtfully.

"While Mr. Tracy was at work, did you say?"

"Night shift—five forty-five to two forty-five. Calls his wife every night during the ten o'clock coffee break to make sure she's all right."

Dr. Youngston took the pill bottle from Shelly's hand and studied the label again.

"Being a physician," he said, slowly, "my mind may run in a rut;

but isn't it possible that the man who came in the cab told Mrs. Tracy that her husband had been injured on the job?"

"Highly possible," Shelly agreed. "But why did he tell her that?"

"She was a very attractive woman," the doctor suggested.

"Is that what you see typed on the prescription label, doctor?"

Youngston didn't answer with words. Instead, he went to his files. A few minutes later, he returned with the information that Linda Tracy had come to him on the seventh of October complaining of severe nervous tension and an inability to sleep. He had given her a prescription for sixty pills, together with the admonition not to use more than two at a time.

"How many pills would you guess are in that bottle, doctor?" Shelly asked.

Youngston adjusted his glasses.

"I won't guess," he said. "I'll just ask. How many, sergeant?"

"Twenty-eight," Shelly said. "That means only thirty-two pills used, or sixteen nights—"

"It's not unusual for a patient to fail to follow instructions," Youngston said.

"—out of better than three months," Shelly concluded. "Has Mrs. Tracy been back since you issued that prescription?"

"No," Youngston said. "If she had, it would have been entered in the files."

"When she came, did she come alone?"

Dr. Youngston hesitated. "No," he said, thoughtfully. "Mr. Tracy was with her. In fact, it was he who made her come. He was always very concerned about her."

"How did he take it when she lost the baby?"

"Hard. No, actually, not too hard. It was Mrs. Tracy's safety that concerned him. He had an almost paternal—" Youngston paused until the silence grew awkward "—possessiveness," he added.

"Did Mrs. Tracy reciprocate?"

Youngston smiled wryly.

"With paternal possessiveness?"

"You know what I mean? Did she love him?"

"That's a peculiar question, sergeant."

"But a necessary one, doctor. For a few months you were close to this woman—closer than anyone. Closer, even, than her husband in many ways. Did she seem a happy woman?"

"Sergeant, a pregnant woman is every kind of woman. Happy, unhappy, fearful, miserable—"

"Dr. Youngston. I remind you, for sixteen nights, consecutively or otherwise, Linda Tracy took the sleeping pills you prescribed for her and, presumably, went to sleep. And yet, her husband told me that he called his wife every night at ten o'clock just before she took her sleeping pills and went to bed. Somebody lied, doctor. Either Chester Tracy lied to me, or Linda Tracy lied to her husband. That's why I asked you if the woman who disappeared last night loved her husband."

Dr. Youngston wasn't naïve. People married for many reasons; occasionally, love. He hesitated a long time before replying.

"I can't answer that," he said.

"Can't, or won't, doctor?"

"Can't, sergeant. You need facts, don't you? Ask me something I can answer factually, and I'll cooperate."

He was adamant. This was the time for diagnosis, analysis, conjecture, or just plain old fashioned gossip; but Dr. Youngston had chosen none of these, and there was a hardness about his mouth that was impervious to change. Shelly recognized defeat when he met it.

"Just one more question," he said. "What was Mrs. Tracy's condition, aside from nervousness, when you last saw her?"

"Physically—excellent," Youngston said.

"Thank you, doctor. If you think of anything else—factual, of course—that might help us, my name is Shelly. Mike Shelly. You can reach me at headquarters."

Twenty-eight pills in a bottle, and dried mud on her walking shoes. The words made a kind of jingle in Shelly's mind. He was still looking for Linda Tracy—not, of course, in that small room at headquarters where Chester Tracy was pleading for action:

"Haven't you found that cab driver yet? My God, my wife's been gone for nearly twelve hours!"

"We've located the cab company, Mr. Tracy. It's one of the big ones, and it took a while to trace the call sheet. The driver was a man named Berendo—Don Berendo."

"What does he say?"

"He's off duty. We've sent a couple of men to pick him up."

"All right, all right! But when are you going to find Linda? My God!"

No, Shelly couldn't take much of Chester Tracy. A man with more control was easier to interview. A man half a head taller than Tracy, wiry but strong. Black curly hair, teeth that gleamed white in an easy smile.

His name was Leo Manfred. He was thirty-ish. He lived in a small apartment over a garage that housed—visible through raised doors—half a section of discarded rental furnishings, a single horse trailer, and a two-year-old convertible with trailer hitch. The interior of the apartment, furnished chiefly by two large couches and a jazz-playing stereo set, was profusely decorated with mounted photos of horses, as well as a small collection of loving cups. Manfred himself was attired in fitted twill pants, a heavy-knit turtleneck sweater, and western boots. Between the white teeth was a rough brier pipe, which he removed at the sight of Shelly's badge. It was still early in the morning, and he hadn't expected a visitor.

"Just got back from the stable," he explained. "Showing a horse I've got to sell to a prospective buyer. A palomino, good strain. I like to work him out early when he's frisky."

"I thought you were on the day shift," Shelly said.

"What? Where?"

"At Flight Research."

And so the call was official, with Leo Manfred involved enough to have given Sergeant Shelly reason to acquire some background. There was no evidence of Manfred's easy smile now.

"Not for a week," he said.

"What happened a week ago?"

"I quit. Life's too short to waste on a job you don't like."

Manfred stepped back to the stereo set and tuned down the volume. The jazz continued behind the conversation like a muted heartbeat.

"Low pay?" Shelly queried.

"Good pay," Manfred said. "I just wanted a change. Look, what is this? Did somebody make off with the payroll?"

"Somebody," Shelly answered, "made off with Chester Tracy's wife."

Mike Shelly appreciated good jazz, and what was coming from the stereo was very good jazz. It was smooth and cool and well organized, and so was Leo Manfred, who took this information with just a trace of muscular reaction in his face that only an expert could have noticed. And then he waited, because, if he waited, Mike Shelly would have to stop listening to the jazz and tell the story that had previously been told to the only other man known to have been acquainted with Linda Tracy.

"Why have you told me this?" he asked, when Shelly finished.

"Chester Tracy mentioned your name."

"Does he think I made off with Linda?"

Manfred's facial expression was controlled, but his voice wasn't. An unmistakable note of derision had crept into his tone.

"Is something wrong with Linda Tracy?" Shelly asked.

"No comment," Manfred answered.

"In that case, I'll have to ask where you were last night at ten thirty."

Chester Tracy had named two men who knew his wife. One was a doctor who didn't smoke; the other was a man with a horse to sell who had one forefinger laced tightly around the stem of a brier pipe.

"Now I'm getting it," Manfred said. "I introduced Linda to Chester—he must have told you that."

"He did." Shelly answered.

"And now you want to know what I know about her. Well, I don't. Linda was half of a double date I once went on. I don't think I even knew her last name before she nailed Chester."

"Nailed?" Shelly echoed.

"She was one of those—that's why I gave her to Chester. She was hunting, and Chester had that certain look."

The face of a kid pressed against the window, Shelly thought.

"The potential husband look," Manfred explained. "I don't have it. Most women sense that right away; to some it has to come subtly—like a blow on the head."

"How did it come to Linda?" Shelly asked.

He was getting tired of jazz. The photos of horses mounted on the walls were more interesting. Some of them had Leo Manfred astride the horse, standing beside the horse; one was of Manfred introducing the horse to a beautiful blonde. Both Manfred and the blonde were wearing dark glasses, but both were recognizable. The blonde was Linda Tracy.

"Who was the other half of the blind date?" Shelly prodded. "A palomino?"

Manfred said nothing for a few seconds. His face was still controlled, but his glands didn't know it. The frown lines on his forehead were getting moist.

"Look," he said, suddenly, "I wasn't even in the city last night. I drove down to San Diego yesterday to see about a job I'm angling for. I didn't get back until almost midnight."

"Did you drive alone?"

"Alone? Sure. Sergeant, I knew this girl a couple of weeks before I introduced her to Chester. We went dancing—things like that. Pairing her off with Chester was a joke. He was afraid of women. I had no idea he'd fall for her. My guess is that Linda was just too much woman for Chester. I think she rigged that whole deal last night in order to get away from him."

"Why?" Shelly demanded.

"Love in bloom. Linda was always the romantic type. She had a big imagination."

"She's not the only one," Shelly said dryly. "If Mrs. Tracy wanted to run off with another man, she could have staged a fight with Chester and then disappeared. We would have classed it as just another domestic quarrel and waited seventy-two hours before issuing a Missing Persons bulletin."

It was good jazz, but it ended. Leo Manfred walked to the stereo set and switched it off. For a moment, his back was to Shelly, and in that moment, it seemed to stiffen.

When he turned around, he said, "I was only trying to be helpful, sergeant."

"Thanks," Shelly answered. "You can be a lot more helpful if you find someone in San Diego, or on the road back, who can verify the story that you were driving home alone at ten thirty last night."

Don Berendo. He still looked sleepy. A pile of comb-resistant black hair crowded for space on the top of his head, spilling over to his forehead. He hadn't had time to shave before being taken in for questioning, and his beard came out black. He wore a brown leather jacket, and twisted his taxi driver's cap in his hands.

"I picked this guy up at the airport," he said. "He came out of the Inter-Continental waiting room and hailed me just as I was getting ready to pull away after unloading a gent and a lady who were flying to Paris. Must have been all of seventy—both of them—but cute as a couple of kids starting out on a honeymoon. Paris." Berendo's face broke in a sleepy smile. "I bet they have a devil of a time at the Folies Bergère."

"The man who came out of the waiting room," Keonig prodded. "What was he like?"

"Him? Let's see. He wore a raincoat—one of those private eye kind, and a brown felt hat with the brim snapped down, and dark glasses."

"Dark glasses *and* a raincoat?" Shelly echoed.

"You get all kinds at International, sergeant."

"How tall was he?" Keonig asked. "How heavy? Fat or thin?"

Berendo scowled. He stared at Keonig; he stared at Shelly. Then he stared at Chester Tracy, who crouched at the edge of his chair listening with his whole body. Suddenly, Berendo brightened.

"He was about my size," he said. "About medium. I didn't get a good look at his face—that hat brim and the glasses."

"Did he have luggage?" Shelly asked.

"No, he didn't. I asked about that. 'It's checked through,' he told me. 'I have to go home. I forgot something.' Then he gave me that address—the place you call Peterson's where this guy, Tracy, lives. He kept telling me to hurry."

"What time was it when you picked him up?"

"Ten after ten. I marked it on my sheet. I got him to the address he gave me before ten thirty. He told me to wait in the drive with the motor running while he went to the place in the back. He was gone about two minutes. When he came back, I thought we'd go again; but he just opened the back door and stood there smoking a cigarette. A minute or so later, the woman came."

"You saw my wife?" Chester demanded. "How did she look?"

"Scared," Berendo said. "No, there's a better word—shocked."

"As if she'd received bad news?" Shelly suggested.

"Something like that. She got into the cab and the guy after her. I backed out of the drive and started back to the airport, thinking we had a plane to catch and wondering, I'll tell you, how a guy could go off and forget a woman like that at home."

"Did they talk?" Keonig asked. "Did you hear any conversation?"

Berendo hesitated. "I was pretty busy driving," he said at last. "Wait—there was something. The cigarette. The guy gave her a cigarette. She must have been nervous because she used three matches trying to get a light."

"*She* used the matches?" Shelly repeated. "The man didn't give her a light?"

"No. He didn't even sit near her. He sat on one side of the seat and she sat on the other—all tense. I thought maybe they'd had a fight and that was why he had to go back for her. Then a funny thing happened. You know where Airport Boulevard crosses Century—that intersection just before you pull into the airport? Well, I was barreling along, still thinking I had a plane to catch, and I started to speed up so's I'd make the green. This guy leans forward and says, 'Turn left here!' I slam on the brakes, thinking he's kidding.

'Look, mister,' I started to say; but he comes right back at me. 'I said, turn left here!' Okay, so he's the customer. I turned left."

"Where did you go then?" Shelly asked.

"Just about half a block—to this engineering place, Flight Research. 'Stop here,' he says, and I stopped. The woman got out and the man got out and paid me. 'Shall I wait?' I ask him. 'Don't bother,' he said. I couldn't figure it, but like I said, you get all kinds."

"Did they go inside?" Keonig queried.

"That's the funny thing," Berendo answered. "I started to pull out into traffic again, but I smelled something burning. I stopped and looked in the back. This woman had dropped her cigarette and the floor mat was smoldering. I stopped and yanked open the back door, and I naturally looked back at where I'd let them out because I was thinking a few choice things I'd like to say, and they were gone."

"What do you mean—gone?"

"What I said—gone! I felt downright spooky."

"Do you mean that they had gone inside the building?" Shelly demanded.

"They couldn't have gone inside the building. It sets way back off the street—one of those real modern places with no windows, just a big glass entrance to a lobby with a reception desk and a row of doors behind it. A couple of months ago, they landscaped in front and put in a long, winding walk of some kind of flagstone, or maybe slate. They put in new grass, that kind you never have to cut, and trees and shrubs so it doesn't look like a factory at all. At night they've got ground lights on the walk, and the lights shining out from that lobby. There was nobody on the walk and nobody in the lobby."

"They might have gone through one of the inner doors," Keonig suggested.

And then Don Berendo smiled sleepily, but knowingly. "That walk goes back a good two hundred feet," he said, "and I hadn't even got pulled away from the curb. What did they use for transportation —rockets?"

There was only one way to check Berendo's story—a trip to Flight Research. It was a little past eleven when Shelly and Keonig arrived. Berendo was right. The walk, slate slabs set in white gravel, formed a huge S curving back to the plate glass entrance. The entire foyer was visible from the street.

"It was dark," Keonig reminded. "The shrubs might have thrown shadows."

"The shrubs might have given shelter," Shelly said.

Halfway to the doors, at the first reverse curve of the walk, a cluster of semi-tropical growth raised a barrier which fanned back to join the edge of the building. Shelly stepped off the walk onto the Dicondra. The growth was tight and cushiony, like a closely woven carpet. It absorbed footprints and sprang back into place. But the foliage, he discovered, was more than decorative. It hid from the street the less scenic tight wire fence which enclosed the loading and parking areas at the side and rear of the building. At first, there seemed to be no break in the fence; then Shelly noticed a small gate, probably for the gardener's use. He started toward it, then stopped. Behind the foliage, there was a break in the grass—a small, round hole about the size of a penny with one side slightly flattened. Nearby, a sprinkler embedded in the earth was leaking, releasing just enough moisture to soften the ground. Shelly's eyes scanned the area. There were no other holes. He continued to the gate, Keonig at his heels, and found it locked. Over a buzzer on the wall of the building was a small sign: RING FOR ADMITTANCE. Shelly rang. Moments later, a uniformed guard appeared, demanded ID cards, and received, instead, police badges. The gate opened. From the inside, Shelly turned and examined the lock.

"Can this be set to remain unlocked?" he asked.

"From the inside," the guard answered.

"That's good enough," Shelly said.

They continued past the guard, past the loading platform, and on to where the parking lot fanned out before them in six rows of double parked vehicles. By this time, a shirtsleeved official, summoned by the guard, joined them to inquire the nature of their business. His badge announced that he was C. H. Dawson, Supervisor, Dept. E.

"How many employees do you have here?" Shelly asked.

"Four hundred and fifty—approximately," Dawson replied. "Three hundred on the day shift and a hundred and fifty on swing and graveyard."

"Skeleton crews," Keonig suggested.

"Somewhat. You see, we produce high precision equipment for the Air Force. The day shift is largely production, but much of our experimental work demands around the clock schedules. We keep skeleton shop and shipping crew at night, but a fairly complete technical force."

Shelly was still staring at the parking lot.

"Precision equipment," he said. "That means ID cards and gate inspection for all employees of all shifts."

"Exactly."

"And no one could enter or leave these premises, by foot or by automobile, who wasn't known to either the guard or the receptionist on duty."

"Not without proper credentials," Dawson replied. "What is the difficulty, officers? We have an Air Force intelligence officer inside."

"It's nothing like that," Shelly said. And then he paused, reflecting. "Around the clock," he said musingly. "Mr. Dawson, do you have anyone in the plant now who was here all last night?"

Dawson smiled wearily. "Several," he admitted, "including myself. We're running some tests—"

"Do you know an employee named Chester Tracy?"

For a moment it seemed that he'd hit a blank wall, and then Dawson brightened. Chester. Of course he knew Chester. He was in charge of the tool crib, night shift.

"Did you see him last night?"

Dawson was puzzled, but still cooperative. Chester'd spent most of the night in the lab, but had stepped out for a coffee—

"At what time?" Shelly asked.

"Time? We lose all sense of time when we're running tests. No, I do remember. It was eleven. Just eleven. I looked at the clock over the coffee machine, still thinking I might get home by midnight. Well, I'm still here."

"Where was Chester?"

"At the machine. The sugar pull jammed and he loosened it for me. 'It's a dull night,' he said. 'I need something to keep me awake.' I think he was making an excuse for being there when it wasn't time for the regular break. Some shop men never lose their awe of the white collar, even when it's open at the neck and frayed on both sides." And then Dawson paused and seemed to reflect on the total conversation. "I hope Chester isn't in some kind of trouble," he said, "—or his wife."

"Why do you mention his wife?" Keonig asked.

"Because she's not well. I know for a fact that Chester telephones her every night during the ten o'clock break. One night—oh, six weeks or so ago—I found him at the phones, frantic. We had a big wind that night and the telephone wires were down. He explained how nervous she had been since losing their child. He was so upset,

I told him to goof off and go home to see how she was taking the storm."

"Goof off?" Shelly said.

"It was a simple matter for Chester. His work is chiefly at the beginning and the end of the shift. He could duck out the loading exit without being missed."

"Did he do it?"

"Yes, he did. About forty-five minutes later, I noticed he was back in the crib. I kidded him about not even turning off the motor, and he told me that his wife was asleep and he hadn't wanted to disturb her. Chester's a conscientious worker, officer. I wouldn't have made such a suggestion to anyone else."

"He still had to drive past the gate man," Shelly observed.

"Yes, he did."

"Would there be any way of finding out if anyone drove out of your parking lot last night between shift changes?"

There was a way. It took a little time, and left everything as it had been in the first place. Two army officers had left the parking lot, and also the wife of one of the late-working technicians, who had brought him a dietetic supper. No one else. That left only one question to ask the cooperative Mr. Dawson.

"Did you know a former employee named Leo Manfred?" Shelly inquired.

This time, Dawson smiled. "The 'Don Juan' of the drafting board," he said. "Leo was a good man, but he's a drifter. He's left us before. He'll be back when it blows over."

"When what blows over, Mr. Dawson?"

"Whatever made him decide it was time to move on—a woman, probably. Leo loves 'em, but leaves 'em." Then Dawson paused and examined the expressionless faces before him. "I don't suppose it would do any good, if I asked what this inquiry is all about," he added.

Shelly gave him the only possible reply. "As much good," he said, "as if we asked what you were testing last night."

Back on the sidewalk, Mike Shelly stood for a while watching the traffic at the intersection in front of the airport entrance. Most of it bound for the airport consisted of taxi cabs. He counted six before Keonig called him back to the radio car. They were wanted at headquarters. Dr. Youngston had come in to make a statement.

Factual. That was the word Shelly had left with Dr. Youngston.

He waited alone in a small room. His statement, he prefaced, was confidential.

"This is Sergeant Keonig," Shelly explained. "He's working on the case with me."

"Very well," Youngston said. "I suppose I should have told you this when you called at my office this morning, but I hadn't had time to absorb the gravity of the situation. Besides, there are moments between a doctor and a patient that are as sacred as those between a confessor and a priest. I told you that I was called to the Tracy home when Mrs. Tracy lost her child. I was called by Mrs. Peterson. It was all over then, but Mrs. Tracy wasn't aware of what had happened. When I told her, she said something that might have a bearing on her disappearance."

"What did she say?" Shelly asked.

"She called out for someone."

"Her husband?"

"Her husband's name is Chester. The name she called was Leo."

Youngston might have said more, but he didn't have the opportunity. There was a sound from the doorway; Youngston, Shelly, Keonig, all turned at once. Chester Tracy stood staring at them with tragic eyes.

"Leo—" he echoed.

"I thought we were alone," Youngston protested.

"He took Linda. Leo. I'll kill him!"

Chester Tracy was in the doorway one instant; gone from it the next. A moment of shocked surprise, and then Shelly led the exodus to the door. The corridor was already empty; the elevator indicator was starting downward.

"Who is Leo?" Keonig demanded. "Where is he?"

Leo was a target on the other side of the city. Leo was in a garage apartment Shelly had visited once, and Chester Tracy probably a dozen times. Now the elevator indicator had reached street level, and Tracy would be racing for his station wagon. With a grim face, Shelly watched the indicator crawl upward again.

"Leo," he said, "is where we're going right now!"

On the far side of the garage apartment, the side not visible from the street, a sliding glass door opened onto a small sun deck. Shortly after noon, the sun leaned across the roof and bathed the deck in winter warmth. Leo Manfred sprawled in a low-slung deck chair. He still wore his boots and western pants, but had removed the sweater. He tossed his dark glasses on a nearby cocktail table and closed his eyes. He might have fallen asleep if it weren't for an annoying sound in the driveway below. Finally, it ceased and Leo relaxed. He remained relaxed until a shadow fell across his naked chest. Without benefit of the direct sun, the air was cold. Leo opened his eyes and looked up. Chester Tracy stood over him with a trench-coat over his right arm and a brown felt hat in his left hand. He watched Leo's eyes open, and then tossed the hat on his chest in a gesture of contempt.

Leo slid one foot to the floor for leverage.

"Chester—" he said.

The coat slid off Chester's arm. In his hand, he held a gun. There was no time for conversation; only an instant for action. Tossing the hat in Chester's face, Leo lunged forward. Chester had time to fire one shot, wildly, and then Leo's arms were about his body, hurling him back into the room behind the glass doors. When Chester fell, Leo broke free and ran for the front stairway. He had scrambled down to the garage level when suddenly brought up short by the solid substance of Mike Shelly, pistol in hand.

"Drop that gun!" Shelly ordered.

Leo whirled. Chester stood above him at the top of the stairs. He'd retrieved the gun and was leveling it at Leo's head.

"I found the raincoat," he yelled, "and the brown hat—"

"Drop the gun!" Shelly repeated.

"I found 'em—in Leo's closet!"

"Drop it or I'll shoot it out of your hand!"

It wasn't just Mike Shelly facing Chester now; Keonig had come up behind him. Slowly, the gun lowered—then dropped.

"Come down," Shelly said.

Chester obeyed. He came down and stood within a few feet of Leo, while Keonig raced upstairs to find and bring back the hat and coat. At the sight of them, Chester found his voice.

"Make him tell what he's done with my Linda," he demanded. "Make Leo tell!"

"I haven't done anything with Linda," Leo protested. "I was in San Diego—"

"You took her away in a taxi! You always were crazy about Linda!"

Shelly took the hat and coat from Keonig's hands. Both showed signs of a lot of use.

"*I* was crazy about Linda?" Leo howled. "Let's get this straight. Linda was crazy about me! Why do you think she married you,

Chester? I'll tell you why. Because she was crazy about me and I wouldn't have her. She married you out of spite—"

Chester no longer had a gun, but he had a body. Before anyone could stop him, he rushed at Leo and hurled him back against the chrome handle of a refrigerator stacked among the landlord's furnishings. Leo groaned and staggered forward, and then the door of the refrigerator slowly opened, bringing Mike Shelly's search to an end. All of the racks had been removed to make room for Linda Tracy's body.

"My God!" Leo gasped. "Oh, my God!"

It was Dr. Youngston who recovered first from the shock of discovery. He went to the body and made a quick examination. Linda Tracy had been struck a blow on the head "—with the usual blunt instrument," he said. "Dead for at least twelve hours."

"A little longer," Shelly said quietly. "Since about ten fifty-five last night."

His words sounded strange against the stunned silence which still pervaded the garage.

"How do you know that?" Keonig demanded.

"Because," Shelly answered, "if it takes eighteen minutes to drive from Flight Research to the Tracy house; it must take the same time to drive from the Tracy house to Flight Research. Think back, Keonig. The cab driver told us that he had picked up a man wearing a trenchcoat, a brown felt hat, and dark glasses at ten minutes past ten in front of the Inter-Continental waiting room at the airport. He drove to the Tracy address, reaching it shortly before ten thirty, picked up Linda Tracy, and drove to Flight Research where he discharged his passengers."

"Where they promptly disappeared," Keonig added. "Completely."

"But they didn't. They stepped behind the shrubbery and started to walk toward the gate in the wide fence, and then—" Shelly handed the coat and hat back to Keonig and went to the body. It was fully clothed—light tan coat, blue suit, black pumps. He wrenched loose the right pump and examined the heel. It was very high and narrow with a tip about the size of a penny with one side flattened. "Dr. Youngston, if a woman wearing a pump such as this were struck a heavy blow, hard enough to kill, from the back, left side, wouldn't the weight of her body fall on the right foot?"

"I suppose it would," Youngston said.

Shelly's thumb pricked at the residue of dried mud on the heel. "The grass on the grounds at Flight Research doesn't leave tracks," he mused, "but there was one small round hole near a leaky sprinkler valve that would just fit this heel. A woman's shoes are very interesting, particularly Mrs. Tracy's. She has a pair of plastic slippers in her closet less than a month old; but the soles are worn down as if she'd been doing a lot of dancing. And she has a pair of walking shoes in that same closet with mud on them. Now there's no mud on the way to the mail box, but there could be mud in the unpaved alley leading to the street."

Still holding the pump, Shelly made his way past a dazed Leo and a stunned Chester to the trunk of Leo's convertible. He opened it and peered inside. A jack, a tire iron, a spare tire, and a folded saddle blanket. He shook out the blanket with one hand and then tossed it back inside the trunk.

"And then," he continued, "there's the matter of the sleeping pills Linda Tracy didn't take—but told her husband she did. What was to stop her, after that ten o'clock call, from slipping out the back way, walking down the alley, and meeting some Prince Charming to take her to the ball? But, like Cinderella, she had a witching hour—three A.M. Before three, when faithful husband returned, she had to be back in bed, asleep."

"Cinderella slipped up," Keonig observed.

"So did Linda Tracy. And so did her killer."

"I was in San Diego!" Leo protested. "I was on the road driving home at ten fifty-five!"

"What about the night the wind blew down the telephone wires?" Shelly demanded. "Where were you then?"

Leo didn't answer. He was still struggling with shock.

"Weren't you waiting in your convertible at the end of the alley—"

"I didn't kill her," Leo protested.

"—wearing that trenchcoat and the brown hat—"

"I went out with her a few times, that's all. Just—just a few times—"

"—under the street lamp where you could be watched by anyone who had cause to be suspicious?"

"I didn't want to go out with her!" Leo cried. "I was sick of her. That's why I put in for this job in San Diego."

"He's lying—" Chester began.

"No," Shelly said, firmly, "I don't think he is. But rumors fly fast in a small plant, don't they? What did you think when you heard that Leo Manfred had quit and was moving south, Mr. Tracy? Were you afraid he was going to take your wife with him?"

The question caught Chester Tracy by surprise. He blinked stupidly, like a man blinded by sudden light.

"It's Leo's coat," he stammered. "It's Leo's hat—"

"Yes, and your wife had seen both of them often enough to have recognized Leo in an instant if he'd been the man who came for her in the cab. But she couldn't have recognized a new trenchcoat and a new hat—particularly not if she'd been called at ten o'clock and told that her husband had been injured on the job and the company was sending someone after her in a cab. The man who came for her was careful not to talk more than necessary. He sat on the opposite side of the seat. When he gave her a cigarette—not the brand he smoked, but a brand picked up in the airport waiting room where he must have kept the coat and hat in a locker—he let her get her own light. There could be only one reason for such caution."

Shelly stood with the black pump in his hands, and the tense faces of four men before him. But one face was more tense than the others.

"If Linda Tracy hadn't been upset," he added, "she would have recognized the man who came for her, in spite of his disguise. She knew him well enough. He was her husband."

"No!" Tracy protested. "It was Leo—"

"It was meant to sound like Leo when the cab driver told his story, as you knew he would do. That cab bothered me from the beginning. It was too easy to trace. Hadn't you been watching your wife since the night Dawson sent you home to inadvertently discover that she wasn't taking her pills at ten o'clock?"

"I work!" Tracy said. "I work nights!"

"But Dawson showed you a way to get in and out of the plant any time you wanted to without being missed. You knew she was going out with Manfred, and you knew Manfred was moving. You killed your wife, Mr. Tracy."

"No—"

"And made a clumsy attempt to frame Leo Manfred. The way you pushed him against that refrigerator just now was a little obvious. If Manfred had put your wife's body in there, he wouldn't have stood within twenty feet of it!"

Chester Tracy's station wagon was parked just outside the open garage. Shelly went to it and opened the tailgate. Early in the morning, the windows had been curtained with fog; nothing inside could be seen. But now he found a canvas tarpaulin, old and dirty but spotted with stains the police lab would find interesting.

"Time of death: approximately ten fifty-five, doctor," he said, "and then the body was carried to the parking lot until the usual time. After that, Chester Tracy went inside to have a cup of coffee before finishing his shift. But it wasn't a dull night, was it, Tracy?"

Shelly turned around and waited for a protest that didn't come. Chester Tracy had lowered his head and was crying, softly.

"Linda," he said. "My Linda—"

He had the face of a kid who had been given the loveliest toy in the shop window—and broken it.

A Good Kid

by James Holding

I was reading the financial news in the evening paper when Garcia called. It was ten thirty at night; I'd been waiting for his call ever since dinner.

"He's here," Garcia said. There was satisfaction in his tone, as though he were personally responsible for Goosens' arrival. "Holed up in the Continental. Fourth floor. Room 429."

I put down the paper. "Good," I said. "Did you pick him up at the airport?"

"Like you told me. Flight 918. No trouble at all."

I nodded. My information from Amsterdam had been solid. "How'd he act?"

"Nervous. He got out of the airplane last and hurried to catch up with the other passengers. Stayed close to the crowd while he waited for his luggage."

"How'd he come into town? Taxi?"

"No, he waited for one of those limousine jobs."

"He's carrying his line, then." I felt excitement beginning to build inside me. "That's the way they act when there's a package in their vest pocket." I paused. "How'd you spot his room?"

Garcia bragged a little. "I got there ahead of him. Once his limousine hit town, it headed for the Point, so the Continental seemed the best bet. I took a shortcut and was in the lobby when he checked in. I overheard the desk clerk give him 429."

"Nice work," I said. I meant it. His ability to sense things like that beforehand was Garcia's greatest asset. "He didn't turn anything in to the hotel strongbox?"

"Not a thing. I watched him for that. He went up to his room and hasn't been down since."

"Then they're still with him," I said.

"He had his dinner sent up to his room." Garcia laughed. "Roast beef and a baked potato with sour cream." I didn't question his accuracy. Garcia had ways of finding out such things, having been a bellboy himself.

"Where's the car?" I asked him.

"The lot behind the Gateway Building. I had to move pretty fast to make the hotel ahead of him, Pete."

I thought for a minute. "Listen. Keep an eye on him till I get there. We've got to know for sure that he doesn't come down to the desk or have any visitors in his room. For sure."

"No problem. I can see his room from the fourth floor fire door."

"I'll be there in twenty minutes. Meet me in the Fiesta Bar if he's still in his room alone." The Fiesta Bar is dimly lighted, and you can see the hotel desk from there.

"Right." Garcia hung up.

I packed the few things I had with me into my briefcase. It didn't take five minutes. I glanced around the hotel room before I left to make sure I hadn't missed anything. Then I went down to the lobby and checked out. I wasn't using my right name at the Carillon.

It was a nice spring night, so I walked the half mile to the Continental Hotel. My briefcase didn't weigh much, and I didn't want any taxi driver to remember me.

Garcia was waiting for me on a banquette seat close to the glass doors of the Fiesta Bar. He was ordering a drink as I walked in.

I said to the waiter, "I'll take one, too, please. Martini on the rocks with a twist, nice and dry."

The waiter went off and I sat down and winked at Garcia. He looked slightly ridiculous in his long sideburns and straggling mustache. "Well?" I said.

"Still in his room. Alone."

"Good. This is the big one, Garcia. The one we've been training for."

Garcia's mustache lifted as he smiled. "About time, too, Pete." I couldn't blame him for being impatient.

The waiter came back with our drinks. Garcia was having one of his sickening grasshoppers. He lifted it toward me. "Luck," he said.

I took a quarter of my martini. "When you finish your drink, go pick up the car from the Gateway lot. Bring it around and park facing south where you can see the hotel entrance. Keep the engine running, and when you see me come out of here, start toward me. I'll cross the street to be clear of the doorman's station. Pick me up there. Okay?"

"Sure." Garcia was nervous now. He drank the rest of his grasshopper as though it was water on an August day.

"Take it easy, Garcia," I said. "This is going to be a breeze."

I stood up, leaving half my martini. I didn't want much alcohol between Goosens and me. "I'll try not to be long," I said. "You pay the bar check on your way out." I picked up my briefcase and pushed through the glass doors of the bar to the hotel lobby.

Nobody as tall and skinny as Goosens had come near the hotel desk during the few minutes we'd been watching from the bar, so I took an elevator to the fifth floor and walked down the fire stairs to the fourth. I opened the door a crack and looked out at the fourth floor corridor that stretched in front of me. Room 429 was two doors up on the left-hand side.

I took my thin gloves out of my briefcase and put them on. Nobody was in sight in the corridor. I stepped out into it, looked both ways, still saw nobody, and knocked on the door of 429.

After a pause, his voice reached me through the door. "What is it?"

"Cablegram, sir." I could hear him put a hand on the door chain inside but he didn't open the door.

"Cablegram?" He'd naturally be pretty careful.

"Yes, sir." I waited a few seconds, then added, "From Holland."

That did it. He took down the chain and opened the door and I pushed in, shoving him back with my briefcase against his chest. It was like shoving a skeleton dressed in pajamas. Two lamps were on in the room. He'd been reading the newspaper in the armchair. He still had the sports section in his hand.

I closed the door behind me as he backed up, off balance. I didn't worry about his making a move for the telephone between the twin beds because his eyes, big and scared, were on my gun.

I said, "Relax," and saw his eyes change as they came up to my face. I'd hoped he wouldn't recognize me, but he did.

He said in a breathy voice, "Wait a minute! Aren't you Piet Westervelt?"

I cut in, "Never mind. I'll take your diamonds."

He was thin and scared but he had guts. "They're in the hotel safe."

I shook my head at him. "No. We've watched you." My eyes went around the room. A pocket-size zippered dispatch case was lying on his dresser next to a regimental striped necktie. Goosens saw what I was looking at and his eyes turned sick.

My silencer kept the gun noise down to not much more than a man clearing his throat. I went over and picked up the dispatch case and kneaded its contents through the soft leather. I could feel the diamonds.

Goosens was a bundle of loose bones on the hotel carpet. He made a little movement with his legs and tried to say something but couldn't get it out. My bullet had taken him through the neck.

I put the gun into my topcoat pocket and opened my briefcase and shoved Goosens' little dispatch case in on top of my dirty shirt. Then I took another look at Goosens.

He was finished. I stooped down and grabbed him and hauled him over to the nearest twin bed and shoved him under it. He was so skinny that he slid under easily, and the bedspread, hanging down to the floor, hid him completely. I half apologized to him as I straightened the bedspread. He must have known that being a diamond salesman was a high-risk occupation.

I looked for blood on the carpet where he went down, but there wasn't any—one advantage of a small gun. The bullet sometimes stays in. They might not find Goosens for days, if things broke lucky. Twelve hours anyway, even at the worst; plenty of time for Garcia and me.

I checked the room to see that I hadn't left any sign behind me. Then I cracked the door quietly. The corridor outside was as deserted as a tomb, so I stepped out, pulled the door of 429 shut behind me, and hung the "Do Not Disturb" sign over the outside knob.

I made the fire door in two seconds, went through it and down the stairs to the second floor. I walked along the second floor corridor to the elevators, sank my gloves under two inches of sand in the cigarette urn there, rang, and waited for a down car. In a minute or so, one stopped for me. Two fancy blondes in mink stoles and costume jewelry gave me the patronizing eye as I stepped in with them. I wondered what they'd think if they knew I had three hundred and seventy thousand dollars' worth of diamonds in my briefcase.

I came out of the elevator with the blondes into a milling crowd of conventioneers that was dispersing in the lobby after a get-to-gether dinner. I left the hotel by the front entrance and nobody gave me a glance, not even the doorman who was standing fifty yards away, whistling up a cab for a couple of drunks I'd seen in the Fiesta Bar earlier.

Garcia drifted up in the car just as I reached the curb across the street. He was leaning over, holding the door open an inch. I slid into the front seat beside him without the car's ever coming to a halt. Garcia headed for the bridge that would take us across the river to the interstate highway going west.

He had a job holding back until we were safely out of town. He kept his mind on his driving, though, for a good twenty minutes before he asked me anything.

When the car was sailing along at sixty and it was pretty plain we were in the clear, Garcia asked, "Did you get them, Pete?"

I tapped the briefcase. "I got them."

He blew out breath. "Great. Any trouble with Goosens?"

"Not a bit. He handed them over like a little lamb." I worked to keep my voice even, for I had the feeling it would come out shrill if I didn't. "Hold back a little, Garcia. We don't want to be picked up on a lousy traffic violation."

Garcia laughed. "I'm excited, but not that excited. I'm five miles below the limit. Tell me about the diamonds." He was all ears.

"He had them in a leather dispatch case on top of his dresser."

"He must be a fool."

I nodded.

"Are they worth as much as you figured, Pete?"

"The diamonds? I haven't looked yet. But I'd say yes. Or more." I gave him a grin. "Try to get this through your thick head, Garcia. We've got it made. Big."

He snuggled back into the seat cushion happily. "I'd like to see the damn things. We've been working on this heist for so long."

"Let's wait till we're a little farther from the action, all right?"

"Whatever you say."

I began to peel off the false eyebrows. The gum stuck and pulled out some of my own eyebrows with it. I threw away the strips of wax I'd had behind my ears to make them stick out. Then I spread my handkerchief on top of the briefcase in my lap and leaned over and popped out the brown contact lenses onto the handkerchief. I didn't expect I'd have any more use for them; my eyes are blue. I tossed the brown lenses out the car window.

Garcia watched me. "Now you look more like yourself."

"Yeah. After I wash the dye out of my hair."

"I can hardly wait to shed these damn sideburns."

"And the mustache," I said. "That crazy, straggly mustache." We found ourselves laughing, as though we'd just heard a very funny joke. I guess we were both a little silly with relief and letdown.

We drove west as fast as we figured was safe. Garcia was full of questions.

"Goosens just passed you his diamonds without a peep?"

"What else could he do? You don't argue with a gun."

"I know. But you'd think a guy who travels around all over the place with diamonds in his pocket would show a little more . . ."

I was patient with him. "Listen. I've told you before, you do something dangerous long enough, and it doesn't seem dangerous any more. You get so used to it you get careless. A diamond salesman is like that. He knows his job is dangerous, sure. He knows he's a prime target for robbery, because diamonds are the best loot in the world. I told you that."

"Yeah. Because they're small, valuable, and untraceable."

"Well," I said, "almost untraceable. The man who cuts a stone can identify it later if the diamond is big enough, say four, four and a half carats or more. Otherwise, no. Anyway, the salesman knows he's likely to be robbed. But he also knows his diamonds are insured pretty good, too, and that the Jewelers' Security Alliance is on his side, along with the FBI and about a million cops, more or less. And he doesn't get robbed for a long time, so sometimes he doesn't bother to be careful. Like tonight. Goosens figured he was safe when he made the hotel room with his line."

Garcia laughed. "I don't think I'd like to be a diamond salesman."

"Think of the fringe benefits."

"Like what? Being knocked cold and robbed every so often?"

"Some of these boys," I told him, "pull down almost a hundred grand a year."

"For selling diamonds?"

"Yeah."

"Who needs it?" Garcia said. "We did better than that tonight in fifteen minutes." He gave me a sideways look. "How come you know so much about diamonds and salesmen, Pete?"

"I used to be in the business," I said.

I tried to take a nap, but I was edgy and couldn't get to sleep. Garcia switched on the radio. There wasn't anything about us on the midnight news, or about Goosens, either. Too soon.

Garcia said, "Well, that's a relief."

I said, "I'll drive for a while. I can't sleep. You might as well catch a few winks."

He pulled up on the shoulder, got out and walked around the front of the car. I slid over into the driver's seat. When he got into the passenger seat, I handed him the briefcase. "You can hold that. It'll give you pleasant dreams."

He took the briefcase and said, "We must have covered a hundred miles already. How about taking a look?"

"Why not?" I was anxious to see them myself. "Go on. Open it up."

I pulled out onto the highway again and drove on west while Garcia opened the briefcase on his knees. Traffic was light going our way.

Garcia lifted the briefcase lid and took out the diamonds in their zippered envelope. The zipper was locked shut. That didn't bother Garcia. He slit the leather alongside the zipper with his pocketknife and dumped a lot of little tissue paper folders out of the envelope into the briefcase on top of my dirty shirt. Each of the tissue paper twists had figures written on it in ink.

"Divided by weights," I said. "Open up a few if you want to have a look."

He opened a twist of tissue paper and there were a couple of dozen beauties sparkling under the dashboard light. It was a pretty thing to see. I kept my eye on the road and our speed at a steady sixty, but I kept grabbing a look at the diamonds every few seconds, too. Garcia opened up more of the paper twists.

He was popeyed. He couldn't believe what he was seeing. "Man!" he said over and over. "Man!" He'd open a paper twist, hold it under the dashlight, admire the fire of the stones and say, "Man!" Then he'd fold up the paper again and put it back in Goosens' dispatch case.

Along about the fifth packet of diamonds, he said something besides "Man!" He said, "When Goosens reports this, there'll sure be hell to pay."

I thought it was all right to tell him now, especially with the sight of the diamonds to brace him up. I said, "Goosens isn't going to report it, kid. He's dead."

Garcia looked up from the diamonds. His face was soft with shock. "What?"

"I had to shoot him, but don't take it too big. I hid him under the bed and hung a 'Do Not Disturb' sign on his door when I left. We ought to have at least until checkout time tomorrow . . . today . . . before anybody finds him."

"You told me you'd just slug him and tie him up," Garcia said. "What happened?"

"He recognized me. Called me by name. Even with the brown eyes, false eyebrows, and bat ears. So I had to shoot him."

"Oh." Garcia folded up a packet of diamonds and started to unfold another. "You knew him before, huh?" he said. "You didn't tell me that."

"It didn't mean anything, not till last night. Then it meant too much to pass up. In a thing as big as this, we can't afford to leave any witnesses behind us who can finger us to the cops."

"I guess not."

I watched the road. "Look at it this way. Those stones you're looking at are worth three hundred and seventy grand, according to the word from Amsterdam. We won't get that much for them in California, of course. Maybe a hundred and a quarter. But all the same, split that two ways and figure if your cut isn't worth it."

Garcia looked at another paper of diamonds. He didn't say anything.

I said, "Besides, Goosens got it from *me*. You didn't hurt anyone."

Garcia brightened up. "That's right. And I guess there wasn't anything else you could do if he knew who you were."

"He knew me, all right, from the old days. We'd never feel safe again if I hadn't cooked him. So forget it."

"Okay, Pete." He moved a paper of diamonds around under the dashlight and said, "Man!" again. Then he said, "Why didn't you tell me about the killing before?" He sounded hurt.

I told him the truth. "I thought it might bug you, Garcia, and I wanted you cool till we were in the clear."

He nodded. He could understand the need for that, all right.

Changing the subject, I said, "Have you seen enough to satisfy you?"

"I could look at these things all night and never get tired of it!"

"I know. Me, too. But we want to get rid of them as soon as we can."

"Get rid of them?" He was surprised. I hadn't told him about this, either.

"Yeah. We'll mail them ahead to California the next town we hit."

"How do we do that in the middle of the night? And what for?"

"The diamonds will be red hot as soon as Goosens is found. Better we don't have them on us for the next few days."

"Who are we mailing them to?" His eyes glinted. "Half of them are mine."

I grinned at him. "There's a mailing box and some sealing tape in the briefcase. The box is already addressed and stamped and ready to go. All you have to do is put the diamonds inside the box, seal it up with the tape, and read the address on the box. Does that answer your questions?"

He rummaged around in the briefcase and came up with the mail-

ing box and tape I'd prepared some days ago. He read the address
on the box. "Who's Henry Anters?" the kid wanted to know.

"Either you or me," I told him. "A phony name I dreamed up to
mail the ice to in San Francisco. It's General Delivery. We call for
the package when we get there. Simple."

Garcia nodded and dumped the papers of diamonds out of Goosens'
slit dispatch case into the mailing box and sealed it up. The next
town we went through, he dropped the box into the chute of one of
those postboxes they had in front of the post office on the main street.
The post office was dark and we didn't see anybody on the street.
It was past two in the morning.

A minute later, Garcia dropped Goosens' leather envelope into a
litter box on a corner. Then he grunted and squirmed down in his
seat and leaned his head back and got quiet. Pretty soon I heard
him breathing heavily, almost snoring. I looked over at him. He'd
pulled off his sideburns and mustache and he looked a lot younger
without them, less like a sharpie.

He'd taken the news, that he was accessory to murder, pretty good
for a kid. Anyway, better he learned it from me than from a radio
bulletin after they found Goosens' body. Maybe his share of the
diamonds would make up to him for it. I hoped so. He was a good
kid. It was a lousy break for both of us that Goosens recognized me
because you can't run fast enough or far enough to get clear after
a job as big as this one if you leave a witness behind you who knows
you pulled it.

I looked at the gasoline gauge and saw we had a quarter of a tank
left. I figured to stop at the next open station and fill up, because
you never know where your next gallon is coming from in the middle
of the night. I drove for another hour. Garcia was sleeping like a
baby beside me. Once his head rolled sideways and even that didn't
wake him up. He didn't come to until I turned into a twenty-four-
hour gas station in a place called Veneta, near the state line, and
pulled up beside the premium pump. Then Garcia opened one eye,
yawned, stretched, and looked out the window.

"Where's this?" he asked me.

I told him. He nodded and climbed out of the car. "Never heard
of the place," he said, "but I guess they have a men's room, anyway."
He headed for it.

An old fellow in a golf cap came out of the station and asked what
he could do for us. "Fill it up with premium," I said. "And check the
oil."

Garcia came back from the men's room and put a dime in the cola machine and said, "You want one, Pete?"

I told him no. The old boy in the cap opened up the hood of the car and groped around for the oil stick. When he showed it to me, it registered full. I asked him to check the water in the battery. Then I went to the men's room myself. It seemed like a long evening.

When I came out, Garcia was standing at the back of the car, jawing with the old gas jockey, who was hanging up the hose, "Seventeen gallons on the nose," the man reported. "It's filled right up."

I paid him cash for the gasoline.

"Want me to drive a while?" Garcia asked me.

"Go ahead. I'll try for a nap again."

We climbed in the car and got going. Garcia said, "The old boy told me we had sixty miles of two-lane before we pick up the interstate again."

"We won't pick up any more interstates," I said. "Secondary roads from now on. The interstate gave us a flying start, but it's on the interstates they'll start looking for us after they find Goosens."

We didn't say anything more after that for quite a while. I leaned back and tried to relax and take a nap but I couldn't seem to unwind, somehow. Instead of getting looser, I was getting tighter. I couldn't figure why. We'd come more than two hundred miles; we'd got rid of the stones; it was a safe bet Goosens' body wasn't found yet. The way it looked, we were home free. All the same, something was nagging at me.

I kept remembering Goosens' legs moving against the red hotel rug, and I kept wondering what he'd tried to say before he cashed in. It didn't make a lot of difference. He couldn't say anything to anybody any more. The cops would never learn about me from him. The only safe witness was a dead one in a job as big as this.

I didn't move or open my eyes, but that's when it first hit me . . . the realization that even with Goosens dead, I wasn't completely in the clear. I give you my word it never occurred to me before that minute. Otherwise I wouldn't have shot my mouth off like a sinner at confession. Believe me, I felt sick.

There was hardly any traffic on our two-lane road. It was getting on for four in the morning now. The road kind of wandered around as though it couldn't make up its mind which direction to go, through farm country, patches of woods, up to a hilltop, down again. For about six miles it ran alongside a little river through a twisting gully. The gully was black as your hat. Every few hundred yards the road went over a culvert that drained off the water from the hillside on one side of us into the river on the other.

I sat up in my seat and said, "Damn it all, I can't get to sleep."

"Nerves." Garcia smiled without turning his head.

"Could be, I guess. Anyway, pull up when you come to a good place and I'll drive."

Garcia pulled up where the road widened a little on a short straightaway. He got out of the car and walked around the front end. Our headlights were on. They probably blinded him a little because he didn't notice that I hadn't slid over under the wheel. When he opened the door on my side, I said, "I'm sorry, kid," and shot him. The bullet took him under the chin and angled up. He was dead before he knew what hit him. I was glad of that. He was a good kid.

I couldn't see any headlights coming in either direction, so I turned off our own. I got out of the car, then, and took Garcia by the slack of his jacket and dragged him along the shoulder of the road to where one of those culverts went under it about twenty yards ahead. I went down into the runoff ditch with him and looked at the culvert. It was maybe three feet in diameter and there was plenty of room for Garcia in it. He wouldn't block the flow of water unless there was a flood. I went through his clothes and took his wallet and everything else he had on him that might give a hint who he was. Then I fed him into the upper end of the culvert and worked him along it until he was out of sight. I left him lying there in about three inches of water and went back to the car.

Still no cars in either direction; my luck was holding up. I took my gun out of my topcoat pocket and heaved it as far as I could out into the river. Then I got Garcia's plastic airplane bag out of the trunk, put his wallet and other stuff in it along with a couple of good-sized rocks from the side of the road to weight it, and slung the whole business into the river after my gun. Finally, I got behind the wheel, turned on the headlights and took off. It would be a long time before they found Garcia, and when they did, it would take them another long time to identify him.

I felt bad about Garcia. You can't work with a kid that long without getting to like him. If only Goosens hadn't recognized me, Garcia would still be alive. I tried to cheer myself by thinking that when I added Garcia's share of the diamonds to mine, I could live it up with the best of them for quite a few years to come. After an hour or so I began to feel a lot better. I even thought that if Garcia were still here to drive me, I could get to sleep at last. Isn't that the way it goes?

I kept on at a steady clip and pretty soon I picked up the interstate that Garcia had mentioned. After a few miles on that, I left it and angled southwest to cut between Cincinnati and Indianapolis and then went northwest again to pick up U.S. 36. I didn't hurry but I didn't loaf, either.

By seven the next morning I was over four hundred miles away from where Goosens was hiding under his bed, and the signs all pointed to another nice spring day.

I stopped for breakfast at a diner fifty miles west of Indianapolis. I needed coffee to keep me awake now. I wasn't hungry but I had a Danish with the third cup of coffee, just to be eating something. Two hours after that, at a wide place in the road called Danforth, I stopped and had the gas tank topped off again. That car used gas like it was going out of style. I thought maybe I'd buy another make of car next time. Then I remembered that I'd soon have enough money so I wouldn't give a damn how many miles to a gallon I got. I drove on west.

A couple of miles east of Springfield's city limits I ran into a roadblock. Two patrols cars were pulled up on the shoulder of the road with their red flashers going. A cop beside the road waved me down. I pulled over and stopped.

The cop, a big guy in highway patrol uniform, walked up to my window and said, "Good morning," in a polite voice.

I said, "Hi," in a voice just as polite as his.

"Would you mind getting out of the car?"

"Getting out?" I was surprised. "What for?"

"Will you please get out?" He was still polite, and opened the door of my car like a silent invitation. There was another uniformed man behind him. A guy in plain clothes with a crooked nose came up on the other side of my car. The traffic went swishing by us on the highway. A third patrolman was waving the cars through.

Whatever they were after, they weren't fooling. I said, "Why not?" and stepped out of the car.

"Put your hands on the roof of the car and stand quiet," the cop said.

I did what he told me. I could feel his hands going over me. They patted my pockets, my belt line, up and down my legs, under each arm. I was glad I'd tossed my gun into that river back in Ohio.

The cop said over the top of the car to the plainclothes boy with the crooked nose, "He's clean, Al."

Al came around the car and said, also politely, "If your arms are getting tired you can turn around now. Would you mind letting us see your car registration and driver's license?"

I dug them out of my wallet and handed them over.

Reading from them, Al said, "Peter Westervelt, San Francisco. Is that you?"

"That's me."

"Is this your address?"

I nodded yes.

"What is it?" he said then, holding the cards so I couldn't see them.

I told him. He didn't look surprised that I knew my own address. He didn't look happy, either. Maybe he thought I'd stolen the car, complete with owner's cards.

I said, "What's the problem, boys? Or is it a secret?"

The uniformed cop said, "We're sorry, we can't tell you that."

"Why not?"

Al took over. "We don't know ourselves," he confessed. He was pretty sore at somebody, and I didn't think it was me. "What happened is, we got word from the highway patrol up the line to stop a blue car with California license plates 156-E-290. And that's you."

I said, "That's me."

Al said, "We kind of understood you were armed and desperate." He wasn't exactly apologizing but it sounded pretty lame.

I leaned against the car. "That patrol up the line must be out of its skull. What would give them a screwy idea like that?"

He looked back up the road. "Maybe we'll find out now. Here it comes."

A cruiser pulled up behind us. A uniformed cop jumped out of it and came running up to us. He looked at me. "You got him?" He was fat and out of breath.

"We got him." From Al's voice, this was the guy he was sore at. "And where did you get that jazz you put on the air about him?"

The fat cop muttered something too low for me to hear, and Al said to the patrol officer beside me, "Keep an eye on him, Joe." Then he went off a little way with the fat cop and they held a conference. Every once in a while one of them would look at me. I watched them, but I couldn't tell what they were talking about.

In a couple of minutes, the fat cop handed something to Al, went

back and climbed in his cruiser, made a fast U-turn, and started
back east. Al came back to me.

He gave me a funny look. "Are you in a hurry, Mr. Westervelt?"

"I am, as a matter of fact."

"Too much of a hurry to stop off for an hour while we try to clear
this up?"

"Clear what up?"

"Offhand, I'd say it's a joke of some kind, Mr. Westervelt. I'd like
to check it out, though, if you'll cooperate by coming to headquarters
for a little while."

"Why should I?" I was feeling edgy again. "You charging me with
anything?"

"I can charge you with going sixty in a thirty-five mile zone, if
you want it that way."

"This is no thirty-five mile zone. That sign right there says sixty."

"I can't quite read it from here." Al was bland as cream.

I said, "All right, damn it, I'll come. But hurry it up, will you? If
it's a joke, it's a lousy one."

Al said, "That's sensible. I'll drive your car, if you don't mind."
He got behind the wheel. One of the uniformed cops got in the back
seat. "You ride beside me, Mr. Westervelt," Al said.

I got in and Al waved to the other cops beside the road and yelled,
"Thanks," as we went by them.

I didn't say anything. I sat there and tried to figure out what the
hell went on. As far as I could see, there wasn't any handle sticking
out anywhere behind me that they could have grabbed to tie me up
with Goosens or the diamonds or Garcia. All the same, I was edgy.
You can understand that. I wasn't exactly an innocent citizen even
if I was sure they couldn't pin anything on me, but they tell me that
even innocent citizens feel uneasy when they deal with cops.

Al took me to a neat squad room at police headquarters, sat me
down in a straight chair with a couple of six-months-old magazines,
and left me with the uniformed patrolman who was supposed to see
that I kept on cooperating, I guess.

As it turned out, it didn't take an hour. Al, the cop told me, was
a Lieutenant Randall of Homicide, and he sent for me in forty-five
minutes. The uniformed cop guided me to Al's shoebox office. There
was only one dirty window in the room, and Al was sitting behind
a beat-up desk in a swivel chair that squeaked every time he moved.
I sat down in a chair across from him without being asked. I tried

to make something out of the expression on his face, but I couldn't. There wasn't any expression on it.

He said, "Well, Mr. Westervelt, it wasn't a joke after all. I was wrong."

I felt a rush of relief. "I'm glad we've got that settled. Can I go now?"

He swung his chair. It squealed like a rat in pain. "Not just yet, no. We're holding you."

The relief went away. "For what?"

"Suspicion of murder, armed robbery, and grand larceny, among other things." He kept his eyes on me. "How does that grab you for openers?"

"Now *you're* joking," I said.

"Far from it."

I took in a breath and said, "Who am I supposed to have murdered?"

"A diamond salesman named Goosens." He came out with it as if announcing that it was going to rain. The words hit me like rain . . . cold rain.

I said, "I never heard of him."

"No? Then there's somebody named John Garcia."

"Him, either."

"And somebody named Henry Anters."

I got out my handkerchief and wiped my upper lip.

Al said, "I'm not going to con you. Westervelt. We've got you good."

"For what? I haven't done anything, I keep telling you."

He tipped up the dog-eared blotter on his desk and pulled out a dirty piece of paper. It had writing on it. "A service station attendant in Danforth found this inside the cap of your gas tank this morning," he told me. He held it up. "The service station attendant called the Highway Patrol and they alerted everybody from Danforth to Pittsfield. Including us."

"What is it?" I asked.

Al grinned. "It's a message from Garcia."

I told him again, "I never heard of any Garcia."

"Let me read it to you." Al folded the paper up so two big words printed on it in pencil showed on top. "See that? CALL POLICE! That's what was staring the service station attendant right in the eye when he took off your gas cap this morning in Danforth. While you were in the men's room, he took out the note and read the rest of it."

"What's it say?" I felt rotten all of a sudden.

"It says, 'This man is a killer. Check Room 429, Continental Hotel, Pittsburgh. Also Henry Anters, General Delivery, San Francisco.' And it's signed 'John Garcia.' "

I dabbed at my lip again.

Al said, "I've been in touch with Pittsburgh. When I asked them to check Room 429 at the Continental Hotel, they found a man named Goosens under the bed, shot to death. A diamond salesman, by his papers. I've also been in touch with the wholesaler he worked for, who says Goosens flew into Pittsburgh last night with three hundred and seventy thousand dollars' worth of diamonds. Pittsburgh says there's no sign of diamonds in his room or on his body."

I thought back. Garcia . . . while we got gas in Veneta, that first time, Garcia had gone to the men's room first, then me. Garcia must have written the note in there, then stuck it into the gas cap while I was in the can. I remembered he was standing at the back of the car, jawing with the old man when I came out.

Al went on, "I'd say that this John Garcia's note checked out pretty good so far, wouldn't you?" Then he added in a hurry, "Don't answer that. I'm advising you of your constitutional rights now. You don't need to answer any questions I ask if you don't want to. And you have the right to have a lawyer present if you want one."

"Who, me?" I said. "What would I want a lawyer for? Ask me anything you like. I haven't done anything. And I don't know what this is all about."

"Never heard of Henry Anters?"

I shook my head. They could never connect me with that name.

"The post office in San Francisco is going to hold anything that arrives in that name. I talked to them, too."

"You have been busy, haven't you?" I had it worked out now. I stretched. "But you've got nothing you can hold me on. I told you once, I'll tell you again, I never heard of Goosens, Garcia, or any diamonds. And nobody can prove I did. A crank note put into a man's gas cap by some nut doesn't prove he's a killer or a diamond thief. And you damn well know it."

Al said, "You sure you never heard of Garcia, eh?"

"Again. I never heard of him."

Al gazed out his dirty office window. "My guess is, Garcia was in on the heist with you. If you killed Goosens during the stickup, maybe Garcia realized all of a sudden what a rough guy he was hooked to, and he figured maybe he was next on your list." His eyes came back to me. "Was he?"

He didn't expect an answer. I didn't give him one. He said, "If you want my opinion, you did know Garcia. And he knew you."

I thought to myself, he did at that, better than I knew him. All the same, he hadn't been as cute as he thought with his little note in the gas cap. Because note or no note, there was nothing to prove a connection between me and Goosens; or between me and Garcia. My gun was on the bottom of a river; Garcia's things ditto and his body missing; the diamonds were in the mail and would never be called for now by Henry Anters in San Francisco. I felt bad about that. Garcia had fouled me up there. But unless the police could tie me in with the diamonds, they had no case at all that I could see.

Al could have been reading my mind. He put his hand into the middle drawer of his desk and brought out two diamonds. He cupped them in the palm of his hand and held them for me to see. "Look what we found in the gas tank of your car," he said.

I didn't have much heart for it, but I kept trying. I said, "What are they?"

"Diamonds." He tossed them and caught them again.

"In my gas tank?"

"Yes."

"Either you're framing me or you're kidding," I said.

The look he gave me would cut grease. "I'm not framing you, and I don't kid with killers. I used to be on robbery detail, and I recognized this paper Garcia wrote his note on as a wrapper for unmounted gems. So I had your gas tank drained just for the hell of it, see? I figured if Garcia put a diamond wrapper in your gas tank, maybe he put the diamonds themselves there, too. You can see I was right."

"What do they weigh?" I asked.

He tapped Garcia's note. "The jeweler's notation here says they're five-carat stones."

That slammed the door. If they'd been smaller, I still had a chance. No expert could have identified them as part of Goosens' line, but with five-carat stones, the man who cut them could identify them in two minutes. I'd told Garcia that, I remembered now, and he'd used the information to cut my throat.

Those two diamonds tied me in with Goosens—but tight—and with Garcia, too. Because it stands to reason nobody is going to show up with two big diamonds in his gas tank unless he's been mixed up in the action somehow, and especially not with Garcia's letter of explanation in the same gas tank.

Garcia . . . I kept thinking about him. The only time he could have palmed the packet of big diamonds was when he was getting the box ready to mail, and that meant he knew I was going to kill him before I knew it myself—before the thought even entered my head.

"This Garcia must have been quite a boy," Al said to nobody in particular. I noticed he used the past tense.

I thought to myself, Garcia *was* a good kid, except for one thing: his creepy way of knowing beforehand what was going to happen next.

Maybe some of it had rubbed off on me, because I already knew what Al was going to say next.

He said, "You want a lawyer now, Westervelt? What do you say?"

I didn't say anything. What was the use?

Enter the Stranger

by Donald Olson

When the young man with the dream-scarred eyes finally found his way to Windfall, De Vore Goring's secluded estate, he stood trembling in the rain under the lighted windows, and not even the thunder rumbling over the wooded foothills behind him sounded louder in his ears than the frantic drumming of his own heart, a disturbance caused less by awe than by joyful anticipation, and when he passed through the gate and sounded the bell he did so without a tremor of shyness.

The aged housekeeper looked at him the way most people looked at him, with that eye-squint of uncertainty he'd learned to counteract, as he did now, with a disarmingly boyish smile. He asked for Goring and when the housekeeper wanted to know his name he said merely that he was a friend of Penelope's.

The woman looked at him oddly for a moment but then responded with a comprehending chirp of approval. "Friend of Penelope's, are you? Oh, ha-ha, yes, I see. Well, come in, then, come in. I'll see if he's still up."

He glanced behind him before following her inside and in a flash of silvery lightning noticed once more how totally isolated the house was.

She returned in a few moments and conducted him to a room at the head of the stairs, leaving him outside the open door.

With the greedy eyes of a traveler overjoyed to be home again, he tried to take in everything at once: the shelves of books, the huge mahogany desk, the marble fireplace, the picture of the young girl over the mantel, so that it was all a shimmery blur made worse by the tears filming his eyes, those dreamy slate-colored eyes that betrayed the presence of some wound or flaw or sorrow lurking just below the surface of his personality.

There was Goring himself, dear old Uncle Dev, with the familiar white hair and mustache, bushy brows and tame-lion eyes.

Goring waited for his tongue-tied caller to speak. When he did not, he lifted a frail hand from his blanketed lap and beckoned the young man closer.

"I'm Goring. Mr. . . . ?"

The visitor stepped eagerly forward to clasp the outstretched hand, somewhat startling Goring, making him feel uncomfortably like St. Peter in the Vatican, fearing for a moment that the fellow might be going to kneel and kiss his toe.

Instead, he moved back as if to give the older man a better look at him and said, with his too-generous smile: "Don't you recognize me?"

Goring stared, murmured an apology.

"I'm Jack!"

"Jack? Hmm . . . I'm still afraid . . . "

"*Jack*. You know—the Mysterious Stranger!"

Goring's hand rose to his eyes. "I'm afraid you still have me at a disadvantage, young fellow. An old man's memory . . . "

The caller looked more impatient than annoyed. "Gee, I recognized you right away. You're just like I knew Uncle Dev would be."

Goring became alert now in a more than socially attentive way. "Wait a minute. You don't mean you're—not *our* Jack."

As he said this he waved toward a certain shelf of books directly behind the desk. The visitor pounced on them, ran trembling fingers across their brightly jacketed spines.

"Yes! Jack, the Mysterious Stranger. I'm him!"

"Are you in*deed?* Well, fancy that." Although truly flabbergasted, a well-trained imagination helped Goring maintain his aplomb.

A blunt-tipped finger plucked one of the volumes from the shelf. *"Penelope and the Coral Reef.* Wow! That was super. But I don't see how Penelope could have thought I was one of the *bad* fishermen. I kept trying to warn her about Chang. But she kept running away."

He raced on in this vein, darting from one book to another, from *Penelope and the Deadly Amulet* to *Penelope and the Enchanted Valley,* from *Penelope and the Travisham Ghost* to *Penelope and the Smugglers' Revenge,* recalling delightedly how in each adventure he had come to Penelope's rescue.

Goring listened to all this with an emotion so singular he could not have defined it; it was as if one of his characters had magically come to life and burst through the study door to confront him at the very spot where Goring had created him. The emotion was certainly disturbing but not ungratifying. Recognition he'd had, to a degree, but this was in its way the supreme compliment.

The *Penelope* books, some two dozen of which had been published over the past couple of decades, had grown out of a simple story he'd written to amuse his young niece, based on one of his archaeological expeditions. He would never have tampered with the stories' formula—his teenage readers would not have tolerated it—and in each book Penelope would accompany Uncle Dev to some distant spot and be plunged into an exotic, danger-filled adventure. A conventional figure in each of the plots was a shadowy young man named Jack, a Mysterious Stranger who invariably popped up when Penelope was about to be fatally bitten by a cobra, suffocated in a mine cave-in, drowned in a scuttled yacht, or shot in a bandit's hideout. Any young reader of average intelligence could have told Penelope—Goring had scores of letters to prove it—that ever since *The Opal Talisman* adventure Jack had been wildly in love with her, yet she remained, book after book, annoyingly oblivious to his affection.

Only now did the visitor become aware that Goring was in a wheelchair.

"Did that bullet wound in *The Mandarin's Hatchet* really injure you, sir?"

Goring sighed and was on the point of explaining that nothing more dramatic than degenerative arthritis accounted for his condition when the caprice seized him to humor the lad's delusion.

Or was the impulse quite that innocent?

It was second nature to Goring to invent fictional plots and already certain elements of a curious scenario may have been shaping themselves in his mind, a mind grown bitter with jealousy and illness.

So he said, "Not really, no. It was that fall in *The Temple of the Sun Dragon,* remember? When I fell down the thousand and one steps?"

The man who thought he was "Jack" looked sympathetic to the point of tears. Feeling guilty, Goring insisted his visitor tell him more about himself. "I could offer you some refreshments, but I told Mrs. Harkins she could go to bed. And I'm quite helpless, as you see."

The visitor's face grew surprisingly hostile. "Is *that* why Penelope's going to marry Howard Rashbrooke?"

Goring's mind, until now only toying with that dangerous scenario, not really believing he could connect those various elements, seized upon the young man's hostility with furtive delight, as if the key to that shadowy plot had suddenly dropped into his hand.

"Er—no. No, of course not."

"Because she mustn't, you know. Rashbrooke's nothing but a fortune hunter. Can't you *see* that?"

The sorrows which had been Goring's only company ever since Sheila had begun the affair with Harry Lawton, the affair she thought Goring knew nothing about, were momentarily forgotten, the pain no pills could conquer half-forgotten.

"Rashbrooke claims to be in love with Penelope," he said slyly.

"Penelope *can't* love *him*. She loves *me*. She always has, ever since I kissed her in *The Opal Talisman*. She slapped my face, sure. Any decent girl would have done the same thing if a mysterious stranger kissed her. But she never forgot the kiss. No! She can't marry Rashbrooke. She can't!"

The young man had jumped to his feet and assumed a pose, legs apart, fists jammed against hips, which Goring recognized as characteristic of Jack. For a moment he felt a bit like Frankenstein and, like Frankenstein, he had passed beyond the point where he might still have abandoned his perilous experiment. It was as if fate had sent him this instrument, this human tool.

Goring implored the visitor to sit down. "You were going to tell me about yourself. How did it begin? I mean, when did you first know?"

"That I was Jack? Gosh, ages ago. When I was still in the orphanage. The other kids, they liked *Tom Swift* and *Nancy Drew,* but the minute I read *Penelope and the Jade Tiger* . . . well, Jack was *me*. He looked like me and he was an orphan and he never belonged anywhere. I must have read that book twenty times. And the others . . . all the others."

Goring was silent, watching the emotions glide swiftly over his visitor's young-old face, while outside the window the artillery rumble of thunder drew closer, and rain, like cold-fingered refugees fleeing before the guns, tapped urgently upon the pane. In spite of what he knew he was going to do, Goring was still deeply touched by the young man's tale, never dreaming that his unambitious labors could have wrought so lastingly vivid an effect upon a childish mind. How dismaying to realize that he had provided another human being with so total an escape into fantasy.

The caller's voice droned on. " . . . and when I read *The Missing Cipher* last month and Penelope actually got *engaged* to Howard Rashbrooke I knew I had to do something. I couldn't let it happen. I knew I had to come here and find her and tell her I love her . . . Where is she, Uncle Dev? Where's Penelope?"

Goring's mind was busy with the various aspects of his scenario that must be made coherent and viable.

"Tell me, Uncle Dev. Where is she?"

Where indeed? *No motion has she now, no force, she neither hears nor sees . . .* Only her name in real life was Polly, that adored little niece who had died in Goring's arms, and with her had died the only thing in the world he'd ever truly loved. He had been unable to keep Polly alive, but he could be sure that Penelope, the shadow child of his imagination whose adventures had so enthralled his little niece, would never die.

This reminded him of Sheila and a wave of hatred darkened his face.

"Uncle Dev? *Where is Penelope?*"

Goring knew it was his last chance to tell the truth, his last chance to scrap the grisly scenario in his mind. And what if he did? What if he were to tell "Jack" that all this time he had been idolizing a dead girl? What effect might such a revelation have on his already clouded mind?

The thunder, closer now, as if the furious armies in the sky were battling above the very roof, seemed to echo the words: *"Where is she, Uncle Dev?"*

"She's not home this evening, Jack. She had to go out."

"With *him?*"

"No. Not with him. She went to visit a sick friend."

Sheila, damn her, had insulted his intelligence with the same brazen excuse. A sick friend! Did she think he was senile, that he would swallow as phony an excuse as that? But then, it gave her pleasure to insult his intelligence just as it gave her pleasure to see him sitting in that wheelchair, helpless and vulnerable and so totally at her mercy.

"That's just like Penelope," the young man murmured. "Where is she, Uncle Dev? Tell me how to get there."

"If you found her, what would you do?"

"Why, tell her, of course."

"That you love her?"

"Yes."

"And want to marry her?"

"Yes!"

"What if she refused?"

"She wouldn't. She loves me."

"But what if she did?"

"I'd kill myself!" All his utterances were as melodramatic as a child's, and as artlessly sincere.

"Ah, my boy, it's no good. She has to marry Rashbrooke whether she wants to or not."

The young man was actually trembling with excitement. "You're wrong, Uncle Dev! I'll help her escape. Like I always do."

"You don't understand, lad. You don't know what Rashbrooke is."

In Goring's mind the scenario assumed its final shape.

"He's nothing but a lousy fortune hunter, Uncle Dev."

"He's more than that. Much more." Goring pointed to the manuscript on the desk. "It's not finished. But read the title."

A sudden shattering clap of thunder seemed to make the house tremble on its foundation as the young man picked up the manuscript and looked at it, his lips shaping and reshaping the words before speaking them aloud. *"Penelope and the Final Escape* . . . I don't get it, Uncle Dev. *Final* escape? That doesn't mean—"

"Marriage will bring Penelope's adventures to a logical conclusion."

Not his idea, never his idea; if he'd had anything to say about it Penelope's adventures would never end, not so long as he had breath in his body. Only he didn't have anything to say about it; he was powerless to cope with Sheila, the woman who had entered his house for the first time as a hired secretary when arthritis had afflicted him shortly after the fourth *Penelope* book and who, as his wife two years later, was writing the books herself. No one knew, of course, not even his publisher; she had become an expert at aping Goring's style. As the royalties had rolled in in greater and greater abundance she had grown indifferent to Goring and his suffering and had begun the affair with Lawton almost under his nose, until finally a day had come when she declared that she was sick of Penelope and she had embarked upon *The Final Escape,* intending to bring the series to a close.

Now Goring wheeled himself to the young man's side and calmly took the manuscript from his hand. "You remember Anaxos in *The Greek Uprising?"*

"Sure. He was one of Chang's men."

"Well, so is Rashbrooke."

The effect of this upon his visitor was enough to make Goring lower his eyes in shame even while his heart pounded with excitement.

"But, Uncle Dev, you can't let her do it!"

Goring spread his hands. "I'm helpless, as you can see. There's nothing I can do."

Gradually a sly, deliberate smile swept the anxiety from the young man's face. "I'm not helpless, Uncle Dev. I can help her get away from Rashbrooke just like I helped her escape from Anaxos."

Now that he could no longer dismiss it, Goring tried to tell himself that the idea for this monstrous scenario wasn't really his at all, but something evil and hideous spawned by the Devil of Pain that had made its home in his crippled body.

"You'd be risking your life, Jack. If you were caught they'd never believe you. You know what they'd say, don't you? That Penelope and Rashbrooke are only figments of the imagination, characters in a book."

The caller's smile grew noticeably slyer. "That's what Mrs. Brooks said when I went back to visit her once at the orphanage and told her all about my adventures. She said I was all mixed up. She said they were only characters in a book. And you know what I said, Uncle Dev? I said, if they're not real, then I'm not real either. She couldn't argue with *that*. That stumped her, let me tell you. Because I was right there talking to her and she couldn't say *I* wasn't real."

The hideousness of what he was doing brought a cold sweat to Goring's hands. "Go away, boy. While there's still time. Forget about Penelope."

"Where is he, Uncle Dev? Tell me where to find Rashbrooke. I'll take care of him just like I took care of Anaxos."

Once more his hand darted toward the desk, this time grabbing up a silver letter knife. "I don't have that Persian dagger I used on Anaxos, but this will do just fine." He smiled at Goring. "How do I find him, Uncle Dev?"

Goring looked very old and very tired. "You'd never find him. Not unless I called him and told him to come here."

Tiny flames burned behind the dream-scarred eyes. "Then call him, Uncle Dev. Right now."

With a curious, passive sense of having delivered himself into the power of an emotion he could neither understand nor resist, Goring picked up the telephone, then paused. "Listen, Jack, while I'm calling him you go downstairs and unlock the front door. Don't make any noise. We don't want to wake Mrs. Harkins."

As soon as the young man was out of the room Goring dialed the number with an aching, stiff-jointed finger. They would be together, of course, Sheila and Lawton. Suppose Sheila were to answer. But of course she didn't.

"Lawton? It's me, Goring, I've got to see you . . . Yes, yes. I know what time it is, but it's important . . . There's something I've got to tell you. About Sheila. Something she mustn't know. You've got to come right now. Sheila's visiting a friend and I've got to see you before she gets home . . . Yes . . . The door will be unlocked. Come straight up to my study." He hung up and pressed his fingers to his eyes. That would give the precious pair something to think about and he'd come. He'd come running to find out what it was all about. Sheila would make sure of that.

When the young man returned, his face was deeply flushed and the paper knife still gleamed in his clenched fist. "Did you reach him, Uncle Dev?"

"Yes. He's on his way." Goring wheeled himself to the door. "Switch off that light, Jack. Just leave the desk lamp burning."

In its greenish glow Goring's face looked as dead-white as a cadaver's. "I'll wait in the next room. Be quick about it, and be silent."

The young man nodded, then spoke just as Goring opened the door. "Uncle Dev?"

Goring looked back at him.

"I just want you to know something. Whatever happens to me, this has been the happiest day in my life."

Goring quickly withdrew. In his darkened bedroom he opened a drawer in the bedside stand, removed the revolver which he kept there, and slid it under the blanket on his lap.

He waited. The sound of thunder was now no more than a distant cannonade.

He didn't hear the car when it drove up and the first sound that reached his ear was a soft but impatient tap on the study door.

For perhaps a second or two he remained immobile, unbreathing, but the wild impulse of remorse which sent him hurtling toward the door came an instant too late. The man he had said was "Rashbrooke" gave a muffled cry as the paper knife drove fiercely into his heart.

Goring froze, then reacted with the calm, fatalistic precision of a sleepwalker, gently pushing the door open wider, raising the gun and firing.

He was almost sure that the young man who thought he was "Jack" never knew what happened, never knew that it was Uncle Dev who killed him.

The sensation it caused was, of course, considerable, but not so great as it would have been had Goring permitted reporters to step foot upon the grounds. His story was simple. A young man had come to the house, Mrs. Harkins confirmed that she had let him in ("he had real funny-looking eyes") and taken him upstairs to Goring's study. Goring stated that the caller had babbled incoherently, seemed to have confused some of the *Penelope* stories with real life, and when Harry Lawton had arrived unexpectedly the young man had gone berserk, seized up a paper knife from the desk, and stabbed Lawton in the heart. Before he could turn on Goring, the older man had been able to reach his revolver and shoot the intruder.

Goring would remember with utmost satisfaction the look on his wife's face when she arrived home just as they were removing her lover's body from the study. He wondered, with no particular alarm, if she would tell the police that Lawton had received a call from Goring. If she did Goring was prepared to deny it, but he didn't really expect her to, since it would mean confessing that she had been with Lawton.

He was right. She said nothing about that call, not to the police and not to him.

Instead of aggravating his condition as it might have been expected to do, the events of that night had quite a different effect upon Goring, for days afterward his aches and pains seeming to enter upon a period of remission, raising his spirits to the point where he actually expressed a desire to return to work.

His wife stared at him in amazement. "Work? *You?*"

"Why not?"

"You haven't worked in years."

"Well, now I feel like working. I've got two or three ideas churning around up here," and he gaily tapped his forehead.

"You're out of your mind," she said coldly. "Dr. Simpson would never approve. And you'd never stand the discomfort. That's why you hired me in the first place, don't forget. Every time you struck a typewriter key you winced with pain, and you know you were never any good at dictating your novels."

"Oh, I don't know. Maybe I didn't have the right *kind* of secretary."

He wheeled himself to the desk, picked up the unfinished manuscript of *The Final Escape* and with a look of infinite satisfaction calmly forced his crippled fingers to rip it into shreds.

"I've got a much better idea. How's this for a title? *Penelope and the Evil Bridegroom.* We'll take the little darling right up to the altar with that scoundrel and then, when things look absolutely hopeless, when there seems to be no conceivable way out of the situation—*enter the stranger.*"

The Crime Machine

by Jack Ritchie

"I was present the last time you committed murder," Henry said.

I lit my cigar. "Really?"

"Of course you couldn't see me."

I smiled. "You were in your time machine?"

Henry nodded.

Naturally I didn't believe a word of it. About the time machine. He *could* actually have been present, however, but not in that fantastic manner.

Murder is my business and the fact that there had been a witness when I disposed of James Brady was naturally disconcerting. And now, for the sake of security, I would have to devise some means of getting rid of Henry. I had no intention of being blackmailed by him. Not for any length of time, at least.

"I must warn you that I have taken pains to let people know that I have come here, Mr. Reeves," Henry said. "They do not know why I am here, but they do know that I am here. You understand, don't you?"

I smiled again. "I do not murder people in my own apartment. It is the height of inhospitality. And so there will be no necessity for you to switch our drinks. I assure you your glass contains nothing stronger than brandy."

The situation was basically unpleasant, but nevertheless I found myself rather enjoying Henry's bizarre story. "This machine of yours, Henry, is it a bit like a barber's chair?"

"To some degree," he admitted.

Evidently we had both seen the same motion picture. "With a round reflector-like device behind you? And levers in front which you pull to propel you into the past? Or the future?"

"Just the past. I'm still working on the mechanism for the future." Henry sipped his brandy. "My machine is also mobile. That is, it not only projects me into the past, but also to any point on the earth I desire."

319

Excellent, I thought. Quite an improvement over the old model time machines. "And you are invisible?"

"Correct. I cannot participate in any manner in the past. I can only observe."

This madman did at least think with some degree of logic. To so much as injure the wing of a butterfly ten thousand years ago could conceivably re-shuffle the course of history.

Henry had come to my apartment at three in the afternoon. He had not given me his last name, which was entirely natural since he intended to blackmail me. He was fairly tall and thin, with glasses that gave him an owlish appearance and hair that tended toward anarchy.

He leaned forward. "I read in yesterday's newspaper that a James Brady was shot to death in a warehouse on Blenheim Street at approximately eleven in the evening of July the 27th."

I thought I could supply the rest. "And you hopped into your time machine, set the dials back to July the 27th and to Blenheim Street, and were there at ten thirty for a ringside seat, waiting for me to re-commit the crime?"

"Precisely."

I would have to discuss this particular form of insanity with Dr. Powers. He is a quite mature and—since I disposed of his wife—wealthy psychiatrist.

Henry smiled thinly. "You shot James Brady at exactly ten fifty-one. As you stooped over him to make certain that he was dead, you dropped your car keys. You said, 'Oh, damn!' and picked them up. At the door of the warehouse, you looked back and lifted your hand in a mock salute to the corpse. Then you departed."

Unquestionably he had been there. Not in that fabulous time machine, but probably hiding among the thousands of boxes and bales inside the warehouse—an accidental witness to the murder. It was one of those unfortunate coincidences that occur occasionally to mar an otherwise perfect killing. But why did he bother to resort to this fantastic story?

Henry put down his glass. "I think that five thousand dollars would be sufficient for me to forget what I saw."

For how long, I wondered. A month? Two? I took a puff of my cigar. "If you went to the police, it would be your word against mine."

"Could you bear an investigation?"

I really didn't know. I am a very careful practitioner of my craft, but it was still possible that here and there I might have made some slight revealing error. I certainly would not welcome the interest of the authorities. Of that much I was positive.

I replenished my glass. "You seem to have fallen into an interesting and profitable business. Have you approached many other murderers?" I looked at his suit. It had undoubtedly been sold with two pairs of trousers.

Perhaps he read my mind. "I have just started, Mr. Reeves. You are the first murderer I have approached."

He smiled primly. "I have done considerable other research on you, Mr. Reeves. On June the 10th, at eleven twelve in the evening, an automobile which you had stolen for the purpose ran down a Mrs. Irvin Perry."

He could have read about Mrs. Perry's death in the newspapers. But how did he know that I had been the driver? A wild guess?

"You parked approximately one hundred yards from the intersection. You kept your motor running while you waited for Mrs. Perry to make her appearance. Ten minutes before she arrived, a collie ran across the street. Seven minutes before she arrived, a fire engine sped past. Three minutes before she arrived, a Model A Ford filled with teenagers raced by. The automobile's muffler was faulty. It was quite noisy."

I frowned. How could he possibly have known those things?

Henry was enjoying himself. "On September 28th, last year, at two fifteen of a chilly afternoon, a Gerald Mitchell 'fell' off an escarpment near his home while he was taking a stroll. You had a bit of trouble with him. Though he was a small man, he showed remarkable strength. He managed to tear the left pocket of your coat before you could throw him into space."

I caught myself staring at him and quickly took a sip of brandy.

"Five thousand dollars," Henry said. "Small bills, of course. Nothing larger than a five hundred. Naturally I didn't expect you to have that much cash lying about. I shall return tomorrow evening at eight."

I pulled myself together. For a moment I had almost entertained the thought that Henry actually might have a time machine. But there was some other explanation and I would have to think it out.

At the door to the hallway, I smiled. "Henry, would you hop into your time machine and find out who Jack the Ripper really was? I'm frightfully curious."

Henry nodded. "I'll do that tonight."

I closed the door and went into my living room.

My wife Diana put aside her fashion magazine. "Who was that strange creature?"

"He claims to be an inventor."

"Really? He certainly looks mad enough for the part. I imagine he wanted to sell you an invention?"

"Not exactly."

Diana is green-eyed and cool and she is perhaps no more predatory or unfaithful than any other woman who marries a man with money who is thirty years her senior. I am fully aware of the nature of our relationship, but I realize that one must pay by various means for the enjoyment of a work of art. And Diana is a work of art—a triumph of physical nature. I value her quite as highly as I do my Modiglianis and my Van Goghs.

"What is he supposed to have invented?"

"A time machine."

She smiled. "I am partial to perpetual motion machines."

I was faintly irritated. "Perhaps it works."

She studied me. "I hope you have no intention of letting that queer man talk you out of money."

"No, my dear. I still retain my mental faculties."

Her solicitude for my money would have been touching, except that I realized that she preferred to spend it on herself. Henry's chances of acquiring any of it were nil as far as she was concerned.

She picked up the magazine. "Has he asked you to see it?"

"No. And even if he does, I have no intention of doing so."

And yet I wondered how Henry could possibly have managed to know the details of those three murders. His presence at one of them could be an acceptable coincidence. But three?

There was no such a thing as a time machine. There had to be some other explanation—something that an intelligent man could believe.

I glanced at my watch and turned my mind to another matter. "I have something to attend to, Diana. I'll be back in an hour or two."

I drove to the main post office downtown and opened my box with a key. The letter I had been expecting was inside.

I conduct most of my business by mail and box number. My clients do not know my name, even on those occasions when personal contact is necessary.

The letter was from Jason Spender. We had exchanged some correspondence and Spender had been negotiating for the elimination of a Charles Atwood. Spender did not give his reasons for that desire and for my purposes they were not necessary. In this case, however, I could hazard a guess. Spender and Atwood were partners in a building concern and evidently sharing the profits no longer appealed to Spender.

The letter accepted my terms—fifteen thousand dollars—and provided the information that Atwood had a dinner engagement tomorrow evening and would return to his home at approximately eleven. Spender would have an alibi for that particular time in the event that the police might make embarrassing inquiries.

I drove on to the Shippler Detective Agency and went directly to Andrew Shippler.

I cannot, of course, employ his agency continuously to follow my wife. But several times a year I made a precautionary use of his services for a week or two. It is usually sufficient.

In 1958, for instance, Shippler discovered a Terence Reilly. He was extremely personable—fair, athletic, and the type to which Diana seems to be drawn—and I cannot blame Diana too much.

However, Terence Reilly soon departed this world. I was not paid for the demise. It was a labor of love.

Shippler was a plump man in his fifties with the air of an accountant. He took a typewritten page from a folder and adjusted his rimless glasses. "Your wife left your apartment twice yesterday. In the morning at ten thirty she went to a small hat shop for an hour. She finally purchased a blue and white hat with . . . "

"Never mind the details."

He was slightly aggrieved. "But details can be important, Mr. Reeves. We try to be absolutely thorough." He glanced at the page again. "Then she had a strawberry soda at a drugstore and went on to . . . "

I interrupted again. "Did she see anyone? Talk to anyone?"

"Well, the owner of the hat shop and the clerk at the drugstore counter."

"Besides that," I snapped.

He shook his head. "No. But she left the apartment again at two thirty in the afternoon. She went to a small cocktail bar on Farwell. There she met two women her age, apparently by prearrangement. It appears that they had been college classmates and hadn't seen each other for years. My man overheard most of their conversation. They discussed their former classmates and what they were doing now." Shippler cleared his throat. "It seems that they were most impressed that your wife had . . . ah . . . caught such a man of means."

"What did Diana say?"

"She was extremely noncommittal." Shippler folded his hands. "Your wife consumed one Pink Lady and one Manhattan during the course of two hours."

"I am not interested in my wife's liquor preferences. Did she see anyone else? A man?"

Shippler shook his head. "No. At four ten she left the two women and returned to your apartment."

The human mind is a peculiar thing. I was relieved, of course—and yet a trifle disappointed.

"Shall we keep watching her?" Shippler asked hopefully.

This time I had had Diana under surveillance for about a week. I mulled over Shippler's question. Shippler charged one hundred dollars a day and that was rather expensive. I smiled slightly. Now, if I had Henry's time machine, I could save a great deal of money. "Watch her a few days more," I said. "And I have something else for you."

"Yes?"

"At eight tomorrow evening, I am expecting a caller. He will be with me ten to twenty minutes. When he leaves, I want him followed. I want to know who he is and where he lives." I gave Shippler a description of Henry. "Phone me as soon as you find out."

I went to the bank and withdrew five thousand dollars.

At seven the next evening Diana left to see a motion picture. Or at least so she informed me. I would find out about that later.

Henry arrived punctually at eight o'clock and I took him into my study.

He took a chair. "He was a clerk with an importing concern."

"Who was?" I asked.

"Jack the Ripper. A timid looking man—in his early forties, I'd estimate. He was apparently a bachelor and he lived with his mother."

I smiled. "How interesting. What was his name?"

"I haven't gotten that yet. You see, people don't go about with signs hanging from their necks, and it can be difficult to find out who they actually are."

He could easily have invented some name for this Jack the Ripper, but this was really more clever—and logical.

Henry said, "Do you have the five thousand dollars?"

"Yes." I got the package and handed it to him.

He rose. "Tonight I think I'll go back to Custer's massacre. I find history fascinating."

I had only one consolation. When the time came to kill him, I would enjoy every moment of it.

When he was gone. I sat beside the phone and waited impatiently. At nine thirty it rang and I quickly lifted the receiver.

"This is Shippler."

"Well, where does he live?"

Shippler's voice was apologetic. "I'm afraid my man lost him."

"What?"

"He transferred from bus to bus and finally disappeared. I think he suspected he was being followed."

"You blundering idiot!" I roared.

"Really, Mr. Reeves," Shippler said stiffly. "It is my man who is the blundering idiot."

I hung up and poured myself some bourbon. This time Henry had eluded me, but there would be other times. He would be back. Blackmailers are never satisfied.

I became aware of the time and realized that I still had work to do that night. I got into my coat and hat and went downstairs to the apartment garage.

Charles Atwood's home was a large one embedded in several acres of wooded property. It was a situation I fancied, since it offered the maximum of concealment.

The dwelling was dark, except for lights on the third floor where I imagined the servants were quartered.

Atwood's three-car garage was detached from the house. I took a stand behind a clump of trees near it and waited.

At eleven fifteen a car swung into the driveway and made its way to the garage. It stopped momentarily while the automatic doors rose, and then it disappeared into the garage.

Thirty seconds later, a side door opened and a tall man stepped into the moonlight. He began walking toward the house.

I had my revolver and silencer ready, and I waited until he came within fifteen feet of me before I left my concealment.

Atwood stopped with an exclamation of startled surprise as he saw me.

I pulled the trigger and Atwood dropped to the ground without a sound. I made certain that he was dead—I do not like to leave things half done—and then made my way back through the woods and to the street where I had parked my car.

The assignment had been entirely successful and, for the first time in thirty-six hours, I felt a certain peace with the world.

I returned to my apartment a little before midnight and I was relaxing when the phone shrilled.

It was Henry. "I see that you killed someone else tonight," he announced pleasantly.

My hands were moist.

"When I arrived home," Henry said, "I got into my time machine and turned it back to the time when I left your apartment. I wanted to see if you had attempted to follow me. I have to be cautious, you know. After all, I am dealing with a murderer."

I said nothing.

"You didn't follow me, but you did leave your apartment and I followed in my machine as a matter of curiosity."

That infernal time machine! Was it possible?

"I'm just wondering," Henry said. "Was that the man you were supposed to kill—the one you killed?"

What was he getting at?

"Because there were two men in the car," Henry said.

I spoke involuntarily. "Two?"

"Yes. You shot the first man as he came out of the garage. The second man left it about forty-five seconds later."

I closed my eyes. "Did he see me?"

"No. You were gone by that time. He just bent over the man you'd shot and called, 'Fred! Fred!' "

I was definitely perspiring. "Henry, I'd like to see you."

"Why?"

"I can't discuss it over the phone. But I've got to see you."

His voice was dubious. "I don't know."

"It means money. A lot of money."

He thought it over. "All right," he said finally. "Tomorrow? Around eight?"

I couldn't wait that long. "No. Right now. As soon as you can get here."

Henry required more seconds to think. "No tricks now, Mr. Reeves," he said. "I'll be prepared for anything."

"No tricks, Henry. I swear it. Get here as soon as you can."

He arrived forty-five minues later. "What is it, Mr. Reeves?"

I had been drinking—not to excess, but I simply found that accepting such an idea—and I was on the verge of accepting it—was painful to my intelligence. "Henry, I'd like to buy your machine. If it really works."

"It works." He shook his head. "But I won't sell it."

"One hundred thousand dollars, Henry."

"Out of the question."

"A hundred and fifty thousand."

"It's my invention," Henry said peevishly. "I wouldn't dream of parting with it."

"You could make another, couldn't you?"

"Well . . . yes." He eyed me suspiciously.

"Henry, do you expect me to mass produce time machines once I get yours? To sell them to others?"

His face indicated that evidently he did.

"Henry," I said patiently. "Having anyone else in the world get hold of that machine is the last thing I want. After all, I *am* a murderer. I wouldn't welcome other people delving into the past, especially my past—now would I?"

"No," he admitted. "Somebody else might want to turn you over to the police. There are people like that."

"Two hundred thousand dollars, Henry," I said. "My last offer." Actually money was no object to me now. With Henry's machine—if it worked—I could make millions.

A crafty light crept into his eyes. "Two hundred and fifty thousand. Take it or leave it."

"Henry, you drive a hard bargain. But I'll meet your price. However, I've got to be satisfied that the machine works. When can I see it?"

"I'll get in touch with you," he said cagily. "Tomorrow, the next day, maybe in a week."

"Why not right now?"

He shook his head. "No. You're very clever, Mr. Reeves. Perhaps you've devised a trap for this moment. I prefer to set the time and terms myself."

I was unable to shake him out of his determination and he left five minutes later.

I rose at seven in the morning and went downstairs to purchase a newspaper. I had indeed killed the wrong man. A Fred Turley. I had never even heard of him before.

Atwood and Turley had returned from the dinner and an evening of cards together and driven into the garage. Turley had gone out of the side door, but Atwood remained behind to lock his car. Then he had seen his briefcase still on the rear seat. After he had recovered it, re-locked the car, and left the garage, he had found Turley dead on the path leading to the house. At first he had thought Turley had suffered a stroke of some kind. When he finally discovered the truth, he had raised an alarm. The police had no clues either to the identity of the murderer or the motive for the killing.

I found myself fretting about the apartment all morning waiting for Henry to phone me. I skimmed through the paper half a dozen times before an item in the local section caught my eye.

It seemed that once again some fool had bought a "money machine."

This form of swindle was probably as old as currency itself. The victim was approached by a stranger claiming to have a money machine. One simply inserted a dollar, turned the handle, and a twenty dollar bill emerged from the opposite end. In this case, the victim had purchased the machine for five hundred dollars—the stranger claiming that he was forced to sell because he needed cash.

People are incredible idiots!

Couldn't the victim have the basic intelligence and imagination to realize that if the machine were actually genuine, all that the stranger had to do to get five hundred dollars himself was to turn the handle twenty-five times and transform twenty-five dollars into five hundred?

Yes, people are monumental—

I found myself reading the article again. Then I went to the liquor cabinet.

After two bourbons, I allowed myself to bask in the returning sun of sanity.

I had almost fallen into Henry's trap. I had, I reluctantly admitted, been just a bit stupid.

I smiled. Still . . . it might be a rather amusing adventure to see Henry's time machine—to see in what manner he hoped to convince me that it actually worked.

Henry came to my apartment at one o'clock in the afternoon. He appeared shaken. "Horrible," he muttered. "Horrible."

"What's horrible?"

"Custer's massacre." He wiped his forehead with a handkerchief. "I'll have to avoid things like that in the future."

I almost laughed. Rather a neat touch. Henry knew how to act. "And now we see your machine?"

Henry nodded. "I suppose so. We'll take your car. Mine's in the garage for repairs."

I had driven him about a mile when he told me to pull over to the curb. I glanced about. "Is this where you live?"

"No. But from here on I drive your car. You will be blindfolded and you will lie on the back seat."

"Oh, come now, Henry!"

"It's absolutely necessary if you want me to take you to the machine," Henry said stubbornly. "And I've got to search you to see that you aren't carrying a weapon."

I was not carrying a weapon and Henry's idea of a blindfold consisted of a black hood that fitted over my entire head and was fastened by strings at the back of the neck.

"I'll be keeping an eye on you through the rear view mirror," Henry cautioned. "If I see you touch that blindfold the whole thing is off."

Automatically I found myself trying to remember the turns Henry made as he drove and attempting to identify sounds which might tell me where he was taking me. However, the task proved too complicated and I finally relaxed as much as I could and waited for the drive to end.

After an hour, the car finally slowed to a stop. Henry left the wheel and I heard what I believed to be the sound of garage doors being opened. Henry returned to the car; we moved forward fifteen feet or so, and stopped again.

The doors closed and I heard a light switch flicked on.

"We're here," Henry said. "I'll take off that blindfold now."

As I had surmised, we were in a garage—but plywood sheets had been nailed over all the windows and a single electric light burned overhead. A stout oak door was in the cement building-block wall to the left.

Henry produced a revolver.

A horrendous thought gripped me. What a fool I had been! I had blindly—literally and figuratively—allowed myself to be lured here. And now, for reasons unknown to me, Henry was about to kill me!

"Henry," I began, "I'm sure we can talk this over and come to some . . . "

He waved the gun. "This is just a precaution. In case you have any ideas."

I was too uneasy to have any ideas.

Henry produced a key and went to the oak door. "This used to be a two-car garage, but I divided it in half. The time machine is in here." He unlocked the door and switched on an overhead light.

Henry's time machine was just about as I had anticipated—a metallic chair with some scant leather upholstering, a large mirror-bright aluminum shield or reflector behind it, and a series of levers, dials, and buttons on a control board attached to the platform on which the chair stood.

The room was windowless and all four walls—with the exception of three grated ventilators approximately shoulder high—were solid cement block. The floor was concrete and the ceiling was plastered.

I smiled. "Henry, your machine looks almost like an electric chair."

"Yes," he said musingly, "it does look rather like that, doesn't it?"

I stared at him. Could he have been so insidious as to actually . . . I studied the machine again. "Naturally I want a demonstration. How does it work?"

"Get into the chair and I'll show you which levers to pull."

The device *did* look a great deal like an electric chair. I cleared my throat. "I have a better idea, Henry. Suppose *you* take a trip in the chair. I'll just wait right here until you return."

Henry gave it thought. "All right. But you'll have to leave the room."

Aha, I thought.

"You see, when I start the machine," Henry said, "it creates quite a disturbance around me. That's why I had to make this room so solid. I've installed ventilators to take care of some of the turbulence, but I'm not too sure how well they work. I have no idea what might happen to you if you remained."

I smiled. "I might possibly be injured? Or killed?"

"Exactly. So if you'll leave and close the door I'll get on with it. And another precaution. When I return, you've got to be out of the room, too."

I chuckled to myself as I left and closed the door behind me. I lit a cigar and waited, amused.

What happened next was most impressive. First there was a low whine, as though a generator were starting. It rose gradually in pitch and then came a rumbling sound mixed with the undulating keen of a fierce wind. It increased in volume and lasted for approximately a minute.

Then it stopped abruptly and there was absolute silence.

Yes, I thought. Altogether a good show. But then it would have to be if Henry expected to extract two hundred and fifty thousand dollars from me.

I went to the door and opened it.

The room was empty!

I stood there gaping. It couldn't be! The only way out of the room was the door I had just entered and even that was certainly too small to pull the chair through. And the only other openings were the three grated ventilators and they were less than two feet square!

The whining suddenly rose again. Strong air currents swirled around the room and I found myself gasping as I fled the room and slammed the door behind me.

The noise became deafening and then, just as abruptly as before, it stopped.

The door clicked open and Henry stepped out of the room. Behind him I could see the time machine back in its place.

Henry appeared thoughtful. Finally he shook his head. "Cleopatra wasn't even goodlooking."

My heart was still pounding. "You were gone only a minute or two."

He waved a hand. "In one time sense. Actually I spent an hour on her barge." He came back to the present. "You can raise two hundred and fifty thousand dollars?"

I nodded weakly. "It will take a week or two." I wiped my forehead. "Henry, I've got to take a trip on that chair."

Henry frowned. "I've been thinking that over, Mr. Reeves. No. You could steal my invention."

"But how? Wouldn't I have to come back here?"

"No. You could go into the past and then return to any place in the world. Perhaps a thousand miles from here."

He pulled a small wrench from his pocket and began disconnecting a section of the control panel.

"What are you doing?"

"I'm taking out some key transistors. I think I'll keep them on my person. That way if someone should steal my time machine he would find it useless."

Henry drove me back to my apartment, taking the same precautions as before, and then he left me.

In America we seem to have a feeling of guilt about discarding old license plates and Henry had been no exception. There had been four old sets of them nailed to the garage wall and I had memorized two of them.

I got Shippler on the phone. "Can you trace license numbers?"

"Yes, Mr. Reeves. I have connections at the state capital."

I gave him the numbers. "The first is a 1958 license number and the second is 1959. I want the name and address of the owner as soon as possible. Phone me the moment you get the information."

I was about to hang up.

"Oh, Mr. Reeves. We have the report on your wife for yesterday. Would you like me to give it over the phone?"

I had forgotten about that. "Well?"

"She left the apartment yesterday morning at ten thirty. She bought some orange sticks and nail polish at the drugstore."

"What shade of nail polish?" I asked dryly.

"Summer Rose," he said proudly. "Then she went to—"

"Never mind all that. Did she meet anyone?"

"No, sir. Just the drugstore clerk. A woman. But in the evening she again left your apartment at three minutes after seven. She met a woman named Doris. My man overheard Doris say that she has twins."

I sighed.

"They went to a show and left at eleven thirty."

I was not going to ask him the name of the picture. "Is that all?"

"Yes, sir. She returned to your apartment at eleven fifty-six. The name of the picture . . . "

I hung up and made myself a whisky and soda.

The idea of a time machine was fantastic. But was it really? We are all aware that there is a fourth dimension. And future travelers in space will eventually have to use space warp in order to reach planets that are physically inaccessible in the present time sense.

Diana came into the room with a manicure kit. "You look thoughtful."

"I have a lot to think about."

"Does it have anything to do with that man who was here? The inventor?"

I sipped my whisky. "Suppose I told you that his time machine works?"

She began working on her nails. "I hope you haven't been taken in?"

I noticed that one of the bottles beside her was named Summer Rose. "And why should a time machine be impossible?"

"Don't tell me he's convinced you?"

I felt a bit defensive. "Perhaps."

She smiled. "Has he asked you for money?"

I watched her use nail polish remover. "How much do you think a time machine would be worth?"

She raised an eyebrow.

I held up a hand. "Let us just *suppose* that there is such a thing? How much would *you* be willing to pay for it?"

She examined her nails. "Perhaps a thousand or two. It might be an amusing toy."

"A *toy?*" I laughed. "My dear, don't you realize the tremendous import of such a thing? You could go into the past and ferret out any secret at all."

She glanced up. "Perhaps try simple blackmail?"

"My dear Diana, not *simple* blackmail, but blackmail extended, doubled, quadrupled. No nation's secrets would be safe from discovery. You could sell your services to the government . . . any government . . . for millions. You could be present at the most important council chambers, the most isolated laboratories . . . "

She looked up again. "Is that what you'd do if you had such a machine, use it for blackmail?"

I had let myself get carried away. I smiled. "Just indulging in fantasy, dear."

Her eyes seemed to calculate me. "Don't do anything foolish."

"My dear, I am the most cautious man in the world."

I decided that I would not hear from Shippler within the next half hour and so I went to the post office.

I had a letter from Spender. He expressed keen disappointment that I had killed Turley instead of Atwood. He had played golf with Turley a number of times and would miss him. He also suggested that I return the fifteen thousand dollars or complete my assignment.

Shippler phoned at three thirty.

"Both of the license numbers belong to the same person," he said. "A Henry Pruitt. He lives at 2349 West Headley. This city."

I waited until ten that evening and then got my flashlight, a tape measure, and my ring of special keys from the wall safe and went down to my car.

Henry's house was in a sparsely populated section of the city—there were empty lots on either side of his house. It was a two story building, but still relatively small. A garage stood next to the alley.

I parked my car a hundred feet down the street and lit a cigar.

At eleven the lights in the living room went out, and a few moments later they reappeared in what was evidently an upstairs bedroom.

After ten minutes, they too went out.

I waited another half hour and then made my way through the littered lots to the garage. It had originally been a common two-car structure, but now the left-hand doors had been replaced by a solid cement block wall. I couldn't peer into the right-hand unit because, as I'd noticed before, the windows had been covered by plywood. Henry clearly believed in absolute secrecy for his invention.

I measured the outside of the garage, the height, width, and length. Then I took the rings of keys out of my pocket and, after a few tries, succeeded in opening the door. I stepped inside, closed the door behind me, and turned on my flashlight.

Yes, this was the place I had been in earlier in the day—the four pairs of license plates nailed to the wall, the workbench at the far end, and the door leading to the time machine on the left.

I switched on the overhead light.

The door to the next room was also locked, but it presented no problem to me. I turned on the light, somewhat apprehensively.

Yes, there it was. The time machine!

For a moment, the idea of stealing it crossed my mind. But then I remembered that Henry had a section of the controls. And besides, how would I get it out of the room? The doorway was obviously too small.

For that matter, how had Henry gotten the machine *into* the room?

I pondered on that and decided he must have brought it in piecemeal and then assembled it.

What really concerned me was how he had managed, earlier in the day, to get the time machine *out* of the room.

That was what I was there to find out.

I began by examining the walls. They were cement block on all four sides and absolutely solid. I took measurements of the room and the entire inside of the garage. My computations showed that there were no secret compartments, no false chambers. I examined the ventilator grates thoroughly. I tried to shake them loose, but they were securely screwed into place. They could not be removed without some time and effort. I examined the floor. It was compact and unbroken cement.

There was one more possibility. The ceiling. Perhaps Henry had some device—some series of hoists—that would whisk the machine into a ceiling crevice.

I got a step ladder from the other room and went over the ceiling with minute thoroughness. The plaster was old and a bit grimy, but there was not even one crack that might indicate access to some secret compartment above.

I got off the ladder and found myself trembling.

There was no possible way out of this room. None at all.

Except by the time machine!

It was ten minutes before the weakness left me. I turned out the lights and locked both doors behind me.

The next morning I began converting my capital into cash.

Shippler called in the afternoon with his daily report. "Mrs. Reeves attended a card party at the home of this Doris at two yesterday afternoon. I found out her last name. It's Weaver. The names of the twins are . . . "

"Confound it, I don't care what the names of the blasted twins are."

"Sorry. Your wife left there at four thirty-six. She stopped at a supermarket and bought four lamb chops, two pounds of . . . "

"She went shopping for the cook," I stormed. "Now do you have anything *important?*"

"Nothing really important, I guess."

"Then send me your bill. I won't be needing you any more."

"Well, if you do," Shippler said brightly, "you know where we are. And congratulations."

"Congratulations? On what?"

"Well . . . on your wife's . . . ah . . . faithfulness . . . this time."

I hung up.

No. I wouldn't be needing Shippler any more. If I wanted to find out anything at all about Diana, I would soon be able to do so myself.

My thoughts went to Henry. He could undoubtedly build another time machine, but I couldn't allow that. In order for my plans to be effective I had to have a monopoly. Henry would have to go and I would see to that after I possessed the machine.

At the end of the week, I had the two hundred and fifty thousand dollars in cash. I was tempted to phone Henry, but I was afraid he might shy away entirely if he knew that I had discovered his identity.

Three excruciatingly long days more went by before Henry rang the door of my apartment.

I drew him quickly inside. "I have the money. All of it."

Henry rubbed an ear. "I really don't know whether I should sell the machine."

I glared at him. "Two hundred and fifty thousand dollars. It's all the money I have in the world. I won't pay another cent."

"It isn't the money. I just don't know if I ought to go through with it."

I opened the suitcase. "Look at it, Henry. Two hundred and fifty thousand dollars. Do you know what that much money can buy? You can make yourself dozens of time machines. You can gold-plate them. You can set jewels in them."

He still held back.

"Henry," I said severely. "We made a bargain, didn't we? You can't go back on that."

Henry finally sighed. "I suppose not. But I still think I'm making a mistake."

I rubbed my hands. "Now let's get down to my car. You may blindfold me and drive me to your place."

"Blindfolding won't be necessary now," Henry said morosely. "As long as you're getting the time machine you'll be able to find out who I am and where I live anyway."

How true. Henry was doomed.

"But I will search you," Henry said.

The ride to Henry's garage seemed interminable, but at last we were inside. Henry fumbled with the keys to the next room and I almost yielded to the urge to snatch them from him and do the job myself.

Finally he had the door open and switched on the overhead light.

The machine was there. Beautiful. Shining. And now it was mine.

Henry took the vital control unit out of his pocket and threaded it into place. He took a sheet of paper from his breast pocket. "These are the directions. Don't lose this paper or you might become stranded somewhere in time. Better yet, memorize them."

I took the sheet out of his hand.

"You may not get the exact date you want at the first try," Henry said. "Because calendars have been changed and besides, once you get back more than five hundred years, you'll find all sorts of errors in history. But you can approximate the time and then use this fine tuner over here in order to pinpoint . . . "

"Stop your babbling and get out of here!" I snapped. "I can read directions as well as anyone."

Henry was a bit miffed, but he left the room and closed the door.

I got into the chair and read the typewritten directions. They were absurdly simple. But I read them again and then put the paper in my pocket.

Now, where would I go?

I studied the controls.

Yes. I had it. The New Year's Eve party at the Lowells'. Diana had disappeared at ten thirty and I hadn't seen her again until two A.M. of 1960. She had never given me a satisfactory explanation for her absence.

I adjusted the time control and the direction knob. I did not know the exact distance to the Lowells' from this point, but I would use the fine tuner directly under the mileage dial once I got underway.

I hesitated a moment, took a deep breath, and then pressed the red button.

I waited.

Nothing happened.

I frowned and pressed the button again.

Nothing.

I took the slip out of my pocket and feverishly reviewed the directions. I had committed no errors.

And then I knew! The entire thing had been a hoax!

I leaped out of the chair and rushed to the door.

It was locked.

I pounded my fists and called Henry's name. I cursed and shrieked until my voice was hoarse.

The door remained closed.

I managed to get some control over myself and darted to the time machine. I wrenched loose a section of the chair piping and returned to the door.

The piece of pipe was aluminum and fiendishly light and malleable. It took me more than forty-five minutes before I managed to force the pins out of the door hinges and get out of the room.

I found an envelope under the windshield of my car and tore it open.

The typewritten pages were, of course, intended for me.

My dear Mr. Reeves:

Yes, you have been thoroughly hoaxed. There is no such a thing as a time machine.

I suppose I could leave it at that and allow you to go mad

attempting to arrive at some reasonable explanation, but I shall not. I am quite proud of my little project and would like the attention of a truly appreciative audience.

I think you will do nicely.

How did I manage to know those interesting details of your last four murders?

I was there.

Not in the time machine, of course.

You are undoubtedly aware that it was not your urbanity, your charm, which attracted Diana to your hearth. She married you for your money—of which you gave indications of having a lot.

But you were extremely reticent about the extent and source of your wealth—an evasion which unquestionably can drive a woman to desperate curiosity. Especially a woman like Diana.

She had you followed and for the purpose employed a detective agency. Shippler, I believe the name was. They are quite thorough and I recommend them highly.

It was indeed fortunate for you—and certainly now for Diana and me—that you did not choose that particular time to commit one of your murders. But it was during one of your periods of unemployment and you were not followed for long. A week.

The reports concerning your activities were mundane, but Diana did fasten on one particular repeated detail they contained. And details are important.

Every day you went to a rented box at the main post office.

Now why would you want a private box? Diana wondered. After all, you do have a home address and that should be sufficient for ordinary mail. Ordinary mail. That was it. This wasn't for ordinary mail.

It was child's play for Diana to get an impression of your box key while you slept and to have a duplicate made, for her use. She made it a practice to go to your post office box each morning—you go there in the afternoon. Whenever she found a letter, she removed it, steamed it open, read the contents, and returned it to the box in plenty of time for you to pick it up the same day.

And so you see it was possible for her to know the details of your negotiations to murder, when the murders were scheduled to be committed and the places where they were to occur. And *that* made it possible for me to be there early, conceal myself, and *watch* you work.

Yes, we've known each other for some time—meeting discreetly—very discreetly. Diana remembers a Terence Reilly and his sudden disappearance. And as an added precaution—since we were on the verge of acquiring a quarter of a million dollars and wanted nothing to prevent that—we have not seen each other for almost a month.

Our original plan had been only blackmail. But again the question of danger arose. How long could I blackmail you and get away with it?

And so we determined to strike once and get *all* of your money.

At the moment you are reading this, Diana and I are increasing the distance between you and us. The world is a large place, Mr. Reeves, and I do not think you will find us. Not without a time machine.

And how did I manage that time machine?

It was an elaborate hoax, Mr. Reeves, but with two hundred and fifty thousand dollars at stake, one can afford to be elaborate.

When you left me alone with my time machine ten days ago, Mr. Reeves, I turned on two devices concealed above the room. One created noise and the other created wind.

And then I quickly *folded* the time machine.

You have no doubt by now noticed that it is extremely light. And if you will look again, you will discover that there are a number of concealed hinges which allow one to fold it into a compact shape.

Then I removed the grate of one of the "ventilators," pushed the collapsed machine through into the small cubicle behind the wall, followed into the cubicle myself, and pulled the grating back into place behind me.

I watched as you re-entered the room, Mr. Reeves, and I allowed you only thirty seconds of astonishment before I turned on the noise and wind machines again. I did not want you to collect your wits and examine the room.

When you left, I simply crawled out of my hiding place and unfolded my machine.

I think that was rather ingenious, don't you?

But you say that is impossible? There *is* no hiding place for the time machine—even folded—and for me?

The room is absolutely solid? You have examined it yourself and you would stake your life on it?

You are right, Mr. Reeves. There is no hiding place here. The room *is* solid.

But you see, Mr. Reeves, there are *two* garages.

The first one, to which I took you blindfolded, is in reality located several miles from here. It is the same type of building—a standard brand erected by the thousands in this area—and I took great pains to make it an exact duplicate of the one you are in now—even to the position of the tools lying on the bench, the ladder against the wall.

The two garages are identical—with some exceptions. The time machine room in one of them is slightly smaller—to allow for the hiding place—and the noise and wind machines are installed under the eaves. As for the ventilators, with the exception of the one I used to enter my hiding place, they are actually blowers.

After I drove you back to your apartment, I returned, packed my time machine, took the license plates off the wall, and brought them here.

Those license plates?

You are a clever man, Mr. Reeves. I grant that and I have taken advantage of that cleverness. I nailed them to a conspicuous place on the wall with the express hope that you would utilize them to track me down—but to *this* place.

I wanted you to examine *this* garage. I wanted you to be absolutely satisfied that the time machine had to be genuine. I was in a neighboring lot watching you after I had turned out the house lights.

I am, of course, not Henry Pruitt. The license plates belonged to the former tenant of the house.

Nevertheless, for the purpose of this letter, I remain, most gratefully,

Your servant,
Henry Pruitt.

I tore the letter to bits and snatched a peen hammer from the workbench.

As I smashed the time machine to smithereens, I couldn't help the horrible thought that perhaps someone, in a *real* time machine might at that very moment be in the room watching me.

And laughing!

The Greatest Cook in Christendom

by S.S. Rafferty

Don't believe the sign outside Rooney's that says, "Bar and Grill." The *bar* is legitimate-enough advertising, but the *grill* is pure fiction. No one, not even Rooney, has ever eaten there, or ever will; but there is a law in this state that came in after Prohibition was sent to the showers that says all drinking establishments must serve hot food. It was one of those nut laws to appease the drys.

However, to uphold the law, or at least give it a nod, all the newspaper people that congregate at Rooney's go through a ritual upon entering the joint.

"What's on the menu?" a reporter, who is probably hiding from his editor, will ask the owner. Rooney will then go through a recitation of edibles that would put a Waldorf headwaiter to shame.

"No *coq au vin blanc?*" the reporter will say, dutifully.

Rooney's face will sadden as he says, "Sorry, only the *vin rouge.*"

"Well, I'll just have bourbon and soda, then," the reporter will say dejectedly.

One morning around three o'clock, when four of us were sitting in a back booth, an old wire editor, Opie Hooter, remembered the time way back when a pilgrim somehow wandered into Rooney's. That in itself is a noble accomplishment, because the place is tucked away in a blind alley that separates two competing dailies and a Sunday rag. It is convenient only to the press and the downtrodden.

"In comes this poor lost soul," Opie was telling us, "and he asks for the menu. Old Rooney gives him the spiel, and the dumb cluck actually orders something. Rooney looked like he was going to have a heart attack. But he's thinking fast, because this guy could be a new state liquor inspector. Rooney beats it back to the rear storeroom. In those days, it had a sign on it that read 'Only Kitchen Personnel Allowed Beyond This Point.' Rooney lurks around in there for a few minutes, and then comes back out with a look of dejection on his puss. In soul-struck tones, he tells the customer that he's out

341

of clams casino, or whatever the numbskull ordered. Undaunted, the boob selects another dish from Rooney's litany. Now Rooney really has a problem. He knows if he tells him he's out of the new dish, too, the guy will probably just order something else. Believe me, fellows, this guy had tenacity written all over him."

"Why didn't he just toss the bum out?" Sid Genderman asked Opie. Sid is a sports writer, so naturally he doesn't follow details.

"Because the creep might be a state snoop," Opie tells him, and goes on with the drama. "Suddenly, Rooney gets a brainstorm. A beaut. He goes into his act and zips back to the nonexistent kitchen, and when he comes out again he has a look of horror about him. 'My chef just dropped dead!' he tells the starving goon. 'No food will be served today.' Now, you'd think that would end it, but no, this fella is a bulldog.

" 'That's terrible,' he says. 'I was with an ambulance unit with the AEF in France. Maybe I can help.' Rooney rolls his eyes toward heaven and tells him the chef is beyond help.

" 'Well, at least I can tell you if he really is dead,' the cluck says. 'It takes an expert eye. He may just be unconscious.' "

"So Rooney was stewing in his own nonexistent soup," Buzzy Lang, the rewrite man on the *Blade,* says with a laugh.

Opie breaks into a sardonic smile. "Not on your life. Rooney is ever resourceful. Back in that phony kitchen, he knows that Oscar Creegan, a *Blade* linotype operator, is sleeping off a two-day binge. Oscar is his ace in the hole. Now the pilgrim starts making for the storeroom door, and Rooney points to the sign. 'Can't break a house rule,' he tells him, but to satisfy pilgrim-boy, Rooney says he will be happy to bring the body out for inspection. I don't know if the cluck was really trying to help or he was just plain morbid, but he gives Rooney the sign to highball the remains into view."

Opie took a short sip from his rye and a long pull on his beer and winked. "It was put-and-call time, and Rooney zips into the storeroom again and ties an apron around Oscar's ossified body and, to insure his cooperation, gives him a thump on the dome with an old chair leg. Then he respectfully dragged Oscar on stage. The cluck looks at the motionless form, pulls back its eyelids, and then puts his ear to Oscar's chest. 'He's dead, all right,' the cluck says, and leaves Rooney to grieve in loneliness while he goes off in search of sustenance."

"Well, if that guy was in charge of death tags with the AEF," Sid

Genderman said, "we'd better get ourselves over to France with some shovels, because that guy didn't know his business."

"Not necessarily," I put in. I work the police beat, and have seen a few corpses and have talked with enough medical examiners to know a few things on the subject. "Determining a body's lifelessness isn't as easy as you may think. Oscar's respiration was probably minimal if he was loaded with booze, and also comatose, courtesy of the chair leg."

"The eyes should have given it away," Sid came back at me. "A coroner down in Mobile told me that the pupil shrinks and is uneven at the rim. I saw it for myself, too. Some bush-league outfielder went to work on an umpire with a number five Louisville Slugger over a bad call. That umpire's pupils were ragged, let me tell you."

Buzzy Lang was toying with his gin and "it" as if his mind were somewhere else. Then he looked up at us suddenly. "That guy—the cluck—couldn't have been with the AEF."

"Why?" I asked him.

"Because I was in the first scuffle overseas myself, and we used the needle test. A needle, a bright one, pushed into any muscle of the body, won't tarnish if the body is dead."

"And if the body says 'Ouch,' it's not," Genderman said, slapping the table.

"No, I mean it. It's a foolproof, one hundred percent test."

"Nothing is one hundred percent anything," Opie said.

"You know," I said, "that yarn about the dead cook reminds me of a time back when I was working a one-sheet weekly out in Christendom, Nevada."

I looked up at the small owlish man who had just come over to the booth.

"Hiya, Doc West, have a seat."

His name is really Richard Sparks, but he's one of the two city medical examiners. He covers the west side, while a counterpart takes care of the east. To keep it simple, we call them Doc West and Doc East. He squeezed in next to Genderman and ordered us all a round.

"We could have used you a few minutes ago, Doc," Buzzy said. "We were discussing how you can tell for sure if a stiff is a stiff."

"No thanks, that's a trade secret. Go on with your story," he urged me.

"Well, you won't have to give away any inside dope on this one, Doc, because we knew this cook was dead. In fact, he was burned to a crisp in a fire. And he would have gone to a peaceable grave if it weren't for Doc Biggs and his X-ray machine."

I looked over at Doc West and said apologetically, "I'm not putting the knock on your profession, mind you. Doc Biggs wasn't a real doctor with a Latin certificate hanging on his wall. He studied some to be a vet, and was pretty good with snakebites and digging bullets out of prospectors after Saturday night debates."

"Sounds like a colorful practice," Doc West chuckled.

"Oh, Christendom was a colorful place, all right. Most of the silver mines were paid out, but there was just enough left to attract the normal cast of scoundrels. Well, I guess Doc Biggs decided to upgrade his standing, so he ordered an X-ray machine from Carson City. Now, it's ironic that the chef and the X-ray machine arrived in town on the same day. Anything new in a small burg can count on the populace giving it the cold shoulder, but the X-ray won hands down. When folks heard that this contraption sent electrical rays through the body, they avoided it like a nest of rattlers."

"He should have called it something less ominous." Opie Hooter said, "like a bone camera. That's the whole secret of advertising."

"Maybe," I went on, "but nothing could convince Christendom that the thing wasn't infernal. Doc Biggs was reduced to experimenting on chickens and cats to prove how harmless it was, but he didn't get any human takers.

"However, the town's cold shoulder didn't extend to Pierre La-Champs. He was greeted like one of the Magi. There was only one cafe in town, run by a mean coot named Tugger McCoy. The slop he dished up tasted like something you'd find on the sod side of a boulder. It was five miles the other side of awful.

"Well, somehow Pierre LaChamps gets Tugger to give him a try, and practically overnight the cafe is a hive of hungry miners. This Frenchman was a master of the pot and pan, and what goes in them. The way he used spices and herbs, he could make a twenty-year-old coyote taste good.

"Everybody was happy as larks, except Doc Biggs. He was still setting busted legs, but no one would go near his machine. Even Tugger McCoy, who never smiled, seemed content. With an A-1 chef handling things, Tugger had more time to spend with his prize hogs, which he kept in a sty just north of town. I swear he thought more of those blueblood hogs than his pretty wife. Those porkers were a vexation to one and all, especially on a hot day, if the main street was downwind from the sty's aroma, but there wasn't much you could do about it. Tugger had been a boxing champ in the Marines, and didn't take criticism lightly. In fact, he claimed the pigs didn't smell at all, which probably explains why his cooking had been so bad.

"So there you have Tugger up with his pigs and Pierre feeding us fine, with a little help from McCoy's wife, Tess."

"Ha-ha," Genderman said, "enter the woman and trouble."

"No, not Tess McCoy, at least. But don't jump ahead."

"Well, for a newspaperman, you sure write a long lead-in. Pigs, X-ray machines, and all."

"They all figure in," I calmed Genderman, "and there was a woman involved. Two of 'em, in fact. Pierre was a real handsome dude. He looked like he just stepped out of a shirt ad. He started keeping company with a Widow Parker, who had a ranch about four miles to the south. That was geographically gratifying to Pierre, because he also practiced his minuet lessons with a lady named Carla Friento, who ran a laundry in town.

"For about two months, everything was fine, and then Pierre started to drop hints that he was thinking of moving on. That caused a bit of civil panic, because our bellies were pampered by now, and we didn't want to return to Tugger's swill. I had a talk with Pierre and suggested that he buy the cafe and settle down. It seems his problem was the same as anybody's—money. He had made such a success of McCoy's place that the coot was asking a fortune for it. That's when I came up with the scheme to solve all our problems in one swoop. If the townspeople came up with the money, we could keep Pierre and his food—and, more important yet, get rid of McCoy and his blasted pigs.

"Well, you'd think I had discovered another Comstock lode, the way the money rolled in. Pierre paid off McCoy and the old coot left town during the night, with Tess. We celebrated with a delicious prize-hog barbecue the next day.

"But life is unpredictable, and after being in business for himself only a few weeks, Pierre's cafe burned down, with him in it. That's when Doc Biggs put in his hand and stirred up a ruckus. Although there wasn't much left of Pierre, he was the first chunk of human anatomy Doc Biggs had bumped into that wouldn't squawk about being X-rayed. He took pictures of every inch of the corpse, and when he developed the negative of Pierre's skull, he yelled 'Murder.'

"It seems the chef had a crack on his skull, and the doc theorized that someone had conked Pierre unconscious and burned down the cafe. At first, we figured that the doc was just looking for publicity. Hell, almost everyone in town had a stake in the cafe, and Pierre had no enemies. When doc showed me the X-ray plate, I was ready to toss him out of the office. The 'crack' wasn't on the back of the skull at all. It was a tiny crack line on the left side of the face, just about where my eyeglass-stops rest on my nose. But I can see that Doc won't take no for an answer, so to shut him up, I send the X-ray plate up to the real doctor in Carson City. I asked him if a man could have died from a small crack like that. It seemed to me that no one ever died from a punch in the nose.

"The Carson City sawbones really knew his onions. He wrote back that the crack was a fracture of some fancy-named head bone, and it couldn't have killed him because it was an old fracture, maybe ten or fifteen years ago. I took the proof over to the sheriff and put the kibosh on Doc Biggs's play for attention."

I took a sip of my drink and looked at my audience. Genderman shook his head. "Is that all? Hell, I thought it was a murder story."

"I didn't say it was a murder story. I just said the Rooney incident reminded me of Pierre's death. That's all I meant to say."

"Well, there's one flaw in it," Opie said. "You said everybody in town had a stake in the cafe, but what about the lady rancher and the laundress? Couldn't one of them have found out he was two-timing her and taken revenge?"

"Not Carla Friento. She was delivering laundry out at the mines and stayed over, with plenty of witnesses to swear to it. As for the lady rancher . . . well, maybe, but there was no murder anyway."

"I believe there was."

We all turned to Doc West, who was lighting his pipe.

"Well, I can't see it," I said.

"You did see it. The sheriff saw it, and your Doc Biggs saw it."

"Where?"

"I admit that it would take technical knowledge, but a trained observer like yourself should have been more acute."

"Go ahead, Doc." Genderman was anxious to see me roast.

"When you wrote to the doctor in Carson City, did you tell him that LaChamps was an expert chef?"

I thought for a moment. "No, I don't believe I did. It didn't seem important."

"Well, if you had, the Carson City man would have been suspicious. You said the fracture was approximately here," and he pointed to the upper side of his nose.

"Yes, that's right."

"That's the ethmoid bone, and I'll wager the fracture was in the cribriform plate. A fracture in that area could cause anosmia."

"Loss of the sense of smell," Opie said.

"Yes, and with the loss of smell, you lose, or greatly impair, the sense of taste. I can't see how a chef could be so good under those conditions."

"Well, I'll be damned." I rubbed my chin. "You mean Pierre was a fake, Doc?"

"More than you realize. I don't mean a fake chef. He obviously knew his business. The corpse was the fake."

"Sure, I see it now." Genderman's eyes popped open. "He wanted to blow town and cover his trail, so he dumped another body in the place and burned it down."

"That's nuts," I told him. "There was no one missing from town."

"More precisely," Doc West said, "there was someone missing. Someone who had been a boxer, and probably got the fracture in the ring. Someone who could work around pigs and not smell them."

"Tugger McCoy!" I said excitedly. "But he left town with his wife."

"Was Mrs. McCoy young?"

"Yes, Doc. And pretty."

"Well, there's Genderman's 'woman means trouble' theory. Pierre falls for her, but covers the affair by being openly amorous with other women. Then he bilks the town for money to buy the cafe, tells people he's paid McCoy off, and sends his true love out of town for a month."

"But where was McCoy all this time?" Opie Hooter inquired of the doc.

"I can only guess. This was desert country. Bodies don't deteriorate rapidly in arid earth. It could have been buried and dug up again on the night of the fire."

Genderman started to laugh. "So old Pierre gets the loot and the girl, and all with the assistance of our esteemed colleague here."

"Now wait a minute," I defended myself. "How was I supposed to know about cribriform plates and anosmia?"

"Sure, pal," Genderman said with some glee, "but you could have given the Carson City doctor all the details."

He was right, so what could I say?

"Don't feel so bad," the doc consoled me. "The whole town overlooked the most suspicious thing of all."

"Like what?" I muttered gloomily.

"McCoy was a pig fancier. Did you really think a true fancier would leave prize hogs to the ignominious fate of a barbecue spit?"

I shot a look at Opie Hooter, who shrugged, "Remind me not to murder anybody in this town," he said, "at least on the west side."

"But, Opie, we're on the west side," I said. "The editor of your paper lives on the west side. Eventually, we'll all murder our editors, and the doc here will get you."

"Not if we use Buzzy Lang's needle test. That will prove he's been dead for years."

"You know," Buzzy said, "that reminds me of a story that never got printed. The cops found this stiff with three needles sticking out of his left big toe."

But that's another story, and it's late, so I'll see you another time. Rooney's is never closed, so drop in.